Devotion

Panic detonated at the base of Ann's skull, a response so reflexive she didn't have time to think. A reaction so black and suffocating she twisted against him, frantic to break away.

Chase let her go.

She stumbled backwards, quivering and panting.

"Ann?" he whispered. "Annie, are you all right?"

Then all at once she realized where she was, who he was, and what Chase had just done for her. For all of them.

He'd saved their lives.

"Jesus God, Annie!" His voice was as shaky as his hands. "Are you all right?"

The notion that she should be so precious to him melted through her like sun through fog. She couldn't remember a time in her life when she'd mattered so much to anyone.

This time when Chase bent his head to kiss her, Ann shivered and offered up her mouth.

Also by Elizabeth Grayson

COLOR OF THE WIND

PAINTED BY THE SUN

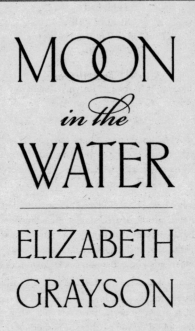

MOON
in the
WATER

ELIZABETH
GRAYSON

BANTAM BOOKS

MOON IN THE WATER
A Bantam Book / April 2004

Published by
Bantam Dell
A Division of Random House, Inc.
New York, New York

Bantam Books and the rooster colophon are registered trademarks of
Random House, Inc.

ISBN 0-553-58424-3

Manufactured in the United States of America
Published simultaneously in Canada

OPM   10 9 8 7 6 5 4 3 2 1

For two of the world's best booksellers,

Steffie Walker

and

Sharon Kosick

gone too soon.

Hope you're sitting on a cloud somewhere

having a smoke and discussing your favorite

books with passion and eloquence,

just the way you lived your lives.

Acknowledgments

This book might have never been written if it hadn't been for my visit to the *Arabia* Steamboat Museum in Kansas City, Missouri. The display of artifacts excavated from the wreck of the steamer *Arabia* would stir the most sluggish imagination, and it most certainly stirred mine.

But while the *Arabia* was the spark, every novel needs fuel in the form of research and encouragement to bring it to fruition. For the former, I turned to Charles Brown and his exceedingly helpful colleagues at the Mercantile Library Association of St. Louis. The resources at that institution continue to astonish me.

Thanks to Chuck Hill of the Missouri Historical Society Archives for unearthing the 1867 diary of Eben Hill (no relation, I'm told) that chronicles his trip to Fort Benton. Without it I might not have been able to recreate that journey with the same insight and accuracy.

I appreciate that Ken Robinson of the River and Plains Society at Fort Benton, Montana, took time to share his expertise. His input helped shape the section of *Moon in the Water* that takes place in that area.

Also thanks to Captain Ron Larson, retired riverboat captain and author of *Upper Mississippi River History*, who was a marvelous help in answering my initial questions about riverboats, piloting, and life on the river.

Certainly the most enjoyable part of my research was cruising on the *American Queen*. If I was able to capture a sense of what being on the water was like, it is because of that marvelous experience. I'd also like to mention Bob Dyer who, in his role of "riverlorian," pointed me to some excellent source material on the river and piloting.

On the technical side, thanks to John Villeneuve for advising me on the workings of Spencer carbines and especially how to disable one. I also appreciate Rick Dreyer's help in checking the bit of German language I used in the story and attempting to explain to me how steam engines work.

On the inspiration side of the equation I must acknowledge Eleanor Alexander for her early suggestions. Also thanks to Julie Beard, Carol Carson, and Adele Ashworth for their ongoing encouragement. Special thanks to Jim—and especially Shirl—Henke for their invaluable insight at a crucial point in the manuscript.

As always I owe a debt of gratitude to Eileen Dreyer, the world's best critique partner, for looking beyond the page and seeing the possibilities.

I thank Meg Ruley, too, for her ever-wise counsel, even if I'm not always smart enough to take it.

Last and always, my love to my husband Tom for his support and, this time especially, for his patience.

Marriage is the highest state

of friendship: if happy it lessens our cares,

at the same time it doubles our pleasures

by mutual participation.

SAMUEL RICHARDSON **from** *Clarissa*

chapter one

March 1867
St. Louis, Missouri

IT WAS A PROPOSITION THAT WOULD TEMPT A SAINT.

Chase Hardesty hitched forward in his chair and stared across the massive mahogany desk in Commodore James Rossiter's well-appointed study. "Let me get this straight," he said. "What you're offering me is the captaincy—"

"Not the captaincy," Rossiter corrected him, "ownership. I'm offering you *ownership* of the Star Line's new stern-wheeler, commissioned out of the Carondelet shipyards just this morning."

Chase had been dreaming about captaining his own steamboat all his life. "And you'll give me the *Andromeda*," he clarified, "in exchange for marrying your daughter."

The commodore nodded. "That's exactly what I'll do."

Chase whistled under his breath. He'd been working

as a pilot for the Gold Star Packets for the past three years, and not once in all that time had the commodore given any sign he favored Chase above the other pilots. Not once had he hinted he might consider promoting Chase to the captaincy of one of the boats, much less offering him ownership.

Not once had Rossiter mentioned his daughter. Which made Chase wonder what was wrong with her.

He'd been away on a run to Sioux City last fall when Ann Rossiter returned to St. Louis after years at some fancy school back East, but Chase's brother Ruben had told him about her homecoming. The commodore had driven his shiny new gig down to the levee to meet her boat. No sooner had the deckhands lowered the gangway than the girl came rushing across it, clearly glad to be home. Rue said Rossiter swept her up in his arms, every bit as pleased to see the girl as she was to see him.

But if Rossiter had held his daughter in such high esteem six months ago, why was he looking for someone to marry her off to now? And what made the commodore offer this sophisticated and pampered young woman to *him*?

Chase made no secret that he came from simple folks. His father had begun as a woodhawk on the frontier, and now sold fuel to the steamers plying the Missouri River west of Council Bluffs. His mother had been the only daughter of an itinerant Baptist preacher. Beyond what she'd taught him reading the Bible, Chase hadn't had so much as a lick of schooling.

All he really knew was the river. He'd climbed aboard a riverboat when he was thirteen and never once been sorry. He'd worked his way up from cub engineer to master pilot. It was a commendable feat, but for all his efforts to better himself, he'd never picked up the polish and social graces some pilots did. And though he was handsomely paid, Chase never seemed to have more than lint in his pockets.

Which made Rossiter's proposal all the more attractive—and all the more puzzling. What kind of man did the commodore think he was to accept such a bargain out of hand?

Chase cleared his throat. "If you don't mind me asking, sir," he began, trying to couch the question as diplomatically as he could. "Why are you offering your daughter to me?"

Rossiter seemed taken aback, either by the question itself, or that Chase had the audacity to ask it outright. He paced to the windows that overlooked the garden at the side of the house and the street of fashionable residences known as Lucas Place.

"Well, you're unmarried, for one thing," the commodore answered with far more candor than Chase had expected. "I like that though you came from humble beginnings, you've made something of yourself. It proves there's grit in you. And I thought that since you might never make captain on your own, you'd find this offer—intriguing."

It *was* intriguing, but Chase couldn't help bristling a little at the commodore's attitude. He didn't much mind admitting where he'd come from, but he resented that Rossiter had drawn his own conclusions about his prospects. The man had as much as said Chase had ambition enough to be hungry and was poor enough to be bought.

"Both the crew and officers like you," the commodore went on, enumerating. "They think you're evenhanded and dependable."

Which was the same as saying he was good at his job and could probably be counted on not to beat his wife. They were, at best, minimal qualifications for what the commodore was proposing. But then, the older man wasn't being all that exacting in his requirements for a son-in-law. Which made Chase wonder all over again what Ann Rossiter had done to deserve such treatment.

Then, clearing his throat, the commodore turned from the window, and Chase knew the time had come to make his choice. He scowled a little as he weighed the possibilities: Rossiter's daughter and a brand-new steamer against the unfettered life he loved and whatever adventures the future might hold for him.

His answer seemed obvious.

"While I'm complimented that you consider me worthy of joining your family, Commodore Rossiter," he began, aware of the gravity of what he'd been asked and grappling for the exact right way to couch his answer, "I've never once set eyes on your daughter. And as far as I know, sir, she's never once set eyes on me."

When Chase opened his mouth to continue, Rossiter cut him short. "You *would* be willing to meet her, though, wouldn't you, Hardesty?"

Chase hesitated, caught between the refusal he'd been about to make and the commodore's new question. "Well, I..."

"Would you be willing to meet her now?" Rossiter pressed him. "This afternoon?"

Chase's nerves tingled in warning.

The commodore raised the ante. "The *Andromeda* is a beautiful steamer, Hardesty. A man could gain a great deal by agreeing to this."

A man could get in over his head wanting things he had no business aspiring to. *Or a man could make his dreams come true.*

Visions of a sleek, freshly painted stern-wheeler flitted through Chase's mind. He could almost see the wide decks and graceful galleries. He pictured a wheelhouse standing tall, ornamented with stained-glass windows and an upholstered lazy bench. He could all but feel the smoothness of the steamer's wheel slide through his hands and hear the roar of her boilers.

He knew how his chest would warm with pride as he nosed a steamer like that in close to the bank at Hardesty's Landing, and what his father would think when he did.

"I can arrange for Ann to meet you in the parlor in ten minutes," Rossiter cajoled.

What could it hurt? temptation purred in his ears.

Chase swallowed uncomfortably and shook his head. "Of—of course, I'll meet her," he answered, in spite of himself.

He regretted the impulse the moment the words were out of his mouth.

$\mathcal{C}\ell$

TRAPPED—HERE. TRAPPED—HERE. TRAPPED—
The needle and thread Ann Rossiter thrust and then pulled through the fabric stretched taut over her embroidery hoop seemed to whisper of her predicament. Trapped in her stepfather's house, isolated, apprehensive, and vulnerable. Trapped by restrictions that chafed her raw and circumstances she could barely bring herself to acknowledge.

She ached to leave, to run away someplace where nobody knew her. She'd packed her things last fall and had gotten as far as Memphis before her stepfather's men caught up with her. Since then, the commodore had kept her too closely confined to try again, but Ann kept watching, waiting for an opportunity.

When the door to the cozy second-floor sitting room started to open, Ann grabbed for the kitchen scissors hidden in the folds of her skirt.

James Rossiter stepped through the doorway. "Hello, Ann," he greeted her. "How are you feeling today?"

Ann released the reassuring weight of the scissors. "Well enough, thank you, Father."

"Good," he answered, sauntering nearer. "Good."

He paused not quite a foot from her chair and compressed his lips. He clearly had something to say to her, something he thought was important.

Probably something she wasn't going to like.

Though her fingers had begun to tremble, she bent even more intently over her stitching.

The commodore cleared his throat and waited. When she refused to so much as look his way, he proceeded anyway. "Since you seem to be feeling well enough, there's someone I'd like you to meet."

Ann raised her head in spite of herself. Her stepfather hadn't allowed her to speak to anyone except family or servants for weeks and weeks. God knows, it had been easy enough to cut her off. She'd been gone from St. Louis long enough to lose track of the boys and girls she had played with when she was a child, and since she'd been back, she hadn't made the kind of friends who'd come banging on the door demanding to see her. She'd been sequestered in these upstairs rooms, shut safely away while the commodore met with his bankers and employees in his study downstairs, or had dinner with his cronies in the dining room.

Ann tucked her needle into the cloth at the prospect of having a visitor. "Who on earth is it you want me to meet?"

"The man's name is Chase Hardesty," James Rossiter answered. "He's one of Gold Star's most reliable pilots."

Ann set aside her embroidery altogether and struggled to suppress the note of eagerness that crept into her voice. "Is there a particular reason you want me to meet him, Father?"

Rossiter lowered himself onto the footstool, then

reached to take her hands. She submitted to his touch, let her fingers lie lax in his, though she didn't like it.

"You know, Ann," he offered almost kindly, "I've been giving your situation a good deal of thought."

"So have I."

"And I think I may well have hit upon a solution."

She raised her gaze to his, succumbing to a thrill of hope. Perhaps the commodore had finally seen things her way. Perhaps he was asking this pilot, this Mr. Hardesty, to escort her to New Orleans or Cincinnati. To someplace where she could live in peace and anonymity.

"What seems to make sense"—her stepfather allowed himself a satisfied smile—"is for you to marry a strapping young man and start raising your family. And I've found *just the fellow!*"

The breath whooshed out of Ann like air from a bellows. Her brain went porous with shock. "You—you want me to m-m-marry this Mr. Hardesty?" she finally managed to gasp. "The man downstairs?"

Her stepfather inclined his head. "I've been watching Hardesty ever since he came to work for me. He's a good, dependable fellow, and an extremely able pilot. I think he'll make you a damn fine husband."

Ann couldn't do more than gape at him. This man— the man her mother had entrusted her to when she lay dying—intended to marry her off to a stranger! To some riverboat steersman!

He meant to betray her all over again.

Cold ran through her veins and pooled in the pit of her belly. Her head swam and her mouth went dry with revulsion. Then blistering outrage roared in on the heels of the shock.

Ann jerked her hands out of James Rossiter's grasp and surged to her feet. The scissors clattered to the floor.

"This isn't the Dark Ages!" she shouted at him. "Men don't arrange marriages for their daughters. Women aren't wed against their will. Surely Mr. Hardesty hasn't agreed to this!"

"He's consented to meet you."

At least Mr. Hardesty was astute enough not to buy a pig in a poke, Ann thought. Still, what kind of a man would be party to wedding a woman he didn't even know?

He'd have to be someone unscrupulous. Someone ambitious. Someone who didn't understand the scope of what he was agreeing to do.

Suspicion swooped through her. "What exactly did you tell Mr. Hardesty about me?" she wanted to know.

"For God's sake, Ann!" her stepfather snapped at her. "How do you expect me to remember exactly what I said?"

That meant her stepfather hadn't told her prospective bridegroom why he'd been soliciting someone to marry her. He was leaving it to her to tell him, to stand there sick with shame as contempt rose in Hardesty's eyes.

"Well, I won't meet with him," she declared. "I won't!"

Rossiter all but leaped to his feet. "Damn you, girl! If you'd only be agreeable, we could get this settled."

"'Get this settled?'" she echoed. "Have you made

some sort of bargain with Mr. Hardesty, Father? Is my new husband already bought and paid for?"

When he didn't deny it, Ann pressed him. "So what *is* the going rate for a man's good name?"

Though his face mottled red, James Rossiter couldn't seem to deny what he had done. "No petty price! I'll tell you that!"

For a moment Ann thought he was going to refuse to say anything more. Then he sucked in his breath, as if he wanted her to know exactly how grateful she ought to be.

"I've offered him ownership of one of the Gold Star's steamers in exchange for a quick marriage and no questions asked."

"Is it really worth giving Mr. Hardesty a boat worth tens of thousands of dollars to strip me of the Rossiter name?"

Her stepfather's jaw clenched. For an instant Ann thought he meant to strike her. He backed away instead.

"I suggest you make the most of the time you have with Chase Hardesty, because you aren't likely to find a better—or a more congenial—suitor."

"Please, Father! Can't you just let me leave on my own?" she all but begged. "If you let me go, I swear I'll never trouble you again."

He paused when he reached the door. "Go see to your appearance, Ann. Put on your good gray gown and repin your hair. I'll show Mr. Hardesty into the parlor once you're ready."

He slammed the thick wooden panel behind him, leaving Ann standing alone in the ringing silence.

AT FIRST CHASE DIDN'T SEE HER.

What he saw when James Rossiter showed him into the town house's deep double parlor was a pair of enormous gilt-framed mirrors that gave back reflections of the soft-green silk wallpaper, the rose and green velvet settees, and plush Aubusson carpets. The room smelled of lemon polish and elbow grease, of bayberry candles and extravagance. But the silence, broken only by the ticking of the ormolu mantel clock, was the most unexpected luxury.

A steamboat was never quiet. The engines roared and banged and wheezed, the paddles sluiced, bells clanged and whistles hooted. People were always about and the hum of conversation, to say nothing of the shouted orders and the cries of the vendors on the levee, added to the cacophony.

The silence in this room was restful, calming, like being submerged in a pool of still, green-water on a summer day.

Only slowly did Chase come to realize that the woman he'd agreed to meet was already here. She was standing motionless, looking out the window at the far end of the room as if there were something of consuming importance taking place in the street.

He slipped silently toward her, soaking up impressions. He noticed first that though she stood gracefully erect, she wasn't all that tall. She held her shoulders a bit too straight to complement the prevailing fashions, but her gown was well-cut and of a soft-gray color that reminded him of winter dawns. Her hair draped thick and golden-brown against her cheeks, then coiled back close to her nape, twisted like a honeybun.

He paused when he stood barely three feet away. "Miss Rossiter?" he said softly.

Her back stiffened and she turned her head, glancing at him over her shoulder. In that moment, Chase took note of a stalk of satiny throat, the thumbprint of a dimple at the tip of her chin, and a delicate mouth, held far too tightly.

Then gradually she turned to face him—and he understood why her father had summoned him.

She was with child.

Chase should have expected it, but the realization thumped into him with force enough to make the breath huff in his throat.

She acknowledged his reaction with a quick, brittle lift of her chin and a bright rise of color into her cheeks.

Her pregnancy was the reason he'd been offered things he hadn't sought and probably didn't deserve. In exchange for ownership of a riverboat, he was supposed to provide Ann Rossiter's bastard with a name.

The knowledge curdled in his belly, a hot mix of cynicism and an odd kind of disappointment.

Judging by what he'd observed when his sisters were carrying their children, Miss Rossiter was fairly well along in her pregnancy. Four months, at least. Yet in the instant before he'd discovered her condition, he'd sensed a daisy-white purity about her, an open-faced innocence that seemed as much a part of her as breathing. But how could she seem so chaste when she'd quite obviously lain with a man, a man who was cad enough to deny her his protection?

As Chase fought to subdue his incredulity, he realized that Ann Rossiter was staring at him every bit as intently as he'd been watching her. She was seeing a tall, ruddy-faced man who'd invaded her parlor, a rough-looking fellow with a day's growth of stubble on his jaw and curly, windblown hair.

Suddenly self-conscious, Chase did his best to tame the waves with his fingers, then flashed her a self-deprecating smile. "I didn't know I was coming courting when I left the levee this morning."

At those few offhanded words, something stark and desolate kindled up in Ann Rossiter's eyes. She immediately lowered her lashes, but Chase knew what he'd seen.

In response, his chest filled with a fierce and improbable protectiveness. It was a thick, tight ache that made him want to curl an arm around her shoulders and reassure her, just as he might have done if one of his younger sisters was troubled or frightened.

Then the impulse to protect Ann Rossiter gave way to something a good deal more appropriate—a sharp jab of annoyance. He groped for something glib and ironic to say, for words to put her in her place and deny the feelings she'd stirred in him. But nothing came.

Instead he became unbearably aware of the rush of his

own breathing and the faint flutter of hers. The drumming of his heart seemed loud, as the silence between them lengthened.

Finally she took mercy on him and raised her head. "So, you're Chase Hardesty." Her voice was low and cool, and blatantly assessing. "One of my father's men."

Chase dipped his head in acknowledgment. "I work for your father as a pilot," he clarified, "but I'm nobody's man."

Her eyebrows arched, lifting like the flicker of a bird's wings. "If you're not one of my stepfather's men, Mr. Hardesty, why are you here?"

Though heat crept up his jaw, he answered as forthrightly as he could. "I'm here because the commodore asked me to meet you. I'm here because he made me a proposition I'd be a fool not to at least consider."

"He's offered you one of his steamers in exchange for marrying me." Her tone was richly flavored with contempt. "Is that right?"

"He offered me the *Andromeda*," he corrected her.

Her soft mouth parted, bowed. "Father's offered you his new stern-wheeler?"

Chase inclined his head.

"He and my stepbrother have talked of little else all winter."

"Then your father must think highly of you," Chase observed, "to offer something so dear to insure your future."

She shook her head as if she was surprised by his assessment of the commodore's motives. "Or he's exceedingly eager to get me off his hands."

"You must be wrong about that," Chase contradicted her. "He's offered to let you stay on here, so there will be people to look after you when I'm away."

Her expression didn't change, but a new desolation crept into her eyes. "He told you that, did he?"

"He mentioned it just now," he said, gesturing toward the hallway. "He's very concerned about your welfare."

Ann turned abruptly and stalked to the far side of the sitting room, her skirts aswish behind her. When she reached the marble fireplace she rounded on him, her expression imperious—a princess considering a commoner.

"Well, then, Mr. Hardesty, tell me just what kind of a man would consider trading his good name for a riverboat?"

Only if you'll explain how a woman like you comes to need my services, he found himself thinking. But he held his tongue and took a moment to assess his motives. To assess himself.

"A poor man would consider it," he answered carefully. "A practical man. A man who can be bought and sold."

She looked back at him, her eyebrows lifted in inquiry. "And which of those men are you, Mr. Hardesty?"

He hesitated, smiled, then inclined his head in a mocking bow. "Why, I'm all of them, Miss Rossiter. But I'm also a man who knows enough to walk away from a bargain when it seems too good to be true."

"Is *this* bargain too good to be true?"

He let his gaze slide over her, let it skim the velvety luminosity of her cheeks, let it follow the slender column of her throat down toward where the black velvet banding at the neckline of her gown skimmed her collarbones, down to where her breasts rose and fell beneath the bodice. He curled his lips appreciatively, letting her know that in spite of her pregnancy, he liked what he saw.

"I'm not sure about this bargain yet, Miss Rossiter. There have been some surprises already. Are there going to be more?"

A fresh flush flared in her cheeks, and she clasped her hands in the folds of her skirt as if to keep herself from slapping him for his impertinence.

Even angry and clearly undone, she was a lovely woman. Graceful, patrician, intriguingly prim, especially considering her condition. In normal circumstances, no one would have thought to introduce her to a man like him, a common riverman, a man who'd run wild in the Missouri bottoms nearly half his life. If he'd encountered Ann Rossiter on one of the packets, he might have inquired if she was enjoying her trip or commented on the weather. Their conversation would never have gone beyond the common courtesies a riverboat pilot afforded a cabin passenger.

It would never have occurred to him that he could marry someone like her. Women with beauty and money and family position didn't take up with river rats. Women with schooling and sophistication didn't wed men who were barely literate. Yet with things as they were, the possibility of marrying Ann Rossiter ruffled the edges of his imagination.

What *would* it be like to take her as his wife?

A simmer of heat rose through him. A frisson of awareness—of her nearness, her scent, her softness. Of what it would be like to take her in his arms. Just thinking about touching her stirred his blood.

Things would never be dull if he were married to her—and things certainly wouldn't be easy. He could see that ideas came and went behind those eyes. There were depths and layers to her that a simple man like him might never penetrate.

But then, he had far more to consider than whether he and Ann Rossiter were likely to be compatible. Taking on a wife—much less a wife and child—meant changes, expenses, responsibilities. Marrying her would mean giving up the freedom he'd relished all his life. It would mean giving up his dreams and the far-flung possibilities he'd never once mentioned to anyone.

It would alter who he was, what people expected from him. *It would change the way he saw himself.*

Before he could think what else marrying Ann Rossiter might mean, she straightened from the soles of those very costly Moroccan leather slippers and faced him.

"The truth of the matter is, Mr. Hardesty," she began, "that Father and I have rather different ideas about how my—my predicament should be resolved."

Chase ambled toward where she stood before the

fireplace, curious about how she meant to remedy this. "So you don't mean to marry me, then, Miss Rossiter?"

She turned the question back on him. "You don't want to be saddled with a woman who's carrying another man's child, do you, Mr. Hardesty?"

Chase watched her, saw her steel herself, and wondered if she expected him to rebuke her for conceiving a child before she was wed. Or was he supposed to say he'd be well-enough compensated that he didn't give a damn about her condition.

"Normally no man wants another man's leavings," he answered, easing nearer. "But sometimes a man takes on this kind of responsibility to give a child a name or to offer his protection."

Her chin came up. "I don't need you to protect me."

He thought there might be more bravado than truth in those words, and that ridiculous concern stirred in him again.

"A man might marry a woman who's with child," he went on, "to acknowledge a long-standing relationship or win some advantage."

"Is the *Andromeda* advantage enough to induce you to spend the rest of your life with a woman you do not love?"

The question took him aback. It hinted at aspirations that could only make his decision—and hers—more difficult.

He deliberately tipped a one-cornered smile in her direction. "I try never to mix love and business, Miss Rossiter," he advised her. "What we're talking about here is riverboats and bargains, your condition and my ambition."

She hesitated for one long moment, then gave a terse nod, acknowledging that if he offered to wed her and she agreed, there would be no pretense of a courtship between them. No boxes of bonbons and nosegays of roses. No protestations of affection.

What Chase wished he understood in all of this was how a man could make love to a woman like her and leave her to face the consequences. What he wished he could ask was whether Ann Rossiter had loved her baby's father, and how the commodore could bargain with his grandchild's future.

But then, Chase figured, even if he had the audacity to ask those questions, he wouldn't much like the answers.

"Well, then, Mr. Hardesty," she began, her voice wavering ever so slightly, "since your priorities are so clear, what are you going to tell my father?"

For an instant Chase couldn't think how to answer. Now that he'd met her and responded to her the way he had, what on earth was he going to say when James Rossiter asked him if he meant to marry his daughter?

"What do you want me to tell him?"

She must have detected the faint rasp of sincerity in his voice, because she raised her head. In that moment he could almost see the thoughts skim through her mind: a spark of hope, a waver of concern at needing to trust a man she barely knew. A brief, bright glint of guilt. Then a darkness, a weariness settled over her, stealing the color from her face and the life from her eyes.

Instinctively Chase reached for her.

She deliberately stepped beyond his grasp. "Tell my father—" She stood like a duelist preparing to fire, terrified but resolute. "Tell my father you wouldn't marry me if he offered you every steamer in the Gold Star fleet."

She left no room for compromise. For compassion or concern.

Chase had no choice but to dip his head in acknowledgment. "Very well, Miss Rossiter. When he asks me what I've decided, I'll refuse your father's offer. And may I wish both you and your child the very best life has to offer."

He turned to go.

"Mr. Hardesty?"

He glanced back to where she still stood before the fire.

"Thank you."

Something in those two softly spoken words, some hint of vulnerability or trepidation made him retrace his steps.

"Ann?" he murmured, searching the depths of her gold-and-green eyes. "Ann, are you *sure* this is what you want?"

She drew a wavery breath. "Yes," she whispered. "Yes."

WHAT HAD SHE DONE?

Ann stood alone in the parlor, just where Chase Hardesty had left her, feeling dazed and breathless.

Though she knew very well what it might cost her, she had thwarted the plans her stepfather had made for her, and she was quivering inside. She was quivering with defiance and pride and sheer hand-wringing terror.

She'd seized the opportunity Chase Hardesty offered—and refused to become his wife. Had she been right to do that, to throw away the only chance she might ever have of securing a name for her child? A name that wasn't Rossiter?

A shudder slid the length of her back.

As if she could outrun her own uncertainty, Ann paced from one end of the room to the other, paused at the wide double doors and pressed her ear to the wood. Chase Hardesty must be in her stepfather's study, facing up to James Rossiter and explaining—she hoped—that he wasn't going to marry her. He should be telling the commodore that no matter how compelling the inducement, Chase wouldn't take another man's leavings.

The truth of that assessment made her belly flutter. She bent and peered through the keyhole, but the hall was empty. She couldn't even hear the sound of voices.

Ann straightened and paced, making a circuit of the room again. She stopped at the window and peered down the street. She had to be sure Chase didn't leave without her knowing, but except for a carter delivering wood, the street was empty. She crossed her arms and chafed her hands up and down her sleeves, trying to dispel the chill that seeped through her.

She could scarcely believe what had passed between Mr. Hardesty and her during the last half hour, how they'd stood right here discussing a marriage between them as if she were goods to be bought and sold and his good name could be hawked to the highest bidder. They had talked with remarkable candor about her condition, and what he'd been offered to make her his wife. He'd been honest about his ambition, and she'd said as much about her reticence as she could.

She didn't know what it was that made him give her the chance to decide her fate, but she was grateful. She'd done what was best for all of them—for her and Mr. Hardesty and her unborn child. It wouldn't have been right to embroil a man of Mr. Hardesty's evident scruples in her stepfather's machinations.

She curled her hand around the curve of her belly. She'd find her own way to protect this baby—if Mr. Hardesty just held to his convictions. If the commodore accepted Chase's refusal. If she could find a way to escape this house before her stepfather drummed up another suitor who'd prove less accommodating than Chase Hardesty—

Just then, the man himself emerged from the town house and took the row of limestone steps two at a time. Ann leaned close to the window, trying to discern from the set of his shoulders and the expression on his face how things had gone with the commodore.

As he reached the iron gate, Chase paused and turned. He looked back at the town house as if he knew she'd be waiting.

Her first impulse was to shrink back out of sight. Instead she pressed her hand to the glass until fuzzy moons of condensation formed beneath her fingertips. Across the patch of winter-yellowed grass, Chase's gaze held her own. He knew why she was there and what she wanted to know.

He lifted one eyebrow and gave her a quick conspiratorial smile that confirmed that at no small price to himself, he'd told her father he wouldn't marry her.

Relief spilled through her, warming her, making her throat burn and her eyes blur with tears. She drew one long, shuddery breath and then another.

Her gaze lingered in the sea-dark depths of his eyes. She wished she could tell him how grateful she was, how much she appreciated that a man she'd never seen before today would sacrifice his chance to be master of the *Andromeda* for her sake.

She inclined her head, holding the pose to indicate her deep appreciation. He gave a quick acknowledging nod, settled a broad-brimmed hat over his curly hair, then turned up Lucas Place. With long, sure strides, he stalked off in the direction of the river. As he did, there was about him an almost electric vitality, a stark, brazen confidence that came from sneering in the face of caution.

She'd done that, too, but she wasn't energized by it the way Chase Hardesty seemed to be. She didn't feel stalwart and dauntless. She was scared to death.

She watched Chase's progress down the block clinging to what confidence she could borrow from him, but when he disappeared around the corner, he took her courage away with him.

She stood at the window shivering and feeling unbearably alone. She was pregnant, without resources, and facing the greatest challenge of her life. She needed to flee this house and make a life for herself and her child.

If only she had some idea how to do that....

CHASE FOUND HIS BROTHER RUBEN WAITING OUTSIDE Mason Baxter's riverfront saloon.

"How'd your meeting with the commodore go?" the slighter, darker man asked him, rocking a little on his feet.

"Interesting," Chase answered, giving nothing away.

"You hear anything about our berths?" It was going to be Rue's first season as a licensed pilot, and he was even more fidgety than usual.

"No," Chase answered, looking out across nearly thirty yards of cobblestone paving to where the bronze-green river lapped at the toes of the levee.

The Mississippi was arguably the longest and the most important waterway on the continent, and more than half a hundred steamers of all sizes and configurations were tied up and bobbing in the stiff spring current. Men swarmed over the boats, finishing up a bit of painting and polishing, hoisting cargo nets and scurrying up gangways, loading goods for the first run of the new shipping season.

Chase nodded in satisfaction at their industry. Like every pilot who'd been dry-docked all winter, he wanted to get underway.

"The assignments won't be posted 'til midday tomorrow," he said for Rue's sake. "So there's no sense getting all wrought up about which boat you'll be on. You'll do fine."

At Chase's reassurance, Rue seemed to settle some, though not a minute later his brother nudged him with his elbow. "You ever see anything so pretty?" Rue all but purred.

Chase turned to where a brand-new stern-wheeler was swinging across the current to tuck into an empty slip between two veteran steamers.

"Bright as a new penny, she is," Rue continued, never taking his eyes off the boat.

"Yes."

"Graceful as swifts winging at twilight. Just imagine how that sweetheart would respond under your hand."

Chase could imagine. Every riverman dreamed about piloting a riverboat as sleek and fast as this one, dreamed about easing her into an upstream crossing and feeling her skim across the current. Dreamed about standing tall in the wheelhouse and surveying the world from bank to bank.

He slid a glance in Rue's direction and read those same aspirations in his brother's eyes.

Then Chase recognized the Gold Star emblem entwined with the wrought-iron cross braces that stabilized the steamer's two towering chimneys. Even before he read the name emblazoned in dark blue and gold across the front of the pilothouse, he knew what ship this was.

It was the *Andromeda*.

Regret caught him hard. His stomach dropped. His chest ached in a way that must be somewhat akin to a broken heart. If he'd agreed to marry the commodore's daughter, this steamer—this magnificent steamer— would have been his.

Chase jammed his hands into his trouser pockets and muttered a string of curses under his breath. Had he been a fool to refuse Rossiter's offer? Had he been a bigger one to allow Ann Rossiter to decide his fate?

Standing toe to toe with him in the parlor, she'd seemed so confident, so sure she knew what was best for her and her child. *She seemed so sure she knew what was best for all of them.*

But when he'd come out of the town house and seen her waiting at the window for an indication of how things had gone with her father, she hadn't seemed all that certain. She'd looked scared, hollow-eyed—and unbearably fragile.

The same clutch of concern he'd experienced earlier nipped his belly. What was it about the expression in Ann Rossiter's eyes that made him feel as if he had abandoned her?

Chase scowled and shoved the impression away. He'd done exactly what she asked him to do. That was the end of it.

He sauntered down the levee toward where the *Andromeda* was tying up. The boat seemed to be everything the commodore had promised. Her hull was sleek and black, narrow enough to slice through the current like a blade. Her decks rose in perfectly proportioned tiers, their graceful promenades inviting passengers to linger and enjoy the river breeze. Each post and railing was adorned with brass or paint or some doodad or another. A prim fringe of carpenter's lace dripped from the lip of the pilothouse roof, giving the place a hint of refinement.

Rue trailed Chase. "Have you heard who gets command of her?"

"Command of the *Andromeda?*" Chase echoed. For a split second he was tempted to tell Rue about Ann Rossiter and her father's extraordinary offer. Instead he shrugged the inquiry away.

"Well, whoever it is," Rue's voice was tinged with awe, "he's one lucky bastard!"

"Oh, hell," a voice drawled from directly behind where the two of them were standing. "It's just another damned steamer."

"There's nothing so special about them Gold Star tubs," someone else put in, "even if their crews do like to claim there is."

Annoyance spiked up Chase's back. Beside him Rue bristled in disagreement.

"I'd as soon pilot a barber's basin as one of them."

Chase and Rue both swung around to where Philo McKee, John Rogers, and Big Teddy Peterson stood amidst the gaggle of businessmen, passengers, and roustabouts who'd gathered to gawk at the handsome new steamer. All three were pilots for the Anchor Line and were well-known along the St. Louis riverfront as men who spent their off hours looking for trouble.

Chase figured a little trouble was just the thing to dampen his disappointment.

Rue fell right in with his line of thinking. "I'd say the *Andromeda* is about as well set up as any boat I've ever seen!" he challenged. "I'd be willing to bet she could out-run any tub the Anchor Line cared to put up against her!"

John Rogers braced his hands on his hips and spat. "So you think this new packet's fast enough to give the Anchor Line steamers a run for their money, do you, Hardesty?"

Chase barged into the argument. "You put Rue or me in the wheelhouse and let Cal Watkins handle the boilers, and we'd show you a race. You'd be chasing our wake all the way to Alton."

"Hell, I admit that new scow can probably maneuver from one sandbar to the next"—Big Teddy gave a snort of disgust—"but none of the Gold Star boats has a chance of showing stern water to an Anchor Line packet."

"The hell you say!" Rue shouted and punched Big Teddy square in the nose.

Chase instantly raised his fists. This wasn't the first riverfront brawl his brother had started, and he was purely looking forward to joining in. He got his guard up just in time to keep John Rogers from taking off his head.

With his ears buzzing from Rogers' blow, Chase staggered back a step. He'd only just regained his balance when Philo McKee blindsided him.

Twisting and grunting with the effort, Chase heaved the redheaded giant backwards. McKee staggered and caught his heels on a coil of rope. He tumbled, howling curses as he went down.

Chase had no more than a moment to stand grinning over McKee before John Rogers came at him again. He scrambled for footing on the uneven stones, and prodded Rogers with his left. The other man feinted right. Chase saw his opening and smashed an uppercut through Rogers' guard.

Rogers went down like a pile of bricks.

Chase danced back a step, shock waves shimmying up his arm.

More than a dozen men had jumped into the fray. Businessmen grappled with roustabouts. Passengers battered one another with their valises. The waterfront taverns spewed drunkards into the midst of the brawl. More men pelted up the levee from where the Illinois ferry was docking.

Philo McKee plowed into Chase again. The two of them went down, thumping and flailing.

McKee grazed Chase's cheekbone with one beefy fist, then landed a bruiser that all but buckled his ribs. Gasping and rabid, Chase fought for breath. He hammered his knuckles into the other man's face.

McKee's nose began to bleed, smearing both of them with red. They kept on punching.

The brawlers roved between the buildings and the waterline, moaning and growling like mongrel dogs. Many of them had been idle all winter and were spoiling for a fight. Everyone else just seemed to catch the spirit. They were a punching, gouging, mass of men thoroughly enjoying themselves, until three sharp, shrill blasts of a policeman's whistle sliced through the babble.

Chase pushed back on his haunches from where he'd pinned McKee. McKee stopped thrashing beneath him. The men around them lifted their heads.

Two policemen came running down Wharf Street. Several more burst out of one of the old stone warehouses that hemmed the waterfront. A paddy wagon with more police rumbled around the corner at Market Street.

The fight broke up as if by magic. With a few last shoves, the brawlers scattered.

Chase stumbled to his feet. He grabbed Rue by the collar and dragged the smaller man up the levee. They ducked behind a head-high pallet of barrels and struggled to catch their breath.

Chase braced his hands on his knees, panting. "Someday that damn Creole temper of yours is going to get both of us killed," he gasped. His side throbbed as if he'd been kicked by a mule.

Rue swiped blood from his split lip and grinned. "I can't help that my mama was a high-spirited octoroon and yours was some prissy white lady."

In truth, Chase didn't know who his real mother was, or his real father, either. When he was about three, Enoch Hardesty had found him huddled in the ash-filled firebox of a burned out cabin. As far as he knew there'd been no sign of his folks. Not a soul for ten miles around knew the family who'd built the cabin, much less whether they had kin to look after the half-starved toddler.

Because he hadn't known what else to do, Enoch had brought Chase home to Lydia. They'd had a baby of their own not long before, and Enoch figured it was as easy for Lydia to raise up two children as it was one.

There in the woodlot on the edge of the Missouri River, Lydia had proved him right. Over the years she'd taken in or given birth to fourteen children. Her easy manner and generous heart had made the Hardestys one of the largest, loudest, most unruly families on the river. A family who teased and scrapped, and would lay down their lives for one another.

Chase had made Rue his personal responsibility twenty-four years before, when a slave escaping North had stumbled up to the Hardestys' cabin and given birth to a baby boy practically on their doorstep. So when a burly young policeman came poking around behind the skid of barrels, Chase just figured he'd be looking after his brother in jail tonight.

"Now, then," the soft-spoken Irish police sergeant wanted to know, "why exactly are you fellows standing over here when a brawl involving half the city went on not twenty yards away?"

Chase had no idea where his hat had gone, but he did his best to smooth down his hair. He was preparing to swear they'd been innocent bystanders to the fight that had already filled one paddy wagon and was rapidly loading a second, when Rue spoke up.

"We just now came out of the tavern for a smoke, sir." He flashed the policeman his most ingenuous smile and produced several slightly mangled cheroots from the inside pocket of his jacket. "Would you care to join us?"

The officer looked the two of them up and down.

Chase had no doubt the man could see their skinned knuckles and mud-spattered clothes. He figured they were as good as hauled off to the police office on Chestnut Street until the sergeant extended his hand for one of the cigars.

"Don't mind if I do have one of your smokes," he said.

Chase hastily pulled a pressed-tin match safe from his trouser pocket and lit the cigars.

"You boys have any idea what touched off this brawl?" the officer asked them, appreciatively blowing out a long, smooth ribbon of tobacco smoke.

"No idea in the world," Rue assured him.

"And you don't know any of the fellows involved?"

Just then, Big Teddy Peterson turned from where he was being prodded into the police van and shook his fist at them.

"I've never seen any of those ruffians in my life," Chase lied earnestly.

The sergeant raised his eyebrows, then took another pull on his cheroot. "Got that lot loaded?" he called to where two of his colleagues were closing the back doors of the paddy wagon.

"You got more brawlers to take to the clink?" a fresh-faced young patrolman called back.

Chase held his breath as the sergeant looked them up and down again.

"Nah," he finally answered, grinning around the butt

of his cigar. "I think we've made all the arrests we're going to. Besides, we need to get that bunch back to the station."

Chase and Rue thanked the policeman, then stood watching the paddy wagon roll south on Wharf Street.

They were just congratulating each other on their narrow escape when the passengers from the *Andromeda* began to disembark. Chase recognized three of the men as officers of Boatman's Bank. He knew two others from his occasional visits to the Carondelet shipyards. The captains of several of the Gold Star steamers followed them down the landing stage and nodded at Chase and Rue as they passed by.

Then Boothe Rossiter stepped into view at the top of the gangway. Chase's stomach curdled at the sight of him.

From his slick, dark Macassared hair to his shiny black boots, Boothe was buffed and polished until he gleamed. He was trim and broad-shouldered and handsome enough to be an actor in one of the shows that played at the Varieties Theatre. He was also the laziest, most mean-spirited and arrogant son of a bitch Chase had ever had the misfortune to be partnered with.

"Surely Commodore Rossiter knows better than to give the command of the *Andromeda* to him," Rue muttered under his breath. "He'll break that darlin's back sure as we're standing here."

But then, Boothe was James Rossiter's son, the heir apparent to the packet line. It made sense that he'd be promoted from pilot to captain and given the most desirable posting.

Chase just didn't have to like it.

Rossiter must have known how he felt, because once he'd given instructions to Jake Skirlin, who seemed to be acting as the *Andromeda*'s clerk, Boothe sauntered down the gangway toward where Chase and Rue were standing. If he noticed they were more than a little battered and their clothes were in disarray, he chose to make no mention of it.

"Admiring my new command, Hardesty?" he asked, smiling to show teeth so white he must spend his evenings polishing them.

"It's a beautiful steamer, Rossiter." Chase almost choked, saying the words, but the steamboat itself was graceful and powerful and obviously of the latest design. "You sure you're the man to captain her?"

"I'm the one who took her out today," Boothe observed. "Who else do you think should get the appointment? You?"

That was closer to the truth than Rossiter knew.

"Why shouldn't he get it?" Rue spoke up. "He's twice the steersman anyone else is. If any pilot deserves to be promoted, it's Chase."

"Standing up for your master, are you, cub?" Boothe sneered.

Chase saw the color come up in his brother's face, but Rue had already started one brawl today, and taking on Commodore Rossiter's son just didn't seem smart. If he crossed the *Andromeda*'s new captain, Rue might lose his hard-won berth with the packet line.

Chase shrugged philosophically. "What people get and what they deserve don't always coincide."

Boothe Rossiter let it go at that. Instead he inclined his head toward the *Andromeda*. "You want to have a look at her?"

Chase knew he was letting himself in for a big dose of envy and a bigger one of regret if he took Rossiter up on his offer. But he'd just defended the *Andromeda* with his fists, and even if the steamer wasn't his, that gave him a proprietary interest.

"Sure," he answered.

Boothe gestured them aboard and led them across what seemed like half an acre of satiny wooden planking to the front of the main deck. A battery of five boilers nearly twenty-four feet long and more than three feet in diameter lay horizontal to the hull. They were an impressive sight.

"The boilers and engines were built by James Rees and Sons, in Pittsburgh," Rossiter told them. "According to the engineers, they'll use less wood and produce more steam than earlier models."

Chase had read about the new designs and was impressed by the iron sheathing above the firebox, the improved mud scupper, and the redesigned safety valves.

Boothe showed them through the open cargo area and stalls amidships to the back of the steamer where the engines lay. Big cylinders with their long, brass reciprocating rods were connected to the central shaft of the paddle wheel.

Chase nodded, recognizing several improvements that

had been made to the engine's design. "Very impressive," he observed.

"Now let me show you the rest."

With rising enthusiasm Boothe led them up the grand double staircase from where the engines and boilers lay on the main deck to the boiler deck above with its salon and cabins.

Chase was immediately struck by the grace of the wide promenades and, as they entered, the beauty of the salon. A line of brass and glass chandeliers ran down the center of the room. Gleaming mahogany chairs and tables clustered beneath them on bright, flower-patterned carpets. The gilt-trimmed doors that led to the first-class cabins were each numbered with a hand-painted china plaque.

Chase had never been a man who coveted things, but he wanted this. He longed to enjoy this beauty and opulence every day, to have something so unique and lovely under his command.

"It's all very grand," Rue mumbled begrudgingly.

Rossiter grinned. "Wait 'til you see the pilothouse."

Pausing to glance into one or two of the well-appointed staterooms and the spotless galleys, the three of them climbed past the Texas deck, where the crew and captain had their accommodations, to the most vital ten square feet on any steamer.

No expense had been spared in furnishing the wheelhouse. The lazy bench that ran across the back of the cabin was upholstered in deep-maroon leather. In the left front corner a squat, potbellied stove radiated heat, while the pilot's private water cooler sat on the right.

But what drew Chase immediately was the huge semi-circular wheel that rose through the floorboards. Set well forward in the alcove created by the side windows and the cabin's open front, the steersman would enjoy a commanding view of the river.

Chase stepped up before the chest-high wheel and curled his hands around the dark, burnished wood. As he did, a sensation he could never remember having radiated from the wheel into the palms of his hands. Warmth penetrated flesh and bone bringing with it a welcome so intense that his chest tightened and his eyes burned.

He wrapped his hands around the broad curve of the wheel, absorbing purpose and resolution and serenity through the very whorls of his fingertips. The *Andromeda* was more than wood and paint and machinery. It was more than graceful galleries, gleaming chandeliers, and opulent cabins. It was the single place in the world where Chase belonged.

"Quite a boat, isn't she, Hardesty?"

Boothe Rossiter's words shattered Chase's haze of wonder. He blinked the wheelhouse into focus around him, and with that clarity came the truth. No matter how right all this felt, the *Andromeda* wasn't his.

It belonged to Boothe Rossiter.

Chase would never stand with his feet braced on this deck and guide the *Andromeda* up the treacherous Missouri. He'd never ease her safely past the sawyers and sandbars that could fool a less proficient pilot. Nor would he ever duplicate this sense of rightness with any other vessel.

Knowing that didn't change a thing.

Chase couldn't think of any way to answer that wouldn't reveal his envy of Boothe Rossiter's new command. He simply nodded and relinquished his hold on the steamer's wheel, feeling as if he'd yielded up some part of himself.

Rue stepped up to take his place. The younger man clasped his hands around the wheel, then turned back grinning. "Oh, yes! She's wondrously fine!"

Though Chase saw the delight in his brother's face, there was none of the wonder or intensity. None of the magic. The *Andromeda* had spoken only to him.

"I can't wait to get her out on a clear stretch of river," Boothe enthused, his voice rising. "We'll tie down those damn safety valves, feed her fatwood, and just see what kind of speed those boilers can give us."

Chase compressed his lips. Rossiter spoke with the kind of reckless arrogance that killed a hundred steamers a year. With the kind of willful disregard for safety that littered the river with wrecks and cost scores of passengers their lives.

And all at once, Chase knew he couldn't stand idly by and let this irresponsible bastard destroy the *Andromeda*. She was his, by God! She was his destiny.

And all he had to do to claim the steamer was go back to James Rossiter and tell him he was willing to marry his daughter.

The idea of confronting Ann Rossiter and telling her what he'd done made his palms sweat. She'd be convinced he was betraying her—and he probably was.

When he had a chance to talk to her, he'd have to be prepared to make concessions, to offer whatever assurances she needed so he could have his way. So he could have the *Andromeda*.

He'd promise her a house with a garden where her child could play in the fresh air and sunshine. He'd offer her money for passage back to Philadelphia. He'd promise her anything so he could claim the *Andromeda* and make it his own.

By the time Boothe had escorted Rue and him back to the landing stage, Chase had made up his mind. He muttered his thanks, then set off up the levee.

Rue caught him as he turned up Locust Street. "Where the devil are you going in such a hurry?"

Chase heard the steel in his own voice when he gave his answer. "I'm going to see a man about a riverboat."

chapter two

M ISERABLE, LYING WEASEL!" ANN ROSSITER HISSED, cursing Chase Hardesty, the man who'd led her on, and then betrayed her trust. *The man she was supposed to marry in less than an hour.*

"Slimy, odious miscreant!"

Ann smacked her silver-backed hairbrush down on her dressing table and stalked across her bedchamber to the pair of tall, lace-curtained windows that overlooked Lucas Place. She'd been shut up in this room for the last two days, alternately weeping and pacing and calling Chase Hardesty every name she knew.

In a little while her stepfather was going to knock on her door expecting to escort her down to the parlor where Reverend Schuyler and her bridegroom were waiting.

"Vile, despicable conniver!"

And once they got downstairs, she was supposed to speak her vows to that *deplorable* man.

God knows, she should have expected Mr. Hardesty's duplicity. Hadn't men been taking advantage of her, *failing her outright*, since she was nine years old? She was the world's greatest fool for thinking—even for a moment—that Chase Hardesty was different.

Yet there had been something in his manner, a warmth in his eyes that swayed her. Because he seemed to care what she wanted, Ann had let herself believe there was something fine in him. Something forthright and honorable. Something she could trust.

Ann stared down from her window to the wrought-iron gate. On Tuesday afternoon Chase Hardesty had stood *right there* and lied to her. He'd given her the secret smile and confirming nod that assured her he'd refused her stepfather's offer.

Ann had gone down to dine with James Rossiter a few hours later, armored with new confidence. She should have noticed the glint in her stepfather's eyes as he held her chair or recognized the lie in his solicitousness, but Ann had been distracted when she saw her stepbrother's place at the table was empty. That's why the commodore's announcement had caught her so much by surprise.

"Chase Hardesty came back to see me late this afternoon," he began as Mary Fairley, their housekeeper, served the consommé.

"Oh?" Ann had said, registering not so much as a twinge of apprehension.

"It seems Mr. Hardesty has reconsidered my proposal."

Ann looked up.

"In exchange for ownership of the *Andromeda*, he's agreed to give your child his name."

Her spoon had clattered into her bowl, spattering the soup down her bodice. "He said he'd marry me?"

"Indeed he did."

"Are you sure?" she'd been surprised enough to ask him.

"I should be. Your Mr. Hardesty and I spent an hour negotiating concessions that include which of my best men will be assigned to the *Andromeda*."

But he promised! Ann had very nearly wailed at him. Chase Hardesty said he'd do what she wanted!

"Now, then," her stepfather continued, "I've gone ahead and made arrangements to have the wedding here at the house on Thursday morning."

"*This* Thursday morning?"

"Reverend Schuyler will come by to conduct the ceremony."

"But Thursday is the day after tomorrow!"

"The river's just opened for shipping," the commodore explained. "The *Andromeda*'s leaving Thursday afternoon."

Ann stared at him, panic burning up the back of her throat.

"Well, I'm afraid you'll just have to send a note around to Reverend Schuyler," she advised him as coolly as she could when her voice was quaking. "Tell him we won't be needing his services. I'm not marrying Mr. Hardesty on Thursday—or any other day, either."

"*Oh, my dear.*" Her stepfather looked at her over the bowl of his spoon. "You most certainly will marry him."

By the set of his jaw and the coldness in his eyes, Ann could see he meant it. Though his conviction lay over her like a heavy snow, she pushed to her feet.

"I have absolutely no intention of marrying some ruffian you lured in off the levee!" she said, her tone nearly as icy as his eyes. "I will not be sold into marriage—not even for the price of so fine a steamer."

"I say you'll wed Chase Hardesty!" the commodore thundered.

"I say I will not!"

Ann had turned and fled upstairs. She was frantically jamming clothes into the satchel gaping open on her bed a few minutes later when she heard her stepfather's tread in the hall outside. No matter what he said or did, no matter how he threatened her, she vowed she wasn't going to marry Chase Hardesty.

But instead of bursting in to argue with her, her stepfather simply turned the key in the lock on her bedroom door.

Ann had scrambled across the room and tried the knob.

"Father!" She smacked her palm against the wooden panel. "Damn it, Father, you can't just shut me up like a prisoner!"

But then, wasn't that exactly what she'd been since her father's men had dragged her home from Memphis? The truth swelled over her like water breaching the lip of a levee. James Rossiter was never going to relinquish his hold on her—or on this child. He was never going to allow her to make a life for herself.

He was going to marry her to Chase Hardesty, whether she wanted a husband or not. She might just as well start embroidering the linens in her hope chest with neat little H's.

Ann wobbled back toward her bed, then slid to the floor beside it. Huddled there, curled in upon herself, she was intensely aware of the fullness in her breasts and belly, intensely aware that she was carrying a child. For weeks she'd tried to pretend it didn't exist, to will it away, but she couldn't deny it any longer.

She splayed her hands over the mound of her stomach and accepted that the child growing inside was hers to provide for and protect. The responsibility terrified her. Tears sprang to her eyes. How was she going to do that?

Was marrying Chase Hardesty the answer? As long as he worked aboard James Rossiter's boats, he'd have to see that there was food on the table and a roof over their heads.

Could Ann promise even that much if she succeeded in leaving the town house? She had no place to go, no clear idea of how she'd make a living, no friends who'd help her or take her in.

In the end, there was only Chase Hardesty. Chase and Chase and Chase and Chase. There was only marriage to a man she barely knew, to a man who had promised one thing and done another. To a man who owed his allegiance to her stepfather.

Ann curled up tighter. How could she make vows to

such a man? To someone who'd proved he had no honor, gave no credence to his promises? What kind of a father could a man like that be to her child?

But then, she couldn't imagine the rawboned riverman wanting anything to do with a baby. She couldn't believe there was enough gentleness in those broad, rude hands to hold one, or enough room in that deceiving heart for someone else's bastard.

She wiped away a freshet of tears and heaved a sigh.

She had hoped for so much more from Mr. Hardesty, far more than she ever expected from the men in her own family. He'd inspired a wonderful and unexpected trust in her, then turned right around and broken his word.

Still, Chase Hardesty was her only chance, her only hope.

Ann had stayed balled up on the floor in her bedchamber half the night, sorting through her options, turning them over in her mind like the pieces of a puzzle she was determined to solve.

In the end she found a way to live with the inevitable—and if marriage to Chase Hardesty didn't give her all she wanted, at least it promised more than she had.

Still, when the commodore came knocking on the door, Ann wished with all her heart she could send him away.

"Ann," he called out. "The parson's waiting."

Her hands started to tremble.

"Ann?"

In spite of her stepfather's growing annoyance, she detected a shading of real concern in his voice. It stirred the rich, dark roux of resentment and promise that had seasoned relations between them since her mother died.

Before she could respond to him, James Rossiter snapped the lock and shouldered his way into the room. He made a quick perusal, as if he expected conspirators lurking in the corners, then let his gaze come to rest on her.

"You look very nice."

Ann did her best not to be pleased. "You ought to like the way I look. *You* picked out my wedding dress."

Her maid had delivered it scarcely an hour before.

"Still, it suits you."

Ann allowed herself a glance at the mirror that hung above her dressing table and saw a slender woman in an ivory-colored gown of silk and lace. Someone pale and gossamer and almost fragile—except for the undeniable rise of her expanding belly.

"I ordered a veil, too, didn't I?" the commodore prompted.

Ann turned to the froth of netting draped across the coverlet. If she were making vows to someone she truly cared for, the circlet of silken flowers and gauzy lace would be a delicious indulgence. As things were, that veil made a mockery of marrying in purity and for true love.

Shame washed her cheeks. "Please don't make me wear that."

She heard her stepfather draw breath as if he meant to insist, and then he shrugged. "Do what you like about the veil."

He offered his arm, and Ann lay her icy fingers against

his sleeve. They were halfway down the stairs when Ann caught the sweet, rich scent of roses and saw through the open parlor doors the towering vases of hothouse flowers that flanked the mantel. Someone was playing the wedding march on the piano, and as they crossed the hall, Mary Fairley smiled encouragement and handed Ann a bouquet of rosebuds.

It was almost as if this was a real wedding, as if what followed was going to be a real marriage.

Ann stole a glance at where the minister stood with her bridegroom and a smaller, darker man before the fireplace.

No matter how she'd tried to prepare herself, Ann wasn't ready to face Chase Hardesty or take her vows. She most especially wasn't ready to take on the duties of this stranger's wife.

In spite of that, James Rossiter steered her into her place before the parson and abandoned her to her bridegroom.

For a moment Ann diligently studied the toes of Chase Hardesty's polished boots. She raised her gaze to the sharply creased pinstripe trousers, then to his black broadcloth frock coat. His linen was dazzlingly white, and his cravat was perfectly tied. She could smell the heavy dose of Macassar oil he'd used to tame his curly hair.

Finally, knowing there was no help for it, Ann raised her gaze to her bridegroom's face—and went cold with shock.

He might be turned out well enough, but his lip was

split. There was a red scuff along the side of his jaw. His left eye was all but swollen shut and the color of ripe plums.

Why, he'd been brawling!

Fiery outrage scalded up Ann's throat and flared in her cheeks. Not only had Chase Hardesty proved himself a liar and a cheat, but here was evidence that he was of a pugnacious and violent nature! How could her stepfather marry her off to such a man?

Ann might have turned and demanded an answer of the commodore directly, except that she'd made her decision. She had no choice if she wanted to get out of the town house.

"Dear-ly Be-lov-ed." Reverend Schuyler launched into the wedding vows, his sonorous voice far more suited to Christ Episcopal Church's vaulted sanctuary than the Rossiter parlor. "We are gathered here before God and this company to unite this Man and this Woman..."

The words of the ceremony broke over Ann like high surf. The magnitude of the charges, the admonitions and implications left her breathless and reeling.

Chase Hardesty spoke his vows clearly and gravely, almost as if he meant them.

The foul, contemptible liar.

When Chase was done, Reverend Schuyler turned to her. "Repeat after me," he directed. "I, Ann, take thee, Chase..."

Ann couldn't help the momentary flare of truculence. To speak another word would seal her fate, bind her to a man who had already proved himself false and unreliable.

It would seal the fate of her child. She didn't want this baby born and raised in this house, did she? She didn't want this child manipulated the way she'd been manipulated for most of her life.

Some final bit of resistance inside her crumbled. She drew a long uneven breath and spoke the words that would change everything.

"I, Ann, take thee, Chase..."

As she continued, Ann did her best to shade the familiar phrases with some semblance of sincerity. In marrying her Chase had agreed to look after her and her child. She supposed she should be grateful.

Yet for all her good intentions, when Chase reached to slide the simple gold band onto her finger, Ann clenched her fist.

He looked down at those balled fingers, then up at her.

She'd closed her hand involuntarily, but somehow once it was knotted up tight, she couldn't bring herself to open it.

Her new husband's lapis-blue eyes iced over as he relentlessly pried open her hand. He forced the gold band over her knuckle and held it in place.

"With this ring, I thee wed," he insisted implacably.

As if he were eager to conclude the ceremony before anything else could happen, Reverend Schuyler rattled off the rest of the ceremony on one long breath. "In as much as Chase and Ann have spoken vows before God and this company, I pronounce them Man and Wife. Amen."

Before Chase could try to seal their union with a kiss,

Ann jerked her hand out of his grasp and turned to where her stepfather was approaching.

James Rossiter bent and bussed Ann's cheek. "You won't be sorry," he promised.

Frankly, Ann doubted that, but she held her peace.

Just then, her stepbrother Boothe, the commodore's son by his first wife, stepped up and caught Ann's arm. Though the gesture might have looked innocuous, his fingers bit deep enough to crush wrinkles into her gown's satin sleeve.

"It must be so gratifying," he all but purred, "to once again prove yourself the favored child. I wouldn't have said it was possible for you to deprive me of my first command, dear sister, but somehow you've managed it."

Ann shivered at the loathing in his black eyes.

"I'm sure Ann appreciates the sacrifice you're making for her sake," James Rossiter put in silkily, "especially in her current situation. But you'll get everything I promised you, if you'll just be patient. Now congratulate your sister and wish her well."

When the commodore stepped beyond her to offer a crisp white envelope to the Reverend, Boothe did as his father had bidden him. "May I offer you my good wishes for a long—and fecund—marriage," Boothe said with a sneer.

Then, before Ann could respond or turn away, he lowered his head and kissed her. Though she closed her eyes and compressed her lips, the high, sharp smell of him washed over her. Her ears rang; her mouth went hot and wet. She fought to swallow the sick, sour burn of bile at the back of her throat.

Just when she thought she might disgrace herself, Chase slipped his hand around her waist and drew her to him. "Just so you know," he interceded smoothly, addressing Boothe over her head. "I mean to take very good care of the *Andromeda* for you."

Ann was grateful when her stepbrother turned the bright beam of his malice from her to her new husband, though Chase didn't seem the least bit quelled by it.

"We'll just have to see if you're man enough to be her master," Boothe snapped and stalked away. For a moment it wasn't clear if Boothe meant the *Andromeda*—or Ann herself.

Though Boothe was gone, Ann couldn't help the tremor that ran through her. "Thank you for running him off," she managed to whisper.

"This isn't the first time I've had words with your stepbrother," Chase assured her, "and I doubt it will be the last."

Chase's dislike of Boothe gave the first hint that there might be some affinity between them.

She'd been at odds with Boothe, it seemed, from the moment she arrived in St. Louis. As a five-year-old, bewildered by her mother's sudden marriage and the neverending trip West, all Ann had wanted was to make friends with the tall, dark-haired boy who lived in her stepfather's house.

But from the moment they arrived, Boothe had set out to show her how unwelcome she was. He made her plead with him not to drop her beautiful bisque doll James Rossiter had given her down the stairwell—then done it anyway. He'd thrown one shoe of each pair she owned into the stove in the kitchen, then taunted her when she was punished. She'd never known when he might jump out at her and scare her, or hit her hard enough to make her cry.

In the six months she'd been home from Philadelphia, she'd found a dozen new reasons to detest her step-brother. One of the reasons she'd resigned herself to this marriage was that no matter how determined her father was to keep her here, she was going to be legally able to gather her belongings and move to Chase Hardesty's rooms in town.

"Ann?"

Chase's voice scattered her thoughts like milkweed down.

"I'd like to introduce you to my brother, Ruben Hardesty." He gestured to the slim, swarthy man who'd been his groomsman.

Ann noticed right off that Ruben looked nearly as battered as Chase did. His nose was swollen and the skin along his cheekbone was black-and-blue. Wherever Chase had been brawling, they'd fought together.

For no reason she could name, the notion pleased her.

"Hello, Ruben," she greeted him and was struck by how dissimilar these two brothers seemed. Chase was big, broad-shouldered, and solidly built. His hair was a ruddy brown and his eyes were bright as bachelor buttons. Ruben was slim and exotic, dark as a Spaniard and lithe as a hickory withe. His thick, black hair curled long on his collar.

Something about the close fit of his clothes and the ornate ruby-red stickpin threaded through his cravat hinted that he was more than a bit of a dandy. He confirmed the notion when he bowed over Ann's hand and brought it to his lips.

"What a pleasure it is to welcome such a lovely and cultured lady to the Hardesty clan."

Ann couldn't help responding to the glint in those warm, brown eyes and the teasing curve of his mouth beneath his closely trimmed mustache.

Ann dipped in a somewhat graceless curtsey. "Why, thank you, Mr. Hardesty. I hope I never do anything to jeopardize your good opinion of me."

"I doubt there's danger of that"—he turned a wide, white grin on her—"especially in *this* family. And just so you know, everyone calls me Rue."

Just then, Mary Fairley came to give Ann a little hug and offer champagne. "I hope your captain proves himself a good papa to the wee one," Mary confided in a whisper before she moved on.

On the far side of the room James Rossiter cleared his throat. "I'd like to propose a toast," he offered, "in honor of my daughter's marriage."

Everyone raised their glasses.

"May Ann and Captain Hardesty enjoy years of health and happiness," he offered.

They all drank.

All except Ann, who, with a stubborn show of pride,

refused to give her stepfather the satisfaction of accepting his good wishes.

They'd barely swallowed the champagne when James Rossiter went on. "Now, then, since I know Captain Hardesty is casting off at four o'clock and eager to get down to the riverfront, I have one last toast to give you." He raised his glass again. "To Captain Hardesty, my new son-in-law, and to the *Andromeda*. May the river always lie deep before the both of you and may your troubles fall quickly in your wake."

"Hear, hear!" everyone agreed and drank.

From the way Chase swallowed the champagne, Ann could see he was impatient to be on about his duties. But Ann had a few things to settle with her new husband before he left.

"I need to have a word with you," she told him. "We can talk in my father's study."

Ann saw Chase cast a glance in the commodore's direction. That he thought he needed her father's permission to talk to his wife boded ill for their discussion. And though Ann's belly fluttered with uneasiness, she refused to back down.

"Follow me," she directed and led him down the hall.

LAST SPRING CHASE'S SISTER MILLIE HAD MARRIED SAM Seifert in the orchard behind his parents' house, then they'd all gone up to the top of the bluffs for a picnic. When his brother Will had spoken vows with Etta Mae

Hoffsteader two years ago, they'd done it on the bow of her family's houseboat, and pretty much everybody ended up in the river.

This wedding sure as hell hadn't been the kind the Hardestys were used to. *His* bride had stood up beside him like a spire of ice. *His* bride had refused to accept his ring, as if she didn't think it was good enough. Now she was sweeping him down the hall toward her father's study like a truant dragged back to school by her ear.

He supposed she had a right to be mad at him. He *had* promised her one thing and done something else entirely. But then, he'd tried to explain.

He'd come to Lucas Place three times in the last two days to see if he could make things right with her. He wanted to tell her what it was like to walk the *Andromeda*'s decks, to stand in the wheelhouse and know it was where he belonged. He needed to make her understand what captaining the *Andromeda* meant to him. But every time he'd come, the housekeeper had told him Ann wasn't seeing callers. Which, he was sure, meant she wasn't seeing him.

Of course, she seemed eager enough to see him now—*now*, when he had pressing duties down at the riverfront.

She gestured him into her father's study, into the room where James Rossiter had first made his outrageous proposition, and closed the door behind them.

Before she could call him in to account, Chase began to apologize. "When I left here Tuesday morning I swear I had every intention of keeping my word. I honestly did tell your father that I didn't want to marry—"

"I don't care why you broke your word to me," Ann interrupted, gone all stiff and imperious. "That you did, says all I need to know about the man I married."

Her condemnation of him was so complete, her refusal to consider his side of things so absolute, there didn't seem room for compromise. But if she was willing to look at the situation logically, there were real advantages to this marriage, things that would benefit both of them—if she'd just cooperate.

"Now, Ann," he began, doing his best to cajole her. "If you just let me explain—"

"I don't want an explanation," she told him crisply. "I don't want anything from you except the keys to your house."

"To my house?"

"To your house, your rooms. To wherever it is you stay when you're not piloting a riverboat."

Chase considered the riverfront hotel where he and Rue had been bunking for the best part of a week. The place was cheap, but barely habitable. The other boarders weren't the kind of folks Ann Rossiter was used to spending time with.

"I don't keep a place in town," he told her.

"But you must!" she insisted.

He shrugged and shook his head. "I don't need rooms during the shipping season, and I spend the winter up-river with my folks, cutting trees for their woodlot."

She stared at him openmouthed. "But—but where do you expect me to live while you're away?"

"Live?" he asked. "Your father said you could stay on here. I told you that."

"Here," she repeated, something terrible and destructive going on behind her eyes. Something that turned the clear, bright hazel dark and impervious. "I can't stay here."

It was a complication Chase hadn't foreseen. That he'd need to find her someplace to live hadn't once occurred to him. If it had, he'd have done his best to make provisions for her, though he didn't have the faintest idea where he might have found her suitable lodgings or how he would have paid for them.

"You're bound to be more comfortable here where there are people to look after you," he offered reasonably. "Besides, there isn't time to find you someplace else. The *Andromeda*'s pulling out this afternoon."

Ann drew herself up straight as a carpenter's rule. "I won't stay here!" she told him, her mouth gone tight.

He supposed Ann had her reasons for wanting to leave. If she was angry with him about agreeing to marry her, she was probably even angrier with her father for buying her a bridegroom. And anyone could see the enmity between Ann and her stepbrother.

Chase's duties aboard the steamer gnawed at him. He ought to be down at the levee meeting his passengers, supervising the loading of cargo, and checking the *Andromeda* over one last time.

"Please, Ann," he urged her. "Stay on with your father while I'm gone. We'll find a place of our own when I get back."

With luck, he'd have wages by then and the captain's share of the *Andromeda*'s profits at the end of the trip. According to the agreement he and the commodore had signed just before the ceremony, full title to the steamer would come to him when he completed the last run of the season.

"And when exactly will you be back?" Ann asked him.

She sounded calmer and somewhat resigned. Chase began to breathe easier. "I'll be back in July."

The room went silent; it was the hollow, roaring kind of silence that followed a clap of thunder.

"*July?*" she echoed incredulously. "How can a packet run to Sioux City take four months?"

Chase could see for all that she was the commodore's daughter, she didn't understand a thing about the shipping business. "On the first run up the Missouri River in the spring," he explained, "the packets are contracted all the way to Fort Benton."

"In the Montana Territory?"

At least she knew her geography.

"The water isn't deep enough most of the year to accommodate steamers as big as the *Andromeda*, but we can navigate upstream on the spring flood and come home on the summer snowmelt. Even at that it's a long, hard trip."

"If shipping as far as Fort Benton is so difficult," she asked, diverted for the moment, "why on earth do you do it?"

"Money," Chase admitted, weighed down all at once by his new responsibilities. "It's the single most profitable trip any of the boats make all season."

She stood for a moment staring past him, her eyes unfocused and her mouth pursed. Something about her abstraction made him uneasy.

Then, all at once, she smiled. "I guess I'll just need to resign myself."

As soon as he got back from Fort Benton, he promised himself, he'd find her as nice a place to live as he could afford, someplace where they'd be able to start their life together. Someplace big enough to accommodate the baby and maybe a child or two of their own when the time came. It was good to know Ann could bend, that she could see things his way.

He turned his attention to more practical matters. "There's a small account in my name at Boatman's Bank you can draw on if you need money," he told her, beginning to wish he was leaving her better off. "If you need more than what's there, I'm sure your father would be willing to advance you—"

"I'll be fine," she assured him hastily.

Chase nodded; it was time to go. For a moment he stared down into his new wife's soft face, focused on the sweet, rosy fullness of her mouth. Her beauty moved him, filled him with a simmering sensual warmth. He and Ann had just spoken their vows, he reasoned, so what could it hurt if he took her in his arms and kissed her good-bye?

Before he could move, Ann stepped back. "Have a good trip," she said.

It was a chilly dismissal, and any hope Chase might have had of kissing his wife abruptly evaporated. "Take care of yourself and the baby while I'm gone," he offered. "I'll be back—"

"Yes, I know. In July."

"July," he echoed. They certainly weren't parting the way he'd hoped, yet somehow they'd maneuvered through the morass of misunderstandings and expectations and had clear water ahead.

He took his leave, making sure to close the door to the commodore's study behind him. He was three strides down the hall when he heard something fragile, and probably expensive, shatter against the opposite side of the wide wooden panel.

chapter three

CHASE BRACED BOTH HANDS AGAINST THE *Andromeda's* big wooden wheel and watched the last of the passengers straggling aboard the steamer, three decks below. He'd already looked over the distribution of the cargo and checked the manifests. He'd greeted most of the cabin passengers. Not five minutes before, he'd rung the bells that connected the pilothouse to the engine room and signaled Cal Watkins to build up steam in the boiler and limber up the engine.

Soon they'd be getting underway, beginning Chase's first run as the *Andromeda's* captain. He'd been dreaming about this moment all his life. He imagined the way he'd stand with his feet planted on the deck of his own boat, how he'd watch the Missouri River country unfurl before him as if he owned that, too.

He drew in a long satisfied breath and let it go. He was

a man in command of his own riverboat, a man in command of his own destiny. What Chase couldn't seem to control was his brother's curiosity—or his impertinence.

While Chase gave the orders that would ready the *Andromeda* for departure, Rue had settled into one corner of the lazy bench that ran across the back of the wheelhouse.

"So," he drawled as Chase consulted his river charts for what must have been the twentieth time, "when exactly do you mean to tell Pa and Ma about the new Mrs. Hardesty?"

Chase was concentrating on the maps, not on his new wife. Still, he knew better than to ignore Rue's question outright. He marked his place with his finger and raised his head. "I'll tell them about Ann when the time comes."

"When we stop home on our way upriver?" Rue pressed him.

"I expect."

"Are you going to mention that Ann's in the family way?" Rue wanted to know. "Or are you going to spring that on them the way you did on me?"

Chase could hear the scorn in his brother's voice that masked his hurt. He truly had meant to tell Rue about Ann, about Ann's baby, and the agreement he'd made with the commodore. He just hadn't been able to find the words.

The bargain sounded so cold-blooded when you said it straight-out. Yet even if his wedding to Ann Rossiter had been more a transaction than a love match, what was

62

wrong with that if both parties were satisfied with the outcome? Though after their interview in the commodore's study, Chase couldn't say Ann seemed all that satisfied.

As much to cover his own discomfort as to get on with his duties, Chase strode to the wheelhouse doorway and shouted for the mate to ring the departure bell, signaling any passengers lingering on the levee to get aboard. He returned to the wheel and stepped on the peddle to blow the departure whistle—*th-oo-op, thoop, thoop, th-oo-op, thoop*—to let the other steamers know they were preparing to leave the levee.

"What I mean is—" Rue continued, never one to be put off. "Well, I wondered about Ann's baby. It isn't yours, is it? You and I must have been at Ma and Pa's about the time she . . . "

In the last two days Chase had spent more time than he cared to admit wondering about Ann, Ann's baby, and especially about Ann's baby's father. Who was he? What kind of man would seduce a respectable, gently reared woman, get her with child, then refuse to marry her?

Chase might speculate about that, but he didn't want anyone else doing it. He turned and faced his brother, meeting his dark gaze head-on. "Ann's baby is mine now," he said simply. "That's all that matters."

Rue paused, then inclined his head. "I see what you mean."

"Good," Chase answered. "Good. And if anybody starts asking questions—especially Ma—I'd be obliged if you tell them that baby belongs to me."

"But if I was able to count back far enough to figure out you aren't that baby's father," Rue pointed out, "don't you think Ma—"

"Let me handle Ma," Chase warned him.

Just then, a horsecab came clattering across the cobblestones at a speed that sent stevedores, transfer agents, and passengers sprinting out of the way. It came to a swaying stop at the foot of the *Andromeda*'s landing stage.

"If that's one of our passengers," Rue observed, coming to stand at Chase's shoulder, "he's cut things pretty damn close."

Chase nodded in agreement and watched the small, bandy-legged driver clamber down from his box. Against a heavy wind, he battled his way back to the carriage door and heaved it open.

A woman emerged somewhat gracelessly, then clamped one hand to the top of her head to batten down her broad-brimmed hat. She glanced once at the ship, then gestured for the driver to gather up her baggage.

Chase didn't recall seeing the name of any lone women on the passenger list, which meant this lady was joining her husband, probably after a day of perusing St. Louis's shops.

As the woman started up the *Andromeda*'s landing stage, her overloaded driver bobbing in her wake, a particularly strong gust of wind molded her deep-blue cloak close against her body.

Chase saw at once that she was pregnant. "*Oh, dear God!*" he breathed.

Rue squinted and bent closer to the window. "Is that Ann?"

"I sure as hell hope not," Chase muttered, then bolted out of the pilothouse. When he reached the main deck the woman in the wide-brimmed hat was standing at the lip of the gangway.

"I'm sorry, ma'am," Jake Skirlin, the *Andromeda*'s clerk, was saying. "We're all sold out of first-class cabins, and even deck passage is at a minimum. Perhaps I can direct you to another..."

Just then the woman raised her head, and Chase saw his worst fears realized. It was Ann Rossiter.

Ann *Hardesty*, he corrected himself.

Before she answered, Ann tipped her chin in that prim, ladylike way Chase was coming to recognize—and detest.

"You misunderstand me, sir. I don't need first class accommodations. I'd like to be shown to the captain's cabin."

"To the captain's cabin?" Skirlin echoed.

For a moment, Chase wondered if he could simply disavow her, say he'd never seen this woman before in his life. He didn't know what Ann was doing here or what she hoped to accomplish, but there was something about the rigidity of her stance and the way the green leather gloves pulled across her knuckles as she balled her fists that made him think he didn't have much choice about claiming her.

"It's all right, Skirlin," he said, coming toward them

around the tall, finialed post at the foot of the grand staircase. "This lady is my wife."

Chase saw the clerk's mouth drop open in astonishment before he turned his full attention on Ann. "Go home," he told her.

"I won't!" The words were sharp, clipped, and, judging from her tone, nonnegotiable.

"We're casting off in ten minutes. I don't want you aboard the *Andromeda* when we do."

Ann gave her head a quick, dismissing shake. "I don't care what you want. I'm coming with you."

He could see by the taut line of her jaw that she meant it and was fully prepared to fight to win her way. Chase didn't have the time or patience to convince her otherwise.

He wasn't about to stand here on the deck with half the crew looking on and argue with her, either. He wasn't going to let Ann Rossiter—Ann *Hardesty*, damn it—ruin one of the most important moments of his life.

He caught her arm and escorted her, none too gently, in the direction of the stairs.

"If we're not back before you hear the order to cast off," he told Skirlin, "load Mrs. Hardesty's baggage and pay her driver. Give him a generous tip, too; those valises look to weigh half as much as he does."

Chase all but dragged Ann up two flights of stairs to where his cabin sat at the front of the Texas deck. Once they were alone he'd set things straight with her, then pack her and her valises back to Lucas Place.

As they approached his stateroom, Chase saw Rue

leaning over the railing outside the wheelhouse on the deck above, his face bright with interest. Chase shot his brother the kind of glare that usually set stevedores trembling, then escorted Ann into his cabin.

The office/sitting room and adjoining bedroom were compact but luxuriously appointed, as suited the master of such a fast and graceful steamer. It was certainly the fanciest place Chase had ever lived. But since he'd taken command, he'd barely had time to notice the intricate millwork, the turkey-red carpets, and the elegant furnishings. For a moment he saw them through Ann's eyes and was pleased at their understated elegance.

Then he narrowed his focus to his wife, standing tall and poker-straight in the middle of his stateroom—where she most certainly didn't belong.

"All right, Ann," he said as reasonably as he could. "What's this all about?"

Ann plucked a long ivory hatpin from her hat, removed the wide-brimmed velvety thing, then patted her hair into place.

The presumption in that gesture made Chase clench his teeth.

"I decided"—Ann tilted her chin up another notch—"that since you don't keep rooms in town, I'd live aboard the *Andromeda.*"

It took Chase a moment to catch his breath. "You can't just move in here!" he protested.

"And why not?"

Several answers flashed across his mind: because women aboard a riverboat were as useless as bulls with udders; because no hothouse lady could bear up to the noise and dirt and rough companions. Because they were headed up the cantankerous Missouri, not on some picnic excursion. Because Ann was carrying a child and needed looking after.

Because he didn't want her here. He didn't want her aboard the *Andromeda* because this moment was his, his alone. He wanted to savor every hoot of the whistle, every riffle of wind across the water. Every prickle of pride.

He didn't want her here because it would be too damned difficult to have someone so young and lovely—and pregnant with someone else's child—living in such proximity. Just thinking about having her here—sharing these rooms, for God's sake—made him itch all over.

Since he couldn't explain that to Ann, he did his best to be reasonable. "Now, Ann," he cajoled, "it would certainly make more sense for you to stay at the town house where you have family to look after you."

"I don't care what makes sense." She faced him, her hands knotted at her waist and color flaming in her cheeks. "I'm your responsibility."

The thorn in his side is what she meant.

"I met my responsibilities," Chase pointed out. "I made provision for you to stay on with your father while I was away."

"Without even asking me what I wanted!"

He hadn't had a chance to ask her; Ann had refused to see him. Besides, he'd done what was quite obviously best for her, and her inability to admit it infuriated him.

Hadn't she vowed to "honor and obey" him just this morning?

"You don't belong on the *Andromeda*," he told her baldly. "The idea of you living aboard is ridiculous, irresponsible."

"Nevertheless," she answered. "I mean to stay."

"Goddamn it, Ann!" he shouted at her. "Why are you here? Why are you so bent on leaving your father's house?"

"Do you think"—her words were harsh and bitten off short—"I'd have come to you if I had anywhere else to go?"

Chase felt the impact of that question in his chest.

"I'm here," she went on, "because the commodore married me off to someone I'd never laid eyes on until two days ago. Because he sold me to a common steersman to save the Rossiter name from scandal.

"I'm here"—her voice thickened, darkened—"because after his doing that, I don't trust him to put my best interests—or the best interests of this baby—ahead of his own."

After his years on the river, Chase had seen Rossiter's ruthlessness in the deals he'd made and the men he'd fired without a thought. That the commodore had married Ann off so hastily and to someone like him, reinforced that the commodore put his own needs and desires ahead of everyone else's.

"So you'll take your chances with me instead?" he asked.

"You've only betrayed me once—" she answered with more than a little bitterness. "At least so far."

Her barb sank deep, and Chase couldn't help grimacing.

"If you stayed aboard I wouldn't have time to look after you," he warned her. "I'm on duty twenty-four hours a day. I stand watches, supervise the navigation and engineering, and make sure the passengers' needs are being taken care of. There are logs and ledgers to keep, decisions to make, and goods to sell at stops along the way."

"You needn't take so much as a moment away from your duties for my sake." Ann stood perfectly still and watched him pace. "You'll barely know I'm here."

"Oh, Ann!" Chase stopped to laugh. "I'd know you were here if I were deaf and blind. Are you really going to be able to ignore me if we're living in these two little rooms together?"

Ann's eyes went wide, as if she hadn't fully considered what their living arrangements were going to be.

"Perhaps you have a vacant cabin," she suggested hopefully.

"Not a one."

She hesitated and pressed her fingers to her lips as if she were casting about for an alternative.

Just then the bell in the steeple of St. Louis Cathedral began to toll. It was four o'clock.

Chase straightened like a shot. He didn't have time to argue with this woman who, in a moment of utter insanity, he'd made his wife. He had his duties to perform.

"I'm going to spare you the humiliation of carrying you

bodily off this boat," he began, "but don't imagine for a moment this arrangement is permanent. I'm flagging down the first steamer we pass that's heading downstream and sending you back to your father.

"Now, before we cast off—should I send word to him that you're here with me?"

"I left a note."

"Good enough," he answered and slammed out of the cabin.

He took the steps to the pilothouse three at a time. Rue was at the wheel when he arrived.

"I didn't see Ann leave," the younger man observed with the slightest of smiles. "Did I miss my chance to say good-bye?"

Chase scowled at his brother and took one last look at the charts. "Whether Ann left the *Andromeda* is none of your concern."

"Well, you have to admire her gumption," Rue went on, "storming aboard this afternoon and demanding passage."

"I can't imagine why I should admire that," Chase shot back. "Now, will you sound that damn whistle to let everyone know we're leaving?"

As Rue blew a single long blast to signal their intentions, Chase made his way down to the hurricane deck. He paused to take one last look at St. Louis, at the cobblestoned levee and the rows of big, brick warehouses rising in tiers beyond it. Then he shouted down to the mate who was waiting on the foredeck.

"Mr. Steinwehr, single up the double lines."

Gustave "Goose" Steinwehr gave the order to his deckhands, and several men scrambled up the levee to loose the ropes that bound the *Andromeda* to big iron links set into the cobblestones.

"Let the stern and aft lines go."

As the hands dropped more of the ropes, the stern of the steamer began to drift out into the current.

Chase turned and called to Rue. "Signal the slow bell ahead and give me some left rudder."

Rue rang the engine room and muscled the wheel around. As the *Andromeda* eased closer to the levee, Chase directed that they drop the bow lines.

Then, once the hands were aboard, Chase signaled for three sharp blasts of the whistle and gave the order for backing down. Graceful as a ballerina, the *Andromeda* eased away from the bank and turned out into the brisk Mississippi River current.

A hot tingle of satisfaction sizzled from Chase's scalp to his toes. He was in command now; the riverboat was his.

"All stop," he sang out once they were well beyond the line of boats tied up at the bank. Facing upstream to the north, Chase sensed the steamer drift a little beneath him and took an intoxicating sip of the river's power before he gave the order.

"Right rudder, full ahead." The *Andromeda* homed to the main channel like a swallow to its nest.

For a long, shining moment Chase stood alone on the hurricane deck and let the cold March wind tear at him. It plastered his clothes against his body and yanked at his hair. It made his cheeks sting and his eyes water. Never had he felt more alive than he did at this moment, like the world was his for the asking. Like he was a man who'd proved himself.

With a whoop of pure elation, Chase spun on his heel and strode back to the wheelhouse.

Once inside, he nudged Rue aside and wrapped his hands around the wheel's elegantly tapered spokes. He caressed the satin-smooth turnings and savored the feel of the engine's vibration in the hollows of his palms.

He closed his eyes and let loose a sigh that felt like it had been building behind his sternum for half his life. He'd never believed he could have this—a boat of his own and a river he could follow into the sunset—the sum total of all he'd ever wanted for himself.

As he guided the *Andromeda* north, the banks of the Mississippi rolled past him. To the east lay Illinois, swampy scrub country that masked its towns and villages in a gray-brown haze of branches. To the west the state of Missouri was slipping by, the St. Louis waterfront giving way to lumber mills and manufacturing plants, scattered farmsteads and forested banks that climbed a low, gray bluff set well back from the water.

Chase rang the bells to the engine room for half-speed as he maneuvered the *Andromeda* toward the mouth of the Chain of Rocks channel. It was one of the most treacherous sections on the Mississippi. In just the last ten years its rocky, saw-toothed reefs had killed seventeen steamboats outright and maimed countless others.

The current was stiff and the Mississippi so swollen by

spring runoff that the *Andromeda* was having to fight up every inch of the Chain's seven-mile course.

"Eddy to port," Rue pointed out from where he was leaning against the breastboard at the front of the pilot-house.

Chase held the wheel over hard, then brought it back. The *Andromeda* came about like a saloon girl ruffling her petticoats at a potential customer.

In the next hour and a half, they clawed their way north, struggling upriver toward the point where the Missouri flowed into the Mississippi from the west. The *Andromeda* bucked as they swung bow-first into the Missouri's current. Then, as they penetrated the mouth of the river that would take them all the way to Montana, she settled again.

"They say boys go up the Mississippi, and the men the Missouri," Rue offered with a grin. "Guess what that makes us?"

"Damn fools for getting into steamboating in the first place," Chase answered and turned into a crossing toward the opposite bank.

"Want me to take the wheel?" Rue asked eagerly.

Chase measured the pleasure of piloting the *Andromeda* against the demands of his other duties and shook his head. "I'll hold her steady for awhile yet."

Rue shrugged, then ambled toward the door. "I'll head down and get us some coffee before the cooks start dishing up supper."

Chase nodded absently and let him go.

Though piloting took most of Chase's concentration, he couldn't seem to keep his thoughts from straying to

Ann. How delicate she'd looked as she'd glided across the parlor this morning. How stubborn and uncompromising she'd been, standing at the head of the gangway this afternoon.

He'd recognized the resolve in her that first day, but it had been tempered by the mortification of being offered in marriage as damaged goods. Chase saw now that when she'd clenched her fist and refused his ring, it had been as much an act of rebellion directed at her father as at him.

But when he'd faced her across the cabin this afternoon, she'd showed such temerity and resolve that Chase found himself wishing he could give her what she wanted. Still, keeping Ann aboard the *Andromeda* was impossible. No matter what James Rossiter had done or how single-minded he was when it came to his daughter, Ann was better off in St. Louis than on a steamer bound for Montana.

Chase stayed on at the wheel for a good deal longer than he'd intended, well into a sunset that turned the river ahead to molten copper. It wasn't until after they'd tied up at Portage de Sioux for the night, that Chase left the wheelhouse, finally resigned to dealing with Ann.

She was his wife, his responsibility, and maybe once they'd shared a companionable dinner, he'd be able to make her see it was best that she take passage home.

Making his way down to the Texas deck, Chase paused outside the door to his cabin. He smoothed his hair, let out a long, gusty sigh, and reached for the knob. It turned beneath his hand, but when he leaned into the panel nothing happened. He jiggled the latch and nudged a little harder. The door didn't budge.

Ann had locked him out of his own cabin!

Chase fought a sharp jab of annoyance. "Ann," he said, leaning close to the door so his voice wouldn't carry. "Open up, Ann. I need to talk to you."

He didn't hear so much as a whisper of movement from inside. Not a rustle, not a murmur.

"Let me in, Ann," His voice was sharper, less cajoling.

He could imagine her sitting in there, knitting or reading with single-minded purpose while he stood out here.

"Ann, please!"

The silence persisted, growing stubborn, insolent, mutinous. Anger chewed along his nerves.

"Ann!"

Nothing.

Damn the woman, anyway. All he wanted was to settle in the captain's sitting room, savor a brandy and a cheroot, and reflect on all he'd accomplished. He'd been working toward this moment all his life. It was his triumph, damn it! His proof that a boy who'd been taken in out of pity could make something of himself.

He wasn't going to let Ann Rossiter—Ann *Hardesty* or whoever the hell she was—spoil his victory. He wasn't going to let her lock him out of his own cabin.

He glared at the door. He could break the lock without half-trying. He could kick his way into that stateroom and show Ann *Hardesty* that her new husband wasn't a man to be trifled with.

He backed up a step, balanced on his left leg and

flexed his right. Did he really want to burst into that cabin and begin married life by bullying his wife into submission? Did he want the crew and passengers to come trooping up here to see what the commotion was about?

That thought sobered Chase faster than a dip in the river. He straightened, let out his breath, braced back against the railing and glared at the door.

He had to get Ann off his boat.

What the devil was she doing in that cabin anyway?

He realized all at once that the sitting-room windows were dark, and the only illumination glimmered dimly between the halves of the bedroom curtains.

He stepped up close to the glass and peered between the velvet panels. He could only see a narrow slice of the room, the bottom half of the bunk, the built-in shaving stand on the opposite wall and the mirror that hung above it.

He saw that Ann lay fully clothed toward the outer edge of his berth. That she was dressed meant either that Skirlin had neglected to have her baggage delivered, or that she thought the layers of clothes might offer some protection.

Against him, he supposed.

Chase let out his breath in exasperation.

As he looked closer, he could see she slept with her knees drawn up and had left the lamp burning, like a child afraid of the dark. And he was suddenly very glad he hadn't gone charging into that cabin like a madman.

Still, a spark of resentment burned in him. Today he

had gotten everything he'd ever wanted for himself, and Ann was spoiling his victory.

Biting back a curse, he turned from the window and took the stairs down to the boiler deck where a few hardy passengers stood in the cold, smoking cigars. He spoke to each of the men in turn, then stepped into the warmth of the pastry kitchen.

Unlike the galleys on most steamboats, Frenchy Bertin's was spotless. The wide wooden tables had been wiped with vinegar, the floors swept, and the food stored away in the pie safe or carefully covered with cheesecloth.

Since he'd elected to remain in the pilothouse right through supper, Chase was hungry. He scavenged two slices of bread, then headed into the starboard galley where Harley Crocker prepared the meat and vegetables. After making himself a sandwich of sliced beef and horseradish, Chase wandered back to Frenchy's side of the boat for a slice of pie and a glass of whiskey from the "nip" bottle Bertin kept hidden in one of the canisters.

Feeling better for having food and a jot of whiskey in his belly, Chase returned to the Texas deck and tried to figure out where he was going to sleep.

When he peered between the curtains again, he saw Ann hadn't moved—and that odd, ridiculous protectiveness stirred in him again. He couldn't quite bring himself to disturb her, which left him one choice about where he'd spend the night.

Cursing under his breath, he entered the officers' quarters, the series of narrow bunk-lined rooms that lay directly behind the captain's cabin. Three men were at the table playing cards: Rue, Cal Watkins, and Beck Morgan, the mud clerk.

They watched without a word as Chase sat down on the nearest berth and removed his boots. In absolute silence they watched as he stripped to his knitted underwear. He tugged back the blankets on the bed and climbed beneath them.

"Good night," he mumbled gruffly.

Not wanting to see his officers' speculative glances, Chase turned his face to the wall. Though not one of them said a word, Chase knew what they were thinking. Here he was, the captain of his own damned steamer, hunkered down in a steerman's cot, humiliated in front of the men he was supposed to command.

And sleeping alone on his wedding night.

chapter four

NOTCHING THE WHEEL TO STARBOARD, CHASE guided the *Andromeda* into another of the scores of channel crossings they'd made since they left St. Louis four days before.

"Is that river the Gasconade?" Rue asked, shouldering into the pilothouse carrying two cups of coffee.

Chase glanced to where another of the Missouri's tributaries joined its already swollen flow and nodded. "I expect we'll make Jefferson City this afternoon."

He accepted one of the steaming mugs, took a sip, and grimaced. He'd forgotten to warn Rue about drinking Harley Crocker's coffee. Still, life was good. The sun was out. The river was running high and fast, and so far at least, the trip had been uneventful.

Because the *Andromeda* was a brand-new boat and making one of the first runs of the season, every cabin was full and cargo was piled high on the guards. There were boxes of cloth, all manner of guns and ammunition, farming implements, boots and tools and patent medicines, tinware and toothbrushes, washtubs and weather vanes. Like every other boat heading west, she was carrying barrels of sugar and salt, flour, whiskey, and pickles. They had everything from dynamite to canned goods aboard, from dentists' tools to hand-painted china.

Some of the load was bound for general stores in towns along the river that had been inaccessible all winter. But most of the cargo was going all the way to the head of navigation at Fort Benton, Montana Territory, where the prices were better.

The passengers aboard the *Andromeda* weren't nearly as diverse as the cargo. Most of the people who'd taken cabin passage fell into one of four groups: folks hoping to homestead in Nebraska and the Dakota Territory now that the war was over, businessmen or speculators intent on making money on people moving West, army officers on their way to postings at the forts along the river, and would-be miners traveling to Montana by boat because the Indians had the trail to the goldfields under seige.

On the main deck, both the accommodations and the company were less refined. "Room" consisted of sleeping in the open with most of the crew, and the "board" was a pan of leftovers from the dining room. Down there, the company ran to adventurers, freed slaves, immigrant families, and barnyard animals.

Rue ambled up beside where Chase was standing at

the wheel. "I didn't see much activity in your cabin when I passed by. You sure Ann's still with us?"

"I imagine."

In truth, Chase hadn't seen hide nor hair of his wife since they'd cast off. He would have been more concerned if the food he'd had set outside the cabin door didn't keep disappearing.

"So what's she doing holed up in there, anyway?"

Chase knew the whole crew was wondering that, and probably half the passengers. "I think she's sleeping."

"Sleeping?" Rue echoed. "For four whole days?"

Chase didn't think Ann had been sleeping the night before when he'd tried the outer door to the cabin and found it unlocked. The way he had it figured, his wife had been poised on the bedroom side of the pocket door, listening as he rummaged through the sitting room and gathered up his logbook and writing utensils, his shaving gear, and a fresh suit of clothes. He doubted she'd have unlocked that outer door at all, except he'd left a note on her breakfast tray explaining what he needed.

Though he supposed Ann had reason to be wary of a man she barely knew, her mistrust rankled him. What did she think he was going to do? Drag her out of the cabin and abandon her on the riverbank? Burst in and ravish her?

Chase steered the steamer into a bend and made note of how the water had undercut the bank. He'd bet two weeks' wages the grove of trees on that little point would be washed away by the time they came downstream four months from now.

"I think women need a lot of sleep when they're breeding," Chase offered sagely.

"I don't remember Etta Mae sleeping this much when she was carrying Samantha," his brother observed.

Chase figured Rue had guessed the truth. "I suppose at least part of the reason Ann's locked herself away is because she's avoiding me," he admitted on a sigh. "I told her I was going to put her aboard the first boat we passed that was headed back to St. Louis, and she isn't giving me the opportunity."

Rue looked up from his coffee. "Do you mean to do that?"

"What are *we* going to do with her?" Chase wanted to know. "Ann's in a family way; she needs folks to look after her. How are *we* going to do that? She'll need a doctor when her time comes. *We're* headed off into the wilderness."

"You could leave her with Ma," Rue suggested. "Ma would look after her."

Chase wasn't about to foist Ann off on his parents. If Ann's baby had been his, he might have considered it. If he were Lydia and Enoch's natural son, he might have felt differently. Though his mother would surely agree, Chase couldn't bring himself to ask more of his parents than they'd given him already. A man didn't expect other people to shoulder responsibilities he'd taken upon himself.

"I'm not leaving Ann with Ma and Pa," he told his brother. "I'm the one who agreed to this marriage, and I'm the one who has to look after my wife. I'm sending

Ann back to St. Louis first chance I get, or my name's not Chase Hardesty!"

HE WAS HERE IN THE ROOM. ANN KNEW IT THE INSTANT she started awake, the moment she opened her eyes. He was hidden, cloaked in the darkness.

But he was here.

She could feel his energy squirm across her skin. She could smell the high, sharp bite of camphor and hear his fervid breathing. He was taunting her with his presence, with his silence. He was waiting to show himself.

He sensed the thick, choking dread condensing inside her. He was relishing her panic, thriving on it.

Gooseflesh crawled along her ribs. All Ann could do was lie there with her mind roaring and her muscles turned to stone. Soon now, between one breath and the next, he would reach out and close his hands on her. He would grab her, tear at her, crush her beneath him.

When he did that, she would shatter. She would splinter into a thousand shivering shards. A sob fluttered in her throat. *If he touched her she would lose her mind.*

Then from somewhere beyond the walls of her terror, beyond the walls of this room, she heard the sound of footsteps and disembodied voices.

"—longer than I figured to scale those damn boilers," one of them said.

"It's hellish work," a second man agreed.

"An' unless I miss my guess," the first continued, "the captain'll want 'er steam up b'fore dawn."

"Then we best grab what sleep we—"

Somewhere to Ann's right a door opened and closed, shutting off the conversation.

Gradually she began to notice other sounds. The gentle *shush* of water and peepers chorusing weren't things Ann associated with her room at her father's house. She gradually came to realize she wasn't cowering in her own bed. She wasn't even in St. Louis.

She was aboard the *Andromeda*, locked up tight in the captain's cabin. Though it might be black as pitch in here, it didn't seem likely someone could have breached the locks on both the outer and inner doors without awakening her. No one was lurking in the dark.

She was safe.

Relief gushed through her. Tears singed her lower lashes; her arms and legs went rubbery. She was safe aboard the *Andromeda*, safe from her demons and from her nightmares.

She nuzzled into her pillow and closed her eyes.

Once Chase had left for the riverfront the day of their wedding, she'd packed her bags and slipped out of the town house while everyone was busy in the aftermath of the wedding. Her hands might have been shaking when she hailed the horsecab that delivered her to the levee, but she'd stood up for herself once she got aboard. Chase hadn't wanted to let her stay. He was still threatening to send her home, but she wasn't going back. Not now, not ever.

Ann nestled deeper into the bedding and lay for a good long while letting the rustle of the river soothe her. Finally, she fumbled toward the head of the berth and peeked outside. What time was it? she wondered. Where had they tied up for the night? How long had she been sleeping?

Long enough at least to need a chamberpot.

Ann pulled herself upright and eased out of the waist-high berth, feeling for the floor with her toes. Once she'd clambered down, she lit a lamp and went about her business.

When she was done, she slipped the lock on the pocket door that separated the sleeping quarters from the captain's cozy sitting room. She saw that Chase had been there again. He'd left papers stacked on the desk, and her covered supper tray was sitting on the table in the corner. Ann crossed the room and raised the cloth. On the plate was a slice of ham and wedges of potato wallowing in grease, a dish of limp cabbage, and a few shriveled grapes.

Though the smell of the cabbage made her swallow hard, Ann realized she was hungry. What she wanted was custard, sweet and creamy enough to roll around on her tongue. Or a big lemon tart with tang enough to make her pucker.

Saliva pooled under her tongue, and her stomach grumbled. What was on this tray was all she was going to get until breakfast—and even then, no one would think to bring her lemon tarts. Which gave her a choice: she could sit here hungry and safe, or brave the open deck in search of something more appetizing.

Though the idea of looking for the galley in the dark turned her hands slick with sweat, Ann teased open the cabin door and stepped outside. Except for lanterns hung at intervals along the rail, everything was dim and quiet.

Did she really want lemon tarts enough to chance this?

Taking her courage in her hands, Ann scurried to the top of the stairs and paused to listen. When nothing stirred, she crept down the flight to the boiler deck. Drawn by the scent of baking bread, she stole along the promenade and peeled open an iron-banded door mid-way toward the stern.

Ripe, fecund heat enfolded her.

Though the galley was only dimly lit, she didn't have any trouble finding the head-high pie safe—or plundering the booty inside. She cut a slice from a tall, elegant coconut cake and another from one of the cherry pies still warm from baking. An enormous tray of plump, golden-brown fried cakes was laid out for breakfast, and tucked back in a corner were three of what must have been yesterday's tarts. They were apple not lemon, but Ann made do.

Then, pulling a stool up to one of the room's three high wooden counters, she forked up a bite of one of the tarts—and moaned with pleasure. The crust was flaky and the apples, still slightly crisp, were perfectly seasoned with sugar and cinnamon.

She devoured the tarts and was chewing her way through the coconut cake when a tall, bone-thin man stalked into the galley through a door that evidently led into the salon.

"*Merde!*" he was mumbling. "Will I ever learn not to draw to an inside straight?"

He'd shambled halfway across the galley before he saw her. "Ah! You there!" he demanded. "What are you doing in my kitchen?"

Ann did her best to swallow the bite of cake so she could answer, but it caught in her throat.

"You cabin passengers," he scolded as he approached her. "You think you can come in and eat my delicacies at any hour of the day or night! What will I serve at dinner if you eat them now, eh? *Eh?*"

Ann scrambled down from her stool and brushed the crumbs off her skirt. "I'm sorry," she said, bobbing her head in apology. "Truly I am. But I was so hungry..."

As she backed away the Frenchman must have caught sight of her belly, because his demeanor immediately changed. "And what kind of a meal is this for a woman carrying a child?" he chided her. "Here, let me fix you something more suitable for that baby than all those sweets."

"Oh, no!" Ann pleaded. "I don't mean to be any trouble."

"Trouble!" he said with a sniff. "Losing all your money at cards is trouble. Having three wives to support is trouble. Fixing you something to eat is no trouble."

He plucked two eggs from the straw in a big, closely woven basket and broke them into a bowl. With a few flicks of his fork, a sprinkling of herbs and cheese, and a swirl or two in a frying pan, he presented her with a perfectly folded omelet.

Ann stared as if he'd conjured the meal out of thin air. "It looks delicious."

The chef raised his impressive eyebrows. "But of course."

As Ann tucked into the eggs, the tall man bowed with a flourish. "I am Guillaume Bertin, but most everyone on the river calls me 'Frenchy'."

"I'm Ann"—Rossiter, she'd almost said—"Hardesty."

Frenchy looked down his long, knobby nose at her. "Ah, the captain's mysterious new wife."

"Mysterious?"

"The captain, he doesn't tell a soul he is getting married." The Frenchman enumerated on his fingers. "His bride arrives and disappears into his cabin. She stays there for five whole days—*all by herself.*"

Ann flushed at his implication. It wasn't her fault Chase had neglected to mention the wedding, and once she'd come aboard and closed the cabin door behind her, all she seemed able to do was sleep. And in spite of the considerable inconvenience and the gossip she'd evidently caused, Chase hadn't disturbed her. Her opinion of her new husband softened a little.

Before she could think of how to respond to Frenchy's words, he took up a wad of toweling and opened the door to one of the ovens. The fire's hot breath rolled over her and inside she could see rows of perfectly browned loaves of bread.

With a long wooden paddle Frenchy lifted them out

one by one, and flipped them onto the counter. Ann went faint with pleasure as the full, yeasty richness rolled over her.

Once Frenchy dusted the shelves of the oven with flour again, he refilled them with unbaked loaves and shut the door with a satisfying *whump*. After that, he turned to where dough was rising in bowls, flopped the contents onto a board, and began punching the fat, white billow with his fists.

"You want to help?" he asked when he saw Ann watching him.

"I've never touched bread dough in my life!"

Frenchy sniffed. "A child could do this."

Before Ann could refuse, he'd knotted one of his big floury aprons around her middle. Leading her to the table, he showed her how to work the dough, divide it in halves, and form it into loaves. Ann was shaping her fourth lopsided loaf when the door at the far end of the galley snapped open.

Chase stepped inside, rumpled with sleep. "Coffee ready?"

Frenchy poured a cup of dense, black liquid. "You come scowling at me every morning wanting coffee. Why not go see Harley Crocker sometimes, eh?"

"He's too busy flipping griddle cakes at this hour of the morning," Chase grumbled, scrubbing a hand across his unshaven cheeks. "Besides, your coffee's better."

"But of course." On the strength of that compliment, Frenchy handed the cup to him.

Chase took a deep swallow, grimaced at the scalding heat, then sighed with pleasure.

"So—" Frenchy went on, stepping aside, "have you met my new assistant?"

Chase raised his gaze beyond the rim of his cup to where Ann stood forearm deep in bread dough. Surprise flashed across his features, as if he couldn't imagine how his very proper bride could be involved in such a common activity.

"I—I didn't know you baked," he finally said.

Ann's first impulse was to tell Chase Hardesty she'd been baking all her life. But she didn't want to lie to him, not about this. Not when there were far more significant lies she might have to tell him.

"Frenchy's offered to teach me," she said.

"Has he really?"

His skeptical tone made Frenchy bristle. "You don't think I can teach her?"

Chase raised his cup in defense. "I didn't say that."

"Soon men will swoon from just one taste of her pies and cakes," Frenchy insisted. "And her bread..."

The Frenchman rolled his eyes as if in an ecstatic swoon and glanced at her. "You come tonight, Ann Hardesty. Together we will show this husband of yours what you can do."

"Is that all right?" Ann turned to Chase and asked permission, just as she might have asked her father's.

Chase's eyebrows levered upward. "Five days ago you stormed aboard the *Andromeda* like a pirate boarding a treasure ship and demanded passage. *Now* you're asking my permission to learn to bake?"

Ann inched backwards, not sure how she should answer him.

"I think you scared poor Skirlin half to death by the time I got there to rescue him." Chase's eyes twinkled, and Ann realized all at once that he was teasing her.

She gave a surprised peep of laughter at the image he'd conjured up of her. No one had ever teased her in her life, and it made her feel light-headed and frivolous.

"Well, I certainly didn't mean to frighten the poor man," she offered tentatively.

Chase rewarded her with a grin. "Oh, I don't think it hurts to give someone like Skirlin a start," he assured her, "at least once in awhile."

Ann smiled back as Chase turned toward the door. "Do what you like about the baking. Just don't expect to be aboard long enough to accomplish much."

His warning doused the warmth that had flickered briefly between them. "I won't go back to St. Louis!" she declared.

But Chase had already left the galley.

THE DEEP BELLOWING HOOT OF THE *ANDROMEDA*'S WHIStle and the clanging of the landing bell awakened Ann at midmorning.

She'd stumbled up to the captain's cabin just at dawn after her first full night as Frenchy's student. She'd learned the exact temperature for water when mixing yeast and how to put the ingredients for bread together. She'd punched down dough, shaped more loaves than she could count, and shuffled them in and out of the oven.

She'd discovered that baking bread was hard, exhausting work. Still, when her first loaves lay in precise brown rows on the long wooden counter, Ann had glowed with satisfaction.

Curled up now, lazing and half-asleep, she could tell from the shouted orders and lagging speed that the *Andromeda* was coming into a landing. She nudged the window curtains aside, but all she could see was a haze of half-budded treetops and an undulating line of distant bluffs.

Where were they?

Ann scrambled to her knees to get a better look, but as she did, a wave of dizziness caught her. She grabbed the berth's low bedrail and hung on tight as the room tilted and her ears rang. Then with a moan, she rolled onto her back and lay there panting. This is what happened these days when she moved too quickly. She had to learn to make allowances since she was carrying a child.

As the spinning slowed, she lay there gathering herself and stroking her palm along the rise of her belly. How full she felt, how warm and firm. She was expanding so fast she could almost feel her muscles flexing and fluttering. It was as if something was stirring inside her, right there where her fingers lay against her...

Ann went still. ·

The ruffling came again. A gentle bump, a faint squirming, a flicker of the faintest restlessness.

It was her baby! Her baby was moving inside her.

Ann laughed in surprise. Wonder filled her chest. Her heart fluttered with unexpected joy. She hadn't doubted there was a baby growing in her, but she hadn't exactly wanted to believe it, either.

Now that she knew what the feeling was, she could feel her child shifting, turning, stretching. Growing right here beneath the palm of her hand, closer to her than any living soul would ever be. A child that was, for awhile at least, a part of her.

How odd and how miraculous.

She never imagined that this child could awaken this joy in her. She hadn't expected to feel such delight—but she did. Tenderness for her baby wafted through her, as soft and airy as dandelion down.

Then tears rose in her eyes, though she couldn't think why she was crying. Swiping at the wetness, Ann rolled onto her side and lay there waiting. When the flutter came again, she drew up her knees and wrapped herself around the wondrous new life astir within her.

Were other women so stunned and astounded by this? Did they wonder about giving birth? Were they as afraid of it as she was?

Ann wished she had someone to ask. She'd been too young to understand what was happening when her mother died. She'd been schooled in the most proper of finishing schools back East. The commodore had cut her off from all female companionship the moment he discovered she was pregnant. There might have been a few women passengers aboard the *Andromeda* she could have asked, but pregnancy and childbirth weren't subjects one generally broached with strangers.

Ann sighed away her concerns and stroked the dome of her belly. God knows, she hadn't wanted this child. She couldn't bear remembering the night it was conceived or how horrified she'd been when she realized she was pregnant. Then why did she feel so possessive, so overcome with pride? How could she feel this need to shelter and protect something that was a reminder of everything she longed to forget?

Yet when the baby stirred, she was astonished and awed all over again.

Ann emerged from the cabin a good while later and rambled across the deck to where Rue was leaning against the railing.

"Where are we?" she asked him.

"We're at a woodlot just north of Arrow Rock," he explained by way of greeting. "We're taking on a full rank of wood."

"How much is that?"

"One of those rows," he told her, gesturing. "Twenty cords."

Along the fringe of the river, a hundred-yard-wide swath of bottomland was piled chest-high with row upon row of split and seasoned wood. At the back of the lot a number of men were working industriously to split and stack even more.

"If a row is twenty cords"—Ann pointed to a peg-legged man and sandy-haired young officer using what looked to be about an eight-foot-long stick to take the dimensions of one of the rows. "—why are they measuring?"

"Beck Morgan, the one with the sounding pole, and our mate Goose Steinwehr are checking because most woodhawks will steal you blind if you let them," Rue answered. "Except our pa. He'd give away one of us kids before he'd cheat anyone. And Ma would have his ears if he even thought about overcharging."

"Is this what your father does?" She and Chase hadn't gotten much past introductions, and Ann was curious.

"Pa has a wood yard between Council Bluffs and Sioux City," Rue said with a nod. "That's why Chase likes having a regular Sioux City run—so he can stop by Hardesty's Landing once or twice a month."

"Will I meet your parents?" she asked him, not at all sure she wanted to. How was Chase's family likely to take the news that their son had married a woman they'd never met? One who was carrying another man's child?

"I wouldn't count on being aboard when we reach Hardesty's Landing," Chase advised her.

Ann turned as Chase sauntered toward where she and Rue were braced against the railing. That he moved across the deck with such rangy grace, with such confidence and self-possession, surprised Ann a little. Back at the commodore's house, his size and rough-hewn looks had seemed coarse and out of place. Here, that broad, bony face conveyed authority and strength—and a kind of blatant masculinity that made Ann's heart beat faster.

"I won't go back," she told him for what seemed like the dozenth time since she'd come aboard.

Chase let his gaze run over her in a perusal so thorough it made Ann flush. The way his eyes lingered on the rise of her belly made his most compelling argument for sending her home.

"A woman in your condition," Chase pointed out, "has no business aboard a boat that's headed for Montana."

Ann shifted away from the rail and faced him directly. "If one of the women passengers was expecting a child, you wouldn't consider putting her off."

"If one of the women passengers was expecting a child, she wouldn't be my responsibility."

Ann knew he was right to be concerned for her. If she was honest with herself, she had to admit the journey frightened her. Carrying this child frightened her. But she was here, and she was staying—no matter what.

"I won't be any trouble," she assured him.

Chase shook his head. "You can't promise that, Ann; no one could. And you've already been trouble.

"By taking your meals upstairs on a tray, you've made more work for the kitchen staff," he enumerated. "You've shut me out of my own cabin and disrupted my work. I don't even have a bed to sleep in."

But his scent still lingered on her sheets, Ann realized with an odd, hollow feeling in her chest. It was a musky masculine smell, tempered with a good dose of woodsmoke. And not in the least unpleasant.

"I'm sorry about the bed," Ann offered.

Chase dipped his head in acknowledgment. "We'll call things even if you stop taking your meals in the cabin. Come eat supper with me tonight, with me and my officers."

Though Ann might be comfortable with Frenchy, the notion of facing Chase's men and a salon full of passengers, intimidated her more than she cared to admit.

"I still prefer," she answered softly, "to take my meals in the cabin."

At her refusal, Chase's eyebrows clashed over the bridge of his nose. "Do you think you're too good to share a meal with me and my men because you're the commodore's daughter?"

Ann retreated a step in surprise. "I most certainly do not think that!"

"Then have supper with us tonight and prove it," Chase challenged her.

Ann bristled at his tone. But before she could answer, Rue's applause cut her off.

"Well done, big brother," he observed laconically, rubbing at one corner of his mustache. "You argue with her, bargain with her, insult her, then expect Ann to want to join you for supper. Ma taught you better; try being polite!"

It was Chase's turn to flush, but after a moment he accepted Rue's advice. "We'll be putting in at a town this evening, Mrs. Hardesty," he tried again. "That means supper will be something a little special. My officers and I would be pleased if you'd agree to join us."

Ann saw the effort Chase was making, and it seemed mean-spirited to refuse him. "I'll join you if you like," she agreed reluctantly.

"I'll come by for you at seven o'clock."

ANN WAS STILL PRIMPING IN FRONT OF THE MIRROR IN the captain's cabin when Chase came by to escort her down to supper. Before she answered his knock, she skimmed her palms down the front of her bodice, then frowned. Even laced as tightly as she could manage by herself, her condition was obvious. Hadn't anyone ever mentioned to Chase Hardesty that ladies who were *enceinte* didn't flaunt themselves in public?

Chase's knock became more insistent. "Ann?" he called out. "Are you ready?"

Maybe she could plead a headache and stay in the cabin. Maybe she could sneak down to the galley once the waiters had begun serving dinner and steal a slice of the chocolate cake Frenchy had been icing this afternoon. Maybe she could...

Ann sighed and opened the cabin door.

Chase inclined his head in a bow. "You're looking very lovely tonight, Mrs. Hardesty."

Ann might have returned the compliment. When he hadn't been brawling on the waterfront, Chase Hardesty cleaned up passably well. Tonight he was freshly scrubbed and barbered, wearing crisp linen, buff trousers, and a deep blue frock coat that emphasized the breadth of his shoulders.

"Thank you," she acknowledged with a nod, and though his words were patented flattery, her cheeks warmed. But then, Ann wasn't sure if it was the compliment or being called "Mrs. Hardesty" that flustered her more.

In that moment of confusion, she missed any chance she might have had to beg off dining with him.

"It's good of you to join me and my officers this evening." Chase extended his hand. "Shall we go on down to the salon?"

Hesitantly, Ann lay her fingers across his palm and let him draw her out into the deepening twilight. It was the first time she'd touched him skin to skin since she'd tried to refuse his wedding band, and she became abruptly aware of his long, rough fingers encircling hers. Of the vitality of his flesh, of the strength and certainty of his grip, of the confidence that seemed to run bone-deep in him.

The power in him disturbed her equilibrium. A strange, warm tingling began in the hollow between their palms. Spangles of sensation crept up her wrist and danced toward the crook of her elbow. Her skin flushed and her chest went inexplicably tight.

Chase inhaled sharply, as if he felt the same connection and was every bit as taken aback by it as she was.

It was as if both of them were caught by a bright river of energy, swept up by a current so strong and swift that they were helpless to deny the affinity suddenly burgeoning between them. It was as if the world around them had dropped away, and they were caught, drawn by some strange force that was as compelling as it was inexplicable.

Whatever it was, the attraction glowed and grew, became as captivating as it was unsettling. Chase turned to her, high color burnishing those strong, broad cheekbones. Ann recognized the wonder in his eyes.

His grip around her fingers tightened. He stepped in close enough that the warmth of his body penetrated the layers of her clothes, close enough that she caught the smoky essence that clung to his skin and hair. She heard the heightened cadence of his breathing, watched as his lips bowed.

Chase Hardesty was going to kiss her.

Ann's nerves rippled with anticipation. Then panic cold as winter's breath sent shivers down her back. The bite of camphor stung her nostrils. Chase's nearness and the clasp of his hand imprisoning hers became unbearable.

With a frantic tug, Ann jerked free. She stumbled toward the edge of the deck and stood there panting.

Chase followed her and lay his hand against her sleeve. "Ann?" he whispered. "Ann, what is it?"

She moaned and threw off his hold a second time. She clung to the railing as if she were dangling above an abyss and ready to fall.

Chase must have sensed how unnerved she was, because he backed away, first one step and then another. Still, she knew that he must be watching her, watching her and wondering, no doubt, what kind of lunatic he'd married.

Ann fought to regain control of herself. She turned her thoughts to simple things: how the spring wind ruffled the tails of her shawl, the way the ropes lay coiled in perfect spirals on the deck below. The breath-soft ripple of the water against the hull of the steamer.

Gradually Ann began to notice that lamps were being lit in the windows of the buildings along the waterfront, that bales and barrels were piled at the end of the gangway, ready to be loaded. The *Andromeda* was tied up at the foot of a town, sharing the landing with another smaller steamer.

"Where..." Ann had to swallow before she could finish the question. "Where are we?"

"We've tied up at Glasgow for the night," Chase answered quietly from where he stood braced against the rail an arm's length away. "Glasgow's about two thirds of the way between St. Louis and Kansas City."

Ann took a better look at the place. Warehouses crouched close along the riverfront. A wide main street lined with businesses, a school, and a church ran up the bluff. The houses that nestled farther up the rise were swiftly being swallowed by the deepening dark.

"They grow a good deal of tobacco hereabout," Chase told her, making innocuous conversation. His voice was low and even, as if he were calming a skittish colt.

She felt like that tonight, all high-strung and wary.

"Is—is that why we've stopped here?" She was still uncomfortably aware of his scrutiny. "Did we put in at Glasgow to load tobacco?"

"To deliver farming implements," he answered and

pushed away from the railing. "Are you feeling settled enough now that we can go down to supper?"

She stole a glance at him and was relieved that the inexplicable sense of connection had dissipated. Certainly a room full of people would further dilute whatever it was that had passed between Chase and her. Dispel whatever madness had induced him to try and kiss her.

He waited for her to nod, then guided her down the stairs with no more contact than the brush of his palm against her back.

"We've got lots of guests for dinner tonight," he told her as they made their descent. "When word gets out that Frenchy's aboard one of the steamers, half the town turns out. Some of the men brought their fiddles and guitars, so I expect we'll have dancing afterwards."

Ann nodded, relieved that her condition allowed her to beg off such exertions. It wasn't that she didn't like dancing, only that she was feeling ungainly. And after what had passed between Chase and her, she preferred to maintain a certain distance between them.

She was grateful that he'd warned her about the crowd. Well over a hundred pairs of eyes followed them as Chase escorted her across the salon. Once he'd settled her at the captain's table, he took the chair to her right.

"So how's the captain's lady this evening?" Rue asked from where he was seated at her opposite hand.

Ann wasn't at all sure she liked being thought of as "the captain's lady." It made her feel like property, something Chase had bought and paid for. Which, she supposed, he had.

"I'm quite well, thank you," she answered crisply.

The young, sandy-haired man she'd seen measuring wood this afternoon, smiled at her. "Glad to hear it. The captain said you'd been ailing."

Ann was taken aback. What Frenchy had intimated must be true, that a steamship full of crewmen had been speculating about her. Knowing that made her squirm, and she couldn't help wondering what else Chase might have told them about her.

"I thank you for your concern," she murmured, then pointedly turned her attention to the cup of oxtail soup the waiter set before her.

She'd barely picked up her spoon when Chase began making introductions. "I believe you've already met our clerk, Mr. Skirlin."

He was the man who'd tried to bar her from the steamer not quite a week before. That day he'd been the soul of chilly officiousness; tonight he was all kindness and cordiality. Ann saw through him like plate glass.

"A pleasure, Mrs. Hardesty." Skirlin's eyes gleamed in a sly, contemptuous way as his gaze slid over her. It came to rest on her belly; he gave her a supercilious smile.

Ann straightened and glared back. "Lovely to see you again, too, Mr. Skirlin."

Oblivious to the hostility between one of his senior officers and his wife, Chase continued with the introductions. "This is our engineer, Cal Watkins. He knows more about what keeps steamboats running than any man on the Missouri River!"

To deflect the praise, the pinched little man to

Skirlin's left reached out a grease-stained hand and patted the black-and-white spaniel settled on the floor beside his chair. "I—I never once in my life thought to be serving on so fine a steamer as the *Andromeda*," he murmured earnestly. "Me and Barney."

Ann could see Cal would be worlds happier down with his boilers and gauges than he was here, so she turned her gentlest smile on him. "And how long have you and Barney been consulting on machinery, Mr. Watkins?"

Cal flushed red, both agitated and delighted that so fine a lady would include his dearest friend as part of her inquiry. "My pa owned a salvage boat," he answered, "so I been working with engines all my life. Barney here come on as my associate about five years back."

"Barney brings Cal his wrenches," Rue put in. "And coaches him at checkers."

"An' amazing enough, ole Barney always knows which move to make so I can beat you!" Cal cackled with glee at Rue's expense.

Chase introduced Gustave Steinwehr next. "Goose oversees the cargo and supervises the deckhands." Ann had noticed the big man with the peg leg this afternoon while they were wooding up.

Only now, close up, Ann could see how huge a man he really was. He was nearly as tall as Chase, but broader, with a deep chest and shoulders as wide as the handle of a broadaxe. His face was hard, blunt-featured, Germanic. The deep creases around his eyes and mouth underlined his air of solemnity.

"It is good to meet you, *Frau* Hardesty," Steinwehr said, his voice rumbling in that massive chest.

"*Und Ihner, Herr* Steinwehr."

"*Sprechen Sie Deutsch?*"

Though it didn't show in his expression, Ann could hear the hopefulness in Steinwehr's tone. Once they left St. Louis, he must not have had much chance to hear his native language spoken or to speak it himself.

"My mathematics teacher was from Darmstadt," Ann answered. "She taught me a few phrases in German."

"Ah," he said, clearly disappointed. "Ah."

"Perhaps you could teach me some more?" Ann found herself suggesting. "I've always had an ear for languages."

Steinwehr's expression immediately lightened. "I would like that," he answered.

Chase indicated the bright-eyed young fellow who'd inquired about her health. "Beck Morgan is our mud clerk," he told her.

"Please, Mr. Morgan," Ann asked, smiling at him, "what exactly is a 'mud clerk'?"

"I'm the one who gets stuck with all the dirty work!" Morgan said and laughed.

"What Beck means," Chase interpreted, "is that when we put in somewhere, it's his job to stand on the bank in the mud and keep the tally of the goods we're loading and unloading."

"Chase can tell how well Beck's done his job by how high the mud goes up his boots," Rue confided in an undertone.

"And when it gets all the way up to his knees, does he get some sort of a bonus?" Ann asked brightly.

"It'd have to go a good deal higher," Chase assured her, "for the commodore to approve money for a bonus."

They all laughed.

The last two men at the table, Roger Brady and Ira Foster, were the captain and the pilot from the *Iowa Princess*, the smaller steamer tied up beside them.

"Where are you bound, Captain Brady?" Ann inquired.

"Downstream, ma'am," Brady answered.

Before she could ask just how far downstream, the waiters swooped in to take their orders for dinner. Harley Crocker, the meat and vegetable cook, was offering a fish course, several meat and game entrees, three hot and three cold side dishes. But as good as the dinner was, Frenchy's desserts were the highlight of the meal.

Ann ate three: chocolate cake light enough to have been baked from fairy dust; a dish of thick, creamy custard; and a slice of pecan pie.

"I've never in my life had such a sweet tooth!" Ann confided to Rue as she set her fork aside.

While the diners lingered over coffee, Chase and Jake Skirlin circulated through the salon, shaking hands with the men, complimenting the ladies, and ruffling the children's hair. It wasn't long before Chase was balancing a sweet-faced little charmer in a frilly dress on one hip, while several boys of five or six trailed after him.

"I had no idea Chase had such a way with little ones,"

Ann murmured half to herself, wondering if it was true that children were good judges of character.

"That comes of Chase raising so many of us," Rue answered.

"Raising you?"

"Ma and Pa loved us and took care of us," he told her, "but in a family as big as ours, the children kind of raised one another, too. Chase, being the oldest, never went anywhere without three or four of us tagging after him. He got good at keeping us out of trouble, and teaching us things."

Ann couldn't imagine growing up in a family like the one Rue was describing. A family where parents showed their children affection, where brothers and sisters played together and looked after one another. Where there was the kind of teasing and honesty and laughter she'd seen between Chase and Rue.

As far back as she could remember it had been just her mother and her. Then Sarah Pelletier had married James Rossiter, and they'd come to live in St. Louis.

The family her mother had tried to cobble together from her and Ann and the commodore and his son had never come to much of anything. Sarah herself had been too preoccupied with meeting her husband's demands to have time for much else. For himself, the commodore had played Boothe and her against each other like pieces on a chessboard, making them compete for his time and his attention.

Whatever connection there had been between the four of them, it had dissolved like sugar in hot tea the day her mother died. Not three weeks after, Ann had been shipped to school back East like so much excess baggage.

Ann leaned in close to Rue, determined to use these few minutes over coffee to discover what she could about the Hardesty clan. But before she could wangle one more insight out of him, a man burst into the salon.

"Fire!" he shouted. "The Fletcher house is afire uptown!"

Chairs scraped across the floor as people jumped to their feet. Shrill voices echoed off the ceiling. Everyone rushed the doorways, draining out of the salon like water from a colander.

From the deck Ann could see an unnatural glow in the windows of a two-story house halfway up the bluff. The townsfolk saw that, too. With cries of alarm, they flooded down the stairs and thundered across the landing stage.

As the mob ran up the town's main street, both crews and passengers grabbed pails and axes, and followed. Ann hurried along in their wake, trying to keep up. By the time she reached the house, a bucket brigade was forming in the yard. Ann took her place in line between one of the *Andromeda*'s roustabouts and a woman from town.

"Is anyone inside?" she heard someone shout.

"Three children in bed on the second floor," another voice answered. "Their mother wasn't able to get them out."

Two men grabbed up feed sacks, wet them in the water trough, and sprinted toward the house. Ann's heart skipped a beat when she recognized Chase was the second one.

She opened her mouth to call him back, but just then someone jammed the handle of a water bucket into her hands. After that, Ann was too busy to either shout or breathe. She took up the rhythm of the line, grabbing a bucket from the man at her left and thrusting it toward the woman on her right, grabbing, turning, and passing. Grabbing, turning, and passing.

As she worked, the strange peachy light in the house's downstairs windows glowed brighter. Smoke poured out the broken door. The roof began to steam.

Ann's eyes stung, and her throat was peppery from the smoke. Between passing one heavy, sloshing bucket and the next, Ann watched for Chase. Why in God's name had he gone charging into that burning house? How could he hope to find the Fletcher children when it must be all but impossible to see in there?

Ann was sweating and gasping for breath when Chase finally burst out the front door. A cheer erupted from a hundred throats as he stumbled toward her, clutching a child against his chest.

Ann's knees wobbled with relief at the sight of him.

"Find this girl's mother!" he instructed as he thrust a child of three or four into her arms.

Ann instinctively clasped the child against her, then reached for Chase. It surprised her how much she needed to touch him, to feel him strong and solid beneath her hands.

Chase didn't give her the chance. He spun on his heel and bounded back toward the house.

"Chase!" she shouted, her heart in her throat. "Don't go back in there!"

But even if Chase could hear her above the roar of the flames, he paid no heed. He grabbed the blanket someone offered, draped himself in the folds, and ducked through the door.

"Chase!" Ann cried, wondering why he suddenly mattered so much to her. "Be careful!"

The fire was chewing through the structure inch by inch. Flames licked up the interior walls and clawed out the broken windows. She could see the fire scaling the stairs. Soon the entire place would be engulfed.

And Chase had gone back inside.

Finally Ann turned her attention to the child Chase had entrusted to her. The girl's round, freckled face was smudged black around her nostrils and at the corners of her mouth. She whimpered, wheezed, and coughed—then vomited all down the skirt of Ann's best gown.

Ann's own supper backed up in her throat. Her ears buzzed. The inside of her mouth went velvety, but somehow she managed to hold herself together until her head stopped reeling.

She fished a handkerchief out of her sleeve, mopped the baby's tear-streaked face and then her mouth. "What's your name, dear?" Ann managed to ask her.

"M-m-marfa," the girl wheezed and began to cry.

"Well, you're safe now, Martha. I'm going to take you to your mother."

They found Mary Fletcher on the far side of the picket fence, lying on the bed of a hay wagon. The blackened folds of her skirts had been turned back, and the doctor was bathing and binding the burns on her legs.

"Oh, Martha!" Mary sobbed at the sight of her daughter. Martha wailed hoarsely and reached for her mother.

Ann lifted the sobbing child into the wagon, and Mary wrapped the girl up tight in her arms. While Martha sniffled and coughed and wailed, her mother stroked and patted her, making sure she'd come out of the fire unhurt.

As the doctor finished bandaging Mary's legs, he turned to Ann. "Is Martha all right?"

Ann thanked God for the bit of nursing she'd done at school. "She seems to have breathed a lot of smoke, and she was sick a couple of minutes ago."

He nodded as if that was normal. "Any burns?"

"None that I was able to see."

Just then, Mary Fletcher clasped Ann's hand and drew her closer. "Have they—" Ann saw the sick terror in the other woman's eyes. "Have they found my other children?"

Ann tightened her hold and did her best to reassure her. "My—my husband and another man are getting them out."

"They'll be all right, Mary," the doctor put in from where he'd begun bandaging one of the volunteers.

Though Mary snuggled her daughter close, Ann could see the impatience and dread in her eyes. She clasped Mary's hand a little tighter and fought to keep her fear for Chase from interfering with the comfort she was offering Mary.

Then Ann looked back at the house and her heart

froze inside her. Flames shot through the second-story windows. Fire gnawed at one corner of the roof and ran in hot orange streaks along the eaves.

Chase was in there somewhere, searching for Mary's other children, risking his life for people he'd never met. It was the bravest thing she'd ever seen anyone do.

And the most foolhardy.

Then a tall man pushed his way through the gate. The steaming blanket draped around his head and shoulders made it impossible for Ann to tell if it was Chase. Whoever it was, he was carrying a boy of five or six.

Ann's throat filled with grateful tears.

"This tyke yours, ma'am?" the man asked Mary and hefted the lad into the wagon bed.

It wasn't Chase's voice. This wasn't Ann's husband.

Mary grabbed the boy and wrapped him against her. "Oh, Jack!" she sobbed. "You're safe!"

"I'm"—the boy's thin chest heaved—"sorry, Ma!" Tears scored thin, white streaks down his sooty cheeks. "I'm sorry. I tried to get out."

Mary buried her face in her son's tumbled hair, then hugged both her children tighter. "It's all right, Jackie boy. Nothing else matters now that you're here with me."

Ann watched the three of them clinging together. A family, not yet whole, but bound together. A family taking comfort among themselves.

When Ann began to feel as if she were intruding, she turned to the man who'd brought Jack out. His shoulders were hunched and his breathing was as labored and ragged as the boy's.

She grabbed his sleeve. "Did you see"—fear squeezed the words up her throat—"anyone else in the house? Did you see my husband?"

"It's like hell in there," was all he said.

She turned from the horror in his eyes and pushed through the gate. As she crossed the yard, the grass crackled beneath her shoes, alive with bits of glowing ash. The smoke rolled over her like lines of breakers. The house wavered and shimmied in the heat.

It's like hell in there.

"Chase?" she whispered. "Oh, Chase."

The house beams creaked and groaned. The walls bowed. Someone grabbed Ann's arm and dragged her back.

Through a film of grimy tears, Ann watched Mary's home disintegrate beam by beam. The roof sagged. The timbers howled and shuddered. The walls crumbled slowly, one at a time. As each one fell, it sent up a shower of angry sparks.

Chase might have rescued little Martha, but that hadn't been enough for him. He'd gone back into that inferno, and he was dying there, searching for Mary's last child.

Ann clasped a hand across her mouth. She'd been wed to Chase Hardesty for less than a week, to someone who'd proved tonight he was a far better man than she'd given him credit for. And now she was his widow.

But then, from somewhere behind what was left of the house, a man reeled out of the darkness. As he wavered across the yard, the steaming blanket slid down around his shoulders. Ann recognized the shape of his head and wild, damp fluff of his hair.

Chase.

She began to run and reached him just as he stumbled to his knees in the brittle grass. His shoulders shook with coughing. As he fought for breath, he curled his body around something clasped against his chest.

Three of the townsmen dragged them back away from the flames and, as they did, Chase offered up what looked like a wad of rags. One of them took the bundle and pulled open the cloth.

Ann heard a baby whimper and knew Chase had saved Mary's youngest child.

"You got the baby out!" Ann cried and cupped his face. "Oh, Chase, you saved the baby from the fire!"

He gave a quick, jerky nod, then reached out and dragged her against him. His frantic energy broke over her. "I came so close—" He gasped and ground his damp, blackened face into her shoulder. "So close to not—finding him. I searched"—he knotted his fists in her clothes—"every inch of those upstairs rooms. I—tried—" His voice broke. "—so hard. But I couldn't . . ."

He bound her tighter. "Oh, Annie, I came so close— to giving up."

Ann all but drowned in the wild boil of his fear and relief as it rolled over her. No woman with a heart beating inside of her could deny Chase Hardesty the comfort he was seeking. Ann wrapped her arms around him and rocked him against her. She splayed her hands against the bow of his shoulders, stroked his crinkled hair.

His skin was hot and wet against her throat. He reeked of sweat and smoke and the residue of terror. She shut her eyes and held him, thanking God in silent, jumbled prayers that this strong, brave man had come through the fire.

"It's all right," she crooned to him. "You got that baby out. All the children are safe."

Chase went still in the circle of her arms. "*All the children?*"

"Yes," she whispered.

His muscles loosened. The last of the energy seemed to drain out of him. "All of them," he rasped deep in his throat. "Oh, dear God! I didn't think we'd get all of them."

His shoulders heaved, and he bent forward, coughing with the effort to draw more air into his lungs.

"Easy," Ann whispered, her own voice raw with breathing smoke. "Don't fight so hard. It's going to be all right now."

Rue materialized over them, hovering, fiercely protective, wavering and unsure of himself.

"Water?" she said.

Rue went off without a word.

Across ten yards of trampled grass, the house shrieked and groaned, shivered and wailed. Ann and Chase watched it settle into a smaller mound of blazing rubble.

In Chase's tearing, smoke-red eyes Ann could see what it had been like in there: a maze of shifting smoke, of scouring flames, and blasting heat. She saw that he'd felt trapped, wild with desperation, crazed with hopelessness. She saw his terror of failing. She felt the shudders take him and tightened her hold.

"I couldn't find that baby," he gasped. "I crawled through those upstairs rooms, feeling my way, knowing I'd never—"

"But you did," she insisted. "You got those babies out. I saw them with their mother. It's all right, Chase; you can let it go."

He nodded, coughing resonant and belly-deep. He hunched forward, exhausted and shaking. Rue came with a canteen of water and Chase drank it down in one long swallow.

They were still kneeling in the grass when one of the townsmen came to get them. "Mrs. Fletcher has asked to see you," he told them. "They've taken her to the house across the street."

When they arrived, Mary was lying in bed in a room to the left of the door. She had the baby cuddled close in her arms. Martha lay with her head tucked into the crook of her mother's shoulder and smiled shyly at Ann when she saw her. Jack was curled up asleep at his mother's side, his arm splinted and tied across his chest.

Ann watched the four of them, understanding in a way she might never have understood before what Chase had given Mary Fletcher.

The woman on the bed reached out and caught Chase's hand. "You saved my children, Captain Hardesty," she said and blinked back tears. "I'm glad to see you got out safe as well."

"I'm fine, Mrs. Fletcher," he assured her.

"I have so very much to thank you for," Mary nuzzled Jack's hair, then hugged Martha and the baby closer. "I never expected to see my wee ones again. I thought they were lost, but you and Mr. Matthews..." Her voice faltered and her eyes filled. "You went into that house and brought them back to me. You risked your lives, and I'll be grateful for what you did as long as I draw breath."

"I did what any man would do," Chase answered.

Ann knew he'd done a good deal more than that. She slid her hand around his wrist and squeezed it gently. She felt him start a little at her touch, and a wave of unexpected protectiveness moved through her.

"You just rest, Mrs. Fletcher," Chase said and turned to go.

As Ann passed the bed, Mary snagged the drape of her skirt between her fingers. "You take good care of him!" she admonished in a whisper. "See that you give him a fine, strong son!"

Ann hesitated, then slowly raised her hand to her belly. "I—I'll do the best I can," she promised.

As they came in sight of the *Andromeda*, the passengers and crew members still milling on deck bounded across the gangway and swept Chase back onto the boat in a flurry of congratulations.

Ann trudged along behind. The furor that had buoyed her up abruptly drained away, leaving her staggering with weariness. Her shoulders ached from lifting buckets. Her head was fuzzy, and she smelled of sweat and vomit.

Halfway up the landing stage, she ran out of energy. She stopped, swaying, not able to move another step.

Cal Watkins and Barney came trotting down to claim her. Cal gave her his arm to lean on and Barney nosed his way through the crowd to a crate where Ann could sit and rest herself.

She just sat for a time, too exhausted to think or move as stories about the fire buzzed above her head. But once she got her second wind, Ann saw that Chase looked even more weary than she, and was wavering on his feet. In the lantern light she could see the angry red burns speckling his face and hands. His hair crinkled at the ends and his eyebrows were singed to stubble. Deep holes pockmarked his once-fine coat, which probably meant there were burns on his chest and shoulders.

Chase clearly needed tending, and Ann could see that no one was going to look after him unless she did it herself.

She heaved to her feet and wended her way toward where Chase was standing. "If you come up to the cabin, I'll see to those burns," she offered.

"I'm fine," he insisted. "Absolutely fine."

But he didn't sound fine. His voice scraped when he talked and his breathing was shallow and rusty. She recognized a tightness around his eyes, and knew that whether he was willing to admit it or not, Chase was in pain.

"He's never liked anyone looking after him," Rue confided softly from somewhere behind her.

Whether Chase liked it or not, Ann meant to look after him. She made the single request she knew he couldn't refuse. "Then, would you mind escorting me upstairs? I'm so tired I can barely stand."

For an instant he scowled down at her, his brow furrowed and his lips compressed. Then, with markedly poor grace, he acceded and offered his arm.

HER REQUEST WAS A RUSE. CHASE KNEW PERFECTLY WELL Ann didn't need *him* to escort her to the cabin. Cal would have done it gladly, or Goose or Rue. But she seemed to feel obliged to look after him, though he most definitely didn't want her to. He especially didn't want her doing it tonight when he had other things to discuss with her entirely.

"Honestly, Ann," he insisted, standing over where she knelt on the bedroom floor, rummaging through her valises. "The burns aren't bothering me."

Ann kept rummaging.

Damn stubborn woman. Damn stubborn, *magnificent* woman. She was the first person he'd seen when he carried the Fletcher girl out of the burning house. He'd spotted Annie—his delicate, well-born, *pregnant* wife—halfway down the bucket line, doing what she could to fight the fire. He'd known right then he could trust her to get that girl to her mother.

What he *hadn't* known was that he could turn to her when he needed someone himself. He hadn't known that she'd kneel with him right there in the grass, that she'd draw him to her when he craved shelter and solidity. He'd never dreamed she could soothe him with the touch of those soft, cool hands; whisper words of calm and comfort and sanity when the world was roaring in his ears.

Ann didn't know what she'd given him tonight, and he couldn't tell her. At least not now.

"Here it is!" Ann said, clambering to her feet as if she'd unearthed a treasure. What she seemed to have found was a jar of thick, brown goo. When she pried off the lid the stench of it blossomed through the room, punky and strong enough to make Chase's eyes water.

"What *is* that stuff?" he demanded, resisting the urge to clamp his hand over his nose.

"Relief," Ann promised.

She dipped two fingers into the noisome gel and started toward him. Knowing what Ann meant to do, Chase backed away.

"My burns are fine," he assured her.

She kept on coming.

"I'll be all right," he tried again. "Thank you for your concern."

Ann got close enough to dab a glob of the vile stuff onto the burn on the side of his chin. At first Chase didn't feel anything but Ann's fingers feathering over his skin. Then all at once, the stinging began to ease. Coolness took its place, and as she'd promised, relief.

"It works," he said in amazement.

Ann nodded and dotted a glop on the hot, raw place

at the corner of his mouth, on the burn on the tip of his nose, and the scrape along the slope of his cheek.

The cool tingling replaced the pain, and now that the ointment was working, he didn't mind so much about the smell. "What is this stuff?" he asked again.

Ann kept dabbing. "A secret concoction the nurse who ran the infirmary at school used to make."

"What's in it?" Chase wanted to know.

Ann gave him the slightest of smiles. "I did mention it was a *secret* concoction, didn't I?"

With the flutter of her fingertips, she stippled more of the balm onto the skin above his left eyebrow, glazed a burn on the rim of his ear, and started working down his neck.

Her touch was quick and matter-of-fact, yet he liked the contact. He liked being able to look down into her face, observe her close at hand. He liked being near enough that he could touch her if he wanted to.

And he most definitely wanted to.

But it wasn't like it was out there in the yard. Every thought and need and fear in him had been laid bare, and Ann had opened herself to him, too. She'd held him and healed him in a way he'd never expected. She was still helping him, easing his pain, but her barriers were back in place. And considering what lay ahead, perhaps that was just as well.

Ann worked over him, seeing to the burns on his face and neck and hands. When she was done, she fastened the lid of the jar and handed it to him. "Rue can see to the spots on your shoulders and back," she said. "Have him reapply the salve every two hours."

Chase knew the instructions were a dismissal, but he had something to say to her. Something he was suddenly even more loath to discuss with her than he'd been before.

He drew a slow, uneven breath; his lungs felt lined with sandpaper. "Do you remember when you came aboard the *Andromeda*," he began, struggling with a surge of guilt and ingratitude, "and I said you could stay until we met a packet headed downstream."

Ann raised her head.

"Well, the *Iowa Princess* is going to St. Louis. Captain Brady has agreed to take you home."

He saw shock and disillusionment dawn in her eyes.

"But we were there in the grass together," she whispered, as if those moments had been as exceptional for her as they'd been for him. As if after what they'd been through, they should be able to trust each other implicitly.

"We've been over this before, Annie," he went on, trying to reason with her. "You can't stay on a boat that's bound for Montana. It's best that you go back."

"It isn't best."

What he was doing was sane and prudent and responsible Chase told himself. So why should he feel such regret? How had she made him feel as if he were betraying her?

He pressed on anyway. "The *Iowa Princess* is casting off

at seven o'clock tomorrow morning. I'll come by a few minutes early so I can take you aboard and get you settled."

Ann didn't say a word. She just stared up at him for one long moment, then turned away.

chapter five

W HAT THE DEVIL WAS GOING ON?

Chase opened the door to Ann's cabin—to his cabin—and stepped inside.

"Ann?" he called out.

He'd come by to escort her to the *Iowa Princess* for the trip downstream and expected to find her waiting with her valises packed. Captain Brady had promised them one of his better cabins if they boarded early.

Instead Chase found the sitting room was cold, dark— and completely empty.

"Annie?" he called a second time.

Nothing stirred.

He crossed the room and opened the pocket door that led into the sleeping area, but Ann wasn't there. Ann's things weren't there, either, he suddenly realized. Not so much as one of her hairpins remained.

Chase slumped against the doorjamb and swiped at his mouth with the back of his hand. He'd spent most of the night bent over a chamberpot, ridding himself of the ash and smoke he'd swallowed during the fire. In spite of Ann's mysterious salve, when he was finally able to sleep, the burns on his back and shoulders had stung like swarming bees.

And now this.

He drew a breath and straightened slowly. Since the cabin was cleared out, he figured Ann wasn't just down at breakfast. So where had she gone?

Not far, he thought. Though she'd all but forced her way onto the *Andromeda,* he didn't think Ann was by nature an adventurous woman. She might well be hidden somewhere aboard, waiting for the *Iowa Princess* to get underway.

She could have gone up into town. But even if she had money for passage, Glasgow wasn't on a rail or stage line. It wasn't big enough to have a livery stable where she could let a horse. With so few options, she couldn't have gotten far.

Now, if she had taken it into her head to leave the boat in Kansas City . . . Chase shuddered at the possibilities.

Moving with far more energy than he could afford to expend, he left the cabin and dispatched several of their most reliable roustabouts to look for Ann in town. After last night, people knew who Ann was. If she'd gone into Glasgow, someone would have noticed, and he'd have her back inside of an hour.

Chase would search the *Andromeda* himself—and he had a very good idea where to start.

Not two minutes later he burst into Bertin's kitchen. "All right," he demanded, "where is she?"

Frenchy and his two breakfast helpers looked up from where they were toasting bread, frying doughnuts, and removing currant-studded coffee cakes from the oven. The scent of cinnamon was thick enough to lick right out of the air.

"Who?" Frenchy asked, his half-moon eyebrows lifting.

"Ann," Chase answered in an accusing tone. "She was supposed to be packed and ready to leave on the *Iowa Princess* first thing this morning."

"So you can send her back to St. Louis, eh?"

"Did Ann tell you that?"

"She didn't have to."

Chase supposed not. It was nearly impossible to have a conversation anywhere on board without someone overhearing, and he'd spoken to Captain Brady right out on deck about taking Ann home yesterday afternoon.

"So can you tell me where she is?" Chase persisted.

Frenchy shrugged. "Perhaps Ann doesn't want to go back."

"I don't care what she wants—"

"*Ah!* Your first mistake," the chef diagnosed sagely.

Chase compressed his lips, hanging on to the tail of his temper with both hands. "She'll be better off back in St. Louis with her father."

Frenchy drizzled icing over a tray of coffee cakes.

"Any pregnant woman would be better off at home than on her way to the Montana Territory," Chase insisted.

The cook set the bowl of icing aside with an emphatic *thump*. "I know nothing about her disappearance."

Chase could feel the color come up in his face. Frenchy's genius in the kitchen had always managed to counterbalance his insubordination—until today. "You're the one she'd come to for help," Chase insisted. "Tell me where she's hiding."

Frenchy wiped his hands on a towel stained brown from being washed too often in the river. "I do not know."

The man had a reputation as a gambler and a liar and a cad, but for some reason Chase believed him.

"All right," he conceded and stomped into the salon. Much to the steward's displeasure, he dragooned two waiters to help him search the boat.

Chase himself started in the pilothouse and found Rue poring over river charts, noting the changes in the channel Captain Brady had warned them about. "Do you have any idea where Ann is?" Chase asked his brother.

Rue paused with pencil poised. "Have you misplaced her?"

Chase scowled at him. "I was to take Ann over to the *Iowa Princess* first thing this morning, but she's gone off somewhere."

Rue stroked the fuzzy ribbon of his mustache. "You suppose she went over to the *Iowa Princess* by herself?"

Chase doubted Ann would go anywhere near the *Iowa Princess*. Still, it made sense to check before they turned the *Andromeda* upside down looking for her. And maybe if he was lucky, he could buy a little time.

Ann wasn't aboard the *Iowa Princess*.

"We haven't seen hide nor hair of her," Captain Brady told him from the head of the gangway where he was greeting his embarking passengers. "I thought you meant to bring her over early so she could have her pick of staterooms."

Chase refused to admit the woman he'd married just a week before had run off somewhere. It was the kind of story that got passed from captain to captain along with channel reports—and he sure as hell didn't want the commodore catching wind of it.

"I must have missed her at breakfast," Chase said and headed back across the landing stage.

"Well, check quick, lad," Brady told him, tapping his pocket watch. "I'm pulling out at seven o'clock. I've got a schedule to keep, you know."

Chase knew; he'd be keeping a packet schedule himself once they got back from Fort Benton. Since Brady was leaving at seven, that gave Chase ten minutes to find his wife and hustle her aboard the *Iowa Princess*.

The rousters who'd gone looking for Ann in town were waiting at the top of the gangway when he got back.

"Ain't nobody seen her," one of them reported. "We looked good, too, Captain. We even checked with the lady that got burnt last night. We thought maybe Mrs. Hardesty went to check on her."

"You did well to think of that." It hadn't once crossed Chase's mind. "How is Mrs. Fletcher?"

"As well as can be expected, I guess," the rouster answered. "She said to thank you again for what you did."

Chase acknowledged the thanks with a nod. "But she hadn't seen my wife?"

"No, sir."

The waiters hadn't had any better luck with their search of the boat. "We opened all the equipment lockers and checked every single one of the upper berths...."

And found nothing.

Chase searched the boat again himself. He opened pantries and broom closets, checked beneath the tarp that tied down the yawl. He ended up standing at the head of the *Andromeda*'s gangway a few minutes later.

Captain Brady hailed him from the deck of the *Iowa Princess*. "Will Mrs. Hardesty be traveling with us to St. Louis?"

Chase lied outright. "Ann's decided to stay aboard as far as Kansas City, but thanks for your offer to see her home."

"Give her my compliments. Your wife's a lovely woman." Brady waved, then signaled for the pilot to sound the whistle for backing down.

Chase stood and watched the *Iowa Princess* pull out. Things would have been so simple if Ann had just agreed...

He ran his hands through his hair and stared up into Glasgow to where the shopkeepers swept their steps and the blacksmith shoed his horses and the children ran laughing on their way to school. He turned his gaze to the charred black hole where a house had stood. To where he'd searched for that baby in a maze of fire and smoke. To where he'd finally battered his way to safety because he'd known that child would die if he gave up.

To where Ann had knelt with him and held him in the steaming grass. To where she'd reached into the heart of his turmoil and helped him find himself again.

He hadn't expected her to be so strong when he needed her. He hadn't thought she'd be willing to risk so much of herself for him. He hadn't imagined she'd join up with the bucket brigade, or take such good care of little Martha. Or charm every single one of his officers at dinner.

Ann hadn't looked down her nose at his men the way most society ladies did. She didn't act as if Goose and Cal were some inferior breed: coarse, unlettered fellows with dirt beneath their fingernails. Ann had treated his men *like men*—worthy of her interest, her kindness, and her concern.

His wife hadn't turned out to be who he thought she was—which made it that much more important for him to find her, look after her, and keep her safe.

He watched the *Iowa Princess* disappear downstream toward Arrow Rock and wished with everything in him that Ann was aboard. He supposed she might have left the *Andromeda* during the night, and if she had, she could be headed off in almost any direction. She could have begged a ride on some farmer's wagon, found someone willing to sell her a horse. She might have set off on foot, or hidden somewhere in town to wait for another steamer.

Or maybe she had plans to rendezvous with her baby's father.

The notion blew through Chase, chilling him to the marrow. *He had to find her.*

Chase straightened and let out his breath. He'd detail men in all directions. He'd send someone to the nearest telegraph office and have Ann's description wired to towns nearby. He'd flag down the next boat headed upstream and send a man ahead to Kansas City. He didn't think Ann would go back toward St. Louis, but just in case . . .

The *ping* of expanding iron and the *hiss* of steam drew Chase's attention. Cal Watkins was back in the engine room awaiting orders. But until Chase found some trace of Ann, he didn't dare leave Glasgow.

He'd just shouted to Watkins to blow off steam and let the fires die when Goose Steinwehr sought him out.

"Are we staying on?" he wanted to know.

Chase nodded grimly, realizing that if they stayed, he'd have to explain to his passengers and pay the shippers' penalties for the delay.

"Are we staying in Glasgow," Steinwehr persisted, "because Mrs. Hardesty is missing?"

As captain of the *Andromeda* Chase didn't owe an explanation to anyone, but there was a concern in Steinwehr's square face that gave him pause.

"You don't know where she is, do you?"

The big man lowered his gaze. "I might have seen her."

Chase's heart chugged a little harder. "When? When did you see her? Where did she go?"

Steinwehr wiped the sweat from his face, then carefully folded his faded blue handkerchief. "She might have come down the stairs with her bags last night. She might have stopped at the top of the gangway. She might have been crying."

"Tell me," Chase insisted.

"I asked her where she was going."

Chase grabbed Steinwehr's sleeve and shook it the way a terrier might try to shake a mastiff. "What did she say?"

"It was very late. She hadn't expected anyone to see her. I frightened her, I think, because she was trembling. 'I won't go back!' she said. 'I won't let him put me on that steamer!'"

"And what did you say?"

Steinwehr dipped his head. "I gave her another choice."

Chase's mouth went dry. "Where is she?"

Steinwehr took a ring of keys from one sagging pocket. He bent slowly and unlocked the padlock on the grilled hatch that led down into the hold. Down into the dark, closely packed underbelly of the steamer.

SHE WAS THERE.

Relief tumbled through Chase like pebbles down a well. He let out his breath in a rush and hung tight to the ladder down into the hold until his knees stopped shaking.

He could hardly believe Ann had spent the night here, here in the shallow slope-sided space that lay between the floorboards of *Andromeda*'s main deck and the steamer's keel. It was close down here, uncomfortably warm, and pungent with the accumulated smells of hemp and resin.

The moment Goose closed the hatch behind her last night, Ann would have been swallowed by pure, undiluted blackness. Yet there she was this morning, curled on a big wooden crate, sleeping peacefully as a child.

A particularly headstrong and infuriating child.

By the faint gray light that filtered through the open hatch, Chase could see that Ann lay with her knees drawn up and had one arm draped protectively around her belly. She seemed impossibly young lying there, a child carrying a child of her own. A woman not in the least prepared for what the birth of that baby was going to demand of her. Yet for all of that, Ann had proved herself to be a warm and capable woman last night—first with his men, then with Martha, and finally with him.

As he stood looking down at her a strange fullness rose beneath his sternum—a sweet, expanding warmth that was not unlike pride or possessiveness. As if here was someone to hold fast and cherish.

But then, Ann had made it abundantly clear she didn't want to be either held *or* cherished. At least not by him.

Still, she'd settled in aboard the *Andromeda* contentedly enough until he'd made arrangements to send her home. She'd taken a terrible chance to escape that fate. If

Goose Steinwehr hadn't intercepted her, there's no telling where she might have gone or what might have happened to her.

Crossing noiselessly to where she lay, Chase knelt beside her makeshift bed. "Ann," he whispered. "Annie?"

When she didn't stir, he reached out and stroked her hair.

She bolted awake hissing and scratching, flailing like a creature possessed.

Chase jerked back as she struck out, but Ann kicked at him, curled her fingers into talons, and tried to rake his face with her fingernails. He caught her wrists and pinned them at her sides. Taking care not to hurt her, he leaned over her and held her down with nothing more than the breadth of his body.

Her eyes shone wide and fierce. Her breathing raged in her throat. She twisted beneath him, lost in some desperate fury.

"Ann!" He spoke harshly, piercingly. He refused to give ground. "It's all right, Ann. It's Chase. Stop, now! Stop! You'll hurt yourself."

She strained against him, gasping.

"*Ann!*"

Either his words or the sharpness of his voice finally penetrated the miasma engulfing her. She hesitated, gave a grunt of recognition, then shuddered and went still.

Though she lay immobile, Chase could still hear the stark, feverish hitch in her breathing. He could feel her muscles coiled and flexed, ready to explode with frenzy.

"It's all right, Annie," he crooned to her. "You were

having a bad dream, but it's over now. No one's going to hurt you."

Ann blinked as if to bring the world into focus around her. Then all at once she seemed to realize where she was.

"I won't board the *Iowa Princess!*" she cried, trying to wriggle free of him again. "You can't make me!"

"It's too late for that, my girl," he said, still holding her immobile. "The *Iowa Princess* left a good long while ago."

She hesitated, trembling under his hands. "It's gone?" she asked and sought the truth in his eyes.

When she realized he hadn't lied to her, he felt her tension drain away. "That's better," he mumbled and released her.

Ann sat up and glared at him, rubbing at her wrists. "So, am I going to be allowed to stay aboard the *Andromeda?* Or is missing the *Iowa Princess* only a reprieve?"

Chase braced his hips against one of the adjoining crates and studied her, taking in the defiant line of her jaw and the fear that lay dark at the backs of her eyes. It wasn't the first time he'd seen fear in her, only now he intended to find out what it meant.

"So, Ann," he asked, easing closer. "Are you afraid to go back to St. Louis? Or were you leaving the *Andromeda* so you could meet the baby's father?"

"The baby's father?" Ann gave a sniff of bitter laugh. "Good God! No!"

"Then what is it about going home that frightens you?"

"I'm not afraid."

But she was. Though she faced him with her back straight and her chin high, it was a hollow gesture. One not of pride but of protection. But from what?

"Is it the commodore, Annie?" Chase pressed her.

"I told you I don't trust the commodore," she answered with a lift of her brows. "Why do you think I keep running away?"

"Keep running away?"

Ann dipped her head. He was suddenly sure she'd said more than she intended.

"Did you try to leave St. Louis before you boarded the *Andromeda?*" he persisted.

She compressed her lips for a moment before she conceded. "Last fall I got as far as Memphis before the commodore's men found me and brought me back."

That's when she'd gotten pregnant, Chase reasoned. Ann had either run off with a man she thought she loved, or been seduced while she was on her own. It explained so much.

What it didn't explain was why she was so eager to get out of her father's grasp. What did she have to fear from him?

Chase considered the possibilities. A single conclusion presented itself. "Does he hit you, Annie?"

She stiffened reflexively.

Something in that faint involuntary response made his belly crimp. "Does that son of a bitch hit you?"

Ann's gaze rose to his. "My stepfather has never laid a hand on me."

Chase didn't believe her. In his years aboard the steamers, he'd seen women beaten by the very men who ought to be looking after them. He'd seen how those women held themselves aloof and cringed when anyone touched them. He'd seen them hide their bruises and heard them lie away their fears because they were ashamed to admit that their husbands or fathers mistreated them.

Chase eased closer. "I need to know if the commodore beats you. I need to know, Annie, so I can protect you. So I can see that he never—"

"The commodore doesn't beat me!" she shouted at him.

Somehow her denial made Chase even more certain that he did. Knowing it sanctioned the protectiveness he'd felt from the moment he laid eyes on her.

Though he weighed his words before he spoke, he knew they were inevitable. "What if I said you didn't have to go back to St. Louis unless you wanted to? That you could stay aboard the *Andromeda*."

"Do you mean it?" Ann asked and raised her gaze to his. But before he could tell her that's exactly what he meant, she glanced away. "But then, you said you'd refuse to marry me, then went right ahead and broke your word."

He *had* done exactly what she said, and never bothered to explain why he'd changed his mind. He hadn't once considered why Ann might want to leave her father's house; he'd just kept threatening to send her back.

"I swear," he said and lay his hand across his heart. "I won't make you go back to St. Louis against your will."

Ann nodded warily. "All right."

"That doesn't mean," he continued as he rose, "that I've given up trying to convince you that you'd be better off there than here."

"I won't go back!"

He shook his head. "You don't know the wild, empty country ahead of us. How far we'll be from civilization."

"Don't underestimate me, Chase." Ann slipped off the crate and faced him. "I might surprise you."

It wouldn't be the first time, Chase thought. As if to prove it, Ann climbed the ladder out of the hold with considerably more agility than he'd expected.

Goose Steinwehr was pacing when they reached the main deck. Chase gave him a quick reassuring nod, then started shouting orders.

"I've given command of the *Andromeda* over to Goose and Rue," he explained as he escorted his wife to the captain's quarters. "They'll get us underway while you and I get a few things settled."

HIS WIFE. GOOD GOD! *SHE WAS HIS WIFE!* CHASE THOUGHT as he closed the cabin door behind them. Somehow, until this moment, he hadn't really thought of Ann as being his wife.

Of course, he'd agreed to marry her, and they'd spoken their vows. She'd taken up residence here in his cabin.

She'd even let him hold onto her last night when he'd needed to be close to someone. Yet she'd remained a stranger.

Why did she feel like his wife this morning? Why did this marriage feel suddenly so real to him?

He heard the steamer's whistle hoot and felt the floor shimmy ever so slightly beneath his boots. The *Andromeda* was backing down. It hung for a moment in the current, then surged ahead and into the channel.

Knowing the steamer was underway, Chase turned to where Ann had settled herself in the medallion-backed armchair to the right of the settee.

"Ann," he began, drawing in a breath that still tasted of smoke. "I think it's high time I explained some things to you."

"What things?" she asked warily.

"Why I broke my word to you, for one."

"You told me you'd do what I wanted."

He could hear the catch of disillusionment in her voice, even now. A sharp residue of regret grated painfully between the man he thought he was and what he'd done.

"I did tell you that," he acknowledged, lowering himself onto the settee. "After I left the parlor that first day, I went directly to your father's study. I told him I wouldn't marry you and refused command of the *Andromeda*."

"But then you changed your mind." The disillusionment in her voice deepened to reproach.

Chase compressed his lips, wondering if he could explain things he wasn't entirely sure he understood himself.

"When I got down to the levee," he went on, deciding to try, "Boothe was just bringing the *Andromeda* in from her inaugural run. Just looking at her, just watching how neatly she nuzzled up to the levee—" He sighed and ruffled his singed hair. "Boothe invited me aboard to look her over."

"To taunt you with him having her."

That's exactly what Boothe had been doing, though he hadn't recognized it as that at the time.

"When I saw how graceful and well-designed the *Andromeda* was," he went on. "When I realized how fast those engines would make her— When I took her wheel in my two hands—" He could feel the throb of that first contact in his palms even now. The conviction that the *Andromeda* was his destiny swept through him again. "I had to have her."

He met her gaze head-on. "I went back and talked to the commodore that afternoon. He signed over ownership the morning you and I were married."

She reached across and touched his hand. "He'll never forgive you for this, you know. For depriving him of his first command. You'll have to watch out for him from now on."

"Boothe?" he asked, surprised by her warning.

He felt the tremor in her fingers before she took back her hand. "You don't know how vindictive he is."

But Chase did know. He'd been partnered with Boothe all of one season and watched him work his subtle cruelties on people who displeased him. Thinking back on that now, Chase couldn't imagine what it must have been like for Ann growing up in the same house as Boothe Rossiter.

"I know this doesn't condone what I did," Chase pressed ahead, determined to get this settled between them, "but I thought I could make things up to you."

"And how did you mean to do that?"

Chase opened his mouth to say he was taking responsibility for a baby he hadn't fathered, to assure her he'd look after her and that child for the rest of their lives. But in the instant before he spoke, Chase realized he wanted Ann and her child to be far more than an obligation.

The notion stunned him, shook him to the marrow.

He wanted Ann to be his *wife*. He wanted her to be his partner and his confidante, his companion and his friend. He wanted to make a life with her, have a home and children, something warm and permanent to come home to. The enormity of the difference between what he'd wanted a week ago and what he wanted now rolled over him and left him reeling.

He couldn't say why he'd changed his mind. Certainly it had something to do with last night—that she'd treated his men with respect, that she'd done her part to fight the fire. That she'd tended him so diligently and offered the comfort he'd needed.

He leaned toward Ann, eager to paint his new vision of their life together in crisp detail. "If this run to Fort Benton is successful"—he could hear the burgeoning excitement in his own voice—"I'll be in a position to buy a house when we get back. Maybe we could find a place a little way out of the city, something with trees and a garden where children can run and play."

He could imagine coming home to her in a place like that, imagine her sitting in the shade of the arbor, waiting for him. Imagine how her face would light with welcome when she saw him.

"You'd give me a place like that?" she asked him, an almost unbearable wistfulness dawning in her eyes.

He nodded, encouraged, wanting it to be all right. "It could be a place where both of us—"

"*Both of us?*" she echoed, stiffening.

He looked up, confused. Had she thought the house he was describing was just for her? Was her idea of their married life so different from his?

"The way I see it—" He pressed ahead, determined to forestall the resistance he could see hovering on her next breath. "—we took vows. We may not have taken them for the noblest of reasons, but we said the words. We made the promises."

His mother's admonitions about the importance of home and family rang in his ears, and Chase realized suddenly how much he'd been dreading facing Lydia Hardesty with what he'd done.

"We made the promises," he insisted. "And it seems to me, we ought to keep them."

Ann scrambled to her feet and backed away. "You've already got what you want! You got the *Andromeda*!"

"What I'm saying," he clarified as he rose, "is that as

long as we're married, we should make the best of it. We should live together as man and wife."

Ann gaped at him, her eyes gone wide. "As man and wife!"

From the moment he'd seen her standing at the parlor window, he'd been aware of her as a woman. He'd wondered how the curve of that graceful throat would feel beneath his fingertips, how that primrose-pink mouth would taste if he kissed her. He hadn't considered what it might be like to bed her.

He hadn't allowed himself to consider it.

But he sure as hell wasn't prepared for the horror that dawned across her features at the prospect of being a wife to him. He might not be the kind of man that women mooned and sighed over, but he could be charming if he set his mind to it, damn it. The women he'd slept with over the years had never complained that he was hasty or inconsiderate of their needs. And he'd always either paid them well or bought something nice for them afterwards.

He changed his linen every other day, and when he was going to be with Ann, he always made sure he'd washed and shaved. He hadn't imagined that Ann might find making love with him so—so revolting.

Instinctively he reached for her. "I wouldn't expect you to lie with me now. Not while you're . . ." Something that felt suspiciously like panic displaced the singe of her rejection. "But—well . . . I'd like more children eventually."

Ann flinched away.

What was it about lying with him that Ann found so damn

distasteful? Chase had barely completed the thought when the truth dawned on him. He wasn't good enough to be her children's father. He was a river rat, an orphan taken out of pity. He had no pedigree, no schooling to speak of, no fancy manners. He was the man her father had bought for her because he couldn't buy anyone better.

Something dark and caustic churned through his insides.

Not an hour before, Chase had stood down in the hold watching Ann sleep, feeling full and warm—and satisfied with his lot. Now she'd managed to drain away every dram of that warmth and pleasure. He felt hollow, vacant, disillusioned, oddly lost. Angry and impatient.

He stepped toward her.

"The future is what we choose to make it, Annie." His voice resonated with convictions he didn't even know he had. "I'm sorry I broke my word to you, but I'm not sorry it got me the *Andromeda.* I don't regret marrying you, either. At least not the way you seem to regret marrying me.

"You've got to accept that what we did has bound us together. I'd like to make the best of that. I'd like to turn this into a real marriage. I'd like to make a life with you."

When all Ann could do was stare at him, he brushed past her on his way to the door.

"Wait!" she called out, halting him. "Tell me you'll keep your word. Tell me I can stay aboard the *Andromeda.*"

He turned with his hand on the doorknob. "I told you I wouldn't send you back unless you agreed to go."

Ann gave an almost imperceptible nod. "I believe you."

Chase jerked open the door and stalked out onto the deck. He didn't give a damn what his wife believed.

Or at least that's what he told himself.

chapter six

ANN STOOD AGAINST THE STARBOARD RAIL AND watched the peach and pink of the sunrise ripple across the paddle wheel's wake. She'd been baking bread with Frenchy Bertin half the night, and now that his assistants had arrived to help with breakfast, Ann slipped out on deck for a cup of coffee and a breath of air.

In this last week they'd put Kansas City, Fort Leavenworth, and Nebraska City behind them as they steamed west. Now Omaha's church steeples were disappearing in the distance, swallowed up by stands of cedars and cottonwoods. Rue said that because the river was high they were making good time, covering between fifteen and twenty miles a day. They'd only run aground twice since they passed the mouth of the Kaw.

Ann braced her forearms against the railing and turned her face into the cool dawn breeze. Though it was strong enough to ruffle the skirt of her gown and tug at her hair, it breathed the promise of spring. The trees along the bank were bursting, greening, humming with new life.

That humming seemed to resonate inside her, too. Her baby was astir this morning, stretching, quickening, quaking. Ann circled her palm at the crest of her belly and smiled to herself, still awed by knowing her child was growing inside her.

Though this certainly wasn't the kind of life Ann had envisioned for herself, she was making her place aboard the *Andromeda*. She'd already learned to make bread and pies and fried cakes from Frenchy. She'd made friends among the steamboat's officers and crew. Occasionally, she even stepped in to act as hostess to the passengers. Oddly enough, even bound by the ties of her marriage and her impending responsibilities as a new mother, Ann had never felt freer in her life.

She was down to the dregs of her coffee when she heard footfalls on the stairs and turned to see Chase descending from the Texas deck. The two of them had been tiptoeing around each other ever since the day they'd left Glasgow. Ever since Chase had defined what it was he expected of a wife.

Ann shivered remembering—angry with Chase for wanting the things he did from her, angry with herself for not being able to give him something that should have been so simple. But the one she was angriest with was her baby's father, for the way he'd pursued her, how he'd treated her, the way he'd ruined her life. The way he'd ruined all their lives.

Deliberately, she shifted her attention away from Chase to where a heron was poised in the shallows fishing. She hoped her husband's duties would take him elsewhere.

Instead he crossed the deck and paused beside her. "You want more coffee?" he offered.

She glanced at him and recognized a sharp impatience in his face, a need to get on with things, settle things between them.

Maybe she wanted to get on with things, too. So she shrugged, surrendered the thick ironstone mug, and waited for him to return from the kitchen.

He came back with two cups of steaming coffee. "So how did the baking go last night?" he asked, leaning against the rail beside her.

Before she answered, Ann took a sip of the coffee. He'd made it exactly the way she liked it, sweetened sparsely with sugar but thick with cream.

"Well enough, I suppose. We baked thirty loaves of bread and twenty-five dozen yeast rolls."

No wonder she was tired.

"And you never baked before you came aboard the *Andromeda?*" He sounded a little incredulous.

"Baking isn't the kind of thing they teach at Miss Amelia Farnsworth's Academy for Young Ladies."

What kind of proper young woman would enjoy dusting her hands with flour or indulge in something so vulgar as plunging forearm-deep in bread dough? Nor would anyone at Miss Farnsworth's have thought to teach their girls something so eminently practical.

"I do quite enjoy it, though," she volunteered.

The way the dough swelled and grew made the simple mixture seem almost alive. The resilience of the stuff beneath her palms awoke something basic and earthy in her. She liked how her muscles warmed as she worked, liked the thick ripe smell of yeast, and the heat of the kitchen.

She liked Frenchy's company, too. His frank, Gallic view of the world, his perspective that, as a man who was no better than he should be, forgave everyone else their weaknesses. Ann found his unquestioning acceptance a great relief.

"Frenchy says I'm ready to try baking a batch of bread on my own." She could hear the faint buff of pride she gave those last three words.

"Could you make a couple loaves to give my mother when we stop at Hardesty's Landing?" he asked her.

Panic slithered along Ann's nerves. Even the baby shifted and squirmed, as if the prospect of meeting Chase's family unnerved her as much as it did her mother.

"Will we reach Hardesty's Landing soon?" Ann managed to ask.

"With any luck, we'll be there day after tomorrow." Chase's voice rose with what Ann supposed was eagerness. "We'll tie up there for the night."

From the things Rue said, Ann had the impression that the Hardestys were a large, unruly lot; blunt, rowdy, simple folk. People so unlike the ones Ann had known in

St. Louis and Philadelphia that they might as well have come from the dark side of the moon.

What Rue had told her made her curious about the Hardestys, yet she needed Chase's reassurance. Would they accept her as his wife, with no questions asked?

Ann slid him a sideways glance. "Will you tell me about your family?"

Chase braced his elbows on the railing and slid a slow speculative glance at her. "Well, we're a mongrel lot; I ought to admit that outright. There are fourteen of us children altogether: six born to Ma and Pa, and eight strays."

Ann could tell by the smile that feathered the corners of his lips that he liked talking about them.

"And which are you?" Ann already knew the answer, but she wanted to hear the story from Chase himself.

He sipped, shifted, shrugged. "I was the first stray Pa brought home for Ma to raise. He found me holed up in the firebox of a burned out cabin. My whole family had been killed."

"How old were you?"

"Two or three."

Glancing at Chase, Ann could imagine the child Enoch Hardesty had taken home to his wife. Chase must have been skinny, tattered, and smudged with ashes and soot. He'd have had a head of matted red-brown curls and wary eyes. Even Ann, who wasn't sure she had so much as a scrap of maternal instinct, would have wanted to gather up that frightened little boy and make him hers.

"I wasn't old enough to remember a thing about my

first family," he continued. "Not so much as their name or what they looked like."

Ann could hear a rime of regret in his voice and felt compelled to speak, though she hadn't intended to reveal anything about her early life to him.

"I don't remember my father, either. I wouldn't have any idea what he looked like except that Mother had their wedding photograph. Rupert Pelletier was a lawyer; a very prominent man in Philadelphia. Or so Mama said. All I know for sure, is that he didn't leave so much as a penny to keep us when he died."

It was why her mother had married James Rossiter, how they'd come to live in St. Louis. In a way, her real father's lack of resources was the reason she was married to Chase Hardesty today.

Or at least one of the reasons.

When Chase didn't volunteer anything else about his childhood, Ann's thoughts returned to the prospect at hand.

"So how many of those fourteen brothers and sisters are likely to be at Hardesty's Landing when we get there?"

He paused to wave at a group of children striding along the bank, probably on their way to school.

"Pretty much everyone should be at the house, except Quinn, who's away at medical college," he answered, "and my sister Millie. She and her husband Sam are proving up a homestead someplace in Nebraska."

"Everyone?" Ann asked weakly. She hadn't imagined she'd be immersed in the Hardesty clan quite so deeply.

"*And* their spouses and children," he added.

"If there are so many, how will I ever keep everyone straight?"

Chase must have seen how intimidated she was by the prospect, and tipped an encouraging grin in her direction. "I expect once we sit down to supper, you'll sort us out. With so many of us being adopted, there isn't enough family resemblance that you'll get confused. Except for the twins, of course."

Ann nodded thoughtfully, then turned her face to the sun. Though she dreaded asking, it would be easier to put her concerns into words now, rather than later.

"What—what are you going to tell your family about marrying me?"

He didn't hesitate. "I'm going to tell them the truth."

She turned and looked at him in spite of herself. "Is that wise?"

His gaze moved over her, a half-amused, half-quizzical expression on his face. "I learned before I was out of short pants that Ma finds out everything anyway. Besides, it's not as if we can hide the fact that I'm in command of the *Andromeda*, or that you're carrying a child."

She turned to him, seeking either reticence or regret in those deep blue eyes. She didn't find either. But then, maybe the truth didn't frighten Chase Hardesty the way it did her.

"Besides," he went on, "Rue can't keep a secret to save his life. Everyone in Hardesty's Landing will know everything about us half an hour after we tie up."

Ann clasped her half-empty cup between her hands,

thankful for its lingering warmth. "What—what will they think of me once you tell them?"

Chase seemed to chew on the answer a little bit longer than he had the previous one. "No two of them will see our marriage the same way, and they'll make no secret of their opinions."

He reached across to curl those strong, rough fingers around her wrist. At his touch, that odd awareness lit in her again. But this time it also awakened a ripple of confidence, the sense that if he was with her, she'd be all right.

She liked the way that felt.

"You know," he continued very softly. "It doesn't matter what they think; it's what I think that's important."

His fingers tightened. She looked up and saw a world of expectation in his eyes. She saw the conviction that they could make something good and strong and satisfying from their marriage. *If they tried.*

But what that would require made Ann's palms sweat and her knees wobble. She disentangled herself from his grasp. She might have stepped away if there hadn't been one last question she had to ask.

"You promised you wouldn't send me back to St. Louis unless I agreed to go," she began, her voice wavering just a little.

"I did promise that."

"Are you planning to leave me with your family at Hardesty's Landing, instead?"

Chase studied her for one long moment before he answered. "You're not their responsibility," he answered.

"You're mine. But I do need to know one thing before we settle this."

Ann nodded, wondering what condition he was going to put on her future. "What is it?"

"How far along are you in your pregnancy?"

Ann flushed to the hairline. How could he speak so frankly about things married women discussed only in whispers? She knew why he was asking and realized that if she meant to stay aboard the *Andromeda*, she was going to have to lie to him.

"I'm four months along," she said, her cheeks going hotter. She was a full five months pregnant and moving closer to six.

"That means the baby will be born in . . ."

Ann calculated hastily. "August."

Chase let his gaze glide over her, studying, assessing. Ann resisted the urge to shield her swollen breasts and wrap a protective hand across her belly.

His mouth narrowed ever so slightly. Ann held her breath.

Finally Chase nodded. "By August the *Andromeda* will be running in and out of St. Louis. We'll find a place for you to stay in town so you can be near a doctor when that baby comes."

Ann went light-headed with relief. Chase was going to keep his word. He was going to let her stay aboard the *Andromeda*. He wasn't going to make her go back to the town house at the end of the run.

"Thank you," she whispered, her voice thick with gratitude. She wished she could have been honest with him about the baby, and about why this meant so much to her. "Staying aboard the *Andromeda* makes me feel ..."

Safe, she almost said, but it was more than safe. Being aboard the *Andromeda* meant she was no longer running away, no longer alone. It made her feel as if she was part of something or well down a road she'd been needing to take.

"Being aboard the *Andromeda* makes me feel as if I'm moving toward something, something I'm supposed to do or be or have." She shook her head in what might have been confusion. "I can't go back, and it's being here with you and the others that convinced me."

She looked up at him to see if he understood, and saw warmth and concern in those deep blue eyes. Warmth and concern and a kind of confidence in the future she wished she shared.

"I'm only trying to do what's best for you."

"This is what's best for me." She spoke the words softly, but with deep conviction. "And it's best for the baby."

Chase wasn't going to send her back—at least not as long as she held to the lie she'd told him. At least not as long as Chase believed her baby wasn't going to be born until after they returned from Fort Benton.

CAN ALL THESE PEOPLE POSSIBLY BE CHASE'S KIN? ANN wondered as she stared at what must be the entire population of Hardesty's Landing, gathered at the foot of the tiny settlement to welcome them.

A band of children had been waiting half a mile up the trace that skirted the river, and they'd done their best to keep pace with the slowing steamer. The men in the crowd looked as if they'd come straight from the woodlot, a few with splitting axes still balanced on their shoulders. A cluster of women and younger children stood well back from the edge of the bank, shouting and waving exuberantly.

The passengers and crewmen not involved in landing the vessel waved back. From her perch on the Texas deck Ann couldn't seem to do more than stare at the crowd. In a few minutes, Chase was going to escort her into that mob and introduce her as his wife.

It *almost* made her wish she was back in St. Louis.

From the roof of the hurricane deck, Chase was shouting orders. When Rue had nudged the *Andromeda* in as close to the bank as possible, two deckhands jumped ashore. Goose Steinwehr threw each of them a line to make fast to the big old cottonwoods at the edge of the river. Rue cramped the wheel around, making the engines grumble, as the rest of the deckhands took up the slack in the mooring ropes.

Finally satisfied with their berthing, Chase gave the order to run out the landing stage and blow off steam.

In spite of being busy piloting, Rue somehow managed to be one of the first people off the boat and was immediately engulfed. Men patted him, women hugged him, and children climbed up his legs, clamoring for the licorice whips he produced from his pockets.

It was a more openhanded and affectionate greeting than Ann had ever imagined anyone would get.

Gradually Rue worked his way toward an older couple standing at the base of the steep stone steps that ran up toward a house at the crest of the rise. Ann hadn't noticed the pair before, but she knew in a single glance they were Chase's parents. Enoch Hardesty was a granite block of a man, standing straight and stalwart beside a wisp of a woman who barely reached the center of his massive chest. Yet even from this distance Ann could sense the wiry strength in her, a toughness that defied the impression of her physical delicacy.

Ann couldn't stop wondering what Enoch and Lydia would think of her—a woman whose father had bought her a husband. A woman who'd come to their son carrying another man's child. She wished all at once that things were different. She wished Chase didn't feel obliged to tell them the truth. She wished...

"So," her husband said, coming up behind her. "Are you ready to meet my family?"

What she longed to do was give in to her sudden queasiness and retire to the cabin. She forced a smile to her lips instead. "Of course."

Pressing his hand to her waist, Chase propelled her down two flights of stairs. As they crossed the landing stage, he bent his head. "Don't let them scare you," he whispered.

Just as she turned to thank him for the reassurance, several children came whooping toward them.

"Chase! Chase!"

Chase scooped a boy of five or six up in his arms.

A delicate strawberry-blonde wormed her hand through the crook of his elbow. "We thought you'd *never* get here!"

Another boy of eight or nine backpedaled in front of them, talking a mile a minute. "Is *that* your new boat, Uncle Chase? How fast will she go? You won any races yet?"

Laughing at their antics, Chase turned to Ann. "The talkative one is my nephew Matt. This one here"—Chase jostled the boy in his arms—"is my brother Tim, and this young lady is my sister Mary Alice."

A lovely mulatto girl of about fourteen came and danced along beside them. "Ooooh, Chase, your new riverboat is very grand. May I go aboard and look around?"

He introduced the curly-haired young woman as his sister Evangeline.

"I've got passengers to think of, Evie. I can't have strange children tearing all over the boat. I figured I'd take everyone aboard once we finish supper."

Evangeline pouted prettily, then took Tim into her arms as Chase and Ann moved deeper into the crowd.

Chase introduced Ann to Will and Stuart and John, the three Hardesty boys who worked in the woodlot. She met Will's wife, Etta Mae, who was balancing baby Samantha on her hip. Ann couldn't help but stare at

Chase's sister D'arcy, whose broad face and hazelnut-colored skin hinted at Indian parentage.

Chase introduced his sister Suzanne, Matt's mother, and the twins, Benjamin and Bartholomew. She met a score of other people—men who worked in the woodlot and their families—people whose names she knew she'd never remember.

Most of the men greeted Chase with a slap on the back or a clasp of his hand—then they invariably asked about the *Andromeda*. The women hugged him and bussed his cheek. Every single one of the Hardestys stared at Ann as if she had dropped out of the sky, their eyes round with speculation.

Chase exchanged a word or two with everyone, but kept pressing toward where his parents were waiting. Lydia Hardesty came forward to greet them, pushing up on her tiptoes to throw her arms around her tall son's neck and claim a kiss. Chase bent so he was easier to reach and hugged her back.

Once Lydia withdrew from her son's embrace, she led both Chase and Ann toward where Enoch Hardesty stood waiting.

As they approached his father, Chase's grip on Ann's hand tightened, and she felt what seemed like reticence flare up in him. Now that the moment was upon him to present her to his family, was he sorry he'd married her?

But when he spoke, his voice rang clear and level. "Ma, Pa," he said, "this is my wife Ann."

Ann heard his family's collective gasp of surprise, followed by a staccato burst of whispers. She spotted Rue standing a little to his parents' left, grinning at the uproar. This was exactly the reaction he'd expected.

"Ann," Chase continued, "I'd like you to meet my mother, Lydia, and my father, Enoch Hardesty."

Up close, Enoch Hardesty wore the hard, furrowed face of a man who'd seen the best and worst life had to offer, and the bright, dreamy eyes of an adventurer. Even in his work clothes and with sawdust sprinkled in his graying hair, there was something vital and romantic about him.

Standing between her husband and her tall son, Lydia Hardesty's fragility was even more pronounced. Her face was angular and sharply molded, her nose high-bridged and narrow, her mouth firm. Her brows arched over incredible eyes, green as bottle-glass and clear enough to see all the way to the bottom.

Lydia caught her son's big hand in one of hers and Ann's in the other. "Congratulations, Chase dear, for finding such a lovely young woman to be your partner in life. And, Ann, I want to welcome you to the Hardesty family."

Ann sensed genuine warmth in Lydia Hardesty—and a germ of real acceptance. Pure unadulterated gratitude made her eyes burn with tears.

"Thank you, Mrs. Hardesty," she managed to murmur and gave Lydia's hand a grateful squeeze before she let it go. "It's an honor to be so warmly welcomed to your family."

But would Mrs. Hardesty be as sanguine about her marriage to Chase once she learned about the bargain her son had made, and that the baby Ann was carrying belonged to someone else?

Beside her Chase stood straight as a jackstaff as Enoch Hardesty's gaze moved over the two of them. It lingered on Ann's face, dropped to her belly, then fixed on his son.

"Both Lydia and I," he finally said in a voice that resonated like a pipe organ, "hope you'll have a long and happy life together."

Ann waited for Chase to respond, but when she glanced across at him, she could see he was caught up in something more complex, something she didn't understand. Nor could she think when she had seen such uncertainty in her husband's eyes—or such hope for approval.

His reaction unnerved her, but somehow she managed to find her tongue. "You're very kind, Mr. Hardesty."

"Thank you, Father," Chase finally managed.

Enoch reached across and patted his son's shoulder. Ann could see that wasn't all Chase had hoped for, but he masked his disappointment and grasped his father's forearm in return.

"We'll fete Chase and his new wife properly at supper," Lydia announced, forestalling another round of greetings and congratulations. With that declaration, she dispatched the women up to the house to get the meal on the table while the men and children went to wash up.

Chase escorted Ann up the stairs and around to the front of a house that rambled along the top of the bluff. Built of blocks cut from the surrounding stone, it looked as if it had sprouted from the rock itself. Wings of matching stone had been added to the right and left, and a number of smaller stone houses and outbuildings were scattered in the meadows on the high ground at the top of the palisade.

"There's a fine orchard over back of the barn," Chase told her, pointing. "Will's started a vineyard just upstream. And then there's my favorite place, a point at the top of the bluffs where you can see for miles. Maybe we'll walk up there later."

The main section of the Hardestys' house was built foursquare, two stories tall with a wide central hall and two rooms to the right and left. Tiers of wooden porches ran across the back, offering lovely wisteria-draped views of the river.

Only because Chase insisted, did Ann send one of the children back to the *Andromeda* for a few loaves of the bread she'd spent half the previous night baking. Shyly, she presented a basket of fragrant, richly browned loaves to Lydia.

D'arcy sliced the bread, then added a plate of it to the ranks of other dishes spread out on a slabbed-pine table that ran the full depth of the basement kitchen. The whole family—twenty people, more or less—settled down around it and waited while Enoch offered a devout but hasty grace.

The moment he said, "Amen," the Hardestys began helping themselves from crocks of beans, bowls of boiled potatoes, and platters draped to overflowing with slices of country ham and fried chicken. There were stewed apples, carrots en casserole, vinegary cold slaw, and two kinds of pickles.

"Try some of Ann's bread," Chase encouraged as he passed the plate to Silas Jenkins, Suzanne's husband. "Frenchy's been teaching Ann to bake. These are the first loaves she's made all by herself."

"Frenchy Bertin is teaching you?" John Hardesty asked, clearly impressed.

Ann nodded and everyone took a slice of bread when the plate reached them. Her stomach fluttered with nervousness as Chase's family buttered and bit and chewed. For one long moment no one said a word.

"*Frenchy Bertin* taught you to make *this?*" Chase's brother Stuart asked skeptically.

Ann's heart dropped into her shoes.

"Look how nicely browned the crust is," Evangeline offered sympathetically.

In spite of the girl's kind words, heat flared in Ann's cheeks.

"It's certainly not bad for a first try," Rue pointed out.

Beside her, Chase chewed determinedly.

Needing to know what was wrong with the bread, Ann helped herself to the last slice, broke off one corner, and put it in her mouth. At first the bread tasted exactly the way it was supposed to, but as she chewed, an odd bitterness filled her mouth, drying the saliva on her tongue. She swallowed hard.

"Pearlash," she murmured after a moment.

"Pearl what?" Chase whispered.

"The sponge, the yeast, was rising too quickly when I

made the bread," she explained. "So—so I added a teaspoon of pearlash to slow it down, but I must not have mixed it as carefully as Frenchy said. That's why the bread has bitter spots."

For a moment they all sat watching her, then D'arcy spoke up. "Well, that's an easy mistake to make."

Suzanne chimed in. "I've done the very same thing myself, haven't I, Silas?"

"Oh, yes," Silas agreed amiably. "Suzanne is quite the worst cook in five states. The children and I would starve if it weren't for Lydia."

Across the table Matt and his sister Katie started to giggle. Suzanne bit her lip to hide her smile. Three places down, Rue gave a snort of suppressed laughter. Enoch chuckled under his breath, and a moment later everyone was laughing.

Even Ann.

She chanced a look toward where Lydia Hardesty was sitting beside her husband at the head of the table, her mouth pursed with mirth and her eyes shining. Across the expanse of crocks and platters their gazes held. The older woman gave an almost imperceptible nod.

At just the hint of Lydia's approval, warmth surged through Ann's veins, turning her breathless and giddy with relief. Maybe she was going to survive visiting with Chase's family, after all.

Her sense of well-being lasted until Lydia and Enoch rose from the table at the end of the meal and suggested she and Chase join them in the sitting room.

The parlor at the front of the main floor of the house

was papered with a blue and yellow sprigged wallpaper and tastefully furnished with a petit-point settee, a massive wing chair, and several lovely pieces of rustic cherry furniture. The fire burning in the cut-stone fireplace gave the room a cozy glow, but at a second glance, Ann suspected it was a sitting room that didn't see much sitting. The upholstered pieces looked too crisp and perfect to have been used by this rough-and-ready family.

Lydia motioned for Ann to take a place beside her on the settee. Enoch made himself comfortable in the wing chair, then set about filling his pipe.

Chase circled the room twice, then finally lighted at the edge of the hearth.

Silence fell, a silence thick enough that the ticking of the iron lantern clock on the shelf in the corner and the scrape of the match as Enoch lit his pipe seemed almost deafening.

Ann resisted the urge to squirm. Chase stood stiff and brittle as broom straw, his forearm braced against the mantel.

"Since your marriage has come as such a surprise to all of us," Lydia began evenly, "why don't you tell us how the two of you became acquainted."

Chase didn't mince words telling them. He began with the extraordinary proposal James Rossiter had made, and explained about Ann's child needing a father. He talked about the advantages that owning and captaining the *Andromeda* would give him.

He told them things Ann hadn't given him a chance to explain: the way he'd responded to the *Andromeda* when he'd first come aboard, why he'd changed his mind about the commodore's offer. She hadn't understood what it was that made him think having the *Andromeda* as his own was worth marrying her for. Ann felt better somehow, knowing how important the steamer was to him.

"But why is Ann here with you now?" Lydia asked when he was done. "Surely you aren't taking her all the way to the Montana Territory in her condition."

"Ann wants to go," Chase explained as if they hadn't been arguing about it for three weeks. "And since the baby isn't due until August—"

"August?" Lydia turned her clear, assessing gaze on Ann, evaluating the fullness of her breasts and the roundness of her belly. "August, you say?"

Ann lowered her eyes. "Yes."

"You're certain?"

Ann nodded, pleating the skirt of her gown between her fingers.

"Is there no place for you to stay in St. Louis while Chase is gone?" Lydia pressed her.

"At first I wanted her to stay on with her father," Chase put in, "but since then I've reconsidered."

"Ann?" Lydia inquired.

Ann raised her head and looked directly into Lydia Hardesty's eyes. She wanted the older woman to understand how determined she was to stay on the *Andromeda*. "I'm hoping that by August we'll have found a place of our own," she explained. "I want my baby born under my own roof, in my own bed."

The older woman studied her with grave intensity, as if she could see the fears that beset her and the secrets Ann would never reveal to anyone.

Lydia turned to her son. "But what if that baby's early? What if that child should come when you're miles from a doctor, miles from help? Miles from any other women, for goodness sake!"

She shifted her gaze to Enoch before she continued. "Perhaps it would be wiser for Ann to stay on here with us until—"

"No!" Chase and Ann spoke as if on the same breath.

"First babies don't always come on schedule," Lydia maintained stubbornly. "Wouldn't it be easier for Ann if—"

"Lydia," Enoch spoke quietly, but with undeniable authority. "They've decided what they mean to do."

Ann saw the glance Lydia directed at her husband. She wasn't pleased by his intervention, but she was bound by it. "Yes, all right," the older woman conceded. "If you're sure—"

With some reluctance Ann reached out to touch Lydia's hand. "We thank you for your concern, but I think this is the wisest choice."

Lydia looked up at her son for confirmation, and Chase wagged his head reluctantly. "Ann's convinced me this is best."

"Very well, then," Enoch agreed and set his pipe aside. "Before he went off to school, Quinn made us some excellent elderberry wine. Perhaps we should have a glass to toast your future before you show us all around that steamer."

When they reached the kitchen only the adults and a few of the older children lingered on at the supper table.

Once Will had passed out small, elegant stemmed glasses and poured Quinn's elderberry wine for each of them, Enoch rose and lifted his glass to Chase and Ann. "May you have at least as many years of happiness together as your mother and I have had."

"May you have big, strong babies," Etta Mae put in, cuddling her daughter close.

"Or even twins," Bartholomew said, toasting with milk instead of wine. His twin, Benjamin, poked him.

"May your new steamer ever find the deepest channel," Silas Jenkins offered.

"And may you settle in a big, fine house in St. Louis so we can all come visit," Evangeline wished.

Once everyone had spoken, they all drank.

Ann lowered her lashes as she sipped the thick, sweet wine so no one would see the sheen of tears in her eyes.

How different this meal with the Hardestys was from the tense, combative dinners Ann had had with the commodore and her stepbrother. Never had Ann been claimed and welcomed the way this family had claimed and welcomed her. Never in her life had she wanted so much to be the woman these people thought she was.

In these few hours she'd come to yearn for the very thing the Hardestys seemed perfectly willing to give her—a family where she belonged.

ilty

CHASE TURNED FROM WHERE THE ROUSTERS WERE loading the last of the wood aboard the *Andromeda* and glanced up toward the captain's cabin. Was Ann up yet? Was she going to come down to bid everyone good-bye?

He'd been so proud of her yesterday. Facing his huge, unruly family had probably scared her half to death. Hell, it had scared him, bringing home a bride no one had ever heard of! But Ann had stood up to all the questions and scrutiny like the gracious lady she was. Ann hadn't even let the pearlash in the bread she'd baked fluster her. She had owned up to the problem and been able to laugh about it afterwards.

Lydia had liked that, and it was very important to Chase that his mother like his new wife. His father had even given their marriage his blessing.

Chase glanced up to Ann's cabin again, fidgety and impatient. Cal was limbering up the paddle wheel. It was nearly time for them to get underway. Where was she?

He looked toward the house and saw his father shambling down the steps toward the landing. The mist rising from the river was thick and cool, making it the kind of morning that stiffened Enoch's joints. Still, Chase had known he'd come. His father was here for a reckoning.

Chase narrowed his mouth to a scowl, then went to meet him. "Morning, Pa," he greeted him.

"Morning, boy."

Chase would be thirty-one this fall. He hadn't lived under his father's roof for more than a month or two at a time since he was thirteen. He'd won his pilot's license, and now he was captaining his own steamer. Just what did he have to do before his father stopped thinking of him as a boy and called him his son?

"Should be a good day on the river," Enoch observed, "soon as this fog burns off."

Chase nodded and stuffed his hands into his pockets. "I expect we'll make a good distance today."

Both of them turned and looked toward the steamer. A few of the rousters were lounging at the end of the gangway. Some of the passengers were out on deck with their trousers pulled on over their long johns, waiting for the steamer to pull out.

"Is Rue doing all right with his piloting?" Enoch asked, breaking the silence between them.

Chase sliced his father a sidelong glance. "I taught him, didn't I?"

"Indeed you did," the older man allowed, rocking a little on his heels. "And I don't doubt your instruction was good. But were you able to teach Rue caution, boy? Were you able to teach him good judgment?"

Every conversation Chase had with his father was like this, gruff and prickly and filled with half-formed rebukes. He could talk to his mother about anything. She might chide him, argue with him, and tell him he was a horse's ass, but he knew Lydia Hardesty loved him. That she would always love him. It had been the single constant in his life.

Chase had never been sure of that with Enoch. He hadn't been sure if his father brought him home to Lydia because he wanted another son, or because he hadn't known what else to do with him.

He had never understood what Enoch expected. Chase only knew that whatever it was, he kept falling short. Which was why he could never let go of anything Enoch said to him.

"Are you saying my judgment's flawed, Pa?" Chase challenged him. "Are you saying I wasn't able to teach Rue caution because my own judgment isn't good enough?"

"I wasn't saying that." His father's voice was tight. "Rue has to learn his own lessons, the same as you."

Chase steeled himself. This was what his father had come to say to him.

"Damn it, Chase! Just look at the mess you've gotten yourself into now."

Chase bristled. "Taking Ann as my wife, you mean?"

Enoch's face was set with disapproval. "Was it smart to jump into marriage with a woman you'd barely met? To take on her problems as well as—"

Chase swung around, addressing his father nose to nose. "I can handle this, Pa. Don't you worry."

"I'm not saying what you did is wrong," Enoch corrected himself. "God knows, I've done my best to look after women and children when they were in need—"

Chase was only alive today because Enoch Hardesty lived by that creed, because he'd scooped a skinny toddler out of a burned-out cabin and brought him here.

"And just in case you're wondering," Enoch went on,

"it doesn't matter a lick to your mother or me whether you're that baby's father."

The anger and confusion built up inside Chase like steam behind one of Cal's pressure valves. "Damn it, Pa! If I'm supposed to look after women and children, and it doesn't matter to you and Ma if Ann's carrying someone else's child—just what the hell did I do wrong?"

The set of his father's chin was like a ledge of stone. "You sold yourself out, boy. A man doesn't buy a boat with his good name. A man doesn't trade his honor for a paddle wheel, some boilers, and a few yards of fancy gingerbread."

"I didn't sell my honor to get the *Andromeda*!"

"What you did, boy, is prove you can be bought. And what's worse, you proved it to a man who'll take advantage."

After working aboard the Gold Star boats as long as he had, Chase knew exactly how ruthless a man James Rossiter was. It was true that some of the things in the contract Chase had signed still rubbed at him, but he wasn't sorry he'd scrawled his name across the bottom. It had given him command of the *Andromeda*. It had pried Ann out of the clutches of the man he'd since discovered was mistreating her.

"If Rossiter's already bought your loyalty and your pride, boy, what's he going to want you to sell to him next time?" Enoch went on. "And how are you going to refuse to be part of his schemes if you're married to his daughter?"

Chase was still fumbling for an answer when the high,

sharp blast of a whistle echoed off the bluffs. The Gold Star Packets' second newest packet, the *Cassiopeia*, came steaming around the bend.

"Who's making all that racket so early in the morning?" Enoch wanted to know.

Chase crossed his arms against his chest. "Ann's stepbrother Boothe was supposed to get command of the *Andromeda*. When I accepted the commodore's offer, young Rossiter lost out. He got the captaincy of the *Cassiopeia* to make up for it."

James Rossiter had had to fire Jeb Bartell, one of the Gold Star Packets' finest captains, in the bargain.

"You didn't much like being partnered with Boothe Rossiter, did you?" Enoch asked.

"I like being family to him even less. And I don't much like the way he's been dogging us all the way up the river—like he wants to beat us to Fort Benton."

They watched the *Cassiopeia* steam past Hardesty's Landing.

"You stay on here too long?" his father asked.

Chase shook his head. "I needed to bring Ann to meet you and Ma. But I don't want Rossiter getting too far ahead of me."

Chase could tell by the smoke streaming from the chimneys that Cal Watkins had the engines humming. They were ready to leave, with nothing to do but say their good-byes.

He hailed Rue in the pilothouse. "Sound the departure whistle."

Having heard that long, single blast, Lydia Hardesty

came bustling down the stone steps with Evangeline at her heels.

It brought Ann out of the cabin, still pinning up her hair. She waved at them from the Texas deck, and a few moments later joined everyone at the foot of the gangway.

Lydia immediately turned to her. "Etta Mae, Suzanne, and I got together a few things we thought might fit you. You'll be needing some new clothes soon, and we figured you wouldn't find many modistes out where you're going."

Trust his ma to put a practical gloss on something so generous. Clothes were turned and re-turned here at the Landing, cut down for the children, then made into quilts when they were all but threadbare. Chase hoped Ann understood what a sacrifice the three women were making for her, but he needn't have worried.

Ann's pale eyes were ashimmer with tears. She reached for Lydia's hand and clasped it to the center of her chest. "I can't tell you how much I appreciate your thoughtfulness."

"Well, it's nothing much," Lydia answered, though Chase could tell his ma was pleased by Ann's gratitude. "Those dresses may need altering here and there—"

"I'm a fair hand with a needle," Ann put in.

"But they're clean and should be serviceable."

"Thank you," Ann whispered and gave Lydia's hand a final squeeze.

Evangeline handed the two big bundles she'd been carrying to one of the rousters, then gave both Chase and

Ann hard, quick hugs. "You'll be stopping on the way back, won't you?"

Chase grinned and ruffled his sister's soft curls. "I expect."

Lydia hugged first Ann and then him.

"You take care of that girl," she whispered in his ear. "She and that baby need lots of looking after."

"I will, Ma," he whispered back.

"See that you do," she admonished him, then let him go.

Enoch said his good-byes. The quick squeeze he gave Chase's shoulder was about as close as his father ever came to expressing affection.

Chase and Ann went aboard and the rousters took in the landing stage. As Chase made his way to the captain's post on the hurricane deck, he heard Rue shout his own good-byes from the wheelhouse.

"Stay off the sandbars, son," Enoch gave the classic Hardesty admonition.

By the time they were free of the bank and backing down, a goodly number of people had gathered to wave them safely away. Ann lingered on deck until they'd pulled out of sight.

For himself, Chase was suddenly very glad they were headed for Montana.

chapter seven

ANN DIDN'T NOTICE THAT THE *CASSIOPEIA* WAS TIED up at the bank in Sioux City until it was too late. She'd climbed midway up the levee on her way to the dry goods store, when a deep, drawling voice froze her in her tracks.

"Well, well, what have we here? The little mother toddling into town all by herself?"

Ann jerked around and saw that her stepbrother had paused in the lee of a head-high pile of crates to light a cigar. For a moment she was rooted where she stood, prey mesmerized by a stalking predator.

The acrid bite of sulphur singed her nostrils as Boothe struck a match and held it to the end of his cheroot. Then, trailing a streamer of smoke, he sauntered toward her. "Well, now, Ann," he said letting his gaze slide over her, "just look how you've filled out. Why, you're big as a house!"

Though she'd stiffened in outrage at his words, Ann couldn't seem to help inching backwards. She tried not to let her stepbrother see how afraid of him she was. But he knew.

He'd always known.

That made Ann angry, both with him and with herself.

"I think it's just as well you left St. Louis when you did," he continued, moving in on her, "especially considering how much you've 'grown' of late. Of course, Father was nearly beside himself when you ran off, with nothing but that note to explain yourself."

"Was he *very* angry?" Ann ventured. Even with Boothe to remind her why she'd been so eager to put St. Louis behind her, Ann felt the sting of her stepfather's reproach.

"You know how he is—pleasant as can be until someone crosses him. But when they do..." Boothe circled closer.

" 'Good riddance' is what I said. 'Let Hardesty look after her; you paid him to do it.' But Father was disappointed. He intended for you to stay on at the house. He wanted to keep an eye on you and that baby. Doubtless he's already making his plans for that poor bastard's future."

Ann felt the color come up her face.

"He'll have his ambitions for it," he went on, "just like he's always had his ambitions for you and me."

Ann did her best to hold her ground. "You know very

well that the commodore's plans aren't why I left St. Louis."

Boothe gave a snort of laughter. "I'd have given a full month's wages to have seen Hardesty's face when you showed up at the *Andromeda.*"

Ann refused to admit that Chase hadn't wanted her aboard, or that he'd done his best to send her back. "Captain Hardesty has been quite accommodating."

"Has he now?" Boothe's booming laughter made her shudder. "Well, Hardesty damn well *ought* to be accommodating, considering that the commodore bought him off with *my* first command."

He leaned in close again. The smell of his tobacco-tinged breath made bile back up in her throat.

"Tell me, Ann," he murmured, "has your husband asked any of the questions that must be plaguing him? Does he want to know how you ended up in such disgrace? Was he curious why no one stepped up to marry you? *Has he asked you who your baby's father is?*"

Ann cupped her hand around her belly, doing her best to shield her child from her stepbrother's malice.

"Chase hasn't asked about its father, has he?" Boothe nettled her. "But he's curious. How long will it be before he questions you? And when he does, what exactly are you going to tell him?"

Heat blossomed in her chest, soared up her throat and jaw. Boothe had no right to ask her that, no right to torment her. She longed to consign him to the devil, but she'd been schooled since childhood to give in to him.

The night before their steamer arrived in St. Louis the

spring Ann was five, her mother had settled on the edge of her berth and taken her hand. "Our whole future depends on meeting your new father's expectations," she'd said, "and on doing everything in our power to make him happy."

One of the things that meant, her mother explained, was that Ann must make friends with her new step-brother, James Rossiter's son by his previous wife. But when they arrived at the elegant town house in Lucas Place, Boothe Rossiter hadn't wanted to be friends. He resented Ann from the moment she crossed the threshold. He detested her more with every hour that passed and with every hint of affection his father showed her.

He'd retaliated by putting spiders in her bed, dropping her bisque doll down the stairwell, tattling to the commodore about money Ann had never stolen and vases she'd never broken. When she tried to fight back, her mother spanked her and locked her in the closet until she promised to apologize. The warnings and the punishment her mother meted out had turned Ann into a perfect victim for her stepbrother's cruelty.

Though Boothe had given her ample reason to be afraid, Ann was standing silent because of the lessons she'd learned in childhood. Lessons, she realized all at once, that were no longer valid.

The notion blew through her like a stiff wind.

In marrying Chase, she'd broken the constraints that had shackled her for years. In leaving St. Louis, she'd escaped far more than her stepfather's town house.

"If Chase asks about this baby's father"—her voice was

breathy with bravado as she faced her stepbrother—"perhaps I'll tell him the truth."

Boothe cursed under his breath and reached for her. But before he could close his fingers around her arm, before he could speak the threats that were surely rising in his throat, someone shouted her name.

"Ann? Annie!"

No one but Chase had ever called her "Annie." She turned and saw her husband striding up the levee. His shoulders were set, and his mouth was pulled taut with concern.

A fizz of exuberance suffused her. She liked that Chase had come after her, liked that he seemed ready to protect her—even from her stepbrother. But what might Boothe say now to retaliate for her temerity?

Chase didn't give Boothe a chance to say anything.

"What were you thinking, Annie," he began, standing over her, "heading off into town all by yourself? The Sioux City levee can be a rough place, and there's no telling"—he tipped his chin in Boothe's direction—"what kind of riffraff you might run into along the way."

Ann all but laughed with relief and looped her hand through Chase's elbow. "I want to start making things for the baby, and I need to get to the mercantile for fabric and yarn."

Chase settled his warm, broad palm over hers. "If you needed to go somewhere while we're tied up in town," he admonished her, "all you have to do is ask me to escort you."

Ann's chest tightened with an odd, sweet satisfaction.

"Good God!" Her stepbrother gave a derisive snort. "She's got you wrapped around her little finger, hasn't she, Hardesty?"

Chase glanced up at Boothe Rossiter, finally acknowledging him. "She's my wife."

It was a deceptively simple answer, one that made Ann stand a little taller, settle a bit more solidly into who she was.

For one long moment Boothe glared at the two of them, his black eyes shimmering. "The devil take you, Hardesty," he finally said. "Go on, waste your life on her and her bastard."

"It is my life, Rossiter. My choice," Chase conceded. "And how are things aboard the *Cassiopeia*?"

It was a professional inquiry between captains of the same packet line, and it required Boothe to answer.

"They're going well enough. We've made good time since Omaha, but then you know that." His smile fell just short of a sneer. "We passed you dawdling at Hardesty's Landing yesterday."

"I suppose you did," Chase answered mildly, then turned to Ann as if Boothe had become invisible. "I can spare half an hour to take you to the mercantile. Will your shopping take longer than that?"

Ann smiled up at him, more than ready to be accommodating. "Not if I know you need to get back."

"Then let's get on about those errands," he said and led her up the levee.

They walked most of the way in silence, but when

they reached Jackson and Toole's Emporium, Ann stopped short. "I want to know why you did that?"

"Did what?"

"Why you came after me. Why you stood up to Boothe. Why you're taking the time from your duties to bring me here."

Chase looked at her as if her question baffled him. "You're my wife."

It was exactly the answer he'd given Boothe, but now a sweet, delicious warmth suffused her. Like sunshine coming to chase away the dark.

"And because you're a Hardesty," he added and pulled open the door to the mercantile. "As you may have noticed, we Hardestys take care of our own."

THE WEST BEGAN AT SIOUX CITY. ANN RECOGNIZED THE difference in the landscape almost as soon as they rounded the first bend. Standing on deck in the ripening dawn, Ann saw a fresh, new country sprawl out before her, a place that was broader, wilder, more exposed to the sky.

Ann's chest filled with anticipation for all that lay ahead: the sheer expanse of the prairie, the scope of the unknown, and the boundless sense of freedom. She felt as if she could breathe out here, and the scent and taste of this wondrous new place was sweet with unfolding promise.

But for all the breadth and scope of the land, the river

ahead was constricted and treacherous. Half-submerged islands hunched in the midst of the stream and a web of floating debris lay like a mantle of lace across the surface of the water.

As Ann watched, men at the bow of the steamer tested the depth of the channel with sounding poles and called their measurements up to the wheelhouse. Others worked to fend off everything from half-submerged branches to full-grown trees, anything that might threaten the *Andromeda*'s delicate hull or paddle wheel.

Because Chase hadn't been waiting on deck for her at the rail this morning, Ann supposed he was in the wheelhouse either piloting the steamer or helping Rue pick his way upriver. Either way, she thought both men might like some coffee and went back into the galley to pour some.

Just as she was setting the cups on a tray, Josh Baldwin looked up from where Frenchy had him sugaring fried cakes.

"I'm mighty obliged to you, Miss Ann," he said, "for fixing my shirt. I ain't got but two and that was pretty near gone at the elbows."

"I hope that checkered patch wasn't too bright," Ann fretted. "It was the only fabric I had just then."

"Makes my shirt look downright festive!" Josh answered.

It had all begun innocently enough. She'd sewn some buttons on for Goose in exchange for the German lessons he was giving her, and word had spread. Now the mending arrived in drifts, piling up in the basket outside her door overnight as if fairies were bringing it. But Ann didn't mind. It was her own small contribution to the crew's welfare.

"Looks like you're missing a button on that shirt, too," Ann pointed out as she balanced the tray of cups against her belly. "Once it's washed, just bring it up."

She turned and left the galley, greeting passengers along the way and pausing to compliment the steward on the wildflower centerpieces he'd used on the tables at dinner. As she climbed the stairs to the wheelhouse, Ann smiled to herself. She was beginning to feel a part of life aboard the *Andromeda*.

When she reached the top, she found Rue hunched over the chest-high wheel, with Chase poised at his shoulder. From here, nearly fifty feet above the water, the river looked utterly impassable.

"See the eddy off to starboard?" Chase coached in an undertone, barely acknowledging Ann when she gave him his coffee. "There's a sawyer underneath just waiting to pop up and nab us."

"I see it," Rue murmured and nudged the wheel to port.

Both men sucked in their breath as the shaft of a submerged tree bobbed to the surface just off the bow. A deep, resonant howl of wood scraping wood shivered from the hold of the steamer to the wheelhouse as the sawyer raked the length of the hull.

"Damage, Mr. Steinwehr?" Chase shouted over the open breastboard the moment things went silent.

"None that we can see, Captain."

Both Rue and Chase's stance loosened a little. Ann

eased down on the lazy bench herself, her knees gone weak.

For the best part of an hour, she clung to the edge of her seat as they skimmed past snags that could have ripped through the *Andromeda*'s hull like a paper sack, past sawyers that could pierce the steamer to its heart. As they picked their way upstream through the rafts of debris, something in the set of Chase's shoulders, in his focus and his calm reassured Ann they were going to come through all right.

At last the islands fell behind them, and the snarl of branches thinned. "Clear water up ahead," Rue sang out and reached for the bellpulls to signal the engine room.

"Never assume that," Chase warned him, ever the older brother. Ever the master pilot. "Gauge the depth of the channel, then give your orders."

Only when they heard the mark sung out from the deck below, did Chase nod in confirmation and turn to where Ann was sitting.

"Thank you for bringing us coffee," he said, settling down beside her. "We need it this morning."

"Will the rest of the river be as difficult to navigate as this?" she asked him.

"It's the islands that cause the jams," Rue replied from where he was squinting out at the water and the deck of dirty clouds hanging above it.

"And that the river's dropping," Chase added. "The channel's even shallower up ahead, so we'll have sandbars and rapids to contend with. I warned you the trip wasn't going to be easy, didn't I?"

Both of them knew the moment the *Andromeda* turned her bow upstream at Sioux City, that Ann was committed to the journey all the way to Fort Benton.

"I'm glad I'm here," she assured him quietly. But now that the excitement was over, Ann drooped with exhaustion.

"I need to rest," she murmured and climbed to her feet. Though she was feeling well enough, it seemed to take more effort to get through the nights of baking than it had a month before.

"Why don't I see you back to your cabin?" Chase offered, rising, too. "There's weather coming in, and I want to be sure you're settled before it starts to rain."

As they left the wheelhouse, Chase called his father's admonition back to Rue. "Stay off the sandbars while I'm gone."

Rue's laughter followed them down the stairs.

Ann was climbing into her berth a few minutes later when she heard the first raindrops pecking at the windowpane. By the time she awoke at midafternoon that soft patter had become a drumming deluge.

She lay drifting for a time, listening to the rhythm of the rain and feeling the baby stir within her. She rubbed her palms over the taut, itchy skin of her abdomen and wished she'd had the gumption to ask Chase's mother about her backaches, the shortness of breath, and her bouts of unexpected tears.

Since Lydia had given birth to six living children, she would have been able to advise Ann about such things. Perhaps she'd have been willing to tell her what it was going to be like when the baby came. How much would it hurt? Would Ann be able to bear the pain? Was she more likely to die in childbirth because her mother had?

Ann did her best to swallow down her anger at being forced to bear a baby she'd never wanted, to bring a child into the world who would constantly remind her of a night she ached to forget.

She wished she'd dared to ask the women homesteaders who'd been aboard about having babies, but ladies didn't talk about such things to strangers. Now that the last of them had disembarked, Ann was marooned in a world of men. If she needed help, the only people she'd have to turn to were the steamer's crew, her officers and chefs and roustabouts, the miners headed for the goldfields or the soldiers with orders to the forts out West. *And what would any of them know about bringing a baby into the world?*

With a sigh of resignation, Ann rolled to the edge of the berth and stretched her toes toward the floor. She could tell by the faint rise and fall beneath her that they'd tied up somewhere. Chase said a pilot couldn't properly read the river if the surface was dappled by rain, so the safest course was to lay-by and wait out a storm.

In the filmy twilight of the rainy afternoon, Ann washed, dressed in one of the gowns the Hardesty women had given her, then coiled her hair. When she pushed open the pocket door into the sitting room, Chase was at his desk.

"There's coffee in the pot," he said without looking up from his ledgers.

Ann glanced toward the stove, then back at him. The light falling from the gimballed oil lamp above the desk cast a sheen of warmth across the broad, blunt bones of his face and set off tracings of red and gold in his curly hair. Tenderness fluttered at the base of her throat as she watched him.

Perhaps it had been the stop at Hardesty's Landing and seeing her husband reflected in his family's eyes, that made her so aware of him. Of how solid and competent he was, of how his men respected him, of the courtesies he paid her. They were simple things: coming to escort her down to supper, insisting that the men keep their voices down as they came and went to the officers' quarters, asking if there was anything she needed when they pulled into a settlement.

Whatever the cause, Ann had begun to look forward to having her time with Chase in the mornings. He usually arrived gruff and rumpled with sleep, responding only in rumbles until he'd drunk his coffee. Still, she appreciated his warmth beside her when the mist rose cool across the water. She relished the things he taught her about the river. She liked that they could laugh together over Frenchy's imperiousness or Beck Morgan pitching face first in the mud at their last landing or the way Cal consistently beat Rue at checkers.

The more time they spent together, the more curious Ann became about the man she married. While he was busy with his duties, Ann had read the logbook and snooped through his things. Though his spelling confirmed his lack of schooling, Chase wrote with insight about the complexities of running a steamer. She discovered he was good at arithmetic and that the clothes in his drawers were of good quality, but old and in need of repair.

The bookshelves above the desk confirmed that he read. He had carefully annotated copies on science, philosophy, and history. She'd found a compact volume of Shakespeare's plays, one of poetry borrowed from the Mercantile Library in St. Louis—and several big, expensive atlases.

But why would a man whose life was constrained by the mudbanks of Missouri have three world atlases?

Chase must have looked up from his work and realized she hadn't moved. "Would you like *me* to get you coffee?"

"I'm fine," she assured him, then asked outright about the atlases.

Coppery color ran up into his cheeks. "I always figured," he admitted hesitantly, "that once Quinn finished medical school, I'd do some traveling."

Ann poured coffee for both of them. "Where would you go?"

Chase shrugged and glanced away. "A good pilot can get a job pretty much anywhere there's a river," he began, "and I hear tell there are castles along the Rhine that are well worth seeing. I've always had a hankering to cruise the Nile and visit the pyramids. And what do you imagine it'd be like to ply the rivers in China?"

Ann had never imagined Chase harbored such big dreams or that he'd entertain such far-flung possibilities.

"I know world travel isn't something a man like me

usually aspires to," he went on uncomfortably, "but I've always had this hankering..."

He flushed again.

"I think your plans sound wonderful," she encouraged him, "but why are you waiting until Quinn gets out of school?"

"Well, you make really good money piloting on the Missouri."

"You're paying for Quinn's education, aren't you?"

Chase toyed with his pen. "When Quinn was little he was always nursing a rabbit that had gotten separated from its mother or a crow with a broken wing. It was Will coming home from the war without his arm that made Quinn decide he ought to be helping people instead." Chase looked at Ann directly. "We're so damn proud Quinn wants to be a doctor."

"But why did *you* take responsibility for putting him through medical school?"

"Well, Pa can't," he said. "And Quinn's family."

It was as simple as that. One of the rules Chase lived by: that family was sacred, something to be treasured and protected and sacrificed for.

Just the way he was making sacrifices for her and her baby. The realization stunned her. For weeks all Ann had been able to see was how much Chase had gained by marrying her. Not once had she considered how much he'd given up.

"You won't be able to go off once Quinn's through school, will you?" she asked him. "Not now that you've married me."

"I might have had a few regrets about the choice when I made it," he conceded in the moment before his bright blue gaze rose to capture hers. "But now I'm not a bit sorry."

The intensity in his eyes sent a frisson dancing along Ann's nerves. A month ago, when they stood up to make their vows, she was convinced Chase Hardesty was a liar and an opportunist, someone who'd betrayed her for the promise of gain. But since that day, her perceptions of him had shifted and shifted again, forming and reforming like the patterns in a kaleidoscope.

They'd shifted again today and somehow struck a balance between them: between his ambition and her needs, between her expectations and his dreams. And in that delicate meshing lay a world of possibilities.

Ann skimmed a hand along his shoulder as she passed on her way to the settee. He hesitated, watching her get settled before he turned back to his work.

Outside the cabin the rain beat noisily against the decks and promenades. Inside, Chase and Ann shared a married couple's comfortable silence.

CAPTAIN! CAPTAIN HARDESTY!"

At the sound of Goose Steinwehr's voice, Chase straightened from where he'd been cutting up one of the trees they'd felled for fuel. He watched as the big, peg-legged Dutchman half-stepped down the cedar-lined ravine.

"Is something the matter, Mr. Steinwehr?"

"No, sir," Goose answered him, then took a moment to catch his breath. "We found ourselves a honey tree."

Chase leaned the axe against his thigh and swiped sweat from his face with the back of his arm. "How'd we do that?"

"One of the sentries found it," Goose reported.

"Did he find any sign of Indians?"

They'd put in to wood up not quite ten miles north of New Fort Berthold, deep in the Dakota Territory. They'd been seeing redskins ever since they left Sioux City a little more than a month before. The *Andromeda*'s sightings had been peaceful enough: squaws washing clothes along the bank, half-grown boys in bull boats, and a crowd of old men milling around the trading post at Fort Sully. Not every boat had been so lucky.

From what Chase and Jake Skirlin heard from the sutler at the fort, war parties were ranging up and down the river, trying to draw the steamers in to shore so they could board them. When the boats steamed by, the Indians fired on them and had succeeded in killing one of the pilots. Which was nothing, the sutler told them, compared to what the Indians were doing out West. The Sioux and Cheyenne had the Bozeman Trail from Wyoming to Montana virtually under siege.

Since Fort Sully, Chase had been posting sentries whenever they tied up for the night or had men ashore hunting or cutting wood. He'd keep right on posting them until they reached Fort Benton, three weeks from now.

"While your sentry was finding that honey tree, did he see any sign of Indians?" Chase asked again.

"No redskins, sir," Goose answered, then grinned like he was ten years old. "So—do you want see the bee tree?"

With a nod, Chase relented. "Where is it?"

"Let me show you."

Chase set aside his axe and followed Goose up the ravine.

Finding a bee tree out here in the wilds was a rare stroke of good fortune. If a hive of honeybees was large and well-established, if the Indians or bears hadn't found it first, a man could harvest gallons of honey from a single tree.

Two hundred yards west and south of the ravine, Chase and Goose reached a hazy, sun-drenched clearing. The air beneath the canopy of the encircling trees was warm and fecund and abuzz with bees. They converged from all directions on a hollow log at the clearing's heart.

Seeing its size, Chase caught a bit of Goose's enthusiasm. The bole had to be an arm's length across and he could see no sign it had been disturbed.

"We'll come back once it's dark," he told Goose in an undertone. "Find four good men who are willing to risk getting stung for a share of the profits. We'll meet on the gangway at dusk. I'll talk to Frenchy about bottling the honey for us."

Goose spoke quietly as if he didn't want the bees to hear. "This honey will be valuable when we get to Fort Benton, *ja?*"

"Worth its weight in gold," Chase said. But instead of

contemplating this windfall, he was thinking of Ann. Thinking about Ann's sweet tooth—and the treat he was going to have for her when this foray was over.

CHASE WAS STILL THINKING ABOUT ANN AS HE LED HIS little band of volunteers up the cedar-lined ravine toward the bee tree. Though the sky above shimmered with bright banners of cerise and gold, the clearing, when they reached it, was shrouded in shadow.

The men held at the edge of the trees, while Chase skulked toward the big hollow log. As he approached, he could hear the faint, almost melodious drone of the nest, and see the last of the worker bees straggling home for the night.

He gestured Rue and Goose forward. They were carrying heavy metal fireman's pails, half-filled with glowing coals.

"Ease the buckets up close to the log," Chase instructed. Then, as Rue and Goose scuttled back, Chase dusted each of the pails with sulphur powder. Thick yellow smoke billowed out of the buckets, blanketing the clearing in a foul-smelling fog.

The bees poured out of the hive, circling and buzzing.

Drawing bandannas up over their faces and narrowing their eyes against the smoke, Chase and Beck Morgan climbed onto the fallen tree and set to work with axes. The wood was dry and powdery with rot, and they'd have made short work of the log, if it hadn't been for the bees.

They hovered in a dark, angry cloud, humming in their ears, buzzing under the brims of their hats, finding ways inside their turned-up collars and tightly buttoned sleeves. Each sting was a sharp, exquisite sear, a spark landing on tender flesh.

In spite of the bees, Chase kept chopping. Beck Morgan stayed with it, too, working with the same tight determination. Finally the log groaned and shifted beneath them. Both of them jumped free as the bole fell apart.

By the light of a single lantern, Chase could see an eight-foot-long cavity inside the broken log filled with shattered comb and oozing honey. With a whoop of victory, he dumped the rest of the sulphur onto the coals and backed away.

The men who'd been waiting in the relative safety of the trees grabbed up their spades and set to work. They scooped shovelfuls of glistening honey from the bee tree into big copper boilers. Some of the gooey harvest was new and translucent, the color of sunshine. Some was old and amber dark, bleeding from a brittle, rust-colored comb.

Chase licked his lips in anticipation, but just that faint swipe of his tongue at the corner of his mouth set his lip to throbbing. The sting he'd gotten while he was splitting the log was already swollen and hot. He could feel more bites twitch to life on his forearms, shoulders, and back.

All of them were swatting at bees and being stung, but everyone had known the risks—and the profits they'd reap when the job was done. Once they'd scraped out the log and filled the copper tubs with honey, they swung into line and headed back to the *Andromeda*.

Most of the passengers were out on deck enjoying the evening breeze when the small lantern-lit procession came striding back down the ravine. Chase immediately spotted Ann just outside the galley door.

Balancing the boiler against his hip, he waved to her. "I've got something for you, Annie, that you're going to like."

Ann leaned as far over the railing as her rounded belly would allow. "What is it?"

He grinned at her. "Come and see."

She was waiting on the main deck when they thundered across the gangway.

"What did you bring me?" she wanted to know, her eyes as wide and bright as a six-year-old's.

Chase held out the washtub for her to see.

"What *is* that stuff?"

"Honey!" he told her. He lowered the tub he'd been carrying onto the deck. Then, dipping two fingers into the warm, sticky ooze, he offered them up to her. Ann laughed, took his wrist, and guided his fingers between her lips.

The moment her mouth closed warm and soft against his flesh, Chase knew he was in trouble. His chest went tight as she sucked the honey from his skin. His ears buzzed and his insides liquefied as she swirled her tongue against him.

Desire condensed in him like humidity on a glass of

lemonade. Ann had absolutely no idea what havoc she was wreaking.

Blood surged into his groin. He went heavy and turgid and hot. His penis rose against the front of his trousers, straining against the fabric. He stood there, knowing a hundred pairs of eyes were focused on the two of them. That each of the men who were watching knew exactly what was happening to him—and were amused by it.

A flush of mortification swept up his neck. Yet Chase couldn't seem to take back his hand. He couldn't seem to step away. He couldn't seem to do more than stare at Ann.

He tried reciting times tables in his head—eight times six is forty-eight, eight times seven is fifty-six, eight times eight is . . . It didn't help.

Then, with a slow final glide that nearly melted his knees out from under him, Ann relinquished his fingers and stepped back smiling. "The honey is delicious."

Her voice seemed muzzy in his ears, and all Chase could think about was her mouth. How warm those lips had been, how slick her tongue. How sweet she'd taste if he kissed her.

"Did you get stung there on the lip?" Ann asked and raised her hand to touch his mouth.

Chase jerked back reflexively.

"Did you get stung getting me honey?"

"We all got stung," Rue broke in, taking pity on his brother.

Ann turned her attention to Rue and the four men standing at the top of the gangway.

"You all did this for me?" she asked them. "Because you knew how much I'm enjoying sweets right now?" She gave Goose's hand a quick, sticky squeeze. "How good all of you are to me!"

Every one of the men blushed to the tips of his ears. Not one of them mentioned the price that honey was going to fetch once they reached Fort Benton.

That riled Chase more than made rational sense.

"Then the least I can do," Ann went on, still beaming, "is look after those stings."

While Ann was dispatching rousters for whiskey from the salon and mud from the riverbank, Chase grabbed up the copper tub and escaped to Frenchy's galley. From there he went on to his cabin.

Her cabin.

The captain's cabin.

He couldn't let Ann near him right now. He was still thrumming with the sensation, all but quivering with his need to take her in his arms. He could think of a hundred things he'd rather do with her right now than feed Ann honey.

He stormed through the sitting room and into the bedchamber. He tore off his shirt, splashed water from the ewer into the gilded basin, and dampened a washrag. He peered into the mirror that hung above the washstand.

Bright red welts splotched his face. More peppered his throat and shoulders. A liberal scattering marked his back and ribs. He soaked a cloth, dabbed it experimentally against a few of the stings, and cursed.

The damn things hurt!

"I wondered where you'd gone," Ann said from the doorway.

Chase started at the sound of her voice, but resisted the urge to grab up his shirt. She was his wife, goddamn it, and she shouldn't be put off by the sight of him.

"You finished doctoring everyone else?" he asked her gruffly.

"Not one of them was stung as badly as you."

"Beck Morgan and I broke into the honey tree."

"Then that explains it." She gestured with the bottle of whiskey in her hand. "If you come into the sitting room where the light is better, I'll look after those stings."

Chase couldn't think of any way to avoid doing that, so he followed her into the sitting room and steeled himself against her touch. Ann stood over him, dabbing him with whiskey.

"You're making me smell like a distillery," he groused. The whiskey wasn't helping; the stings felt worse.

"I rather like the smell of whiskey," Annie confessed.

"I could take to swilling some in the evenings," he offered, "if you like."

He saw her bite back a smile. "I can't imagine it would enhance your reputation as a steamboat captain."

"No, probably not," he agreed.

He wanted to make love to her so much he could barely sit still. The feather-light brush of her hands against his skin was exquisite torture. Her nearness was making him dizzy. He wanted to draw her onto his lap and kiss her until both of them were wild with desire. But he didn't dare.

"Those stings feeling any better?" she asked and picked up the plate of mud. She started dabbing again.

He'd been aware of Ann before, but he hadn't ever *wanted* her the way he did tonight. He hadn't thought about running his hands the length of her legs, tasting the skin at the small of her back, or cupping her breasts in his two hands. He hadn't thought about lying down with her, rubbing skin to skin, or coming inside her. Because of her reticence, because she was carrying someone else's child, he hadn't let himself think about what that might be like. But he was thinking about it tonight.

He was thinking about *her* tonight.

Ann was possessed of a deep, quiet beauty, the kind that would linger all her life. The kind a man discovered and rediscovered a hundred times as the years went by. Chase wanted so much to be with her, to savor that breathless loveliness when she turned thirty and forty and fifty. He wanted to be with her and hold her and cherish her forever.

He'd committed himself to a life with her. He just had no real idea of how rich that life could be—until today.

Ann set the pan of mud aside and stepped back to admire her handiwork. "There," she said. "That should help."

He'd been anointed with whiskey and dabbed with mud that was drying and starting to itch.

"Thank you," he said.

"It seems the very least I can do since you were injured for my sake."

He hadn't imagined she'd be so delighted by a gesture that had begun, at least for everyone else, with the hope of gain. He supposed he should put their raid on the honey tree in its true perspective, but he didn't want to disillusion her. He liked that she thought that he, that all of them, had done this to please her.

"I'm glad you like honey," he said as he rose to go.

"At least you all should be able to sleep tonight," she offered, following him to the door.

Chase looked down at her and thought that sleep didn't seem very likely—at least for him. He had fallen in love with his own wife, and he didn't know what to do about it.

THE RIVER CHANGED AGAIN WEST OF COW ISLAND, BE-coming shallower, rockier. Ann had watched the low earthen banks that hemmed their progress for weeks give way to bare, broken hills, then to striated bluffs of shale and sandstone. Even the air seemed different once they breached that endless stretch of prairie. The breeze had turned chilly, astringent, and it was spiced with the sweet bite of sage.

Early morning was Ann's favorite time on the river, and today the silky gray surface of the water was flushed with the light of dawn. In the silence she could hear the *chuff* of the steam engine echoing back from the banks and the shrill cry of eagles circling.

Just as the birds wheeled and soared off into the sun, the galley door snapped open behind her.

"Damn it, Annie!" Chase barked. "What in the name of all that's holy are you doing on deck? You know the Sioux have been shooting at steamers!"

They'd been seeing Indians along the banks for weeks, small family groups at the edge of the river, riders in the distance, and a few sad, solitary fellows who came down to the boat to trade. Though Ann knew mountain boats had been shot at and an engineer killed on this stretch of river not a week before, the Indians she'd seen seemed harmless.

"It was so hot in the kitchen," she complained, fluttering the damp neckline of her gown. "I needed a breath of air."

Never had she been so affected by heat as she was this summer and the weight of her advancing pregnancy seemed to make it worse.

Chase drew her back from the rail, then squinted to where the sun was gilding the water in the steamer's wake. "You're usually done baking by this hour, aren't you?"

Just thinking about the three dozen crusty brown loaves laid out on racks in the pantry made Ann's throat knot with pride. Who would have thought when she was learning French and dancing and fancywork at school back East, that she'd find such satisfaction in doing something so practical as baking bread?

"I *am* done baking."

"Then let me take you up to the cabin." He cupped his hand around her elbow and steered her toward the stairs. "It's just not safe for you to be waltzing around on deck."

"I'm far too ungainly to waltz anywhere."

Chase grinned, but he didn't refute her.

"Please, Chase," she asked as he eased her up the stairs. "The river's beautiful here. It's the most interesting it's been since we left Iowa. And it will be so *hot* inside the cabin."

"Would you rather come up to the pilothouse with me?"

Ann loved being in the *Andromeda*'s wheelhouse, loved the openness and the view, but she always waited to be invited.

"I'd like that," she agreed.

It might have been the climb to the wheelhouse that stole her breath, though she preferred to think it was the scope of the landscape spread out before her. Low rounded peaks ran off to the southwest like lizards crouched in the sun. Directly ahead, dun-colored buttes rolled out of the earth like a line of ocean breakers.

Chase displaced his brother at the wheel and sent him down to breakfast. "You can linger over coffee if you like."

"I'm going to write Ma a letter," Rue said and turned to go. "Now, you stay off the sandbars while I'm gone."

Chase snickered at the admonition and turned his attention to the channel.

For a time Ann was content to sit high on the lazy

bench and let the wind blow through her hair, content to watch the world reel out before her in a dazzling panorama of golden landscape and cerulean sky. But as sharply cut spires of stone began to rise to their right and left, Ann crossed to the front of the wheelhouse to lean against the breastboard.

"The last time I was out this way, I found seashells in the rock at the top of those bluffs," Chase told her, gesturing toward the pinnacles cut by water and wind. "Some folks think that means that this land was once an inland sea."

Ann looked at him instead of the rocks. She studied that high, broad brow and fine, strong chin, those sharp blue eyes, narrowed against the glare. For a man with no formal education, Chase knew amazing things.

"So what do you think?" she asked him.

"I think the world must be immeasurably old for rocks to have crumbled into sand," he said, and smiled at her. "And those seashells must have come from somewhere."

The river meandered for a space, then as they eased around another bend in the river, walls of white and ocher stone closed in around them.

"This section of the Missouri," Chase told her, "is faster, shallower. We'll be running rapids day after tomorrow."

Low-treed islands appeared in the midst of the stream, a string of them to starboard, with half-submerged sandbars at the upstream ends. Chase picked his way around the first one, passing close to a tumble of house-sized boulders at the base of the wall on the opposite side of the river.

As they broached the second island, a band of painted Indians galloped out onto the beach. They gestured the steamer nearer as if they meant to trade. As Chase steamed past, they began to fire at the *Andromeda*.

Chase cranked the wheel to port, and as the boat came about, a second fusillade of gunshots boomed from the cluster of boulders on the opposite side of the channel.

"Get down!" he shouted and shoved Ann to the floor.

Ann curled up in a ball and grabbed her belly. Above her Chase shouted orders and dragged on the bellpulls to signal the engine room.

She could hear Indian rifles cracking from both sides of the river. Bullets *ping*ed and *thud*ded into the steamer. Footsteps thundered, and men started yelling on the decks below. A moment later Ann heard a spatter of return gunfire.

The engine room responded to Chase's orders. The *Andromeda* trembled and surged ahead.

The shooting both on the bank and from the steamer intensified. One of the windows in the pilothouse exploded in a hail of shattered glass. Ann curled up tight and covered her head.

Chase muscled the wheel to port again. "Brace yourself!" he shouted.

Just as Ann wedged herself against the wall, the *Andromeda* battered into something solid. They hung there stalled, trapped. Run aground on what Ann guessed must be a sandbar.

The Indians whooped as if they'd won. The gunfire picked up sharply from the island and the bank.

Terror washed through her. Were they going to be boarded, overrun, and massacred?

Ann squeezed her eyes shut and prayed for deliverance.

Rifles rattled from the deck below. The smell of hot gunpowder burned up her nostrils. Were she and her baby going to die here, staring at the toes of her husband's boots?

Chase kept yelling orders and ringing the engineering bells. Three decks below, Cal seemed to be answering. The engines shrieked louder than the Indians; the steam valves whistled. The *Andromeda* nudged hard against the bar.

Chase rocked back and forth as if his weight could push her over. "Come on, sweetheart!" he shouted. "Come on!"

The floor of the pilothouse shivered and shook. The shaking became a trembling. The steamer rattled so hard Ann's teeth clattered together.

The Indians seemed to be whooping from right alongside the steamer.

"Please!" Ann whispered, though she wasn't sure if she was praying or offering encouragement. "Please! Please!"

A deep guttural groan ran the length of the steamer. Sand gritted beneath her belly. Slowly, very slowly the *Andromeda* floundered forward.

She broke free all at once and surged ahead, skimming across the water so fast they might have been flying.

Ann fell back laughing with relief. All over the steamer, men bellowed. Someone started ringing the landing bell, and Chase gave the whistle a long echoing *thoop* of victory.

As the *Andromeda* sped upriver, the sound of the Indians' rifle fire fell farther and farther behind them. Still, Ann stayed huddled on the floor of the wheelhouse, shaking too hard to try to stand.

Chase stood over her, signaled a change of speed, then steered them into a deeper channel.

"Annie?" he finally said, bending over her. "Annie, are you all right?"

When she nodded, Chase hauled her to her feet, then stood for an instant looking down at her. Then, without a word, he grabbed her and crushed his mouth over hers.

Panic detonated at the base of Ann's skull, a response so reflexive she didn't have time to think. A reaction so black and suffocating she twisted against him, frantic to break away.

Chase let her go.

She stumbled backwards, quivering and panting.

"Ann?" he whispered. "Annie, are you all right?"

Then all at once she realized where she was, who he was, and what Chase had just done for her. For all of them.

He'd saved their lives.

She saw all at once that he was trembling nearly as hard as she was. In that instant she reached for him, felt the tremor in his arms as he enfolded her. His face was damp against her, his palms clammy as he smoothed them down her back. She could smell his sweat.

"Jesus God, Annie!" His voice was as shaky as his hands. "Are you all right?"

And all at once Ann understood it wasn't the Indians or their narrow escape that had put the stutter in his breathing and the fear in his eyes. It was concern for her.

The notion that she should be so precious to him melted through her like sun through fog. She couldn't remember a time in her life when she'd mattered so much to anyone. That Chase cared for her astonished her, bemused her, made something stark and cold inside her liquefy.

This time when Chase bent his head to kiss her, Ann shivered and offered up her mouth. This kiss was less frantic, no longer balanced on the sharp, gilded edge of panic.

Instead it became fleet and tender, fluid and sweet. Chase feathered his lips over hers. He brushed gently and slowly, taught her the cadence of his kiss. He showed her the way intensity could blend into something softer, something delicate and fluttery.

They glided from one kiss to the next with languorous grace, shifting, merging. Ann's mouth tingled and warmed, slackened and savored. She opened to him and caught her breath when he nibbled gently at the bow of her upper lip. When he slicked the sensitive inner margins of her mouth with the tip of his tongue. When he delved deeper and touched his tongue to hers.

She shivered from her scalp to her toes, but not with fear.

With a murmur of approbation, Chase slid the palm of his hand the length of her spine, fit the fullness of her body against him. She nestled closer and wrapped herself around him.

Their kisses deepened and expanded, filling Ann with a wonder she had never known. For what seemed like a good long while, Ann wasn't aware of anything but Chase's mouth on hers and his arms around her.

She wasn't aware of anything until Rue came pounding up the stairs and burst into the pilothouse.

"For the love of God!" he shouted. "Chase, are you all—" He stopped dead in his tracks and stared at them openmouthed.

Chase raised his head, his own mouth drawn up in a smile. "Is something wrong?" he asked.

Rue waved frantically toward the bow of the steamer.

Both Ann and Chase turned and saw a wall of trees not thirty feet away—and advancing toward them.

Rue finally found his voice. "We're about to hit an—"

The *Andromeda* grounded with a lurch that nearly knocked the three of them off their feet.

"—island," he said.

chapter eight

"IS *THAT* FORT BENTON?" ANN ASKED, STARING OUT THE window of the pilothouse in disbelief. "We've traveled all this way to get *here?*"

"It's as far up the Missouri River as steamers can navigate." Chase said, maneuvering the *Andromeda* toward an empty spot at the landing. "That's what makes it important."

"The Great Falls is only a few miles upstream," Rue went on from where he lounged on the lazy bench, thumbing through a copy of a two-month-old Omaha newspaper.

From her vantage point in the *Andromeda's* wheelhouse, Ann could look beyond the cluster of steamers, beyond the fifty-yard-wide swath of riverbank piled high with barrels and crates, to the cluster of shacks that passed for a town. She could see beyond the buildings and across a barren strip of bottomland to a string of hump-backed hills every bit as stark and uninviting as the rest of the place.

"I don't suppose they settled Fort Benton for the scenery," Ann observed.

"It was built for the fur trade," Chase informed her. "And now that the Indians have pretty much closed Bozeman Trail, Fort Benton has taken on new importance. It's the only way for people and goods to reach to the Montana goldfields."

He leaned over the breastboard and shouted orders down to Goose before he continued. "Fort Benton's full of folks either outfitting would-be miners or catering to the ones who've already struck it rich. And it most certainly is *not* the kind of place where a lady should go wandering by herself," he went on, warning her. "Besides the *Cassiopeia's* here."

Ann hadn't noticed her stepbrother's steamer tied up at the levee until Chase pointed it out. The prospect of encountering Boothe the way she had in Sioux City very nearly guaranteed that she wouldn't be going off on her own.

Yet something about Chase's careful and determined protectiveness made her smile. Things had changed between them the day he'd run the *Andromeda* aground.

The day he'd kissed her.

The day she'd shocked herself by kissing him back.

She sensed his comings and his goings now as if the energy he generated moved like the warmth of sunshine across her skin. She seemed able to catch the deep timbre of his voice even if he was speaking to someone three decks below. She'd learned to recognize the rhythm of his tread on the stairs.

Chase had turned up the wick of her anticipation and made her look forward to dinner and dawn when the two of them had time together.

She thought Chase was more aware of her, too. He was more proprietary and solicitous. He almost always took time to wash and shave before he came to escort her to supper. He'd arranged for tea and a bite of something sweet to be delivered to her cabin in the afternoon. She'd even caught him badgering Frenchy about having her work fewer hours in the galley.

Oddly enough the growing affinity between them harbored a certain restraint. They were careful with each other now, as if they were passing something precious and incredibly fragile back and forth between them.

"Ann?" Chase's voice cut into her thoughts. "I'll be happy to escort you into town tomorrow, if you like."

"Today he has to see about getting that busted rudder fixed properly," Rue pointed out, "after he ran the poor *Andromeda* up onto that island."

Chase flushed red. He'd taken a good deal of ribbing from the crew about the accident. The heckling would have been a whole lot worse if Rue had told anyone what he'd found Chase doing when he arrived in the wheelhouse. But for once, Rue had managed to keep a secret.

As it was, they'd lost two days mending one of the rudder blades as best they could and refloating the *Andromeda*.

"Didn't I warn you to stay off the sandbars?" the younger man gigged him as he shoved to his feet.

Chase called his brother a name Lydia never would have approved of as Rue sashayed out the door.

Ann laughed and reached across to pat her husband's arm. "I'd love for you to escort me into town tomorrow afternoon."

Chase was waiting for Ann at the head of the gangway the following day at two o'clock.

"Are you sure you're up to this?" he asked as she swayed awkwardly toward him.

"I'm a little unwieldy these days," she acknowledged and adjusted her hat, "but it will be good to get off the boat."

The wagon ruts cut deep into the mud gave the levee the texture of corduroy, and Ann had to take Chase's arm as they navigated around head-high piles of barrels and crates. The single row of business that comprised Fort Benton's main street included the Overland Hotel, several freight offices, two mining outfitters, and a handful of saloons. At the end of the street rose the walls of the fort itself.

Ann found what she was looking for—a fine, white cotton flannel for baby blankets—at I.G. Baker's store. While Chase was paying for her things, Ann ambled out into the sunshine.

As she stood waiting, a family of Indians rode past her. She couldn't help but stare in fascination at their smooth brown faces and night-black hair. She took note of the man's fringed shirt and split-feathered headdress and how the woman rode with her baby's cradleboard braced against the pommel of her saddle.

"Those folks are Blackfeet," Chase said, coming up behind her. "They're headed to the Indian Agent down at the fort."

"Do you suppose they live around here?" Ann wanted to know.

"Some Blackfeet do. There's an encampment back of the fort if you're curious and don't mind the walk."

"I'd like that," she said and took his arm.

"I generally do a little trading while I'm here," Chase told her. "There are a couple of collectors in St. Louis who'll buy what I bring back. We'll stop and see what my friend Red Dog has for me this time."

Red Dog's tepee was on the river side of the wide circle of tents. It was a fascinating conical structure of sticks and skins, painted with bright designs of birds and animals. As Chase and Ann approached, a stocky, dusky-skinned man rose from where he'd been sitting on a blanket in the company of a pretty young woman.

Chase spoke a few words of greeting in what Ann supposed was the Blackfeet language, and Red Dog answered in English.

"You come to trade, Hardesty?"

"I came to see if you have anything I like," Chase offered noncommittally. "Then we'll see. This is my wife, Ann Hardesty."

"Hello, Ann Hardesty," the Blackfeet trader greeted her.

"How do you do, Mr. Red Dog," Ann answered him, then felt ridiculous speaking so formally when the man she was addressing was bared to the waist.

Red Dog looked bemused by her address, then gestured to the woman by the fire. "This is my wife. Her name in your language is Spotted Fawn Woman."

At the sound of her name the young woman with the thick black braids rose slowly and gracefully. As she did she let the blanket she had draped around her shoulders drop to the ground. Beneath it she was round as a pumpkin and even more full of baby than Ann was herself.

The two women looked at each other, then laughed.

"Spotted Fawn Woman carries my first child inside her," Red Dog said with a nod of approval, then turned to Chase. "Come, I will show you the beadwork and skins I have for you. You will pay me a good price for them because you are going to be a father, too, and are feeling generous."

"We'll have to see about that," Chase answered and followed Red Dog into his tent.

After the men were gone, Ann and Spotted Fawn Woman didn't have so much as one word in common. They stood staring for a moment, then the Indian woman smiled graciously and gestured for Ann to join her on the blanket.

Ann descended somewhat clumsily, but managed to make herself comfortable. Once she had, Spotted Fawn Woman pointed to Ann's belly, raised one finger and made a gesture Ann interpreted as a moon crossing the sky. It was an amazingly accurate guess as to when her baby was due.

Ann nodded and pointed to the other woman.

Spotted Fawn Woman began what looked to be the same moon sign she'd used before, then abruptly closed her fist and lowered it to her lap.

"Any day now," Ann interpreted. "Are you scared?"

But there were no hand signals to pantomime her growing feelings of anticipation and doubt, and no way for Spotted Fawn Woman to answer.

Yet as if she'd understood what Ann meant, the Indian woman patted Ann's knee and brought out a tiny pair of beautifully beaded moccasins.

"Are these for your baby?" Ann asked, turning the little shoes over and over in her hands. The colored beads were arranged in intricate leaf designs, and the stitches were small and neat. "You do fine work. The moccasins are wonderful."

But when Ann tried to give the moccasins back, Spotted Fawn Woman shook her head. Ann offered them again, but the other woman refused her.

"I can't take them," Ann told her. "They're the most precious little things I've ever seen, but you made them for your own baby."

The Indian woman pursed her mouth insistently.

Just then, the men pushed out of the tent.

"You must take the moccasins," Chase encouraged her once he realized what was happening. "To refuse would be an insult."

Ann glanced up at him for confirmation, then pressed

the tiny shoes against her heart. "Thank you for your kindness to someone from another place."

When Red Dog translated Ann's words, Spotted Fawn Woman smiled and nodded. It seemed as if in these last few minutes she and Ann had become friends.

Chase helped Ann to her feet and left the encampment amid a flurry of thanks and good wishes.

As they strolled—a good deal more slowly than before because Ann was tiring—back to the *Andromeda*, Chase told her not only about the hide and beaded pieces Red Dog would be delivering to the *Andromeda*, but about an invitation he'd received from Mr. Baker.

"He's giving a party tomorrow night on one of the steamers," Chase told her, as they recrossed the levee, "and I thought we should attend."

"Oh, Chase," Ann demurred. "A woman in my condition is hardly fit for polite society."

He laughed outright and shook his head. "No one could possibly mistake parties here at Fort Benton as polite society," he told her. "There will be food and music and probably a bit of storytelling. Baker throws some sort of a shindig every year when the boats come in. I think you might enjoy it. And I promise we'll leave before the fighting starts."

Four months ago, Ann would have thrown up her hands at the idea of attending such a crude gathering. But after traveling more than two thousand miles in the company of miners and rivermen, Ann thought she just might enjoy herself.

"All right," she agreed. "We'll go."

CHASE SHOULDERED UP TO THE BAR IN THE STEAMER *Independence*'s crowded salon and ordered a drink.

"So Ann decided to come to the party, did she?" Rue greeted him, turning from where he'd been talking to two other rivermen.

"I didn't even have to coax her," Chase answered and glanced toward where Ann was chatting with the only two other respectable women who'd come tonight. Mrs. Tyson and Mrs. Young would be taking the stage to Helena in the morning to join their husbands.

"Well, she certainly seems to be enjoying herself."

Chase nodded and sipped his whiskey. In a roomful of miners and soldiers and riverboatmen, Ann stood out like a diamond in a dish of sand. Even round and full as she was with her child, she maintained the elegance and refinement he'd admired in her from the first time he'd set eyes on her.

Of course he had absolutely no business bringing a lady like her to a place like this. But then, Ann hadn't had any business marrying up with a man like him, either. Chase just hoped she wasn't sorry.

Somehow that notion snagged in his throat like a burr, and he washed down the sting with a swallow of whiskey. "She *is* a lovely woman, isn't she?"

Rue grinned and nodded in agreement. "I bet she'll be glad to be getting home."

"I think she's liked being aboard the *Andromeda*." And no matter how unwilling he'd been to have her there at the start, he couldn't imagine what it would have been like to make this trip without her.

Still, Chase hadn't realized how close Ann must be to delivering that baby until he'd seen her at a distance yesterday. How pressing it suddenly felt to get her back to St. Louis, find her a place to live, and a doctor to look after her.

The commotion at the door of the steamer's salon drew everyone's attention, and as the newcomers piled in, Chase nudged his brother. "I thought the *Cassiopeia* was supposed to leave this afternoon."

"Cal said they were having trouble with one of the boilers," Rue replied as Boothe Rossiter bellied up to the bar three or four miners down from where they were standing.

Chase considered collecting Ann right then and getting her out of harm's way. But before he could, officers from several of the other steamers converged on them.

"They tell me James Rossiter entrusted you with his brand-new boat," the *Julie B*'s captain, Barnaby Greene, greeted Chase with a grin. "Can that possibly be right?"

"The commodore barely drew breath all winter for talking about how fine and fast that steamer was going to be," Zeb Mortimer chimed in, "so we all figured young Rossiter would get the captaincy."

"Hell, Zeb!" George Rush smacked Chase on the back. "Don't you know this boy can pilot rings around Rossiter? For once in this life, the prize has gone to the man who deserved it."

"Well, you ride high on those Gold Star fortunes, boy,"

Greene advised, dropping his voice to an undertone, *"while you still can."*

Chase turned and looked at the *Julie B's* captain directly. "What do you mean, Barnaby?"

"Oh, nothing much," Greene answered, reaching for the drink the barkeep set before him. "Just that I hear tell Gold Star boats are making unscheduled stops."

Chase knew better than to ignore Greene's information. The river trade lived and died on messages passed along from man to man. "Just what kind of unscheduled stops have the Gold Star boats been making?"

"The kind of stops"—Greene lowered his voice even more—"where unrecorded cargo gets unloaded in unexpected places."

Chase leaned closer, hoping he was wrong about what the other captain meant. "What kind of cargo?"

Greene shrugged. "Contraband, maybe. Things that might eventually find their way to the Indians."

Guns and ammunition.

Chase's gut tightened. Someone thought the Gold Star boats were running weapons? Chase couldn't believe it and would have questioned Greene more closely, except that Zeb Mortimer interrupted them.

"George here says you got command of the *Andromeda*, Captain Hardesty, because you married the commodore's daughter. Is that right?"

Chase had known someone would ask that sooner or later, and he couldn't see much point denying it.

"I got both Ann Rossiter *and* the *Andromeda*," he drawled and lifted his glass toward where his wife was still visiting with her new friends. "Which as far as I'm concerned is a damn fine bargain."

All the men turned to stare at her.

"A lovely woman," Captain Greene pronounced and drank to Ann's health.

"You brought your new bride way out here?" Mortimer asked incredulously. "And her in a family way!"

"Ann wanted to see the West before the baby came."

"Well, your Ann must be an intrepid woman," Rush offered. "Mrs. Rush thinks going to The Planters House Hotel for tea is high adventure."

Talk turned, as it always did among rivermen, to business—steamers and cargo and the most recent changes in the river. When Chase looked up a few minutes later, he saw Boothe had cornered Ann, and he immediately set his drink aside.

Rue lay a hand against his sleeve. "Ann's been contending with her brother since they were children. It'll be better if you let her handle him."

"Her family's not like ours," he said shortly and shook off his brother's hold. Rue hadn't seen the venom in Boothe Rossiter's eyes that day in Sioux City; nor did he feel a husband's responsibility to protect Ann from her stepbrother.

Yet tonight, Ann seemed to be holding her own. Her chin was tilted at a defiant angle, and she seemed to be ignoring whatever Boothe was saying. But as she turned to leave, he grabbed her arm and swung her around.

It was all Chase needed to see him do. He started toward them, slicing a path through the closely packed bodies like an otter through the scum on a pond. He was too far away to keep Rossiter from pushing Ann back against the wall, too far away to hear what it was Boothe said that made her eyes fill with tears.

Whatever it was, Chase hurdled the last few feet and jerked Rossiter away from her.

Boothe spun around and raised his fists to defend himself. Chase slammed a punch right through his guard.

The slimmer, darker man reeled and staggered backwards. Chase caught a glimpse of Ann cringing back against the wall just as her stepbrother came back at him. He brushed off the other man's blow and hit him as hard as he could.

Pure feral joy surged up his spine.

Fort Benton didn't have a reputation as "the wildest town in the West" for nothing. Men who'd been drinking companionably moments before set to brawling. Strangers pounded strangers with their fists. Furniture flew and windows shattered. Fighters reeled from one opponent to another. A table of bottles and food went over with a clatter. The air reeked of whiskey and pickled onions.

When Rossiter came at him again, Chase jabbed him even harder. He ducked Boothe's answering blow, then rammed his fist right into Boothe's belly. Chase followed with an uppercut. Rossiter went over like he'd been poleaxed.

Chase stood grinning down at him, ferociously pleased with himself.

Then, before anyone else could grab him—or her—Chase gathered Ann up in the crook of his arm. Together they scuttled to the right and to the left, through the maze of howling, brawling men. They stumbled out onto the steamer's deck, both of them breathless.

Chase swept Ann down the gangway while he had the chance and dragged her into the shadow of one of the piles of goods on the landing. "Are you all right?" he asked, skimming his hands over her to make sure she was.

"Fine," she answered, though her voice was shaking.

"Did that bastard hurt you?"

If Boothe had done more than muss Ann's hair, Chase was going to go back inside and—

"He didn't hurt me."

Still, there was something wrong. Though her head was bent, she was standing so stiffly she might as well have bathed in starch. So if she wasn't hurt, she must be . . .

Chase's breath caught fire halfway up his chest. The elation he'd been savoring, dimmed.

She must be angry.

Ann had made it clear enough what she thought about brawling when he showed up at their wedding all battered and bruised from that dustup on the levee. Now, just when things seemed to be going a little better between them, he'd picked another fight.

He supposed it might not hurt to apologize. "Now, Ann," he began. "I'm really sorry I started that fight—"

"Chase."

"—but when I saw Boothe put his hands on you—"

"Chase."

"—I wanted to pound that bastard to kingdom—"

She lifted her hand and pressed her fingertips to his mouth.

Chase caught his breath. The feel of those cool, soft fingers against his lips made it almost worth a reprimand.

"I want you to understand," she said. Her eyes were wide and shining in the dark. "I want you to understand that you needn't apologize to me for starting that fight."

Surprise skipped through him. "I—I don't?"

"I—I can't say anyone has ever stood up for me like that." Her mouth softened in a way that made him want to kiss her. "And the very idea that you would—"

"You're my wife," Chase insisted. "What did you expect me to do when Boothe was plaguing you?"

It was an odd notion that she'd be surprised that he'd protect her. In his family, the women always had a father or a brother or a husband watching over them—whether they wanted to be watched over or not. But then, all Ann had was Boothe, who hated her, or the commodore, who attended to what was good for Ann only when he benefited from it himself.

Chase looked down, seeing his wife in a whole new light.

"I wanted you to do exactly what you did," Ann admitted.

"You don't mind that I punched Boothe?"

She looked flushed, chagrined. "I hoped you'd knock him halfway to Helena!"

Chase did his best not to laugh. He could see the admission wasn't an easy one for her to make—and not just because it sanctioned fighting. What Ann was saying was that she liked him protecting her, that she trusted him to do it. That he had a right to defend her if he saw fit.

Knowing that's how she felt gave him a kind of validation Chase hadn't even known he needed.

He stepped in a little closer, smoothed a strand of her hair. "So, Mrs. Hardesty," he said, "do you mind if I go on protecting you?"

"From Boothe?" she asked him.

"Well, yes. Boothe," he said. "But I suppose I could protect you from other things, too."

"Other things?"

Chase eased close enough that he was aware of her warmth against him, caught the faint, clean scent of lavender in her hair. He felt suddenly flushed, suddenly light-headed and breathless.

"Well," he drawled, "I suppose I could protect you from the mice in the pantry."

"Really?" She giggled and looked up at him with glistening eyes. He wasn't sure he'd ever heard her giggle and the sound of it made his chest swell with warmth.

"Maybe I could protect you from drinking Harley Crocker's coffee," he suggested. "Or tyrannical French cooks."

Ann laughed outright. "How about protecting me from the bat-sized mosquitoes along this river?"

"I'm not sure I can promise to protect you from the mosquitoes." He lowered his head, focusing on her soft, bowed mouth. "But I think I can handle some of the other things."

"Thank you," she whispered, leaning into him. "I'd like that."

But just when he might have kissed her, might have taken her in his arms and drawn her against him, two drunks staggered out of the *Independence*'s salon. Halfway down the landing stage, one of them fell in the river.

Chase stepped out from between the crates to make sure the man could swim, and by the time he turned back, Ann had begun to wend her way back toward the *Andromeda*.

Aɴɴ DIDN'T HURRY VERY WELL THESE DAYS, AND SHE needed to make the trip from the *Andromeda* to the Indian encampment and back before the steamer pulled out of Fort Benton at noon.

As she walked, Ann fingered the square of downy flannel folded over her arm. After Spotted Fawn Woman had given her the tiny pair of moccasins two days before, Ann decided to make a gift to repay her kindnesses. She had worked most of the previous day binding a blanket with claret-colored ribbon and embroidering clusters of daisies in the corners. Ann just hoped her new Indian friend would like it.

As she plodded the length of the landing in the direction of the fort, Ann glanced back at the boats lined up at the edge of the river. The *Cassiopeia* had left at dawn. Only when she saw the river mist erase it line by line, did she feel as if she could breathe again.

For awhile at least, she needn't worry about Boothe's threats, what he might say to Chase about her child, or how she would respond to him if he did.

Yet terrifying as Boothe's malice was, the way Chase had taken her part filled her with a kind of wonder. She couldn't remember another person in her life who'd done that. Not even her mother.

"We've come to St. Louis to stay," Sarah Pelletier Rossiter had explained to her when Ann complained about the way Boothe treated her. "We both need to learn to be accommodating."

Chase hadn't accommodated anyone last night.

When Boothe threatened her, Chase had dispatched him with his fists. Ann was a little appalled at the pure, intemperate joy she'd felt at seeing Boothe laid out on the floor. She shouldn't have sanctioned fighting, shouldn't have felt such pride that Chase was willing, and completely able, to protect her. Still, she couldn't seem to help what she was feeling. Somehow she was able to stand taller, was able to protect herself better just knowing Chase was there if she needed to turn to him.

As Ann entered the Indian encampment behind the fort, several of the women nodded at her and nudged one another. Two children stopped and stared. Feeling like an intruder, she quickened her pace, heading purposefully toward Red Dog's tepee. Ann had hoped to find Spotted Fawn Woman sitting outside in the sun, but there was no sign of her.

Then Ann saw the thin blue vapor trailing from the tepee's smoke hole and scratched on the stiff, elk-skin door. "Spotted Fawn Woman, are you there?" she called out, then scratched a little more insistently.

Red Dog himself thrust the hide back out of the way.

Ann gasped at the sight of him. The man's skin and clothes were caked with ash. His chest-length hair was hacked off short and hung in tangles that were gray and powdery with dust. Long, freshly bloodied cuts ran down his chest and arms. His face was streaked with soot.

He glared at Ann with bloodshot eyes. "Why are you here?" he demanded.

Ann held out the blanket in both hands. "I made this for Spotted Fawn Woman and your baby."

He glared at her with what could have been either fury or anguish. "I have no baby." His voice was raw and guttural. "I have no wife. My wife is dead."

Ann stood staring, suddenly feeling breathless and gone at the knees. "What—what happened?"

A fierceness came into Red Dog's eyes, a grief so bright it was like staring into the sun. He refused to speak, but Ann didn't really need him to explain. Just knowing passed a cold, threatening hand over the child in her own womb.

Tears for Spotted Fawn Woman and the man who mourned her rose in Ann's eyes. "What—what would you have me do with this?" she asked him.

Red Dog hesitated, then took the soft, flowered blanket into his hands. He held it for one long moment, then he turned. Just as the hide door dropped back in place, Ann saw him lower the blanket into the fire.

Ann stumbled back through the encampment,

Spotted Fawn Woman had been so young, hardly more than a girl. She'd seemed so happy to be carrying a child, so full of life and hope. *How could she be dead?*

Ann knew women died in childbirth. She'd heard society matrons whispering behind their fans about some young wife who'd died without delivering her child. Girls at school had talked about older classmates who'd bled to death or succumbed to childbed fever.

Ann slowed her steps as she crossed the rutted landing. As with so much else about this child, Ann hadn't thought beyond the moment: the moment she'd realized she was pregnant or the moment she'd felt the baby stir within her. Why would she have dwelled on the dangers of childbirth when her baby wasn't coming for months? How could she think about death when being out on the river made her feel so vital and alive?

Besides, Ann never really knew anyone who died in her travails—*except, of course, her mother.*

Ann's steps faltered as she climbed the *Andromeda*'s gangway. A wave of childish grief rolled over her. Her mother had been reading to her the day before the doctors began to arrive with their black satchels and scowling faces. She remembered now how her mother's screams had echoed through the house for most of the afternoon. Then toward evening James Rossiter had come into her room with tears on his face and told her that her mother and baby brother were dead.

Ann shivered with the memory as she trudged up the stairs toward her cabin.

If her mother and Spotted Fawn Woman had died giving birth, Ann knew she could die, too. She could die birthing a child that had begun in shame, a child she'd tried to deny she was even carrying. She could die screaming in agony, with no one to help but a boatload of rivermen.

Still, Ann had made this choice and she wasn't sorry. She loved her life on the river. She loved that she'd found someone to watch over her the way Chase had last night, someone who cared about what she thought and how she felt.

Ann had changed since she'd barged aboard the *Andromeda*, then fought to stay. She'd made fast friends of people she might never even have noticed in her other life. She'd seen things and done things and learned things—and found a family. She didn't regret a moment of her months on the river, no matter the cost.

But now that it was nearly time to deliver her baby, Ann couldn't help being terrified. She crossed the cabin to the bedroom and climbed into her berth. Whispering a prayer for Spotted Fawn Woman and her child, she curled up tight and pulled the blanket over her.

A NNIE?"

Ann started awake, realizing between one heartbeat and the next that *he* was here with her. She could feel his energy squirm across her skin, hear the tempo of his breathing, and smell the high, sharp bite of camphor.

She could see him silhouetted in the lighted doorway,

his shadow reaching out to her. Her heart throbbed in her throat and panic roared along her nerves. Her ears rang; her muscles froze.

"Annie, are you all right?"

Those weren't the words or the voice she'd been expecting. This voice was soft and deep and filled with concern.

Ann's fear evaporated. She pushed herself upright and sat at the edge of the bed, becoming aware all at once that her hair was straggling down her back and her dress was bunched in a wrinkled mass around her.

"I looked in on you before I went down to the salon," Chase said coming toward her. "But you seemed to be sleeping."

"I was tired," she said. It was the easiest explanation.

Chase smiled a little. "My sister Suzanne spent the whole last month she was carrying Matt sitting on the back porch at my parents' house, staring at the river."

Ann grazed his sleeve with her palm to thank him for encouraging her.

"I brought you supper on a tray," he coaxed her. "Frenchy gave you three desserts."

A stroke of appreciation tickled through her. "I'll eat it later."

"Is your stomach upset?" Chase asked and lifted his hand to feel her head. "You're not feverish, are you? That baby's not coming, is it?"

"I'm fine."

But Chase seemed to know she wasn't fine. He stood

looking down at her. "Rue said he saw you heading into town this morning. Where did you go?"

She averted her eyes and didn't answer.

"Annie?" Even in the half-light she could see a score of worry slice between his brows. "Did something upset you?"

For a moment she tried to hold her peace, but it seemed useless to try to evade the truth. "I walked to the Blackfeet encampment to give Spotted Fawn Woman the blanket I made for her."

She'd been so pleased with the piece, she'd showed it to him the night before.

"It was lovely," he offered carefully. "Did she like it?"

"Red Dog was there alone," Ann went on, thinking how silent and desolate their camp had seemed. "He'd hacked off his hair and was covered with ash."

Chase made a sound low in his throat and cupped his hands around her forearms. "What happened?"

Ann's throat worked to form the words as tears spilled down her cheeks. "Spotted Fawn Woman died," she said. "The baby died, too."

"Oh, Annie." Chase pulled her to him, accommodating the full, ripe bulk of her in his arms. Ann leaned into him, pressed her face to the wash-softened cotton of his shirtfront.

"She was so young," she whispered. "She seemed so happy to be carrying Red Dog's child. How could she die?"

He seemed to know her fears, hear the things she hadn't said. "Don't be afraid, Annie. You'll be all right."

"How do you know?"

"I know," he said and wrapped her up tight in his arms. "I know, because I'm going to get the finest doctor in St. Louis to take care of you. I know you and that baby are to be fine."

Ann nodded and nestled close, wanting so much to believe him.

chapter nine

THE PAINS BEGAN ABOUT THREE O'CLOCK. ANN WAS kneading the night's last batch of bread dough when a sharp catch near the base of her spine made her straighten. The tightness rippled low along the sides of her abdomen and bunched at the base of her belly. She rubbed at the spot with one floury hand.

She'd been having pulls and twinges for weeks, and at first she'd marveled at the changes taking place in her body. But now that the spasms were a daily occurrence, they seemed a dark portent of what lay ahead.

Ann bent gingerly sideways to relieve the strain and heaved a gusty sigh. What the devil was she doing here, anyway? She hadn't come down to bake since they left Fort Benton two weeks before. She was tired and hot from the blast of the ovens, and for the life of her, she couldn't remember why she found dumping flour into yeast so fascinating. Yet here she was with one last batch of dough to knead and form into loaves.

She stretched, then bent back to her work.

The next pain caught Ann hard enough to make her gasp. It began with another constriction low in her back, then wrapped around her belly like two grasping hands. She gripped the edge of the counter in surprise and panted until the pain was over.

She swiped the sweat off her forehead, then glared across at Frenchy. He was singing as he slid one pale loaf after another into the roaring ovens.

She ought to tell the man to finish his own damn bread. She ought to throw off her apron and stomp...

Another sharp roil of discomfort grabbed her and squeezed her hard enough to send a hot trickle of liquid running down between her legs. Ann pressed her thighs together to stanch the flow, but the trickle became a stream, and that stream a gush that soaked right through her underdrawers and pooled around her shoes.

Ann froze, utterly mortified. She hadn't wet herself since she was three years old.

Frenchy must have noticed something was wrong, because he hurried toward her. "Ann? Are you all right?"

A fiery blush scorched up into her hair.

"*Merde!*" he cried when he rounded the counter where she'd been working and saw the floor. "You're going to have that baby, aren't you?"

"Now?" Ann asked him, horrified.

He grabbed a chair and made her sit, then tore out of the galley. He returned with Chase not three minutes later.

Chase's hair was ruffled with sleep. His open shirt flapped around his hips and his feet were bare. He looked at the puddle on the floor and then at her.

"Are you having labor pains?" he asked her.

Is that what they were?

"How bad are they?"

She didn't have any idea how bad "bad" was. She didn't see how Chase could know that, either.

All Ann knew was that the ordeal was beginning, the ordeal that had taken her mother away, the ordeal that cost Spotted Fawn Woman her life. The ordeal that set the very marrow of her bones to trembling.

Her belly bunched again, and she started to squirm.

Chase must have realized what was happening, because he bent and swooped her up in his arms. "Don't you worry, Annie," he assured her. "You and this baby are going to be fine."

She wrapped her arms around his neck and hid her face against his throat.

Chase gave Frenchy directions in a low, terse voice. "Go rouse Cal. Have him stoke up the boilers. Get Rue up, too. Tell him to get us to Hardesty's Landing as fast as he can."

Frenchy, whose position usually precluded such mundane work, went without a word of complaint.

As Chase turned to leave the galley, Ann saw smoke

curling around the edges of the oven door. "Wait!" she cried. "The bread is burning!"

"To hell with the bread," Chase snapped, then took the stairs to the captain's cabin two at a time.

Fifteen minutes later Ann was snugged up tight in the captain's berth. "How—how far is it to Hardesty's Landing?" she fretted as another of the pains tightened its grip on her.

Chase hesitated, and she thought for a moment he was going to lie to her. "Forty miles, more or less," he finally answered.

"A full day's run," she whispered, horrified.

"It's downstream, Annie." He took her hand. "We'll get you to Ma before the baby comes, so don't you worry."

Pressed palm to palm, she soaked in the calm that was so much a part of him, savored the comfort in his promises. No matter how their marriage had begun or what she thought of him four months ago, she knew Chase Hardesty would stand by her. She knew she could count on his strength and his concern.

"Is there anything I can get you?" he asked gently. "Do you want someone to come and sit with you?"

Ann didn't want anyone but him, but she'd probably need him far more later than she did now. "You go on up to the pilothouse," she told him. "I'm going to rest for a little while."

Ann hadn't expected to sleep, but when she awoke at midday, Frenchy was settled in a chair beside the bed.

"Did the bread burn?" she asked him.

He gave his head a contemptuous shake. "Those rousters! They'll eat anything. But for you, I made some good beef consommé. Women need strength to push their babies out."

Ann managed to eat a little.

"And now we walk," Frenchy instructed when she was done. "It will bring the baby sooner."

Knowing better than to argue with him, Ann wriggled to the edge of the bunk. She'd barely gotten to her feet when one of the pains swelled over her.

"Breathe!" Frenchy ordered. Then taking liberties only a Frenchman would take, he pressed his fist against her spine and massaged, none too gently. The pressure eased her constricted muscles and gave her something to press against.

"How did you know to do this?" she panted.

"I have"—he flushed as he answered—"wives. I have children. Frenchy Bertin, he knows about such things."

When Chase came by a good while later, the cabin had grown warm and close with the heat of the afternoon.

"How far to Hardesty's Landing?" Ann asked fitfully. The pains were coming harder and more regularly.

"We'll be there soon, Annie," he promised, wiping her face and throat with a cool cloth. "Soon."

In the steamy dimness of late afternoon, Ann's thoughts ran in fragments, focusing and then fading into the hot, yellow air. Visions of her mother and Spotted Fawn Woman rose up before her. Had they died panting and writhing in pain? Had they succumbed sobbing with weakness and despair? Would she die that way, too?

Terror climbed her chest, ripped hot through her throat and belly. Was she going to be punished for not wanting this child? And if she managed to deliver it alive, would Chase take one look at the baby and realize what she'd done?

She wrapped her arms around her belly and drenched her pillow in hopeless tears.

When Chase came next, it was almost dark.

"Where *are* we?" she pleaded. "How far is it to Hardesty's Landing?"

Before he could answer, one of the contractions roared in on her like a rogue wave. She clutched his hand as the constriction tightened inside her. She squeezed harder as the pain rose and poised and crested. She moaned as it crashed over her. When it finally ebbed away, she was sobbing for breath.

"Are they all like that?" Chase asked. His hand was steady around hers, but she could hear his voice shaking.

Ann didn't answer; tears slid from the corners of her eyes.

"Hang on just a little while longer, Annie, please," he whispered. "I'll get you home. I swear I'll get you home."

Home, she thought hazily, to a place where she'd been accepted without question. Home to a woman with kind eyes and knowing hands, to a family who brought their babies into the world safe and whole.

Home. It sounded like heaven.

"Hurry," she whispered. "Hurry!"

CHASE RAISED ONE SHAKING HAND FROM THE *Andromeda*'s wheel and wiped the sweat from his eyes. The sky had long since faded from dusty blue to midnight-black, leaving not so much as a star or a sliver of moon to light their way. The Missouri lay ahead like an undulating ribbon of crepe, dead of all reflections, all movement.

They were just a few miles upstream of Hardesty's Landing, picking their way through the dark, running for home as fast as they dared.

Chase strained his ears for some sound from the cabin below, where Goose had gone to sit with Ann. All he could hear was the roar of the furnaces, the low-pitched *huff* of the engines, and the paddle wheel's ceaseless churning. Those sounds, the circumstances, and the heat tugged at the raveling edge of Chase's patience.

He'd chosen to gamble with all their lives to see that Ann got the help she needed. He mopped his face on his sleeve and squinted at the small, flat-bottomed yawl bobbing a hundred yards ahead of them. Across a skim of ink-black water the lantern in the bow illuminated a desperate scheme unfolding in pantomime.

As two deckhands, Bill Whalen and Kit Harvester, eased the boat forward, Rue stood in the bow and felt out the bottom of the channel with a sounding pole. Once he was satisfied with the measurement, Rue gestured to Beck Morgan who sat in the stern.

As Chase watched, Morgan took one of the contraptions they'd knocked together an hour ago—a six-inch-square block of wood with a candle affixed to one side and a weighted line dangling from the other—and lit the candle's wick.

Old-timers referred to what they were doing, following the channel one candle at a time, as "eating up the lights," but Chase had never done it. He'd never seen it done, and he couldn't be entirely sure if it wasn't a story the seasoned pilots had made up to bamboozle unsuspecting cubs. Still, after seeing the kind of pain Ann was in, he was desperate enough to try anything.

In the skiff, Morgan sheathed the lighted candle with a collar of stiff paper to protect the flame and set it gingerly on the surface of the water.

The rowers moved the yawl ahead. Rue probed; Morgan launched another of the little glowing rafts. They moved again.

When half a dozen lights were laid out like a path of fallen stars, Chase rang the engineering bells. Cal responded to the orders, the deck shimmied, and they crept ahead by inches.

Chase followed the pinpricks of light until he thought he'd go blind. Then the high gray bluff just north of Hardesty's Landing loomed out of the dark. The rider they'd landed two hours ago and sent galloping ahead must have reached the house, because his mother was standing at the foot of the steps, waiting for them.

Though his nerves clamored for a quick French landing, Chase brought the boat round and nuzzled her up to the bank with his usual care. When he reached the Texas deck a few minutes later, Goose Steinwehr stood braced against the wall beside the door to the captain's cabin.

"Your mother's with her," the mate informed him.

Chase nodded his head. "How's Ann faring?"

"She makes me glad it's *women* who have babies," the big German said with a laugh. Chase could see by the slump of his shoulders and the way Goose's hands shook as he lit his cigar that sitting with Ann had taken its toll on him.

"Thank you for staying with her."

Steinwehr nodded and pushed away from the wall. "When this is over," he said, thumping down the stairs toward the salon, "we will drink to the health of your new son."

Chase could have used a swallow of whiskey right then, but instead of following Steinwehr, he gathered his gumption and went into the cabin.

The air was so hot and thick he could feel it against his skin. It had breadth, volume, and a smell—sweat and blood and a faint lingering drift of Ann's perfume. He kicked past a pile of damp, pink-tinged sheets on the sitting room floor, stepped into the bedroom—and stopped dead in his tracks.

Annie lay so white and still she might have been carved from alabaster. Her hair straggled against her shoulders, corded and dark with sweat. Her nightdress was plastered to her skin as if she were glazed with icing.

I didn't get her to Ma soon enough, he found himself thinking. *I should have pushed harder, done more....*

"'Bout time you put in an appearance," Lydia said.

Chase instantly recognized his mother's tone. He was in trouble, and he didn't even know what he'd done wrong.

"I—I had to get us here," he stammered, still not able to take his eyes off his Annie's face.

"Couldn't Rue have done it?"

Chase opened his mouth and closed it again. Once Ma set her mind on something, arguing was pointless.

"You should have been down here with your wife," she went on, "instead of asking that *Dutchman* to sit with her!"

Ann spoke without opening her eyes. "I *asked* for Goose."

"It's all right, Annie." Chase didn't want her spending her strength defending either Steinwehr or him.

"There's absolutely no excuse," his mother began, "for a husband passing off his responsibil—"

Ann made a little warning trill deep in her throat as a spasm took hold of her. Chase had seen her through one of the pains before, and it left him quaking. This one was worse, *a hundred times worse*.

He stood helpless as the contraction grabbed her, grew in her, mastered her, and made her writhe. Ann arched her back, her head thrown back and her shoulders lifting right off the bed. Her face contorted as wavering cries pushed up her corded throat.

"Good girl!" he heard his mother say. "You're doing well!"

Doing well? Chase couldn't swallow, couldn't breathe,

couldn't do more than stare at what was happening to his wife. He couldn't seem to leave her, either.

"The pain is cresting," Lydia encouraged her. "Take a breath."

Ann gulped down air like water at an oasis. She tossed and strained some more. The tension finally seeped out of her. She lay back, panting.

"Tell her she did well," his mother prompted him.

"You did well." Chase's mouth was so dry he could barely speak the words. He knew now why Goose had looked so worn and exhausted out there on deck. Chase needed to leave himself while things were quiet.

His mother had other ideas.

"What I want you to do," she instructed, "is climb up into the bunk and sit behind your wife."

"You want me to what?" Chase started to sweat.

"Ann's going to need your help to push this baby out," Lydia said, managing to sound both instructive and none too patient.

"Please, Lydia." Ann sounded unbearably fragile. "Don't make Chase stay."

"Now, honey"—His mother turned and glared at him, though her voice was gentle—"wouldn't it help to have Chase here with you?"

"I—I suppose."

Panic backed up in Chase's throat. A desperate need to run pushed at him. "But Pa never stayed..."

Once Ma went into labor, Pa would send for one of the neighbor women and take the children fishing. Sometimes they fished all night. Twice they'd had to cut through the ice to fish, but when they went home, there Ma would be, tucked up snug in bed, cuddling another new baby.

None of them, *not even Pa*, had been within earshot when Ma was having a baby. Chase didn't want to be in earshot now.

Lydia scowled at him again, and he could hear her unspoken admonition in his head. *She'll die if you don't stay with her.*

Chase looked down at his wife. In the light of the oil lamp, her face was translucent, milky pale. Veins ran in delicate blue-gray traceries beneath the surface of the skin. Her lips were bitten raw, and each breath she took seemed to require determination, effort.

He'd long since recognized the steely core in his wife, but giving birth to this child seemed to be demanding more strength and will than Ann could muster. It seemed to be demanding things only he could provide: encouragement, tenderness, his own determination to see Ann safely through this. If he cared for her, how could he deny Ann the help she needed?

Without another word, Chase climbed aboard the high, wide berth. It took a good deal of maneuvering to get the two of them settled. He ended up sitting with his back to the wall at the head of the bed. Ann lay between his raised knees, her back supported against his chest.

She hadn't weighed much when he'd carried her up the stairs this morning. She seemed even less substantial now. She sprawled limp as wet wash, slack and flaccid against him. That scared him even more than his mother's scowling admonitions.

Could Ann get through the rest of this?

Before he'd finished the thought, he felt her gathering what fortitude she had to meet the pain that grabbed at her.

As she stiffened and writhed in his arms, he looked along the length of her. He saw the muscles in her belly bunch and contract, realized the almost unimaginable force being brought to bear on her. She moaned as the agony caught her in its grip and dragged her down.

How could this sliver of a woman stand so much? he kept wondering. And just how long could she stand it?

By the time the tension ran out of her, Chase was panting and nearly as spent as Ann herself. She slumped against him and began to cry.

"Promise me," she whispered, "promise me you'll bury me in a proper churchyard..."

"Oh, Annie, don't," he murmured and wiped her tears away. "I'm not burying you anywhere. We're going to get through this."

Down near the foot of the bed Chase saw his mother nod at him, encouraging him.

"Maybe it's better," his Annie went on, her tears falling faster, "if this child is never born. Maybe I have no right to ask you to take my child as your own. Maybe I don't deserve..."

Chase wrapped himself around her, gathered her close in his arms. "Damn it, Annie, I don't care what you did or what you think you deserve. It doesn't matter where this baby came from. It's *my* baby now."

"Yours?" Her voice faltered.

"Mine since the day we spoke our vows," he swore to her. "Mine the same way you are my wife."

Tears hung on her lashes. "Truly yours?"

"Yes."

Ann looked to Lydia as if she needed permission to take what Chase was offering her.

"And who does this one—" Lydia tilted her chin toward Chase. "Who does *he* belong to if not to me? Blood's not all that matters when it comes to loving a child. Wouldn't Chase understand that better than anyone?"

Ann nodded as if she realized what Lydia meant. Chase was proof that blood wasn't the only thing that made men fathers. Or women mothers, either.

"All right, I'll try," she promised.

And she did. The next pain came stronger than the ones before, making her thrash and twist, grind her heels into the mattress and push back against Chase's chest. She flailed and sobbed as the contraction escalated. Then after what seemed like forever, she finally sagged against him.

Almost before that pain subsided, another began. To Chase it was like riding a skiff across the wake of a fast-moving steamer. They'd fight to the crest of one pain, slide into the trough between, and up the crest of the next.

Chase lost track of how many of the contractions they

struggled through together, lost track of the time of night and where they were. He lost track of everything but Ann, writhing in his arms, straining against him. Of pouring every ounce of his strength, every ounce of his will into her.

She was fighting so valiantly to have this child, but each fresh effort drained her more. He could see how worn she was, how weak and tired of fighting, how discouraged and frightened.

The words she'd whispered earlier came back to him: *Promise me you'll bury me in a proper churchyard.*

He'd agreed to appease her, but now he was afraid. He knew Spotted Fawn Woman must have died struggling just like this, and maybe even Ann's own mother. He knew women died in childbirth far more often than anyone talked about. What would he do if his Annie died?

Then as the next spasm began, Lydia stepped in close at the foot of the bed. "I need you to push now, Annie girl. We need to get that baby born."

"Can—can I do that?" Ann whispered.

"It'll come soon," Lydia answered. "Fight just a little longer."

"I'll help all I can," Chase swore to her. "I'm eager to see my new son or daughter."

Ann seemed somehow stronger and more focused as she strained against him this time. Chase curled himself around her and pushed back, holding her, supporting her.

"Good," Lydia told her. "Lie back and breathe."

All of them took a moment's respite. When the next pain came, they began again.

Ann pushed until every muscle was trembling, pushed with her teeth bared and a low growl rising in her throat. She pushed until she ran with sweat, and tears of effort slid down her face.

As she fought to bring their baby into the world, Chase willed her his fortitude, willed her his strength. *He willed the goddamned baby to come out before it killed her.*

Lydia bent nearer and spread her hands at the apex of Annie's legs. "Here it comes!" she cried.

Chase bowed his body, and Ann strained against him. They struggled and panted.

Then all at once, the child slid from Ann's body in a gush. Before it was fully born, it gave an impatient, high-pitched yelp.

At the sound, Chase laughed, then felt himself go soft and quivery inside. Ann sobbed with pure relief.

"This one will never make a secret of what she wants," Lydia prophesied and held up a red-faced dab of humanity, small and squalling and utterly perfect.

Chase had to swallow before he could speak. "Oh, Annie," he whispered and nuzzled her temple. "Just look what you've done! You've given us a wonderful little girl. Have you ever seen a baby so pretty?"

"I've got a little girl?" Ann's voice was soft with wonder and muffled with weariness.

"Indeed you do," Lydia assured her. "She's the sweetest little thing I've ever held in my arms."

She settled the baby on her mother's belly, and Ann ran her fingertips down her daughter's cheek. She stroked the damp filaments of her dark hair, the tiny, almost star-shaped hands.

His Annie cried with joy this time.

"So what are you going to call her?" Chase asked when her tears were over.

"I want to call her Christina," Ann said, then turned to Chase as if his willingness to claim the child gave him a right to object to that.

Chase just nodded.

"That's a lot of name for someone so little," Lydia warned.

"She won't always be little," Ann answered as if to confirm her choice. "And she won't always be weak. No one's going to force their will on my Christina."

"Then Christina it is." Chase grinned. "Christina Hardesty . . . I think I like the sound of that."

THEY WERE UNDERWAY. ANN RECOGNIZED THE MOVEMENT and the sound of the engines even before she was fully awake. Well underway, she realized, blinking at the angle of the sun. How long had she been sleeping?

Hours, she figured. Hours and hours. Ever since the gaggle of Hardestys had cleared out of the cabin just before sunup.

She hadn't been sleeping nearly long enough.

She rolled over, moaned, and lay still again. She felt as if she'd been stretched like a wishbone, but not quite broken in two. The muscles of her back and belly and legs protested her slightest movement. Her jaw ached from grinding her teeth, and her throat was raspy.

Every part of her hurt—but somehow it was a good hurt, a productive hurt. It was a hurt that had accomplished something wonderful. It had accomplished Christina.

Christina, her daughter. *Her baby girl*.

Ann yearned to hold her, to feel the weight of her baby in her arms as she had last night. To cuddle her, stroke her, and breathe her in.

But first Ann had to get out of bed.

She moved again, slowly and with exaggerated caution. She wriggled to the edge of the berth and eased her feet toward the floor. Her knees nearly buckled when she tried to stand, but she wobbled as far as the laundry basket Lydia and Chase had pressed into service as the baby's bed.

The basket was empty.

Ann jerked around. Concern surged up her chest. Where was Christina? Who had taken her? Was she all right?

Weaving on her feet, Ann palmed her way along the wall toward the sitting room, then sagged against the doorjamb in relief.

Chase had settled in one of the big, rush-seated rocking chairs just outside the cabin door. He was rumpled, half-dressed, and barefoot, holding Ann's tiny blanket-wrapped daughter close against his chest. Something about the way his broad workingman's hands cradled her child, something about the way he bent his head above her wrinkly red face, something about the quiet tenor of his voice when he spoke to her awakened the deep, powerful ache of tenderness beneath Ann's breastbone.

She loved this child with all her heart—and she'd come to love the man who was holding her. She might as well admit it, at least to herself.

The two of them were breathtakingly beautiful nestled together in the rocking chair, the soft, buttery sunlight melting over them. They were beautiful, inexpressibly precious, and undeniably hers. Ann's eyes blurred with tears.

Last night Chase had wrapped her up close in his arms. He'd told her how brave and strong she was, how good a mother she was going to be. He'd convinced her she could give her daughter life, then lent her the strength to do it.

This morning he held that baby in his arms, claiming her with quiet tenderness. Just watching the two of them together, Ann could see how seriously Chase was taking the responsibilities of fatherhood, and how Christina was going to grow to adore him.

Drawn by the serenity and love she saw between the two of them, Ann eased close enough to hear what Chase was saying.

"—far as I know, there's never been a woman pilot," he was murmuring to their daughter. "But that doesn't mean there can't ever be one. And it seems to me that actually being born aboard a riverboat gives you a leg up on the competition."

Another swell of love for him broke over her.

"What if she doesn't want to be a riverboat pilot?" she asked, her voice as soft and lulling as his had been.

Chase looked around in surprise, then came to his feet in a single lithe movement. "I think our daughter should be whatever in the world she wants to be," he told her, then gestured for Ann to take the rocking chair. "Are you well enough to be up and wandering around?"

"There's no one here to say I'm not, is there?" Ann asked him. She settled herself gingerly in the chair, and he hunkered down beside her.

"Well, no, there isn't. Ma didn't leave any instructions except to be sure you got some rest. Then she lent us Evangeline to look after Christina, so you can. Evie's had nearly as much practice tending youngsters as I have."

Ann wagged her head. "I wish you'd awakened me before we left Hardesty's Landing so I could thank Lydia again for all she did, and say good-bye."

"Wake you and risk making Ma mad?" Chase gave a delicate shudder. "I take care not to do that deliberately."

Ann reached out to stroke her daughter's hair. "I'd never have gotten through last night if it hadn't been for Lydia."

If it hadn't been for you.

"Ma says babies pretty much bring themselves," he said with a shrug. "All they need us for is the fancywork."

"Rue told me the chance you took to get me to Hardesty's Landing," Ann went on, marveling. "I've never once heard of anyone running the Missouri River in the dark."

"I hardly did it by myself. Rue helped, and Beck Morgan..." He lowered his gaze from hers. "I'm just sorry it took so long to get you someone who could help."

Still, she knew he'd risked his steamer and everyone on it so she could have this morning, this child.

This chance.

Ann reached out and brushed his cheek by way of thanks, reveling at the sun-drenched warmth of his skin.

He turned his gaze from Christina to her. His eyes were a brilliant blue, clear all the way to the bottom. They were honest eyes, trusting eyes. Eyes that held the promise of a life she was just beginning to dream about claiming for herself.

She spread her fingers, cupping his face with her hand. She stroked the corner of his mouth with her thumb, sought the bristle of his whiskers with the hollow of her palm, felt his breath fall warm against her wrist. No matter what had brought them together, here was a man strong enough to protect her, solid enough to build a life on, and tender enough to win her heart.

But then, he'd already won it, hadn't he?

Over these last months, he'd proved he was someone she could count on, someone she could trust. Last night he'd been with her when she'd needed him so desperately. This morning she'd found him cradling her daughter in his arms as if it was the most natural thing in the world for him to scoop up her child and comfort her. As if Christina was as precious to him as she was to her. As if after their marriage's rocky start, they might be able to make a life together.

Just then Christina gave a high, squeaky cry and nuzzled against the half-open placket of Chase's shirt. The words of commitment Ann had been about to speak fell abruptly silent.

Chase laughed and rose. "The baby was happy enough to be with me when I changed her diaper and let her suck my fingers," he said, "but what I think she wants now is something only her mother can give her."

Balancing Christina against his shoulder, Chase helped Ann to her feet and tucked her back in bed. Then he scooped the baby up in his hands and offered her to Ann.

He does this so easily, she thought, amazed. *As if he knows how to hold Christina so she won't break.*

Ann found she wasn't nearly so deft. She fumbled for a grip on the squirming child. Only gradually did she discover how to cup her hands and nestle that small dark head in the crook of her arm. Chase stood over them, giving Ann the time she needed to get the baby settled.

Finally Ann drew her daughter against her and smiled at him. A current flowed between them, a current so warm and sweet she might have lingered in the light of his answering smile, except that Christina squalled, impatient for her dinner.

Once Chase had gone, Ann opened the front of her bedgown and put the baby to her breast just the way Lydia had showed her the night before. As Christina suckled, Ann looked down at her little girl, and the soft, crooning words she had been about to speak died to silence on her lips.

Because what Ann saw in her baby's face, was the very essence of Christina's father.

chapter ten

THE CITY OF ST. LOUIS ROSE IN TIERS FROM WHERE HALF-a-hundred steamers nuzzled up close to the foot of the levee. The mile-long expanse was swarming with wagons and drays, with steamboat agents and stevedores, with passengers and pursers. Goods—both inbound and out-bound—stood in mounds along the cobblestoned slope that lay between the river and the solid block of ware-houses fifty yards back from the water.

"That, my love, is your new home," Ann said, stand-ing at the head of the Texas deck, holding Christina in her arms. "At the end of the season your papa's going to find us a fine, new house up there in town. We'll have a garden where you can play, and I can sit and do my needlework."

Christina gurgled and waved her arms.

In these last two weeks Ann had picked up Chase's

habit of talking to Christina as if she understood every word. In truth, Ann had learned most of what she knew about taking care of the baby from him. She'd learned how to lay Christina across her knees to burp her, how to hold her daughter with one hand and diaper with the other. But Ann had perfected her parental sway—a rhythmic shift from foot to foot—all by herself.

Just then, Chase's sister Evangeline turned from the railing beside her. "Is *all* of that St. Louis?" she asked, wide-eyed.

Hearing the faint waver in the girl's voice, Ann reached across and patted her arm. As grown-up as Evie sometimes seemed, she was still only fifteen and had never set foot outside Hardesty's Landing until she boarded the *Andromeda*.

Ann introduced the city to her bit by bit. "The warehouses store the goods we brought downriver," she pointed out. "Up at the top of the rise is the business district. It's full of hotels and offices and shops—"

"Shops?" Evangeline perked up. "Oh, Ann, will you take me to some of those shops while we're here?"

Chase was giving the girl a stipend for helping with Christina, and the money must have been burning a hole in her pocket.

"We leave for Sioux City at midday tomorrow," Ann reminded her, "and I suppose my stepfather will expect to see us while we're here. Maybe Rue will have time to take you shopping."

"I'll go ask!" Evie cried and darted toward the wheelhouse.

"Don't distract Rue until the Andromeda's tied up!" Ann shouted after her, but the girl was gone.

That left Ann alone to consider her reunion with James Rossiter. She'd left the town house and boarded the Andromeda without his permission, committed the unpardonable offense of altering the plans he'd made for her. Now he'd make her pay dearly for defying him.

He'd insist that she and Christina come back to live at the town house, at least for the rest of the shipping season. But Ann had come a long way since the morning she'd taken the commodore's arm and gone down to marry Chase. She wasn't going to allow her stepfather to order her life—or Christina's, either.

Chase would help her make her stand against the commodore, if she asked him to. But she didn't want to ask more of Chase than what he'd given them already.

"Well, at least we won't have to face your grandfather on our own," she whispered to Christina and turned to the hurricane deck where her husband was bawling orders.

From the way he stood with his feet planted wide on the planking and his head held high, Ann could see how proud he was to be bringing the Andromeda safely home. Judging from the figures he showed her last night, not only had the trip to Fort Benton gone smoothly, but it had also been extremely profitable.

The Andromeda had been tied up at the levee not quite ten minutes when a messenger bounded up the gangway and delivered an invitation to dinner written in the commodore's own hand.

Ann immediately lost her appetite.

Chase studied the missive for one long moment before he handed it back to her. "So he's summoned us to the town house, has he?"

The hint of censure in his voice surprised her. "I suppose he has," she acknowledged.

"To upbraid you for leaving?"

"I expect."

"And pass judgment on Christina?"

Ann glanced up, surprised that he'd seen the invitation for what it was. "Dare I send him our excuses?" she asked him.

"We'll beard the lion in his den—" A smile quirked one corner of Chase's mouth. "—But perhaps things won't go quite the way the commodore expects."

Ann wasn't sure what that meant and spent the afternoon worrying. By the time Mary Fairley, the commodore's longtime housekeeper, led them to the town house's parlor, Ann's heart was throbbing against her corset stays.

Chase must have sensed her uneasiness because he closed a hand around her elbow. "You're presenting the commodore with his first grandchild," he whispered. "No man alive could spurn such a beautiful baby."

Ann had certainly never expected Enoch Hardesty to cuddle and croon over her newborn daughter the way he had. But Ann's hopes that Christina would melt the commodore's heart were dashed the moment the three of them crossed the threshold. Instead of speaking so much as a word of welcome, James Rossiter waited in frigid silence as they crossed what seemed like an acre of flowery Aubusson carpet.

"Good evening, sir," Chase greeted him.

James Rossiter ignored the words and turned a scowl on Ann.

"You damned ungrateful girl!" he spat at her. "You left this house without my permission! After I'd taken responsibility for you when your mother died, after I'd sent you to that exclusive school back East, after I found you a husband when you disgraced yourself, you show your gratitude by ignoring my wishes."

If half of what he claimed was true, Ann wouldn't be married to Chase, she wouldn't be standing with Christina in her arms. She wouldn't have had reason to run away. A need to speak the truth clawed at the back of her throat.

"Didn't I make it perfectly clear," he all but snarled at her, "that I intended for you to stay on here at the town house? It was a damned generous offer, and instead of having the good grace to accept it, you slunk away without a single word."

Beside her, Chase shifted back on his heels preparing to come to her defense. Ann stayed him with a touch.

"Indeed," she admitted, drawing Christina close as she faced her stepfather. "I did leave without your consent. But I was a married woman by then and no longer your concern. My place was with my husband, even if it meant following him all the way to Montana."

The commodore's face darkened and his fists knotted at his sides. For an instant Ann thought he meant to strike her for her impertinence, and she shielded the baby with her hands. But the commodore managed to regain control of himself.

He turned on Chase instead. "You knew I meant for her to stay on here while you were gone. It's what we agreed."

Chase gave a laconic shrug. "I don't recollect that Ann's living arrangements were any part of the bargain we made."

"She defied me—and you helped her do it!"

"All I did was accede to my wife's wishes—as any good husband would."

Ann sliced a startled glance at her husband. Chase hadn't "acceded to" anything; he'd done his best to send her home. Now he was defending her, lying for her sake.

The commodore's eyes narrowed as he looked from Chase to her. Clearly he hadn't expected they'd form an alliance, stand united against him. A scowl furrowed his wide face. Then, as if he could see he'd gain no ground with them today, the commodore's stance softened, and he drew a breath.

"Well, then," he said, "let's have a look at that baby."

"At your *granddaughter*, you mean?" Ann asked, determined to press her advantage while she could.

Rossiter grimaced. "I'd like a look at my *granddaughter*, if you please."

Though Ann had pressed for that acknowledgment, she had to fight down a surge of protectiveness as she folded back the baby's lace-trimmed blanket. If James Rossiter said so much as one disparaging word...

Christina blinked up at her grandfather as if she knew she was on display.

The moment James Rossiter clapped eyes on her, his face changed, falling into lines of tenderness and delight that looked like they might once have been habitual and well-used. Ann wondered if it had been the struggle to rise from the corruption and squalor of Natchez-under-the-Hill when he was a young man that had turned him into such a tyrant. Or were there other things that made maintaining his power and control so important?

As her stepfather stroked Christina's thick dark hair, the hard knot of Ann's misgivings eased. Perhaps for all his guile and manipulativeness, the commodore had a gentler side, one he'd never been able to show to Boothe or her.

But when he turned his black, speculative gaze from the baby to Ann, she knew enough to shield herself. "Well, my dear," he drawled. "I can't say I see much of *you* in the child."

The comment seemed innocuous enough, but his words resounded in Ann's head like a slap. What he meant was that with her shock of black hair and widow's peak, with her dark eyes and narrow mouth, Christina looked exactly like her father.

For Ann, that resemblance was not only a reminder of things she longed to forget, but a fuse burning toward detonation. How long before Chase saw the likeness, too? How long before he guessed the truth? And what would he think when that moment came?

Yet, for now at least, Chase seemed oblivious.

"What we hope," he told the commodore, resting his hand at the small of Ann's back, "is that Christina will have her mother's grace and wit, as well as her generous heart."

Ann's cheeks warmed. For the second time since they'd arrived at the town house, her husband had taken her part against the commodore. Not wanting either of the men to guess how much Chase's words had meant to her, she drew Christina close and turned away.

And all but collided with her stepbrother.

Boothe reached out to steady her. But as considerate as the gesture might have appeared, his grip bit deep into her upper arm. In the moment before she jerked out of his hold, the scent of moth-chaser and malevolence nearly overwhelmed her.

"You had the child," he said, his black eyes holding hers.

"Yes," Ann confirmed. "A little girl."

"And what do you call her?"

Chase turned at the sound of Boothe's voice. "We call our daughter Christina."

"*Your* daughter?" Boothe scoffed, his voice ripe with irony.

"Annie's and mine."

For a moment, a frisson of antagonism that had nothing to do with Christina or Ann danced between the two men.

Then Boothe shot Ann his viper's smile and reached to grasp one of the baby's flailing hands. "Is she his, indeed?"

Ann shrank back against her husband's chest, not wanting her stepbrother's touch to sully her daughter. Refusing to tread the dangerous ground of Christina's paternity.

She fumbled for a reason to get away. "Perhaps I should go and feed Christina so she'll sleep through dinner."

"You may use my study if you like," the commodore offered. "And while you're gone, I mean to offer these two gentlemen some of my excellent brandy. From what I hear, both the *Andromeda* and *Cassiopeia* did very well on their runs to Fort Benton, and we have a great deal to celebrate."

Once Ann was settled in one of the armchairs in her stepfather's study, she opened the bodice of her gown and guided her nipple into Christina's mouth. The baby snorted with delight and suckled noisily.

"You *were* hungry, weren't you?" Ann murmured, smoothing the baby's hair. How could any child conceived the way Christina had been, have become so precious to her?

Christina nursed for a good long while, and just as the baby was falling asleep, a chill of uneasiness slithered up Ann's back. Instinctively she turned and saw Boothe standing in the doorway to the servants' stairs, watching her. For a moment their gazes held, then with a feral smile, he sauntered toward her.

Cold speared Ann's heart. She tugged at the baby's blanket, veiling both Christina and herself from his view. "How dare you intrude on us here?" she hissed at him.

He settled himself at the edge of the commodore's desk, an arm's-length away. "Goodness, Ann," he observed quietly. "Who'd have thought you'd take to that bastard child the way you have?"

Ann drew the blanket higher. "I refuse to make an innocent child pay for her father's sins."

"Or for her mother's?"

Ann felt the blood flood into her cheeks. "Her mother was blameless in this!"

Boothe shrugged. "The little girl's dark-haired," he observed mildly. "And she's going to have her father's eyes."

"She's not a thing like him!"

He snickered, showing his teeth. "I thought you liked him well enough when you lay with him."

"He took me against my will—as well you know."

"Perhaps he's sorry," he suggested and reached for the blanket. "Perhaps he'd like a chance to know his daughter."

She slapped his hand away, hot, black loathing bubbling beneath her sternum. "Her father has no rights at all where Christina is concerned."

"What if he chose to make a place for himself in her life?" Boothe proposed. "As a dear friend, or even a doting *uncle*?"

"Christina's father should understand that if he comes near this child"—Ann clutched her daughter—"if he even hints to her about who he is, he'll answer to me."

Boothe threw back his head and laughed—a harrowing sound that reverberated off the study's paneled walls. "My dear Ann," he scoffed. "You've never been able to defend yourself. How do you expect to shield this little girl if her father chooses to make himself known to her?"

Something ruthless and maternal coalesced in her, a force that was powerful and ages-old. A fierceness that ran soul-deep, one she sensed would endure to her last breath.

"I might never have been able to defend myself," Ann said in a deceptively quiet voice, "but I'll do whatever I have to do to protect Christina. No matter what went on before, I will never—*never* let you hurt my daughter."

CHASE STUDIED THE COMMODORE OVER THE RIM OF HIS glass, taking note of the blunt, big-knuckled hand wrapped around the cut crystal tumbler. Had those hands ever grabbed his Annie hard enough to leave bruises? Had he shaken her hard enough to set her head reeling? Had this man ever struck her?

Though Ann denied it, Chase thought he had. Certainly something that happened in this house had marked her: made his Annie start when someone came too close or made her recoil when someone touched her. He'd seen the shadows in her eyes, and he suspected...

Chase wasn't exactly sure what he suspected. But from what he'd seen and heard today, he knew James Rossiter had been belittling and bullying and manipulating Annie all her life. Once he'd met his obligations and owned the *Andromeda* outright, he'd call the commodore to account for what he'd done. In the meantime, he meant to keep his Annie safe from both the commodore and her step-brother.

But for the time being, Chase had his obligations aboard the *Andromeda* to see to, and some business to discuss with the commodore that had nothing to do with Ann. He needed to tell James Rossiter about the allegations he'd heard at Fort Benton.

"Refill, Hardesty?" the commodore offered from where he was refreshing his own drink. Chase swallowed down the last gulp of brandy and shook his head.

"While we were out West," he began and set his glass aside, "I heard something about the Gold Star boats that worries me."

"Oh?" Rossiter turned from the side table, glass in hand.

"It may be nothing more than talk...." Chase couched the rumors as diplomatically as he could, especially considering that what Barnaby Greene said that night in Fort Benton had been chewing at Chase all the way home.

The older man settled himself in one of the parlor's graceful settees. "Let's hear it, anyway."

Chase rose and paced to the fireplace. "What I heard was that Gold Star steamers have been making unscheduled stops out west of here."

The commodore sipped from his glass, unconcerned. "We've always made unscheduled stops. Anyone can flag us down."

"Well, yes," Chase agreed, beginning to wish he'd saved a swallow of brandy to lubricate the words. "I know most steamers respond to signals from shore. What worried me was the implication that the stops the Gold Star boats are making involve delivering illegal cargos."

"Illegal cargos?" The commodore shifted and braced his hands against his knees. "And what would those illegal cargos be?"

Chase knew the man was baiting him and did his best not to squirm. "Contraband," he answered.

"What kind of contraband?"

"Armaments to the Indians."

"Guns, you mean?" the commodore roared at him.

Chase stood his ground. "The Indians are causing trouble out West. From what I heard at Fort Sully, the Sioux and Cheyenne menacing the Bozeman Trail are armed with Spencer carbines. Guns the army hadn't even been issued yet."

"And you think the Gold Star boats are delivering those carbines to the Indians?"

Chase shrugged. "I'm just telling you what I heard."

"Only the *Andromeda* and the *Cassiopeia* have ventured far enough west to have had truck with the Indians," Rossiter pointed out. "I know Boothe wasn't carrying contraband. Were you?"

A flush warmed Chase's cheekbones. He glanced back at his father-in-law. "I would *never* transport contraband."

Rossiter eyed him speculatively, as if to say he knew Chase had his price. Since he'd proved he did when he bargained his name for the *Andromeda*, Chase's face went hotter.

"Most of the Gold Star captains," the commodore went on, "have been with me for years."

"I know."

"I refuse to call their honor into question on the strength of a rumor you picked up out in the wilds."

Chase shifted on his feet. He could see he'd been a fool to bring this up.

"If you get proof that any of my captains are involved in running contraband"—Rossiter slugged down the rest of his brandy—"you come see me. In the meantime, you keep these damn rumors to yourself."

Chase couldn't fault James Rossiter's stance. It was exactly the kind of backing *he* would want from the head of the steamboat line he worked for.

"I just thought you should know," Chase said by way of apology. "Stories get passed up and down the river faster than the collection plate at Sunday services. Even if the rumor isn't true, it could damage the Gold Star's reputation."

Rossiter gave a grunt of acknowledgment and rose to pour himself another drink. "I'll see what I can do to squelch it," he conceded. "And while we're talking business, I have something else I need to discuss with you."

Chase nodded for him to continue.

"I'm reassigning Goose Steinwehr to another vessel."

It wasn't what Chase had been expecting. "The contract we signed when I married Ann gave me my choice of officers."

"And you had it—*for the run to Fort Benton.* But the

men work for Gold Star, not for you. And Steinwehr's expertise is needed elsewhere.

"Besides," the commodore went on slyly. "You don't take full ownership of the *Andromeda* until the end of the season."

Nor was the commodore likely to relinquish control of the steamer one minute sooner than the contract specified. His father-in-law was putting him in his place, and Chase didn't like the feel of that.

As sorry as he was to lose Goose Steinwehr, Ann was going to miss him even more. Chase said as much, and Rossiter dismissed his concerns with a snort of derision. "Ann has no business whatsoever living aboard the *Andromeda*, much less fraternizing with the crew."

"I promised her I'd rent us a house here in town," Chase said to appease the commodore. But in truth, Chase himself was spending more and more of his time thinking about how good it would be to come home to Annie and Christina at the end of a run. To sit down to supper with them and play with Christina afterwards. To turn to Ann in bed and have her open her arms to him. It was the life he wanted for all of them.

"Ann would be far better off staying on in the town house with me," the commodore insisted, breaking into Chase's thoughts. "She's got no business gallivanting up and down the Missouri River when she's got a baby to tend. She's your wife, Hardesty. You tell her you've decided she ought to stay on here with me."

Chase nodded as if he'd agreed. But since he'd begun

to suspect why Ann refused to live under James Rossiter's roof, he wasn't about to force her.

"So who are you assigning to the *Andromeda* in Goose's place?" he asked instead.

"Joel Curry is my choice."

Chase did his best to hide his contempt. Curry was one of Skirlin's cronies and not half the mate Goose Steinwehr was. But since Chase had no choice, he put the best face he could on the commodore's decision.

"I'm sure Curry will work out fine."

Just then, Ann returned to the parlor with Christina asleep in the crook of her shoulder. As she nestled the baby in the basket they'd brought for her and drew up the blanket, Chase saw that her hands were trembling.

"Are you all right?" he asked quietly, catching her wrist.

Ann cast a glance at her father, then to where Boothe was returning to the parlor himself. "I'm fine," she whispered.

Chase didn't think she was fine. But before he could discern what was wrong with her, the commodore shepherded them all into the dining room.

O N HER WAY BACK FROM BREAKFAST THE FOLLOWING morning, Ann found Frenchy Bertin sitting slumped and disconsolate at one of the counters in the galley. The way he'd braced his head in his hands and kept mumbling in

French made her think what was bothering him was far more serious than burning a tray of pastries.

She paused to ask. "Is something wrong?"

"Ah, *mon Dieu*!" he moaned. "I have had the worst news!"

"Frenchy, for goodness sake!" she exclaimed, noticing the closely written letter lying on the countertop between his elbows. "What's happened?"

"It's from my wife Anouk in New Orleans."

"Is she ill?" Ann asked, rubbing his bony shoulder. "If you need to go to her I'm sure we can—"

"*Non*, she is not ill. She is coming here to live with me!" He picked up the letter and waved it at her. "Anouk and the children are moving to St. Louis! She wants to be with me when this new baby is born!"

"Why that's wonderful!" Ann exclaimed before she recognized the panic in his eyes. "Isn't it?"

"I can't have Anouk living in St. Louis!"

"Whyever not?"

"How will I visit my wife Marie in Natchez and my wife Charmaine in Dubuque?"

Ann gaped at him. "You mean you really *do* have three wives?" she asked incredulously.

The dramatic lift and droop of Frenchy's shoulders was all the admission Ann needed.

"How on earth did you end up married to three different women?"

"The priests insisted," he answered with a sniff. "They said Marie and Charmaine would go to hell if I didn't marry them."

"And you'd lain with these women, I suppose," Ann guessed. She'd never had any illusions about Frenchy's weaknesses for cards and women.

"*Oui.*"

It was an outrageous situation, yet somehow it had always been Frenchy's foibles that endeared him to Ann, that made her own difficulties and deceptions seem modest by comparison.

"And which wife is Anouk?" she wanted to know.

"My first," he answered on a heavy sigh. "I apprenticed at her father's bakery; Anouk sold bread in the shop. She was so pretty in her big white apron and embroidered cap—and even prettier *out* of them."

Ann saw the gentle melancholy that came into his face as he remembered. "You still love her, don't you?" she asked softly.

"Of course I love her!" He ran his big hands through his lank hair. "I love them all. What am I going to do about Anouk? What can I say to keep her from moving to St. Louis?"

In spite of what he'd done, Ann found herself consoling him. "There has to be a solution to this," she promised him.

Just then, Chase pushed open the door from the salon. "Annie," he called and gestured her closer.

Ann gave Frenchy a final pat and crossed the galley.

"Someone's come to see you," Chase told her quietly. "A man named Throckmorton. He says he's a lawyer."

Uneasiness blossomed beneath Ann's ribs. "A

lawyer?" she breathed. "Why would a lawyer want to talk to me?"

"He didn't say what he wanted."

The image of her stepbrother flashed through her mind, and then the commodore. "I can't have done anything wrong, can I?"

"That isn't the only reason lawyers look for people." Chase trailed his hand along her arm, and for all its brevity, his touch was comforting. "I had Mr. Throckmorton wait in the salon. Why don't you go see what he wants, while I check on Christina and Evie."

Ann caught his wrist as he turned to go. "I won't go back to the commodore's!" She hadn't meant to let her fear slip out, but the visit to the town house the night before had stirred up a kind of dread she hadn't felt in months.

"Oh, Annie." Chase squeezed her hand. "You're my wife now. You belong with me."

It was both the reassurance Ann needed and a reminder of her own doubts about the future. She drew a breath to calm herself, then smoothed her palms down the front of her bodice. "I'll go see what he wants."

Quite a few of the cabin passengers had already come aboard in preparation for the *Andromeda*'s midday departure and were seated at tables in the steamer's long main room. In spite of the crowd, Ann spotted Mr. Throckmorton immediately.

He was a trim, gray-haired man who sat with his knees together and a lawyer's satchel in his lap. Though he didn't look particularly intimidating, Ann's legs were rubbery as she made her way toward him.

The moment he realized who she was, he sprang to his feet. "Mrs. Hardesty?" When Ann inclined her head, he continued. "Are you the former Miss Ann Pelletier Rossiter, daughter of Rupert and Sarah Pelletier of Philadelphia?"

"Yes," Ann answered. What could her parents possibly have to do with this?

"And you recently wed Chase Ezekiel Hardesty?"

Chase's middle name was Ezekiel? She hadn't known that!

"I recently married Captain Hardesty," she confirmed.

"Then please allow me to introduce myself." He gestured her into one of the chairs at the table and resumed his own seat. "I am Thomas Willis Throckmorton of Throckmorton and Latham Solicitors, and I believe I have some rather good news for you."

"Do lawyers ever bring good news, Mr. Throckmorton?"

He smiled benevolently. "Why don't you be the judge of that, Mrs. Hardesty." He took a sheaf of papers from his satchel and placed them on the table between them. "It seems that not long before her death, your mother received a sizable inheritance from one of her aunts."

"My Aunt Isobel?" Ann asked, calling up a memory of the diminutive, papery-skinned woman whose house had always smelled of oranges and cloves.

"The very same," he confirmed. "Your mother, in turn, used that money to set up a trust for you."

Ann pressed a hand to her lips, too surprised for a moment to speak. "You mean, I've inherited money from my mother? After all this time?"

"Indeed," Throckmorton continued, thumbing through the paperwork. "There were several conditions to the trust."

Ann should have known there would be. Hadn't there always been restrictions and qualifications to every good thing that came her way?

"And just what are those conditions?"

"The main one, the reason I've come to you now after all these years," Mr. Throckmorton went on, "is that your mother stipulated that the inheritance was to come to you only after you were married."

But why would her mother make that particular provision? Ann wondered.

"The other term of the trust," he told her, "is that you must agree that the monies you inherit must be held and controlled solely by you as long as you live."

Ann stared at him taken aback not only by the gift, but by the stipulations her mother had put on it. How old must Ann have been when her mother decided this? And why on earth had Sarah Pelletier been so adamant about Ann coming into the money only after she was wed?

If she'd had this money last spring, Ann found herself thinking, she could have left St. Louis. She would have had the means to go where her father would never find her. She could have started a new life, a new life for her and her daughter.

But then, she might never have met or married Chase.

She might never have been embraced by his wonderful family, might never have lived aboard the *Andromeda*, had adventures or given birth to Christina. The very idea made her throat knot tight.

Mr. Throckmorton went on, breaking into her thoughts. "When most people receive news of an inheritance, Mrs. Hardesty, the first thing they ask is how much money is involved. Of course if you have other questions you prefer I answer first . . ."

"Can you tell me why my mother made these specific stipulations? What was it she hoped to accomplish by providing this money to me the way she did?"

"I'm afraid it was my father, God rest his soul, who wrote the will. I'm just not privy to your mother's motives."

Ann clasped her hands in her lap and nodded. "Very well, then, Mr. Throckmorton. I suppose I *am* curious about how much money's involved."

The lawyer gave her the slightest of smiles. "I hope you will not think ill of me if I tell you, ma'am, that our firm has a certain reputation for husbanding their clients' funds wisely."

"I'm glad to hear that."

"In your case," he said with a twinkle of pride, "we've managed to increase the initial amount by about a third."

Ann nodded again.

"Which means that your inheritance now, Mrs. Hardesty, is a little in excess of fifty-two thousand dollars."

Ann blinked at him, then burst out laughing. "Oh,

Mr. Throckmorton! There must be some mistake. My mother never had that kind of money in her life!"

The lawyer looked affronted. "I assure you, ma'am. I have the figures right here."

Ann stared at the financial statements, trying to imagine how much fifty-two thousand dollars really was. It was enough to buy a second *Andromeda*. A magnificent house in town. Land out West that stretched as far as the eye could see.

Or the life she'd dreamed about forging for herself and her daughter last fall.

"Now if you'll just sign these papers, Mrs. Hardesty"—Throckmorton put a pile of legal notices before her—"I'll begin to put things in order. And of course you'll have to decide if you prefer to have us continue to administer your holdings, or whether you want to take control of the monies yourself. Either way, it shouldn't take more than a month or two to get everything finalized."

Ann nodded, too stunned by her mother's bequest to think beyond the astonishing thing Throckmorton had revealed to her. "I think I'd like you to oversee the money for a little while, at least," she murmured.

Still shaking her head, Ann read over the documents, asked questions about the passages she didn't understand, and finally signed her name.

"I wish you well, Mrs. Hardesty," Mr. Throckmorton said as he gathered everything into his satchel and offered her his card. "And if there's anything else I can do for you..."

"Oh, Mr. Throckmorton!" Ann laughed again. "I

think you've done more than enough for me already. Thank you."

Ann walked the lawyer to the head of the grand staircase, said good-bye, then hurried upstairs. Her meeting had taken most of the morning, and Ann knew Christina would be hungry.

"She was just starting to fuss," Evangeline reported as she bustled into the cabin.

Ann took the baby in her arms, then shooed Evie out on deck. "It's too nice a day to be shut up in here," she told her.

Yet the moment the girl was gone, Ann closed the door and drew the curtains. With the news Mr. Throckmorton had brought, Ann's world had suddenly become too wide, too bright, too filled with choices she had no idea how to make.

By carefully husbanding her inheritance, she could have the freedom to do whatever she wanted to do, to go wherever she longed to go. She could find a place where no one knew her, where she never need acknowledge the misfortunes that had befallen her. She could escape the commodore's domination and Boothe's malevolence. She could protect her sweet Christina from scandal. She could start all over again.

But if she chose to leave, she'd forfeit the life she'd begun aboard the *Andromeda*. She'd have to deny her love for Chase, turn her back on a man who'd accepted her without question, and given her the happiest months of her life. She'd have to take Christina away from a father who adored her and a family who'd claimed the two of them with no questions asked.

Yet in order to stay, she'd have to tell Chase the truth. She'd have to acknowledge what Boothe had done to her, and how Christina was conceived. She'd need to find the courage within herself to go to Chase, to open herself to him, and show him in the most intimate way possible how much she loved him.

Ann didn't know if she could do that. The very idea sent hot blood scorching through her, made her hands shake and her breath catch in her throat. Ann squeezed her eyes shut and tried to fight down the sear of panic, to silence the clamor in her head.

She did her best to concentrate on where she was and the child in her arms. Gradually the weight of her daughter, the scent of her skin, and the rhythmic pull of her baby's suckling helped Ann settle.

She stroked Christina's face, wondering if her own mother ever held her like this. Had she taken Ann into her arms for the pure joy of holding her? Had Sarah Pelletier ever bound her close against her heart and wished she could hold her safe forever? Was this unexpected legacy Sarah's way of providing her little girl with a kind of security Sarah herself must always have wanted?

Ann struggled to part the veil of her own feelings for her mother and was dismayed by how little she found behind it. She remembered Sarah Pelletier's thick, honey-brown hair and the dimple in her chin because Ann faced them in her mirror every morning. She recollected that her mother had worn a small lion-head stickpin in her collar because it had belonged to Ann's father. She could still call up the scent of her mother's lily of the valley perfume and the swipe of her lace handkerchief against her cheek. She remembered her mother had liked buying hats; some of Ann's best memories were of milliners' shops.

But Ann had no idea who her mother was or why she'd made the choices she had while she lived. Regret and a kind of childlike longing, tugged at her. She missed her mother today as she had not missed her in years.

Now that Ann was older, she understood the decisions women were forced to make for the sake of their children. Had Sarah Pelletier married the commodore to make sure she could provide for Ann? Had she subjugated her will to make a life with a man who ruthlessly oversaw every facet of their lives? Had her mother left Ann this inheritance with its odd stipulations, so that when her time came to marry, Ann would have a kind of independence and security Sarah never had?

Ann wished all at once that she could clasp her mother's cool, petal-soft hand in hers, pillow her head on her rustling skirts, and tell the woman who'd left her so long ago that she thought she understood. She wanted to tell her mother—after all these years—that she'd forgiven her for abandoning her. She wanted Sarah Pelletier to know that now that Ann had a daughter of her own to consider, she understood so much more about love—about resignation and sacrifice.

Ann was still holding her sleeping daughter when Chase came into the cabin a good while later.

"We'll be pulling out in a few minutes," he told her, "but before I got too busy, I thought I'd see how you made out with that lawyer."

Ann looked at Christina. "Oh, things went well enough."

"What was it he came to see you about?"

For reasons Ann couldn't in any way justify, even to herself, she lied to Chase.

"It wasn't anything important. Really nothing at all."

IT WAS A BEAUTIFUL NIGHT. MOONLIGHT LAY IN A SHIM-mering silver band across the breadth of the river. Ann could hear the high, bright notes drifting up from the main deck where someone in one of the immigrant families was playing a mandolin. The sultry smell of distant rain drifted on the freshening wind, and she paused at the head of the Texas deck to tuck the tails of her shawl more securely around herself.

Chase stepped up beside her, close enough that she was aware of his solidity and his warmth. Usually she enjoyed the time they managed to spend together: their coffee at dawn, an occasional stroll on deck in the afternoon, and these quiet moments after supper. But tonight Chase couldn't seem to keep still; she sensed a restlessness about him that wafted toward her like the scent of his shaving soap.

"Wasn't it good of Mary Fletcher to bring the children

down to see us?" Ann said, needing suddenly to fill the silence between them.

It had been five months since the night the *Andromeda* had tied up at Glasgow, five months since Chase had rescued two of the Fletcher children from the house fire. Ann could almost feel the waves of heat and see the flames flaring treetop high. She could almost hear the timbers moan as the roof gave way.

"I was pleased to see they'd all recovered," Chase agreed, shifting uneasily beside her.

Ann could remember watching the house disintegrate board by board. She could remember praying for Chase's safety, though she'd been sure he was lost. Then he'd come stumbling out of the fire with the Fletcher baby clutched close against his chest.

When he spoke again, Ann knew the memories were as clear to him tonight as they were to her.

"Do you have any idea how much it meant to find you waiting for me in the yard that night?" Something thick and husky in his voice made Ann turn and look at him. "You were my anchor, Annie, someone to hold on to."

She remembered how he'd knotted his fists in her clothes. How he'd shivered beneath her hands. And whispered his fears into her hair.

"I needed you so much that night." He raised his hand and touched her face, grazed along her throat with his fingertips. He cupped his hand around her shoulder and drew her toward him. "And it didn't take seeing Mary Fletcher and her children to remind me how much I still need you."

He lowered his head and kissed her. His lips grazed hers in a slow, sentient slide, moved over hers gentle as a flutter of breath. He began to nibble the tender curves of her mouth.

Ann tilted her chin, offering up more of herself.

Chase deepened his kisses, until their mouths meshed and clung, until that languid exchange became something sweeter, richer, hotter.

Ann wrapped her arms around his neck and was surprised all over again at how much she liked kissing him. How much she liked the taste of him, the shape and texture of his lips, the way he gathered her up in his hands as if she were something delicate and infinitely precious. She liked the way his tongue sought hers in the sweet, humid hollow of their mouths. A thick, lulling tide of warmth seemed to rise between them.

"I'm so glad that you're my wife," he breathed. "That you're here for me to kiss and touch."

Beneath the soft drape of her shawl, Chase raised his hand and cupped her breast. Ann's pulse rate leaped at her wrists and in the hollow of her throat.

He held her in his open palm, caressing gently, almost reverently. In spite of her best resolve, her muscles tightened; she fought the urge to pull away.

"As much as I needed you the night of the fire, Annie," he whispered. "I need you even more now."

She did her best to put some small space between them. Somehow she had to have that distance.

"The *Andromeda*'s tied up for the night," he proposed.

"Evie's looking after Christina. There's an empty stateroom just downstairs. No one will miss us if we slip away."

She fumbled for a way to put him off.

"Annie, please." His voice was deep, persuasive; the timbre shot a quiver deep into her belly. "I want so much to be with you tonight. I want so much to make love to you."

You want to strip away my clothes. Lie over me and crush me. Force yourself inside me.

The idea of someone doing that, even Chase, sent a jolt of panic ripping through her. She braced her palms against his chest and pressed away.

"I can't do that now," she said, her voice tight with both reticence and regret.

He looked down at her as if he could see right past the evasions to the fear. "You know, Annie, not every man who touches you is going to hurt you. You don't have to be afraid of me."

Ann felt the color drain out of her face. Just how much did Chase understand? Did he still believe the reason she kept her distance was because the commodore had beaten her? Or did he suspect . . .

"I just can't!" she blurted out.

She knew she ought to tell him the truth. But how could she explain what had happened to her, then watch the concern and respect in his eyes change to pity or disappointment or regret? How could she risk losing his regard when it was what she'd built her new life on?

"Please try to understand that I can't be with you," she entreated him.

"Why?" he asked her.

She hesitated, wanting to tell him everything, but she just couldn't seem to form the words. "It's just too soon, too soon after the baby."

It was a lie, and Chase knew it. She could sense the hurt and concern in him, as well as the need and longing. Still, he seemed willing to be patient. But for how long? And how, in God's name, would she ever find the courage to do what he wanted, when the mere thought of it made her quiver inside?

Chase skimmed his fingers along her cheek, stroked the length of her throat, then curled his palm around her shoulder. He looked deep into her eyes. "Then I guess we'll just have to wait a little longer."

chapter eleven

HIS LIFE WAS VERY NEARLY PERFECT—OR AT LEAST that's how it seemed to Chase Hardesty as he stood braced against the *Andromeda*'s railing on this fine mid-summer morning. He was master of the fastest and most beautiful steamer on the whole of the Missouri River. His first run of the packet season to Sioux City had been so profitable that once the cargo was unloaded, he'd taken Ann, Christina, and Evie on a spree in town.

Now, two days into the homebound run, Chase had cargo stacked to the guards and nearly every stateroom was occupied. When he'd peeked into the captain's cabin a few minutes earlier, both his baby daughter and his sister were tucked up in their beds and fast asleep. Now he was braced against the rail on the boiler deck, waiting for his wife to join him for coffee and a few quiet words before their responsibilities claimed them both.

Maybe he was a simple man for taking such joy in simple things—but he was content.

Or at least almost content.

Chase glanced off to the east, where the swath of sunlight on the horizon was spreading seamless black and gold reflections across the surface of the Missouri. The river was so still this morning, it was impossible to discern where the sky and trees and bank merged into lovely liquid illusion.

Ann stepped out on deck a few minutes later smelling of yeast and warmth and perhaps just the slightest hint of vanilla. He turned and smiled at her, then reached to dust a smudge of flour from her chin. Her skin was warm beneath his fingertips, flushed and dewy from the heat of the ovens.

"Long night?" he asked her.

Her elbow nudged his as she leaned against the railing.

"No longer than most." She scuffed out of her shoes and wiggled her bare toes against the decking. "We made white bread, rye bread, and *twelve dozen* shortcakes."

"I hear Frenchy drafted half of Joel Curry's deckhands to pick raspberries last night when we wooded up."

"I doubt Mr. Curry was pleased with him," she observed with some asperity.

Ann resented Joel Curry because he'd taken Goose Steinwehr's place, and Goose had been Ann's special friend. On the long trip to Fort Benton, he'd taught her German, picked her flowers, and found her a honey tree. He'd been the only man aboard brave enough to sit with her through those last long hours of labor.

Chase couldn't say he was much more pleased about having Joel Curry aboard than Ann was. Goose led men; Curry drove them. Goose knew where he put every paper of pins when he packed a cargo; Joel Curry's methods were a good deal less exacting. Still, the commodore had assigned Curry to the boat, which meant that until Chase took full ownership of the *Andromeda* at the end of the season, he had to make the best of it.

Chase put thoughts of Joel Curry aside and turned to his wife. Ann had changed since she'd come aboard the *Andromeda*. She baked with Frenchy every night, had become a gracious hostess to his cabin passengers, and forged friendships with his crew.

When she took Christina in her arms, she simply glowed. Chase loved watching Ann with the baby and listening to her explain the world to their wide-eyed daughter. Ann was gentle with her, warm and tender and playful in a way Chase hadn't expected she'd be.

Drawn by his appreciation of that warmth, Chase leaned nearer. Now that the light was stronger, he could see Ann's mouth was moist and faintly tinged with purple.

"It looks to me," he teased her, "like you've been sampling Joel Curry's raspberries."

Ann smiled guiltily.

"And were they sweet?"

She licked her lips and laughed. "Delicious!"

For a moment all Chase could do was stare at her, at that soft, raspberry-tinted mouth, at the flush of color in her cheeks, and the tendrils of butterscotch hair trailing against her throat. Never had he wanted to kiss her more than he did right then. He wanted to wrap his arm around her and draw her to him. He wanted to trail his tongue along her lips, sip the tartness of those raspberries, and the sweetness of Ann herself.

He wanted to take her to bed and make love to her.

It was something that might have been as natural as breathing for another man and another wife, but as congenial as their life seemed, Ann foiled every attempt he made to become more intimate. He ached to touch her and hold her, but invariably when the moment came for them to steal off alone together, she pulled away. He was willing to be patient, but the constraint between them was something Chase had no idea how to breach.

He'd seen the contradictions in Ann's eyes the day they met, and he'd been as drawn by the shade in them as the sunshine. He'd been drawn as much by the longing and the reticence he'd sensed in her, as by her integrity and her resolve to do what she thought was right.

What he'd seen had made him want to take care of her, and he had. He'd wanted her to trust him, and she did.

Just not enough.

So Chase stared out at the dawn instead of turning to Ann. He drank down the dregs of his coffee instead of taking her in his arms and licking that raspberry color from her mouth.

Ann put the "very nearly" in his otherwise perfect life, and Chase didn't know how to set things right between them.

Just then, Ann leaned over the railing for a better look at what seemed even to Chase, who knew every eddy and every bend, an unremarkable stretch of riverbank.

"Where are we?" she asked him. "Why are we stopping?"

"I don't know." Chase braced his palms on the railing and leaned over, too. "This is northeastern Nebraska; there can't be more than a handful of homesteaders here yet."

Still, the *Andromeda* was making a landing. The engines changed their pitch and the wheel its tempo. The deck shivered underfoot.

Chase peered ahead even more intently. He knew they were far enough down the Missouri that they didn't need to worry about being set upon by Indians. Yet something about this place, about the man waiting at the edge of the river, and the heavy, high-sided wagon parked back in the trees made Chase's palms itch.

Rue nuzzled the steamer up tight to the sandy bank in a feat of impressive steersmanship. Cal held the boat against the brisk downstream current as the deckhands ran out the gangway. Jake Skirlin strode across it with a sheaf of papers in hand. Joel Curry and his roustabouts followed, straining under the weight of four heavy wooden boxes.

"Mr. Skirlin," Chase called down. "I don't recall seeing a landing scheduled for so early this morning."

Skirlin glanced up at him. "Morning, Captain," he said, his expression as bland as tapioca. "We missed this delivery on the way upriver."

Chase knew that happened sometimes, especially in such swampy, broken country as this. It was easy to steam right past a transfer point unless someone was there to flag them down. Yet something about this landing felt wrong to him.

"Is there more to be off-loaded, Mr. Skirlin?" Chase pushed back from the railing. "You need any help?"

Curry answered him from where he and his rousters were wrestling the boxes into the back of the wagon. "No, sir. This is the whole of it."

"There's just the bill of lading to see to," Skirlin told him, "and we can get underway."

In spite of his misgivings, Chase nodded and let his officers get on about their work.

He didn't even think about Barnaby Greene's allegations until they were a good long way downstream. When he did, Chase swung around and stared upriver. Had this been one of the "unscheduled stops" Barnaby claimed the Gold Star boats were making? Had the *Andromeda* just off-loaded contraband?

Chase did his best to remember everything he could about that sandy stretch of riverbank, the tangle of scrub trees, and especially about those big, oblong boxes. His impressions just weren't sharp enough to answer the questions plaguing him. Had the boxes they'd just delivered to this godforsaken corner of Nebraska been full of rifles?

Beside him, Ann drained her coffee and slid her feet into her shoes. The sun was up. The passengers were stirring, taking their morning constitutionals or making trips to the privy.

"The girls will be rising anytime now," Ann said as she pushed away from the railing. "And the minute she's awake, Christina is going to want her breakfast."

Chase caught her arm, needing to have Ann to himself for a few moments longer. He wished she would turn and smile at him. He wished she'd say just one word that would make him feel that if he was steadfast and patient, everything would turn out the way he wanted it to.

He wished she'd say something that would divert him from the suspicion knotting his belly.

But Ann didn't smile. She didn't reassure him.

"I need to go," was all she said and slid away toward the steps that led up to the Texas deck.

ANN WAS ALL TOO FAMILIAR WITH THE LONGING IN Chase's eyes—and she fled from it. She darted up the steps two at a time, darted toward the cabin where her daughter lay sleeping. Once she got inside she'd be able to close the door on Chase's hope and his boundless expectation. Until she did, his need for her would follow her like smoke.

"Annie?"

Chase's voice caught up with her as she reached the top of the stairs. That deep, rich timbre stroked goose-flesh up her back and made her turn to him, almost against her will. He stood where she had left him braced against the railing, magnificent in all his rangy grace, big and rumpled and unabashedly masculine, limned by the copper light of the early morning sun.

Her mouth went dry just looking at him.

"Annie," he asked, "shall I come and escort you to supper?"

He liked doing that. He liked knocking on her door, draping the shawl around her shoulders, offering her his arm. He liked that she dressed just for him and wore the silver filigree earbobs he'd given her as a belated wedding gift. He liked that she took extra time with her hair and dabbed lavender water on her wrists and throat.

And Ann liked doing it.

She liked pleasing Chase with these simple things. But he wanted so much more from her than a little primping and her company at dinner.

He'd made what he wanted clear enough that night three weeks ago, and Ann wished with all her heart she'd been able to give in to him.

God knows, Chase deserved what other husbands had. He'd married her and given her his protection. He'd lent her his strength the night Christina was born and given her baby his name. He'd opened his world to her and made her a part of his family. Never in her life had anyone been so generous or so patient or cared for her so much.

And Ann loved him for it.

But Chase wanted it all, everything a marriage could be. He wanted a place to come home to at the end of a run, a wife who would welcome him with open arms, and children who were truly his. He wanted kisses and caresses, tenderness and trust. He wanted to lie with her and hold her and touch her in ways Ann couldn't even bear thinking about. He wanted her to open herself to him and accept him as her true husband.

Ann couldn't do that.

Chase was poised and waiting for their life to start, waiting for it to turn into something wonderful. Ann didn't know if she could go on from where they were. Her reticence made her ache with shame and regret.

She loved this good, strong man with all her heart, but she couldn't give him the things he needed. She couldn't be the kind of wife she ought to be to him. And if she couldn't give him what he deserved, she knew the longing she saw in his eyes would turn to disappointment. It would become bitterness or anger, and he would end up hating her—or hating himself. Ann refused to let that happen.

She had to leave.

As long as she was who she was, she had no choice. The money her mother had left her, gave her—and Chase—a chance to make new lives for themselves. And since she couldn't give Chase a home and family, she at least owed him his freedom.

Without her and Christina to encumber him, Chase could set off and see the world. He could find another woman, someone who was able to give him the warmth and affection Ann never could. He could start a family of his own.

She blinked back tears at the thought of someone else

going down to supper on Chase's arm, of someone else smiling at him and turning her face up for his kisses. Of him holding some other woman's baby in his arms. Yet Ann knew that if she couldn't be the wife Chase needed her to be, then she ought to give him the chance to be happy with somebody else.

She'd speak to Mr. Throckmorton when they got back and make arrangements for a bank draft to be waiting at the end of the *Andromeda*'s next run.

"Annie?" Chase called out, still looking up at her from the deck below.

Looking up at her as if the world hadn't changed in this single moment.

"Shall I come get you for supper?"

Ann swallowed hard and nodded. "I'll be ready."

Aɴɴ ᴡɪsʜᴇᴅ ᴛʜᴀᴛ ᴘᴜʟʟɪɴɢ ɪɴ ᴀᴛ Hᴀʀᴅᴇsᴛʏ's Lᴀɴᴅɪɴɢ didn't feel so much like coming home.

She took delight in the way the children came running at the first blast of the *Andromeda*'s whistle, appreciated how the men in the woodlot lay down their tools and headed to the riverbank to greet them. She loved that the women scurried down from houses at the top of the bluff, waving and shouting their hellos. But today Ann watched through a veil of tears as the Hardestys gathered to welcome them.

She'd made her choice. Yet as sure as she was that she

must give Chase back his freedom, Ann was going to miss coming here, being a part of this.

Even now a contingent of women was clustering at the foot of the gangway to visit with her and Christina.

"Oh, isn't Christina the dearest little thing?" Chase's sister D'arcy crooned the moment Ann's shoe soles hit dry land. "May I hold her?"

Ann eased the baby into her sister-in-law's arms and watched D'arcy's wide mouth bow and her broad face soften as she cooed to her niece. Clearly D'arcy needed children of her own, and Ann decided to ask Evangeline if there was a particular suitor her sister fancied. Then all at once, Ann realized she wasn't going to be around to see D'arcy marry. She'd never meet Chase's brother Quinn who was away at medical school, or Millie who'd gone with her husband to homestead in Nebraska.

Ann's throat clogged with regret when she considered a hundred conversations she'd never have, the family recipes she'd never learn to make, and all the years she'd never share with the people who'd become so dear to her. She might have wept right then and there if Silas Jenkins hadn't poked his head over Suzanne's broad shoulder for a look at the baby.

"You know, Ann," he offered. "She may not have your coloring, but I think Christina is going to have that dimple in her chin, just like yours."

"And there's something about the shape of her eyes..." his wife agreed.

Ann could have hugged both Suzanne and Silas. She

hadn't realized how eager she'd been for someone to see a resemblance between her and her daughter.

"What I want to know," Benjamin asked as he and Bartholomew insinuated themselves on either side of D'arcy, "is whether that baby is ever going to get real hair."

"Benjamin!" the women chorused, admonishing him.

"As I recall," Lydia said, coming up behind her son and ruffling his curls, "you and your brother were bald as horse chestnuts 'til you were a year old."

"Aw, Ma!" Bartholomew shouted and both boys ran off.

Lydia watched them go, then turned her attention to the baby. "I'm claiming a grandmother's privilege," she declared and gathered Christina out of D'arcy's arms.

She held the baby in the crook of one elbow and stroked her cheek. Christina gurgled contentedly.

Lydia glanced from the baby to Ann. "You've taken to mothering like a duck to water, now, haven't you, girl?"

No words had ever caught Ann so much by surprise or pleased her more than Lydia's praise. She lowered her lashes to shield a sudden wash of teary gratitude. "Chase and Evangeline showed me what to do."

"No, it's more than that," Lydia continued, beginning to sway. "Some women take to mothering like it's natural as breathing. I think you're one of them."

"Now, me," Suzanne said, saving Ann from having to answer. "I barely knew which end of my children to diaper until they were six weeks old."

Then, as if to belie his mother's words, Matt ran up

and threw his arms around her waist. "Can I go with Cal and Barney to see the engine room?"

When she nodded, he ran off whooping.

"It's not 'til children get about Matt's age that they get interesting," Suzanne qualified. Silas slipped his arm around her waist and gave her a proprietary squeeze.

Ann glanced hastily away. She and Chase would never share that kind of easy affection. They would never set off sparks when they looked at each other the way Etta Mae and Will did. They could never aspire to the kind of enduring love that had kept Enoch and Lydia together for more than thirty years.

Just seeing the Hardestys together reinforced her decision to leave. She'd failed as Chase's wife, and she couldn't think of anything in her life that had grieved her more.

AFTER TWO DAYS OF TRYING TO SPEAK TO RUE ALONE, Chase finally caught up with his brother just as he was passing out the last of the candy he'd brought for the children.

"That's all the licorice," the younger man announced with a flutter of his hands.

"Next time, Uncle Rue," Katie asked him, "could you bring us *my* favorite candy?"

"I'll bring anything you want, sweetheart," Rue promised.

"Then bring peppermints," Katie cried and scampered away.

"Ma won't thank you for giving them sweets if it rots their teeth," Chase admonished as he ambled closer.

"A little treat never hurt anyone," Rue retorted and produced two cheroots from the inside pocket of his jacket.

Chase accepted one of the cigars, and then a light. He wasn't sure how to broach the subject he'd come to discuss, but Rue saved him the trouble.

"What you want to ask me is about the landing yesterday morning, isn't it?"

The hair rippled at the back of Chase's neck. "Did Skirlin tell you what we were delivering?"

Chase had gone over and over that landing in his mind, doing his best to convince himself it was just like the scores of others they made in the course of a run.

"Skirlin came up to the wheelhouse about half an hour after we got underway," Rue went on. "He told me we'd missed a delivery on the upstream run and that someone would flag us down."

Chase licked his lips before he spoke. "Did you—did you think about what Barnaby Greene said that night at Fort Benton?"

"Not until I saw the boxes."

"Jesus, Rue!" He ran his hand through his hair. "Do you think we just delivered Spencer carbines for the Indians?"

Rue reached across and squeezed his arm. "We don't know that's what they were."

Chase was suddenly glad for the din of half a hundred voices around them. "God knows, there'd be big money in running guns. With the troubles the Sioux and Cheyenne are causing along the Bozeman Trail, repeating rifles are worth their weight in gold."

"It's a long pull between here and Wyoming," Rue argued. "Though that fellow was a freighter, wasn't he?"

A frisson of recognition ran the length of Chase's back. He'd noticed the mules and his high-sided wagon parked back in the trees. "You think Curry and Skirlin are the ones behind this?"

"Whatever's going on," Rue said with a shake of his head, "we're going to need proof before we go to the authorities."

Chase knew that, too.

"And, Chase—" Rue waited until Chase acknowledged him with the lift of his chin. "There's no way you could have known we were carrying rifles."

"The *Andromeda*'s my responsibility," Chase said under his breath. "I should have known."

They were just finishing their cigars when Lydia Hardesty came bustling in their direction.

"She after you or me?" Rue asked laconically.

"Can't be me she wants," Chase murmured. "*I* haven't done anything wrong."

But it was him his mother wanted.

"So how's Evangeline doing on her own?" Lydia demanded once she'd hugged Rue and sent him ambling back to the boat.

Chase glanced toward where Evie bent her dark, curly head close to Mary Alice's blonde one. "Evie's been wonderful with Christina," Chase reported, "and a big help to Ann. She wouldn't be back to baking if Evie wasn't aboard to help with the baby."

"Well, it was time Evangeline saw a bit more of the world than we can show her. She was getting restless," Lydia confided, "and I wasn't sure what to do with her."

"We're glad to have her."

"And how is Rue?"

She wanted an accounting, so Chase told her.

"I can see how Ann is. How are you?" she finally asked him.

Chase's gaze lingered on Ann, the clean, graceful lines of her profile, the way the honey-colored swag of hair draped along the line of her jaw as she bent over their daughter. Something powerful and bittersweet tightened in his chest.

"I'm fine."

"Are you, boy?"

Ma had always seen through him like he was water, so it shouldn't have surprised him that she'd recognized the longing in his eyes when he looked at his wife.

"I love her, Ma," he admitted, "but I'm not sure this marriage is going to work out. She doesn't want—" Chase flushed at what he'd been about to admit to his mother, then went ahead anyway. "Ann doesn't want to lie with me. Everytime I try to touch her she draws away. It makes me wonder if something happened. If she was—"

The word stuck in his throat.

Lydia pursed her lips, and Chase thought for a moment his mother wasn't going to answer him. Then she reached up and smoothed back his hair as if he were a child and not a man towering over her.

"You give Annie time," she advised softly. "I think she needs all the love and understanding you've got to give her. If that's what happened, then she's got good reason to be afraid, and probably some things to figure out before she can see her way clear to turn to you. So you be patient."

"I'll try, Ma."

"And when you and Ann come together—"

Chase nodded.

"—you take care with her."

"I will."

Her green eyes glowed when she smiled up at him. "You were always such a good boy, Chase, and you've grown into such a good man. Your father and I have always been so proud of you."

He turned to look at the tall, broad-shouldered man talking to Rue at the foot of the *Andromeda*'s gangway.

The notion that his father might be proud of him whip-sawed through him, cutting once with the quick, sharp joy of thinking it might be true and again with a bitter surge of disbelief.

"I'm glad, Ma," he said with an edge to his voice.

Lydia opened her mouth and closed it again.

Just then, Joel Curry shouted that the wood they'd

needed was stacked in the bow. Chase could hear that Cal was limbering up the paddle wheel.

He bent and gave his mother a final hug, then stared toward the steamer. It was time to go.

And maybe he was glad of it.

chapter twelve

A NN CHERISHED EACH DAY OF THE *ANDROMEDA'S*
second packet run as if they were pearls on a string. She
took joy in the boats they passed, the landings they made,
the banks lush with summer growth. She lingered over
the luminous dawn and glowing sunsets, savored the
sound of crickets *cheep*ing in the dark and the sultry scent
of the evening breeze.

She spent extra time with the passengers and the crew.
She visited with the women in the ladies' salon and sat
with Barney and Cal after supper when Cal smoked his
pipe. She helped Beck Morgan write a love letter to a girl
in Cairo he was sweet on, and did another mountain of
mending for the roustabouts. She took delight in her
nights in Frenchy's galley. She savored their outbound
stop at Hardesty's Landing—the second to last time she
and Christina would visit Chase's family.

She hoarded memories of everyone aboard—but especially of Chase. How he'd brought her an armload of black-eyed Susans one afternoon while they were wooding up. The way he tucked Christina into the crook of his arm and carried her around as he went about his duties. How sometimes when he was standing watch on the hurricane deck, he'd grin like he owned the world.

Now that she was leaving, Ann realized just how deeply she'd fallen in love with Chase. But instead of that love bringing her joy, it intensified the ache of regret. Loving him couldn't free Ann from the past; it didn't change who Christina's father was. It didn't alter that no matter how much she wanted to, she couldn't be the wife Chase needed her to be. She had to leave for all their sakes, before she ruined everything.

The *Andromeda* was a day and a half out of Sioux City on the downstream run when one of the deckhands *thumped* on the door to Ann's cabin.

"Mr. Watkins said to come see if you have anything for burns," he told her.

Since the incident with the bees, Ann was the one the men came to when they needed tending. So she left Christina in Evie's care, and grabbed up her basket of ointments and bandages.

When she reached the steamer's wide main deck Cal Watkins was ranting at two young rousters who were stripped to the waist and draped in dripping compresses.

"You damn fools!" he fumed. "Why the devil were you sleeping under those steam gauges? Didn't you know you could get burned?"

Judging by their reddened skin, neither Billy Martin nor Nate Ogden had realized the danger.

Ann hunkered down among the barrels and crates in the open section of the steamer's lower deck and quickly examined both the men. "Those burns may hurt," she sympathized when she was done, "but they really aren't all that serious."

"It was good of you to come down, Mrs. Hardesty," Cal offered in aggravation, "to look after such fools as these."

"Well, I've got just the thing for those burns," she said, and pried the lid off a jar of thick, brownish ointment. All three of the men leaned away to escape the smell.

"I don't know which is worse, Mr. Watkins," Billy Martin began, "the burns or *that a-romer!*"

Just then the bells in the engine room rang, and Cal hurried off to answer them, with Barney romping at his heels.

"Go ahead and use that stuff on them," he shouted back. "Can't make 'em smell much worse than they do already!"

Ann was still dabbing Nate and Billy when Rue happened by a few minutes later. "Why on earth are you anointing those boys with that noxious goo?" he demanded, taking out a handkerchief to wave beneath his nose.

"We run afoul of them steam gauges," Billy spoke up. "This stuff may be rank as a skunk's hole, but Mrs. Hardesty claims it works wonders on burns."

"Well, it does," Rue agreed, flashing a grin. "But I'd

think twice about letting her dab me with a mixture of bear grease, scorpion gizzard, and horse piss!"

Both men turned to Ann askance.

Ann refused to be outdone by Rue's blandishments. "It's an old family recipe," she averred, "passed down from a witch in medieval France."

"My ma's folks was from the middle of France," Nate put in.

Rue burst out laughing. "Well, the captain certainly does swear by that salve's curative properties."

"You used this on the cap'n, ma'am?"

"The night he brought those two tykes out of the fire," Ann assured them. "Only the captain didn't snivel about the smell."

Both men looked awed, as if they hoped the ointment would inoculate them with that same kind of daring. "Well, you know," Billy ventured, "it *does* kind of smell like horse piss!"

Ann bit back a laugh and glared at Rue. "Thank you so much for opening this particular avenue of conjecture."

Rue grinned back. "Glad to help."

But when Ann glanced up a moment later, Rue seemed intent on something going on at the far side of the deck. Though Ann craned her neck, she didn't see anything unusual—just Joel Curry and Jake Skirlin wrestling boxes out of the hold.

"Rue?" she began.

Though Rue gestured her to silence, Curry turned at

the sound of her voice. The mate said something to Skirlin, then Skirlin looked across at them, too.

It was an odd moment, though Ann couldn't say exactly why.

Then Rue pushed to his feet and ambled toward them. He made some comment Ann couldn't hear, laughed at Skirlin's answer, then continued on back to the engine room.

Ann had just finished bandaging Nate and Billy's burns when Barney started barking on the far side of the deck. Something about the sharp, frantic sound of it brought Ann to her feet and sent her rushing in that direction. She reached the starboard side just as Rue crashed through the steamer's railing and fell backwards into the river.

"Rue!" she screamed, knowing he'd be dragged right under the boat and into the paddle wheel. "Rue!"

"Man overboard!" Curry bellowed from just behind her, then flung one of the steamer's long, cork floats into the water.

The *Andromeda*'s speed immediately lagged.

"Rue!" Ann yelled, leaning over the edge of the deck and peering into the water. "Damn it, Rue! Where are you?"

There was no sign of her brother-in-law. Not so much as a trail of bubbles.

She heard footsteps thunder overhead and a man leaped from the deck above. As he plunged into the water, Ann caught a glimpse of his clothes and hair—and realized it was her husband.

Ann grabbed one of the uprights and hung as far over the guard as she dared. How deep was the water here? Were there rocks at the bottom to break Chase's legs, or branches to snag him? Could Chase even swim? And if he could, what chance did he have of finding Rue down there in the silt and the darkness?

Endless seconds dragged by. Ann's heart rattled around inside her chest like a coin in a box.

"Please," she whispered, her entire prayer in a single word.

At last Chase bobbed to the surface a good way upstream and off the starboard side. He glanced around to get his bearings, gasped for breath and dove again.

Beck Morgan leaped into action. "Throw more floats!" he shouted. "Prepare to launch the yawl!"

The deckhands scrambled to obey.

Once the skiff was afloat, Morgan, Curry, and several deckhands climbed aboard. They rowed out a half a dozen yards and held their position, preparing to haul either living men or dead ones out of the river.

Ann stared at the water, but could see no more than its dark, impenetrable surface.

Her breath quivered in her throat. How could Chase hope to find his brother in that murk and debris? If finding Rue became hopeless, would she be able to convince him to stop looking? *And if Rue died, would her husband be able to live with himself?*

Then from near at hand Ann heard a tremulous, high-pitched whimper and turned to find Evangeline standing at the foot of the stairs clutching the baby against her chest.

"Oh, Ann!" Evie sobbed. "Did Rue really fall overboard?"

"Chase has gone in after him," Ann reassured her, sweeping both Evie and Christina up in her arms. "Beck Morgan's taken out the yawl. He'll pick them up as soon as they surface."

"Chase *will* save Rue, won't he?"

Ann looked into Evie's teary eyes. "Hasn't Chase been pulling Rue out of scrapes his whole life long?"

Evie's sniffle ended in a nervous giggle. "Then of course he'll rescue him!"

Ann held Evie and the baby close as they waited.

"There!" someone on the boiler deck shouted. "There's someone in the water a hundred yards astern and off to starboard."

The men in the yawl set off rowing.

Ann shaded her eyes, trying to pick out a swimmer amid the tucks and the ruffles in the steamer's wake.

"I see them!" Evie crowed.

Ann struggled to find the single dark shape on the river's shifting surface. It was too far away to say if it was one man or two. She held her breath until the skiff pulled up alongside, until she saw Beck Morgan drag first one body and then a second into the boat.

A cheer went up as the yawl turned toward home.

Ann's knees wobbled with relief. Then, because she didn't know if both Chase and Rue were even going to be alive when the yawl pulled up alongside, she steered Evie toward the stairs.

"You take the baby on up to your stateroom while I—"

"Please, Ann!" the girl begged. "Don't send me away."

"I'm going to be busy taking care of your brothers," she argued, "and I need to be sure Christina—"

"I *have* to know if they're all right!"

Before Ann could think what more to say, the yawl bumped up against the side of the steamer. Chase sat hunched in the bottom of the skiff with Rue's head pillowed in his lap.

"Is Rue all right?" Evangeline demanded.

"He's still breathing," her brother answered.

Ann read volumes in those three words. "There, you've seen your brothers," she said. "Now go and do as I asked."

Evie cast one last glance at where the deckhands were lifting Rue out of the yawl, then she started up the steps.

Cee

"HE LOOKS LIKE HE'S ALREADY DEAD."

Ann did her best to ignore her husband's words as she worked over where Rue lay limp and gray in the center of the captain's bunk. Except for the faint rattle when he breathed and the bloom of red seeping through the bandage around his head, she might have thought that, too.

"Are there any doctors aboard?" she asked him. "Does anyone know more about taking care of an injured man than I do?"

"Skirlin says there's a faith healer among the deck passengers. He's offered to lay on hands."

What could it hurt? Ann found herself thinking as she ran her palms along the sleek, angular lines of her brother-in-law's body. She checked Rue's right leg for breaks, then gently rotated his left to a more natural position. She braced it with pillows and wondered what she could use for splints.

"How is he?"

She could hear the dread in Chase's voice and looked across to where he stood braced in the doorway between the bedroom and the sitting room. He was battered and scuffed himself, shivering in spite of the heat, and dripping all over the floor.

He could have been hurt every bit as badly as Rue. He might well have drowned trying to rescue his brother. Her hands shook knowing that, but she stifled the need to go to him, wrap Chase up in her arms, and hang on forever.

She turned to Rue instead. "Since he hasn't stirred," she began, "I think it's likely he's suffered a concussion. His left leg is broken, and while he's unconscious I'm going to do what I can to stabilize it."

Chase crossed the room and stood looking down at Rue.

"Considering how long he was in the water," she went on, "his lungs sound remarkably clear."

"That's good, isn't it?" Chase asked quietly.

"What isn't good," she said and dabbed at the bright

pink foam forming at the corners of Rue's mouth, "is that there's blood in his saliva. . . ."

Ann couldn't say what that meant exactly, but she did know enough to be afraid for Rue's life.

"I've given Lucien Boudreau orders to Hardesty's Landing," Chase went on.

She knew he'd do that, run for home. For Chase, home meant care and security and people who would be every bit as concerned for Rue as he was. If there had been a sizable town between here and Hardesty's Landing, Ann might have argued. As it was, getting Rue to Lydia seemed his best chance for survival.

God knows, it was pure serendipity that young Boudreau, a pilot who'd begged passage downstream, had been in the wheelhouse when Rue went overboard. If he hadn't, Chase couldn't have left his post, and Rue most certainly would have been lost.

Ann slid her arm around her husband's waist and, though it broke her heart to say the words, she knew Chase had to hear them. "You've got to accept that Rue may be too badly hurt for anyone to help him."

He shook his head. "We'll get Doc Meyers to tend him," he insisted, laying a hand on his brother's shoulder. "Doc pulled Pa through snakebite and some of the younger children through scarlet fever. He'll get Rue through this, too."

Just then Rue coughed again and the froth of pink bubbled to his lips. Ann wiped it away, fear weighing on her heart.

"Doc Meyers will fix Rue up as good as new, Annie," Chase insisted. "Just you wait."

NEITHER LYDIA NOR DOC MEYERS WERE ABLE TO FIX RUE up "as good as new." That's why the Hardesty family had gathered in Lydia's parlor—to worry and wait. Silas Jenkins stood over Suzanne, who knitted fiercely in the chair by the fire. Will had tucked Etta Mae into the crook of his good arm. Evangeline sat sniffling into a handkerchief while D'arcy patted and consoled her. Enoch hadn't once left Lydia's side since they'd brought Rue up to the house.

While the rest of the Hardestys seemed to draw strength from being together—Chase sat with his head in his hands. Beyond the orders he'd given when they left the steamer, he hadn't said a word to anyone. Ann could see in the sag of those wide shoulders and the stain of responsibility that darkened the blue of his eyes, that Chase blamed himself for Rue getting hurt.

She hitched as close as she could to him on the wide settee, but Chase was oblivious. He didn't stir until Lydia came in.

"How is he, Ma?" Will asked, speaking for all of them.

Lydia's face was scored with lines of concern, but her voice was level. "Rue's lucky to be alive," she began. "He hit his head and has been drifting in and out of consciousness. His leg is broken, and he's cracked at least one of his ribs. Those are injuries we can take care of; they're things that will heal."

Everyone seemed to sense the gravity of what she was about to tell them. John straightened in his chair. The twins' eyes went round. Even Suzanne's knitting needles fell silent.

Ann clasped Chase's hand in both of hers.

Lydia settled back on her heels as if she were steeling herself. "Doc thinks Rue might be bleeding inside. If he is, there's not a thing any one of us can do to help him."

Evie sobbed and buried her face against D'arcy's neck. Etta Mae nestled close against Will's side. Silas closed his hands on Suzanne's wide shoulders.

"You mean, Rue's going to die?" Benjamin asked, his boyish chin trembling.

"What I'm saying is that he's in God's hands." Lydia's mouth pinched tighter, as if she was going to have a few words to say to the Almighty about hurting one of her children. "What I'm saying is that while Doc and I are going to do everything we can for him, Rue's fate isn't up to us."

Chase dropped his head into his hands again.

"You did everything you could," Ann whispered, her palm pressed to his bowed back.

"I should have done more."

Stuart Hardesty, square and bluff and two years younger than Rue, shook his head in protest. "How could he have fallen overboard? Rue's lithe as a cat."

"Maybe he caught his foot on a rope," John suggested.

"Maybe the railing was loose," Bartholomew offered.

"Maybe he took some ridiculous dare," Will put in.

"Like the time you bet him he couldn't walk the barn's ridgepole?" D'arcy reminded him.

"And he slid right into the manure pile?" John recalled and everyone snickered.

"It doesn't matter how he fell overboard," Etta Mae pointed out, ever practical. "What matters is that there are people here to take care of Rue as long as he needs us."

"Doc Meyers has agreed to spend the night," Lydia told them, matching her daughter-in-law's resolution. "Your father's with Rue now. I mean to go back in a little while."

"I'll stay tonight," Suzanne volunteered, covering Silas's hand with her own as if drawing on his strength. "To keep Ma company."

As the others made their plans, Lydia crossed the room to where Ann and Chase sat together on the settee. "I want to thank you," she began, her gaze intent on her eldest son, "for bringing Rue home to me. I know the risk you took going into that river, and I want you to know—"

"How could I have done anything else?" Chase sounded impatient, almost angry.

A frisson of distress creased Lydia's brow. "You've always looked after him, Chase, right from the day he was born."

"I'm sorry I didn't do a better job of it this time."

She cupped his cheek and tilted his face so she could look into his eyes. "I won't have you blaming yourself for this."

Chase pursed his lips, then glanced away, not able to accept the absolution his mother was offering him. Still, Lydia's hand lingered on his skin almost as if she were seeking amid the planes and angles of that hard, masculine face the boy she'd held and comforted.

Then she turned to Ann. "I want to thank you for what you did, as well. Doc Meyers said you immobilized Rue's leg every bit as well as he could have done it himself."

"Chase and Beck Morgan helped," Ann answered.

"I'll make sure I thank Beck before you leave."

Ann hadn't even considered that they had a schedule to keep. No matter how Rue was, they had goods to deliver before they spoiled, passengers who needed to make connections, and mail contracts to fulfill. But how was Chase going to climb aboard the *Andromeda* and head downstream? How were they going to leave Hardesty's Landing not knowing if Rue was going to live?

Just then, Enoch appeared in the doorway. "Lydia," he said sharply. "Rue's coughing blood. Doc says come."

Lydia brushed past her husband and hurried down the hall.

Enoch lingered in the doorway, his gaze drifting over each of his children. The way his eyes gleamed said how much each of them meant to him: Will who'd returned from the war battered but unbowed, D'arcy with her dark beauty and quiet strength, the twins only half-grown but already shining with the promise of the men they would become. He turned to each of them in turn as if he were drawing his own strength from seeing his family together.

Finally, Enoch looked long and hard at his eldest son. Though a scowl pinched the corners of his mouth, Ann saw beyond that rough, weathered face to the tenderness in his eyes. They shone bright with pride and approval, things Chase had never been able to see because he was too stubborn—or too afraid—to look for himself.

Chase never saw that his father understood the burden he was carrying by putting his love for the people in this room beyond all else. Enoch understood, because it was him, not Lydia, who'd taught Chase what family could mean to a man.

Enoch's gaze lingered a moment longer, then moved to Ann herself. She immediately felt the weight of Enoch's expectations. Silas had settled Suzanne's fluttering with his touch. Etta Mae had taken up the mantle of Will's leadership. D'arcy was looking after Evie. Even the boys, for all their youth, seemed to have banded together.

In that moment Ann saw that Enoch expected her to stand by Chase, to see to him and console him. But what did Ann have to offer when Chase didn't think he deserved to be comforted? What could she give him when she was leaving Chase and the *Andromeda* when they reached St. Louis?

Then, with a reassuring touch on Evangeline's shoulder and a murmur to Will, Enoch turned and went back to the room at the end of the hall.

Once he was gone, Ann rose hesitantly.

"Where are you going?" Chase demanded, glaring up at her.

"I'm going back to the *Andromeda*," she said, "and I'd

like you to come with me. We have a schedule to keep, and even if Lucien Boudreau is taking Rue's watches in the pilothouse, you have duties of your own to see to tomorrow, don't you?"

"But Rue—"

"Ann's right," Suzanne insisted as she jabbed her knitting needles into the knob of wool. "Rue has all of us here to look after him."

"Go on, Chase," Will encouraged him. "You got Rue here; you did your part. We'll do the rest."

"If we need you," Silas assured him, "we'll come get you."

D'arcy rose and glided toward them. "Since Christina's already asleep upstairs, why don't you let Evie and me look after her tonight."

Seeing how these people took care of one another made Ann's throat ache with tenderness. She hugged D'arcy by way of thanks, then with Chase unwillingly in tow, she knocked on the door at the end of the hall to say good night.

"He's holding his own," Lydia reported.

Beyond the open door, Ann could see that Rue lay pale and inert in the middle of Enoch and Lydia's big bed. He looked even more battered than he had this afternoon and far more fragile.

"Are you going back to the *Andromeda?*" Chase's mother asked.

"Ann's making me," he protested.

"As well she should," Lydia answered and wrapped her arms around her tall son. "You risked your life to pull Rue out of the river when any other captain would have considered him lost. You think on that tonight, Chase, instead of blaming yourself."

Chase nodded and stepped away.

As Ann said her own good-nights, Lydia pressed her warm, wrinkled cheek to Ann's far smoother one. For a moment Ann wallowed in the scent of rosewater and the comfort of having Lydia's arms around her. It had been so long since anyone had mothered her, longer still since she'd experienced this sense of belonging. The knowledge that in a week's time she was going to turn her back on the Hardestys tore her heart anew.

"Thank you for taking such good care of one of my sons this afternoon," the older woman whispered. "Now I'm asking you to look after the other. See that Chase rests. See that he doesn't spend the night brooding over something he couldn't help."

"She'll do her best, Lydia," Enoch said, coming up behind his wife and resting his hands on her shoulders. "You will do your best to take care of him, won't you, Ann?"

"Yes," she agreed quietly. "I promise."

ANN SAW ALMOST IMMEDIATELY THAT SHE WASN'T GOING to be able to keep the promise she'd made to Enoch and Lydia. Chase wasn't going to let her get close enough to take care of him. She saw how agitated he was, and though he spoke barely a dozen words the whole way back to the *Andromeda*, she could hear the litany of blame and self-doubt that ran beneath his silence.

When they reached the door to the captain's cabin, Ann grabbed his wrist and asked, "What are you going to do now?"

He shifted skittishly from foot to foot. "What I *want* is to go sit with Rue, but I know Ma won't let me."

She squeezed gently. "You did your part this morning. You saved his life."

He glanced back toward the house. "That isn't enough."

"This isn't your part of the fight. Leave Rue to your ma and Doc Meyers."

He swung around and glared at her. "And what would you have me do in the meantime?"

"You need to rest."

"Hell, Annie!" he burst out. "How do you expect me to rest when Rue might be dying up there?"

"All right, what can we do instead?"

"Do?"

"Is there someplace we can go for a little while?" she suggested. "Someplace cool, someplace quiet?"

Chase hesitated, then grabbed her hand. Barely a minute later, they bolted across the gangway as if the hounds of hell were at their heels. They ran the length of the woodlot and scrambled up a steep, twisting trail only someone who'd followed it a thousand times could navigate in the dark.

They climbed until Ann was stumbling and gasping for breath. At the top of the path, Chase led her through woods so close and dark she could barely see his silhouette ahead of her. They clambered through a maze of towering rocks, then stepped into a clearing at the top of the bluffs.

A world veiled with midnight opened up before them. The Missouri, dimpled with moonlight, shimmered a hundred feet below. The sky spread clear and black, sliced by a sly smirk of crescent moon and stippled with stars. The valley that stretched to the horizon lay cloaked in crepe.

"Where are we?" Ann asked breathlessly.

"This is the point," Chase told her. He seemed calmer somehow, as if the climb had burned off some of that frantic energy. "It's the highest spot for miles around. When I was a boy, I'd come up here and watch the river."

"Is this where you decided to become a riverboat captain?"

"Oh, I never aspired to anything so grand as that. But I knew even then the river was where I belonged."

Ann stepped into a shallow grassy bowl just back from the edge of the cliff and sat down on her heels. From far below, she could hear the faint hush of the river's passage and smell the rich fecund dampness of earth and night. A soft, sultry wind feathered up the cliffside, and the trees along the edge of the bluff sighed with pleasure.

"The view must be glorious in daylight," she whispered.

Chase dropped down on the grass beside her. "You can see half of Nebraska across the river."

Ann lay back and stared up at the sky. "I think I can see a million stars. . . ."

Chase stretched out beside her. "Look," he offered, pointing. "There's the constellation Andromeda."

They lay in the soft, whispery grass listening to the river and watching the sky. The cool and the quiet worked their magic.

"I remember the night Rue was born," Chase said.

Ann rolled toward him. "You do?"

"It was just about nightfall when his mama came knocking at our door." Chase was calling up the memory to keep Rue close tonight. "Francie was an octoroon and had been a white man's mistress somewhere in Louisiana. She decided to head North so her first child would be born in freedom."

Ann reached out to squeeze his shoulder, encouraging him.

"The people who'd been helping Francie had rowed her across the Missouri a few miles south of here. She was supposed to keep to the woods and bypass Hardesty's Landing."

"But she needed help."

"It was her time," Chase confirmed. "Ma took her in and made her as comfortable as she could. Francie must have been in labor, though I don't suppose I knew that then. What I do remember is Ma waking me in the middle of the night and handing me this squalling baby—"

"Rue," she guessed with a laugh.

"My God, Annie! He was little and red-faced and yelling like he wanted folks in Omaha to hear him. 'He's yours to look after,' Ma told me, ''til I get his mama in the ground.'"

"Rue's mother died giving birth?" Ann couldn't seem to help the waver in her voice. The night Christina was born came back to her, how frightened she'd been. How sure she'd been that neither she nor Christina would survive.

Chase slipped his arm around her and pulled her close. Ann turned her face into his shoulder, accepting the comfort he was offering, though she knew she ought to be comforting him.

"I was used to tending little ones." His breath stirred her hair. "But Rue just kept hollering."

"That hasn't changed, has it?"

Ann hadn't realized how tightly Chase was holding himself until he laughed. More of that terrible energy burned away.

"He was so noisy, I took him out onto the porch so he wouldn't wake the others. I rocked him—and rocked him and rocked him." His voice wavered a little more with every word. "I rocked him until it was light, rocked him so long that when Ma came to take him back, I really did think he belonged to me."

Ann splayed her hand across his chest and felt his warmth melt into her palm. He covered her hand with his, as if he relished her touching him.

"From then on," Chase said, "when Rue cried only I could quiet him. Once he was able to toddle, he followed me everywhere. I did my best to teach him things, and I kept him out of trouble when I could.

"I was a pilot myself by the time he decided to sign on as a cub, and since then I've taught him everything I knew about the river. Everything I learned from my own master, from the pilots I'd partnered with, and everything I picked up on my own."

He turned to her and she could see his eyes had gone liquid with tears. "Oh, Annie! What will I do if Rue dies?"

Ann gathered him up in her arms and bound him close. He was a strong man, a brave man, but even the bravest men crumbled when it came to losing someone they loved.

"He's young, Chase," she murmured, smoothing his hair. "He's healthy and he's strong."

"I can't imagine being on the river without him."

"He'll be all right."

Ann had never had much reason to believe in things, but she believed in this man. She believed in his family's power to heal and hold onto their own. She also believed that if Rue was hurt so badly that they had to let him go, this family would find a way to accept his loss.

And they'd recover afterwards, *even her husband.*

At least she was here tonight to help Chase endure the wait. "It will be all right," she whispered, and knew in the ways that mattered most she spoke the truth.

They lay curled together there in the hollow at the top of the bluff as if they were cupped in God's own hands, blessed by the silence and the solitude. By being together.

Ann had never lain like this with a man, never nestled her head in the crook of his shoulder, never savored his warmth along the length of her, never pressed her hand against his heart and felt it beating.

She never realized how tall Chase was lying down. How big, how broad and powerful.

How small she was beside him.

From the black ooze of another night months before came a swell of unbidden memories—of rough hands binding her wrists, of her clothes being torn away, of a man thrusting hard between her legs. Of peril and help-lessness, pain and degradation.

Ann fought the haze of red that fogged her brain, the dread that gripped her chest and belly, the rime of fear at the back of her tongue. She squeezed her eyes closed and did her best to crush the memories.

There was no room for fear between Chase and her tonight, so she drew in one long breath and then another. She concentrated on the splendor of the bluffs and the trees and the sky. She focused on what Chase needed from her.

Lying so close beside him, she sensed the last of his frantic energy burn away, felt him nestled against her as he drifted toward sleep.

Ann knew she should be sleeping, too. Instead she lay vividly aware of Chase beside her—of the solidity of his shoulder beneath her cheek, of the protective arc of his arm around her, of how well she fit against him. No mat-ter what the future held for them, tonight Chase was hers to claim and hold, soothe and protect. Tonight as he slept she could touch him without fear of consequences.

Tempted by the unexpected opportunity, Ann gently

traced her fingers over that rugged face: the high, hard ridge of brow, the turning of his jaw, the column of his neck. While he was lost in exhaustion, she tracked the wide yoke of his collarbones and his broad, hard chest; the pleated arch of his ribs and muscle-banded belly.

He was so dense and substantial beneath her hands, so strong and darkly masculine. Ann turned her face into the whiskery hollow beneath his jaw and breathed him in, the sweetness of woodsmoke, the hint of Lydia's lye soap and his father's whiskey, the musk of Chase himself.

At those innocuous intimacies, something akin to awe or exhilaration stole through her. A strange, delicious warmth swelled beneath her sternum. It seeped to the base of her belly, pooled in the hollow of her hips and melted between her legs.

Ann hesitated in astonishment. Never had she felt so breathless and aware, so beguiled and enticed. Drawn to him, she stretched along the length of his body and pressed her mouth to the pliant, beard-roughened column of his throat. Her heart thumped loud in her ears as she tasted the bristle with the tip of her tongue and savored the salty tang of his skin.

She pressed even more intimately against him, close enough to feel his chest expand, close enough to feel his breath feather over her skin. A slow, unfurling thrill moved through her, a shiver of delight and daring and recklessness.

Bit by bit she began to understand that the mysterious warmth flowed not from him—but from her. It flowed from the deepest well of her own femininity. It sprang from her own curiosity and appreciation, from her own feminine need to respond to all that was male in him.

And it was lying with Chase and touching Chase that set things simmering inside her.

Because this new sensation abided in her, Ann wasn't afraid. She was emboldened enough to push up on her elbow and nibble the sharply angled turn of his jaw. She nuzzled the crest of his cheekbone and the hollow beneath it. Barely able to believe what she was doing, Ann kissed the corner of his mouth and swept the bow of his upper lip with the tip of her tongue.

She might have done the same with the lower one if Chase hadn't shifted, hadn't stirred. He mumbled in his sleep, flexed his arm reflexively and bound her closer.

That left Ann sprawled over him, dizzy with a mixture of her own impetuousness and his nearness. How hard and trim he was against her, how manly and solid. How safe she felt, tucked up tight in the crook of his arm.

How trembly and curious.

What might Chase do if he awoke and found her curled so intimately against him? A shiver moved through her at the thought. A blush sluiced across her chest and throat. Her nipples stiffened. Her belly fluttered. The muscles between her thighs drew taut. Responding instinctively, Ann curled closer, pressing that tightness against Chase's hip.

She rubbed against him and the feeling of pleasure grew even more compelling and sensual. She discovered a slow, sinuous rhythm that seemed so much a part of her she might have known it all her life. She recognized a yearning within herself she never dreamed existed.

This was why men and women came together.

This was why a woman's eyes shone when she looked at her husband. It was why a man cherished and protected his wife to his last breath. It was the reason two people chose each other and spoke their vows—to savor this strange and mysterious alchemy.

Ann shut her eyes, stunned by her discovery. She hadn't understood that relations between men and women could be more than demand and submission, pain and degradation. She hadn't known that women could want, that women could need. But now she saw a wondrous possibility in coming together. *Of making love.*

A flood of goose bumps rippled warm across her skin.

The notion of making love with Chase teased her imagination. What would he do if he awakened now? Would he take her in his arms and return her kisses? Would he touch her in ways that would heighten these new sensations? Would he want her to be a wife to him? *And now that she'd begun to feel this fascination, would she be able to . . .*

Before she'd completed the thought, the memories swooped in, terrorized and overwhelmed her. She turned from Chase and began to weep in the thick, sweet grass.

Now that she'd begun to understand what loving was, why shouldn't she be able to lie with her husband if that's what she wanted? Would she always be haunted by what Boothe had done to her? Had he ruined her as a woman?

Ann balled up tighter, hating that Boothe's cruelty

was denying her everything she wanted for herself. She cursed him for the children she'd never have, the love she'd never be able to share. The life she was being forced to forfeit because she couldn't give herself to the man she loved.

She shivered with silent sobs, longing to put what Boothe had done, behind her—and knowing she could not.

Then, as if even in sleep Chase sensed how much she needed him, he rolled toward her, wrapped his arm around her, and snuggled her close against his chest.

She must have fallen asleep there in Chase's arms, because the next thing she knew he was bending over her.

"Annie," he whispered, trailing one finger from her brow to the corner of her mouth.

His eyes were bright and his touch both delicate and beguiling. She stared up at him, gone warm and weightless inside. She held her breath, needing to see what happened next.

"Lovely as it's been to sleep with you, sweet Annie," he went on as he climbed to his feet. "It's time to go."

Ann saw that high above the stars were fading and the sky had lightened to the color of chambray.

"We need to stop at the house and get Christina," he said as he helped her to her feet. He didn't say a word about Rue; he didn't have to.

Ann rose stiff and damp, and more than a little rumpled, then let him lead her back along a path that skirted the edge of the bluffs. They were a good deal closer to the house than she'd imagined, and the sight of it standing stalwart in the dawn cheered her.

Lydia met them at the door. "He's better," she whispered.

Chase brushed past his mother, needing to see his brother for himself.

Ann slid her arm around her mother-in-law. "I knew if anyone could pull him through, it would be you."

"Last night I wasn't so sure," she confessed and leaned into Ann, letting her weariness show, confiding the doubts and fears she hadn't dared to share with anyone else.

Ann treasured the moment, feeling honored that her mother-in-law had turned to her, had trusted her and relied on her to give her the comfort she needed. Now that Ann was preparing to say her final good-byes, Lydia had made her her confidante, made her truly one of them.

"It was a near thing with Rue," Lydia sighed and conceded, easing back a little. "He only stopped coughing blood an hour ago. But praise the Lord, he's finally breathing easier."

"He has a hard road ahead," Ann murmured in concern.

"His leg is badly broken," the older woman agreed, "but Rue's young and strong—and one of the scrappiest human beings God's ever created. In the end he'll be all right."

She let out another long, deep sigh. "I thought this would get easier once the children were grown."

Before Ann could consider how to answer, Evie came

bounding down the stairs with Christina tucked in her arms.

Ann and Lydia stepped apart, but as they did their hands lingered on each other's elbows and forearms and wrists. An instant of affection unlike anything Ann had ever known, passed between them. It was filled with pride and resolve—and a kind of grief so deep it tore her heart.

Ann felt the tears well up and turned to claim her daughter so Lydia wouldn't guess what she was feeling.

"Christy was such a good girl," Evie cooed. "She slept right through the night, but I think she wants her breakfast."

Ann settled Christina in the crook of her elbow and wrapped her opposite arm around the younger girl. "I want to thank you, Evie, for coming with us this summer. I don't know how I would have managed Christina without your help."

Evie tossed her curls. "I liked doing it. I liked seeing the river and all the towns. I'd be glad to stay on with you, except for Rue."

"Except that school is starting," her mother reminded her.

Evie nodded, resigned.

Just then, Chase and Enoch came out of the room at the end of the hall. "Rue's still sleeping," Chase reported, "but he looks so much better."

"He's going to be fine," Enoch confirmed, though Ann could see the toll the night of worry had taken on him, too.

"Now, boy," he went on, addressing Chase, "haven't you got passengers waiting and a schedule to keep?"

It was time to go. Suzanne and D'arcy came out of the parlor to hug both Chase and Ann.

Then Lydia wrapped her arms around Ann and the baby one last time. "You did well by Chase last night."

"I did what I could."

"I'm so glad he found you," her mother-in-law said as she let Ann go. "I think you're the perfect wife for him."

Ann couldn't say a word. She didn't dare acknowledge what Lydia's praise had meant to her. Not when she knew she was leaving the *Andromeda* in St. Louis, not when the woman who'd trusted her and been so kind to her would discover on Chase's next run how wrong she'd been.

chapter thirteen

EVERY MAN STORES UP MEMORIES, FLICKERS OF TIME that crystallize in the chambers of the mind, instants of beauty and simple truth that warm him when the world goes cold. Images that resonate as long as he draws breath.

Chase paused on the wheelhouse steps, staring down at where his wife and child sat in one of the *Andromeda*'s big, rush-seated rocking chairs on the deck below. The sun caught in the soft honey-brown drape of Ann's hair as she cooed over the baby in her lap. He drank in the rosy perfection of her features, the glow of love in her eyes. He savored the burble of Christina's laughter. The moment soaked into him and stained his soul.

They were his. No matter how they'd come to him, no matter what had passed before, Ann and Christina belonged to him.

Nearly losing Rue had reminded him how fragile life really was. It made him realize the time had come for Ann and him to build a future for themselves. For so long, Ann seemed reluctant to do that. But since the night at the point, the night she'd consoled him and slept in his arms, she finally seemed ready to move ahead.

And if she was . . .

Just then, Ann looked up and saw him on the stairs. She smiled at him, and her smile made the sun shine brighter.

"So," she called, "have you finally managed to entrust the wheelhouse to Lucien Boudreau?"

"Boudreau's hardly the steersman Rue is," Chase grumbled as he made his way to where she and Christina were sitting. "But now that there's a bit more water under us, I'm leaving the man to his own devices."

Steamers universally extended the courtesy of bed and board to officers between one assignment and the next and, because of that goodwill, Boudreau had been in the wheelhouse when Rue went overboard. He had volunteered to stand Rue's watches for the rest of the run, probably in hopes of securing a berth on one of the Gold Star boats when they reached St. Louis.

Thinking about Rue made Chase remember something Cal had mentioned the night before, something that made him unaccountably curious. He hunkered down beside Ann's chair and took a moment to stroke the baby's fluff of dark hair.

"Why didn't you tell me," he asked, "that you were down on the main deck when Rue went overboard?"

Ann glanced up at him. "What with everything else, I didn't think much about it. It was the day Nate Ogden and Billy Martin got burned. I was down there looking after the two of them when Rue came by."

"Did he say why he was down there?"

"I thought you'd sent him with a message for Cal."

Chase didn't remember doing that. "I suppose he could have gone down to pay Cal the money he'd lost at checkers."

"They bet on checkers?" Ann asked incredulously.

"Men'll bet on pretty much anything."

"Like Frenchy." Ann frowned and lifted the baby against her.

Chase knew Ann was worried about Frenchy, worried that he gambled too much. Especially for a man who had a family in—Dubuque or maybe it was New Orleans—to support.

"So what did Rue say when he talked to you?" he persisted.

She looked up, and he could see the concern in her eyes.

"There's not a thing you could have done to change what happened," she scolded. "You need to stop tormenting yourself."

He wished he could. But until he found out how Rue had ended up in the river, Chase had to keep nudging people and asking questions.

"Just tell me what Rue said," he insisted.

Ann slanted him a sidelong grin. "Mostly he teased me about the burn ointment I was using on Nate and Billy."

"The one that smells like ten-year-old socks?"

"Rue told them I'd made it from bear grease, scorpion gizzard, and horse piss."

Chase gulped with laughter. "I suspected that!"

"Though you know," she went on, frowning a little, "Rue did seem kind of preoccupied with what Joel Curry and Jake Skirlin were doing."

A shiver feathered up Chase's neck. "And what was that?"

"Just moving boxes."

Chase went still inside. "What kind of boxes?"

Ann shrugged, patting Christina. "Big boxes. Heavy boxes."

Boxes of guns. Certainty squeezed his belly. Chase had to wrap his hands around the arm of Ann's chair to keep his balance.

"What were Curry and Skirlin doing with the boxes?"

"They were handing them up out of the hold."

"As if they were getting ready to deliver them somewhere?" He could hear the escalating pitch of his own voice.

"I suppose."

The *Andromeda* was only a day and a half into their homebound run when Rue was hurt. Things to be delivered that early in the trip should have been stowed on deck. So why had Curry and Skirlin been manhandling big, heavy boxes out of the hold? And why had they been doing it themselves when hauling cargo was the rousters' job?

The only reason those boxes would have been down

there, Chase figured, was to keep them out of sight. *Or because they'd been aboard since the upstream run.*

His gut tightened.

When they'd off-loaded that first set of suspicious boxes, Skirlin said they'd missed making the delivery on their way upstream. Was that how he meant to explain landing these boxes, too? Or was delivering the contraband on the downstream run a way to hide that the shipments of rifles had really been loaded in St. Louis?

Of course it wasn't illegal to transport firearms. All the steamers in the Missouri River trade carried guns at one time or another. Either they came as private consignments from gunsmiths back East, or as part of regular orders to the shops and mercantiles in the towns along the river. The larger shipments of rifles were earmarked for the western forts, and a detail of soldiers usually accompanied them.

Chase could see only one reason to be delivering those big boxes, *those crates of guns,* to the Nebraska shore: so they could be sold to the Indians.

He rubbed his hand across his mouth.

Could the guns possibly have come aboard in St. Louis without him realizing what they were? Had they been stowed in the hold for over a month, without him catching wind of it?

If that was so, what kind of a captain did that make him?

Since the *Andromeda* had headed directly to Hardesty's Landing after Rue was hurt, and Chase was certain they hadn't delivered the boxes Ann described to any of the stops they'd made since then, the guns should still be aboard.

The realization rocked Chase back on his heels.

If he searched the boat and found them, he'd have the proof he needed to charge Curry and Skirlin with running contraband. He'd be able to stop at least these guns from reaching the Indians, and he might even discover who was behind the smuggling.

It wouldn't make up for what had happened to Rue, but he might be able to sleep through the night again.

Chase pushed resolutely to his feet. He'd start by checking the manifest and bills of lading to see if he could discover how the guns had come aboard. Then he'd search every crate and box and barrel on the *Andromeda* until he found the rifles.

Impulsively he bent and pressed a kiss to Ann's forehead.

"What's that for?" Ann called after him as he strode toward the steps.

He could hear the curiosity in her voice and didn't want to explain himself. He clattered down the stairs without answering.

ONCE ALL HIS OFFICERS HAD GATHERED FOR THEIR EVEning meal, Chase excused himself and went to search the *Andromeda* for the crates of rifles.

As he descended into the hold by the forward hatch, the air grew close and fetid. The reek of the hides they'd shipped down from the mountains had permeated the wooden beams and mingled now with the sweetness of fresh-picked apples and the dusky bite of cured tobacco. If there were guns and ammunition hidden anywhere, they'd be here amid the bales of short-fiber cotton and sacks of grain.

Chase began at the bow end and searched his way back. Setting his lantern aside, he shifted a few boxes of goods from one side of the hold to the other so he could look beneath them. He prodded under sacks of grain with a sounding pole and listened for the *thump* of something solid.

Once he'd carefully searched from front to back, he climbed out of the hatch at the stern and inspected the cargo on the main deck with the same dogged thoroughness. But as diligently as he looked, Chase could find no sign of the boxes Ann had described to him. No sign of what he was growing more and more certain were guns bound for the Indians.

But where had the boxes gone? He'd checked the manifest against the bills of lading and found nothing suspicious. He'd searched every inch of the hold and hadn't discovered a thing. Surely the contents of those boxes were too valuable—and too damning—to abandon indiscriminantly.

Were the guns and ammunition hidden somewhere Chase hadn't thought to look? Had Curry and Skirlin found a way to deliver their contraband in spite of the change in plans? Who else aboard might know about the guns besides the two of them?

When he was done looking and thoroughly thwarted, Chase washed his face and hands. He tidied his clothes and returned to the salon in time for dessert. As he forked up a helping of Frenchy's pecan pie, he wondered what Skirlin and Curry would make of what he'd done.

The deckhands and the roustabouts had seen him climb into the bow hatch and emerge from the stern. He'd searched the cargo on the main deck in full view of a score of crewmen and several dozen deck passengers.

If there were conspirators aboard, Chase had declared himself. Now all he had to do was wait and see what happened.

NOTHING HAPPENED.

No one let on that Chase's search of the hold in the midst of a run was in any way unusual. Curry didn't ask him why he'd done it. Skirlin spoke not one word of complaint when Chase reviewed his records for a second time, and as far as Chase could see, there wasn't one discrepancy.

When they arrived in St. Louis four days later, Chase stood on the levee and watched the rousters unload every barrel, box, and bale. The crates Ann described, the ones Rue had taken such an interest in, never turned up. Chase walked the empty hold from end to end before he admitted defeat.

What in the name of God had become of those boxes?

Furious and frustrated, Chase decided he ought to see

the commodore and report what he suspected. He hopped a horsecar to the Rossiter town house and arrived mere minutes after Ann and Christina had left.

As Chase entered the commodore's study, Rossiter looked up from the papers spread out across his desk. "I've just been going over the *Andromeda*'s accounts," he greeted him, "and I'm very impressed!"

Though Chase nodded in confirmation, he noticed Rossiter didn't so much as ask after Rue—as if one pilot more or less, one brother more or less—didn't matter much.

The commodore pushed to his feet instead and strode to the ornate mahogany sideboard. He poured two glasses of brandy and offered one to Chase. "You're proving yourself to be a very resourceful and competent captain."

"I'm glad you're satisfied with my efforts."

Though he didn't usually hold with taking spirits in the middle of the day, Chase welcomed the heat of the brandy in his belly to bolster his courage. It chaffed at him that someone had managed to load contraband aboard the *Andromeda* without him knowing, especially after the assurances he'd given the commodore. What bothered him more was to have to admit that two of his senior officers were running guns and might well have tried to kill his brother.

Chase set his glass aside and turned to the commodore. "There's a matter of some importance I need to discuss with you."

"Keeping Lucien Boudreau on in your brother's place?" the commodore guessed. "Ann told me about the accident. It's just short of miraculous that Ruben survived. How is he faring?"

Chase wished he knew. "When we left Hardesty's Landing a week ago, Rue seemed to be holding his own."

"Well, the young heal fast," James Rossiter said, swirling the brandy in his glass. "Now, about Boudreau... If you're satisfied with his work, perhaps you should keep him on for the rest of the season. I don't have another pilot available who—"

"I didn't come here to talk about Boudreau."

Rossiter must have recognized the gravity in Chase's tone, because he gestured him into one of the armchairs and lowered himself into the other.

Chase took a swallow of brandy. "I believe," he began, "that Jake Skirlin and Joel Curry are part of a conspiracy to smuggle guns to the Indians."

"Are you on about *that* again?" the commodore burst out.

In spite of the older man's evident exasperation, Chase forged ahead. As he did, the commodore's mouth drew tighter and tighter. When he was done, Rossiter sat for a moment and stared at him.

"When you first came to me with allegations that the Gold Star boats were running contraband, you swore that the *Andromeda* would never be involved in anything illegal," the older man chided him.

Heat rose in Chase's face. "I'm afraid I was wrong."

"You're making some serious charges, accusing two of your senior officers of smuggling contraband. You're not wrong about this, too, are you, Captain Hardesty?"

346

Smuggling was an ugly claim to make against men he'd worked with most of the shipping season.

"I take it you have proof against them," the commodore challenged.

Chase had known Rossiter would want proof. God knows, he wanted proof himself, confirmation that his suspicions were based on more than coincidence, supposition—and a knot in his gut that wouldn't go away.

"I haven't been able to find"—Chase began and Rossiter snorted in disgust—"any tangible proof. But on each of the Sioux City runs, we've delivered or been ready to deliver several suspicious-looking boxes—"

"We move hundreds of boxes every trip," the commodore countered. "Tens of thousands in the course of the shipping season. How many of them are 'suspicious?'"

"Not many are big enough or heavy enough to hold a dozen carbines," Chase persisted. "I saw Skirlin and Curry deliver what I believe was the first shipment of rifles myself."

"And you didn't stop them?"

"I didn't suspect what they were doing until afterwards," Chase said, angry at himself all over again. "And this time Ann—"

"Ann!"

"—saw Skirlin and Curry preparing to off-load some big, heavy boxes . . ."

. . . *the afternoon Rue went overboard.*

Chase sucked in a breath of air and felt the chill all the way to his diaphragm. Why hadn't he made that connection before?

Ann had said that while Rue was down on the main deck he'd taken a particular interest in the boxes Curry and Skirlin were moving. Not ten minutes later, Rue ended up in the river.

Had it been Curry or Skirlin who'd tried to kill his brother?

The commodore's harsh tone drew Chase's attention. His eyes were slitted and dark with anger. "Did you—did Ann—see anything besides two of my officers doing their jobs?"

The chill in Chase oozed deeper.

"No," Chase answered, instinctively shielding Ann—*shielding Ann from her own father.* "Ann didn't see anything except the boxes. Still, it seems best if we notify the federal authorities that we suspect—"

Rossiter slammed his hand down on Chase's wrist, pinning it to the arm of his chair.

Chase looked into those black eyes and felt the older man's rage roll over him. Is this what Ann had faced when she tried to oppose the marriage the commodore had planned for her? Is this how her stepfather looked when he hit her?

"Listen here, you young jackanapes," he said, the strength of his grip reinforcing the menace in his voice. "You're not going to tell anyone anything."

"You know all about the contraband, don't you?" Chase's mouth went dry. "You're the one behind it. Are all the Gold Star boats running guns to the Indians?"

The commodore blew out his breath in a huff, as if he were amazed that it had taken Chase so long to figure that out.

"Making the most of opportunities is how men like you and I get rich," the commodore advised him.

Chase jerked his arm out of Rossiter's grasp and lurched to his feet. "You're willing to put the lives of people on the frontier in jeopardy to build your fortune?"

"We're supplying a demand," he said simply. "The redskins want guns. The freighters are willing to pay a premium to have a few boxes of carbines landed inconspicuously. We're just one link in the chain, boy. It's how our business works."

"Not my business!"

The older man stared at him with an almost reptilian calm. "If you mean to stay in the shipping business, Hardesty, you'll do as you're told."

"I'll go to the authorities," Chase threatened.

"Then you'll lose the *Andromeda.*"

Chase froze where he stood.

"You look over the terms of the agreement you signed the day you married Ann," Rossiter went on to advise him. "The *Andromeda* only comes to you at the *end* of the shipping season. She only comes to you if you're still married to Ann *and* you're still the *Andromeda's* master."

Chase knew the terms well enough.

"If you cross me on this, Hardesty," Rossiter threatened, "I'll order the *Andromeda* burned to the waterline before I let you have her."

Chase had known the moment he stepped aboard that the steamer was part of him. Since then, he'd courted his wife on her decks. His daughter had been born in the captain's cabin. He'd felt like his own man for the first time in his life on the day they pulled the *Andromeda* in at Hardesty's Landing.

Losing the *Andromeda* struck at the very heart of him. She was both his livelihood and an extension of himself. *But how much of the man he was would it cost to keep her?*

He'd have to forfeit his reputation, his honor, and his self-respect. He's have to break the law. He'd have to turn a blind eye to the people who were dying out West because he was smuggling guns to the Indians. He'd have to give up everything he believed in, the kind of man he'd been raised to be.

It would cost too much.

"Take the damn boat," he muttered and wheeled toward the door. "Do what you will with her."

"Well, if losing the *Andromeda* doesn't matter, ask yourself how you're going to provide for Ann and Christina when you lose your command?" Rossiter's voice stopped him in his tracks. "Once I put the word out that I had to let you go because you're reckless and unreliable, no one between St. Paul and the Mississippi delta will hire you. How would your wife and daughter fare if you were arrested for smuggling contraband?"

"I haven't known I was smuggling contraband."

The commodore laughed. "There's not a judge here in St. Louis who would believe that a captain with your reputation could have had contraband aboard his steamer without knowing it."

Chase turned on him. "My God, man!" he shouted. "Do you think so little of your daughter and granddaughter that you'd put them in jeopardy to get to me?"

The commodore shoved to his feet. "And what will your precious Ann think of you if you go to the authorities and make charges that could send her father to prison?"

Ann knew what kind of man the commodore was, Chase told himself. God knows, Rossiter had manipulated her, forced her into marriage, and maybe even beaten her to bend her to his will.

Still, she cared enough about this man to bring Christina to see him everytime they landed in St. Louis. And wouldn't both Ann and her daughter be dishonored if the commodore was tried and convicted?

"How can you threaten the people who love you, and live with yourself?" Chase demanded.

"What my life has taught me, Hardesty," the commodore said as if he knew he'd won, "is that a man who wants to survive thinks first of himself."

Chase nodded, knowing he was trapped. Knowing that while he might have been able to walk away from the *Andromeda*, he couldn't ignore his commitment to Ann and Christina.

"Now, then," Rossiter went on with a self-satisfied smile. "Some of those boxes you've been so curious about are going to be delivered to the *Andromeda* this evening. As a show of good faith, I expect you to take delivery personally. I want you to sign the receipt, and when the boxes reach their destination, I'm going to hold you responsible for seeing them delivered."

"You're making me complicit in the smuggling."

"I'm giving you the chance to hold on to all that's dear

to you," the commodore clarified. "So do as I tell you, Hardesty, and you won't lose a thing."

Except decency and honor.

"You can go to the devil, Rossiter!" Chase shouted and slammed out the study door.

He could hear Rossiter laughing all the way down the hall.

CHASE WAS WAITING AT THE HEAD OF THE *Andromeda*'s gangway when the boxes arrived. There were six of them, about five feet long and back-breakingly heavy. It took two husky stevedores to lift one of them from the wagon, heft it up the gangway, and stow it away in the hold.

Chase followed the boxes down and watched as Curry directed the rousters. "Put them there at the back," he ordered. "We'll pack lighter things around them."

Once all six boxes were in place, Curry handed Chase the invoices for his signature. "Commodore's orders," he said with a sneer.

Chase nodded and took the papers in his hands, but he couldn't seem to focus on the words. Still, he didn't have to read them to know what they said.

What they meant.

They said that Chase Hardesty was a criminal and a coward, and once he affixed his name, James Rossiter would own him. He'd have the proof he needed that

Chase was a smuggler, that he was a failure as both a captain and a man.

Chase fought a quick, fierce skirmish with his conscience, weighing what was right against the way Annie and Christina had looked sitting in the rocker the other morning. He weighed the things he'd always believed about himself against his fears for the future and his new responsibilities.

This wasn't about keeping the *Andromeda*. It might tear out his heart to lose the boat, but Chase could give her up if it came to that. What he couldn't sacrifice was his wife and child for principles and his good name.

He scrawled his name across the receipts, refolded the papers and handed them back to Joel Curry.

Now Chase was as guilty as the rest of them.

Curry smiled as if he enjoyed seeing the mighty fall, then followed the rousters up the ladder to the deck.

Chase stayed behind, listening to the muffled conversations and the footfalls crossing the landing stage. Only when he was sure everyone had gone on about their duties did Chase pry up the lid on one of the boxes.

There *were* guns inside. Spencer carbines that gleamed sleek and deadly in the lantern light. Here was the proof he needed to take his allegations to the authorities.

If he did, he'd save the lives of who-knew-how-many miners and settlers and soldiers out in Wyoming and Montana. If he chose to march right up to General Sherman's house in town and report the smuggling, Sherman would order the provost marshal to confiscate the guns. They'd arrest James Rossiter and gradually round up the rest of the men who'd been part of the con-spiracy.

There'd be a trial and Chase would testify. In the end Rossiter and his cronies would be found guilty and go to prison.

It was the right thing to do. But Chase couldn't move. All he was able to do was stand staring down at the car-bines.

If he stayed this course, if he said nothing and trans-ported these guns west, he'd turn against the way he'd been raised and everything he believed in.

How was he going to be able to face Ma and Pa when they pulled in at Hardesty's Landing with these guns in the hold of the *Andromeda*? His mother would know there was something wrong the moment she laid eyes on him. And if Enoch ever found out, he'd know he'd been right all along, that Chase was unworthy of being his son.

And Rue...

Oh, sweet Jesus! How would he face Rue after he'd made an alliance with the men who'd almost killed him?

Chase moaned and hunched over the box of rifles, gripping the edges with trembling hands. He was doing this to protect Ann and Christina. To make sure he could provide for them. He was doing this to keep Annie from discovering that her stepfather was brokering the death of innocent people out in the plains.

But after tonight, how much less guilty was Chase himself of that?

He stared down at the carbines' sleek steel barrels, gleaming faintly in the lantern light. He'd just sold himself for this box of guns, sold himself to protect the people he loved and a life that had grown precious to him.

Yet in making that choice, he'd decimated who he was and forfeited everything he believed in. He'd relinquished his pride in his accomplishments, betrayed the honor he'd held close to the bone since he was a boy.

There was no going back.

Chase closed the crate of carbines and pounded the lid in place. As he did, self-loathing seared through him, and despair wrapped around his heart like a cold, black snake.

chapter fourteen

ODAY," ANN CONFIDED TO HER DAUGHTER AS Christina nursed, "while your papa was unloading cargo, I went and met with Mr. Throckmorton. He gave me some of the money your grandmother set aside for us, and tomorrow we leave for Cincinnati. That seems as likely a place as any to start our new life, don't you think?"

Only when she'd stood with the steamer tickets in her hands, did Ann admit to herself how much she loved this life and how much it grieved her to leave. How could she go when Rue's recovery was still in jeopardy? How could she turn her back on the Hardestys after the way they'd opened their hearts to her? How could she leave the steamer that seemed like home and a crew who had taken to her and her daughter as if they were family?

How could she part from the man she loved—the man who'd become a true papa to her little girl and a wonderful husband to Ann herself? *Yet how could she stay, knowing that she could never be the wife Chase needed her to be, that she would never lie with him or give him the children she knew he wanted?*

Ann was making the only choice she could possibly make. So she'd tucked the tickets away and gone to see her stepfather one last time.

Now that Christina had nursed herself to sleep, Ann needed to find Chase and tell him she and Christina were going away. There was a time when she might have simply left a note for him to find, but she was braver now. Being aboard the *Andromeda* had made her braver; being Christina's mother had made her braver. Being Chase's wife had given her a kind of courage Ann hadn't imagined she was even capable of.

Besides, she owed Chase the truth—or at least as much of the truth as she dared to tell him.

Her hands were trembling as she shifted the baby from her breast to the crook of her shoulder. "I'll be such a good mother to you, Christina," she promised, patting her, "that you won't even mind if Chase isn't your papa anymore."

After she'd settled her daughter in her basket, Ann refastened her clothes and went to look for her husband.

She didn't have far to go.

Chase was right outside the cabin door, a dark silhouette against the yellowish bloom of St. Louis's gaslights. He stood with his palms braced on the railing and his shoulders hunched.

Whenever she thought about Chase, it would always

be out here on deck, standing tall and shouting orders, sitting in the sun with Christina gathered close against his chest, or waiting for Ann to join him in the rosy freshness of dawn. She'd never forget how a grin could transform that rugged face, that his eyes shone with the color of the summer sky, or that Chase was the only person in the world who called her Annie.

Though she knew lingering over the memories could only make the things she'd come to say more difficult, she dwelled on them anyway. She clung to the final moments of her marriage, waiting through one more breath, one more heartbeat. Finally she drew herself up and spoke her husband's name.

He turned with a start and stared at her, his eyes as hollow and stark as the craters of the moon.

"My God, Chase!" Ann ran and clutched him to her. "What is it? What's happened? Is it Rue?"

"I've had no word of Rue." His voice was as desolate as his eyes.

Had he discovered the truth about her, about Christina?

Ann's heartbeat lumbered. But if Chase had unraveled her most closely guarded secret, he wouldn't be standing here on deck. He'd have sought her out and confronted her, or gone off to tear Boothe Rossiter limb from limb.

Whatever this was, it was worse than that.

Ann knotted her fingers in his clothes and tugged him closer. "Tell me what's happened!"

"Nothing for you to be concerned about."

Ann wasn't concerned; she was terrified.

He was knotted up tight as a monkey's fist. His muscles

coiled like cables beneath his skin. His breath came in the harsh, quick puffs of a man in almost unendurable pain.

"Tell me what this is about. You mustn't try to protect me."

He gave a mirthless laugh. "As if I could protect you."

He was coming apart before her eyes. "I'm your wife, Chase," she implored him. "Let me help you."

"Why?"

She flinched at that single softly spoken word. It called her feelings for him into account: her respect for him, the trust they'd built, the love she hadn't dared to admit. It made her question her own intent, her offer to make this better. How much help could she be if she was leaving in the morning?

"Every time I've been in trouble," she began because she couldn't turn away, "you've stood by me. You've protected me, taken care of me. Whatever this is, I'll stand by you."

He shifted on his feet and stared past her toward the river.

"You've held my hand when I was afraid," she went on in a whisper. "You stayed with me when I needed your strength. Tell me what's wrong, and we'll find a way to work it out."

Chase hesitated as if he were weighing her words, then he turned the harsh beam of his desolation on her. The anguish she saw in his eyes nearly drove her to her knees.

"Annie..." His voice was so raw and frayed she barely recognized her own name. "Annie, do you believe in me?"

How could Chase ask that? Chase whose family loved him. Chase who was respected and revered all up and down the river. Chase who'd worked miracles in her life since she'd come aboard the *Andromeda*.

But then, it didn't matter why he was asking. What Chase needed was her answer and her reassurance.

She raised her hands to cup his face. She looked up into those eyes, so dark with pain and doubt. "I believe, Chase Hardesty, that you are the finest and most honorable man I've ever known."

He seemed to falter under the weight of those words. "Am I, Annie?"

She saw how shaken and depleted he was, and all she wanted to do was hold him, give to him, and fill him up again.

"You are to me." Tears welled in her eyes and her own voice caught. "I've believed in you when I didn't have anything else to believe in."

Ann pushed up on her toes and kissed him.

Chase did his best to turn away, as if he didn't deserve what she was offering, but Ann clasped his face in her hands. She drew gently on his mouth. She caressed his lips, giving back the simple intimacies Chase himself had taught her. He tried to deny himself the solace she was offering, but with a shudder he gave in to his need for consolation. His need for her.

"Oh, Annie," he moaned and kissed her as if he meant to devour her, as if she was the only one in the world who could ease his pain. He dragged her against him, his hands tightening and letting go. Claiming, relinquishing, and reclaiming.

Ann clung to him, her fingers skimming the planes of that rugged face, slicing through the strands of his thick hair.

He pulled her nearer, so close she could feel his ribs rise against her as he breathed and feel the surging of his heart.

"Oh, Annie."

All at once it didn't matter what was plaguing him. Chase needed to be held as tenderly as she could hold him and soothed with the stroke of her hands. He needed to be convinced that no matter what he'd done, he was worthy of the love she had to give him. The only way to do that, she saw suddenly, was to trust him, to offer up the thing he wanted most. What she hadn't been able to give him.

Herself.

She needed to go to him tonight with a glow of love in her eyes and show how much being his wife meant to her. She needed to offer up her faith and ardor, her body and the solace it could give him.

But when the moment came to give herself, would she be able to offer Chase everything?

Ann eased back in his arms, fighting down the squeeze of panic and resistance. Chase must have sensed her indecision, because he lowered his hands and stepped away.

And in that acquiescence, Ann recognized the truth: that Chase would never hurt her. He would never tear at her clothes or crush her beneath him. He would never force himself on her.

If she was ever going to overcome what happened to her, if she was ever going to be with a man and make love to him, it had to be Chase. It had to be here tonight, when he needed her so desperately.

Ann drew herself up and extended her hand in invitation.

Chase looked down at her open palm, then up at her. "Annie, are you sure?"

Was she?

"Yes."

He waited a moment longer, as if he were giving her a chance to change her mind, then he placed his hand in hers.

She led him across the deck, through the silent sitting room, and into the captain's shadowy sleeping chamber. They paused before the high, wide berth and stood with their hands linked and the flutter of their breathing roaring in the silence. The air hung thick with anticipation. Long moments slipped past them, slipped away.

"Annie?"

"It's all right."

"I understand why you don't want to be with me."

Her head came up. "You don't understand." *He would never understand; she didn't want him to understand.*

It took everything in her to admit the truth. "I—I don't know what to do."

"What?"

She all but suffocated on the wave of mortification

that swept up her throat. "I don't know what happens next. I—I don't know *how* to be with you."

Chase stared down at her, saw the earnestness and confusion in her eyes. How could Ann have lain with a man and borne a child without having tasted seduction? Unless his suspicions had been right. Unless someone had taken her against her will.

He stared down at those delicate hands clasped in his own, at the fine-boned face and vulnerable mouth. How could anyone have hurt her?

The very idea cauterized his mind. Yet he was suddenly very sure they had. Knowing that made him want to roar with rage, gather his Annie up in his arms and protect her. Chase hesitated, trying to catch hold of himself, trying to tamp down the questions suddenly howling through his brain.

"Would you—" He gave her hands a gentle squeeze. "Would you like me to show you?"

Her chin came up, her mouth gone soft with disappointment. "This—this is something *I* meant to give to *you*."

Something shifted in his chest.

"That's very generous, Annie," he murmured, "but when two people come together and make love, it doesn't much matter who gives and who takes. If it works the way it should, things come out even in the end."

"Oh?" Ann sounded perplexed.

Chase allowed himself the slightest of smiles; it was going to be such pleasure teaching her the way of things.

"When a man and a woman come together," he went

on instructively, "what they find can be wonderful. Just the simplest touching"—he traced a slow, deliberate circle on the back of her hand—"can become intimate and beguiling.

"And kissing is a pleasure"—he bent his head and brushed her lips with his—"that mustn't be hurried. And lying down together—" He felt her shiver and did his best to believe it was in anticipation. "—can lead to other things. Things you'll like, Annie. Things I'll like showing you."

Ann nodded and drew in a shaky breath.

"Do you trust me, Annie?"

"Yes."

"Do you believe me when I tell you that I would never in this life do anything to hurt you?"

"Yes."

"Will you let me show you how wonderful loving can be?"

She looked up at him and nodded.

Chase lowered his head and pressed what he hoped was the tenderest kiss a man had ever given a woman to Ann's lips. He began with a flutter of contact, a graze of sensation, a glide of touching mouth to mouth. He turned that kiss into a delicate tracery; a tender exploration; a slow, simmering exchange of breath.

Ann leaned into him and offered up more of herself.

Chase took what she gave, tasting the plush, warm, fullness of her mouth, letting one kiss trail into the next. He took up a slow, lazy cadence that was meant as much to tantalize as beguile. He nibbled the soft, sleek margins of her lips, delved deeper and tickled the tip of her tongue with his.

Ann shivered with what might have been daring and tickled him back.

He splayed his palms against her back and fought down the almost overwhelming need to lift her onto the bed, spread her body beneath his, and lose himself in her. Yet even as his arousal grew, Chase knew Ann needed soft words and encouragement, tenderness and courting. She needed every gram of patience he could find within himself.

"Oh, Annie!" Even as his breath raged hot and ragged in his throat, his caress was gentle. "I want so much to lie down and hold you in my arms. Do you think we could do that?"

"Will—" her voice wavered. "Will it be like that night at the point?"

The memory of the thick, cool darkness circled through his brain. Of how soft she'd been against him. Of how right it seemed to hold her and sleep with her in his arms.

"It will be almost exactly like that, Annie," he promised. *"Only so much better."*

He felt her shiver again and stepped away, giving her a moment to collect herself.

While she considered what he'd said, Chase stripped off his shirt and boots, made short work of his trousers and underdrawers. He hoisted himself into the captain's berth and pulled the sheet up over him. Once he had, he turned to see if Annie was watching.

She'd turned away instead and was pinching open the row of whorled steel buttons at the front of her bodice.

"You need any help?" he asked her.

Ann glanced at him, flushed when she realized he was teasing—and naked—then turned away.

Once she'd opened the very last button, she hesitated. Then, with her back still to him, she eased the close-fitting jacket down her arms.

All Chase could do was stare at that pale expanse of nape, the fragile symmetry of her shoulders, at the sweep of her spine and the row of laces that strung the edges of her corset together. When he had her within his reach, he was going to tear that corset away, and graze every inch of that warm, ivory flesh with kisses.

But then Ann turned to him, still mostly dressed, and he couldn't think of anything else to do but shift deeper into the berth and extend his arm in invitation.

"I'm lonely up here," he whispered.

Ann hesitated, nodded, and stepped out of her shoes.

"It'll be all right, Annie," he whispered as she stretched out beside him.

"I know it will."

Her absolute trust reminded him just how patient he needed to be with her, how gentle. How hard it was going to be to wait when he was hard and heavy with his need for her already.

Still, he gave her time to settle in before he reached across and teased one of the hairpins from her hair. She wasn't fast enough to push it back in place, and he stole another.

"Do you have any idea how long I've wanted to do this?" he murmured as he drew more of the pins from her hair. "How long I've wanted your hair loose around your shoulders?"

Ann laughed and gave her head a quick little shake that sent her tightly wound chignon unfurling down her back.

Chase combed the tangle back from her face then savored the cool, silky slide of those honey-brown strands against his skin. He wrapped a ribbon of tresses around his palm and wound her closer.

"Do you have any idea how beautiful you are, Annie, or how long I've wanted to be with you?" He bent his head and kissed her slowly, relishing the fullness and the texture of her mouth.

She kissed him back, the brush of her lips was hesitant at first, soft and light. But as her courage grew, her kisses became an exploration of his mouth—and his intentions. Of his desires—and her own. Then seeming satisfied with what she'd discovered, Ann nestled closer.

The friction of mouths and bodies tangled together seemed to kindle a fierce, hungry need in both of them. Their hands strayed, lingering and possessing. Their mouths merged; their kisses gathered intensity. Pressed chest to chest and thigh to thigh, heat spiraled up between them.

"Oh, Annie," Chase murmured against her lips. "I've watched you all these months, watched you the way a man watches the moon in the water. He's enchanted by its radiance, mesmerized by its beauty." He trailed trembling fingers down her back. "He longs to reach out and touch the moon, but he's afraid.

"He knows that something so wondrous can't be real. He knows that if he tries to catch the moon in his two hands, he'll ruin everything."

"Oh, Chase."

"That if he tries to claim it as his own, he'll destroy everything that's beautiful in his life. Everything he cherishes."

He recognized the edge of longing in his words, but he wasn't sorry he'd spoken. This woman was his wife. He loved her beyond all else, and now that she was here with him, he had to tell her what she meant to him.

In the half-light Ann's eyes shimmered with tears. She raised her hand and brushed his lips with her fingertips. She contoured her palm to the curve of his cheek.

"Oh, Chase." He could hear her voice waver. "I don't want to be the moon in the water anymore. I want you to touch me and hold me. I want you to make love to me."

"Annie, are you sure?"

As if to show him how she felt, she clasped his hand in hers and pressed it into the hollow above her heart. "I want to be your wife tonight. I wouldn't be here if I wasn't sure."

He leaned over her and kissed her, tasting the salty tang of tears at the corner of her eye, the downy-soft skin at the crest of her cheek, the delicate crease at the corner of her mouth. He nibbled along her jaw. He licked her ear and smiled as she squirmed against him.

Holding back his baser urges, Chase fluttered kisses along the length of her throat. He laved the delicate half-moon hollow at its base, sketched a slow, moist line down her chest with the tip of his tongue. He paused to loosen the satin string at the neck of her chemise and breathed sultry heat across her breasts.

She was so lovely draped across his arm, her chin tilted to grant him access, her damp, rosy lips parted in wonder. "I didn't think you could make me feel—like this."

"Like what?" he asked, teasing her again.

"So warm," she confessed, "yet like I'm shivering inside."

He knew just how that felt, and his blood surged with wanting her. "Annie," he promised. "There are so many things I want to show you."

He teased open the ribbon at the neckline of her chemise and brushed the tissue-thin lawn aside. The full bloom of her femininity spilled into his palm. Her flesh was lush and warm, the nipple ripe and puckered from Christina nursing. He lowered his head and circled the wide, dusky-pink areola with his tongue.

Ann arched against him. She tangled her fingers in his hair and offered up even more of herself.

He took what she gave him, yet yearned for so much more. He wanted her willing and unencumbered beneath his hands. He wanted to kiss every inch of her, to clasp the fullness of her hips and buttocks in his hands. He wanted to draw her against him, claim her as his bride, and initiate her to the pleasures marriage could afford both of them.

He made more promises as he reached for the hooks at the back of her skirt and pinched them free, as he loosened the tapes at the waist of her petticoats, as he eased her skirts and petticoats away. It took some tugging, some whispered consultations, and a good deal of cooperation to loosen the laces on her corset and draw the garment over her head. When she was free of it, he teased her lawn drawers down her hips.

But when he reached to lift the hem of her chemise, Ann grabbed his hands. "Please," she implored him. "Please!"

"It's all right, Annie. I won't do anything you don't want me to."

He smoothed his hands the length of her back, molded her to him as if he were sculpting clay. He loved the sweet solidity of her against him, the faint lavender tang that clung to her skin, and the silken warmth of her throat.

As they lay together, Ann touched him, too. She spread her small, cool hand against his breastbone, and he wondered if she could feel the jarring of his heart. She scuffed the hair on his chest with her fingertips, then followed the flow of it down his ribs, down the midline of his belly to where the bedsheet blocked her way.

His erection rose hard and full beneath it as he shifted toward her, courting her with soul-deep kisses, with murmured endearments, and gliding caresses. He eased closer, and when he sensed the desire well up between them, he whispered her name and rolled over her.

Panic shrilled along Ann's nerves. The world went white around her. The smell of camphor burned in her nostrils.

Ann struck out blindly, frenzied, flailing, kicking, trying to buck off the man restraining her. She wouldn't be
crushed and manhandled, held down and violated ever
again. She clawed at the arm that clamped around her
waist, at the man who bound her to him.

Abruptly he rolled onto his back, dragging her with
him.

Ann sprawled over him trembling, coming back to
herself one sense at a time. She recognized Chase's voice
calling her name, smelled his woodsmoke scent surrounding her, felt his callused hands stroking the length
of her back.

"Easy, Annie," he consoled. "I didn't mean to scare you."

Ann's memory of her night with Boothe was still too
vivid, too close. For a moment it had blotted out everything else.

"Don't you know I'd never hurt you...."

... the way he hurt you. Ann knew Chase hadn't spoken the words, but she heard them in her head as if he
had. He didn't know—*couldn't know*—what had happened to her. Still, he seemed to understand how much
she needed to be calmed and comforted.

"Annie, you'll always be safe with me."

Ann willed the fear away, let the beating of his heart
against her own, soothe her. She was safe to stretch along
the length of him, safe to press her lips to his, safe to let
him enfold her and kiss her back.

As their mouths brushed and their bodies tangled
close, a faint, familiar humming tuned up in her. As they
kissed it intensified, becoming an insistent mumble of

awareness, a slowly rising timbre that set her nerves to trembling. It seemed to vibrate the length of her spine, reawakened a deep, rich yearning in her. It was what she'd felt that night at the point—the night she'd turned away from Chase because she was afraid.

Now she refused to turn away. She felt sure of herself and brave enough to chance whatever came.

Chase must have sensed that boldness because he lifted his hips against her. As his arousal nestled between her legs, pressed hard and hot against her mound, the humming in her became a chorus. A wave of sensation ruffled the surface of her skin. Her breath caught in her throat; her heart fluttered. The heat in her belly seeped down into her loins.

Something powerful and female awoke in her, something that was hungry and atavistic and soul-deep. She *wanted* him.

Ann tipped back on her knees and straddled his hips. She rose above him, glorying in what she'd discovered within herself.

"I want you." She spoke the words with joy and awe. A brazen thrill swept through her. "I want you!"

Chase looked up at her, his heart in his eyes. "I want you, too, Annie."

He breached the hem of her chemise, and beneath the drape of the lacy undergarment he slid his hands up over her. He grazed her thighs and hips, cupped her breasts and feathered her nipples with his fingertips.

He engendered a rich and powerful voluptuousness in her.

He stroked from the arch of her ribs to the small of her back, rode the swell of her buttocks to the inner curve of her thighs. He caressed the nest of curls at the apex of her legs—then began to stroke more deeply. He opened that soft, mysterious part of her with the pads of his thumbs, as if it were the petals of some rare and exotic flower.

Ann closed her eyes and sank into the sensations. He sought her tiny, tender places, her secret, sensitive places. Her suddenly wet and wanting places. She seemed to be melting inside, going malleable and damp with something she was beginning to recognize as desire.

"What are you doing to me?" she murmured, startled by the slurred throaty sound of her own voice.

"I'm making love to you, Annie," he whispered. "Didn't I tell you it would be wonderful?"

Before she could think how to answer, he touched her in a way that sent shivers bursting the length of her back. Her head went light and the very core of her flesh constricted, mingling the intensity of longing with the incipient promise of pleasure.

"That's only a taste of what's to come, Annie," he promised her. "Will you let me show you all of it?"

Ann could do no more than nod, do no more than shift her weight as he pulled away the sheet that had separated him from her. She became acutely aware of the sinuous warmth of him along the inside of her legs, of how big and hard his manhood was pressing against her.

How easy it would be for him to take her if he wanted her. Instead he hesitated, offering her a choice.

"Annie, are you sure?"

"Yes," she answered on a sob. "Yes, I want you."

They brushed intimate flesh to intimate flesh, and when he clasped the flare of her hips and eased her over him, Ann was ready.

As he penetrated her feminine core, she waited for the pain to come. But there was only a fullness, a rightness, a breathless sense of completeness. Never in her life had Ann experienced a connection so deep, a bond so profound.

Ann quaked in awe at being one with him, and now that she was, his kisses seemed more intense. His caress left a lingering afterglow. The endearments he whispered into her mouth set her head to spinning.

Never had she felt more deeply, more purely.

With the brush of his hands against her skin, with the lift of her hips against him, they wove yearning into wanting, tenderness into need. They caught a slow, sinuous meter that seemed to resonate in each of them; a graceful sequence of movements that made the delight Ann had felt at being one with him more ardent, more intense.

"I've imagined making love to you just like this a thousand times," Chase whispered, his voice feverish with desire.

Ann's eyes drifted closed and she lost herself in wonder. Only Chase could touch her like this, mind and heart, soul and body. Only Chase could make her feel so safe, so beautiful, so utterly cherished. Only Chase could draw her from desire to desperation, from fervor to frenzy.

Their harsh breathing tore the quiet of the night.

Their whispered endearments mingled with their gasps of pleasure. Their need for each other grew and grew.

"Oh, Annie," Chase cried out, and the sound of her name in his mouth seemed to call her home.

Ann came apart in his arms. Delight condensed inside her. It burst at the base of her belly and spun along her nerves in a spangle of shivers. It rose in her, awakening a kind of incandescent freedom, a kind of shattering elation, a kind of intemperate joy that she had never imagined she could feel.

Chase cried out her name as he reached his peak and they gave themselves over to the wild, fierce splendor of fulfillment.

When Ann came to herself a good while later, she was spilled across Chase's chest, boneless and spent. She felt his hands move with almost unbearable tenderness to smooth her tumbled hair, and she reveled in the serenity and joy between them.

"I didn't know it could be like that," she murmured without so much as opening her eyes.

"I know."

"Why didn't you tell me making love could be so wonderful?"

She heard a smile come into his voice. "Would you have believed me?"

What had gone before was as different from what she'd discovered with Chase as daylight was from dark, as love from hate. As different from the girl she was when she'd married him from the woman she'd become.

"Thank you," she whispered, raising her head so she could look into his eyes, "for what you've given me."

He reached up and stroked her cheek. "You mean the world to me, Annie."

His hands were gentle on her skin, at the turn of her jaw, along the slope of her neck and the rise of her collarbone. He drew her down and kissed her.

At the core where his body was still joined to hers, Ann felt him stir. Her own body responded to his with a provocative, carnal tightening. She hadn't expected that response, hadn't expected to want him so soon again.

"Is it possible for us to—to do that—" The heat of a blush ran into her cheeks, "—more than once?"

"Did you like what we did?" he asked her. His voice deepened to a husky timbre she had begun to associate with desire.

She flushed darker. "Y-y-yes."

He was growing inside her, swelling, hardening. It was both a strange and heady sensation.

"Would you like to do—that again?"

His hands crept up inside her chemise, stroking the sensitive skin of her chest and belly. At the spot where they were joined, her body pulsed.

"Yes." The single word turned her breathless.

"I'd like to, too," he told her. "But this time I'd like to see all of you."

"You—you would?" He was touching her intimately, pressing himself more deeply inside her.

"So could you take off your chemise?" he asked her.

Ann's head was muzzy with wanting him. There was such respect and tenderness and longing in her husband's eyes, that she couldn't refuse.

She reached for the hem of the chemise and pulled the garment over her head.

chapter fifteen

THERE WAS NO GOING BACK.

Ann knew it the moment she opened her eyes, the moment she heard the blast of the *Andromeda*'s departure whistle. The instant she recollected where she was—ensconced all rosy and naked amidst the tumbled bedclothes in the captain's berth—she realized how irrevocably she'd altered her future.

She dragged the covers over her head and considered what she and Chase had done right here last night to change it. Her lips still tingled with the remnants of what might have been a thousand kisses. She could feel the slow, sensual glide of Chase's hands along her skin. Low in her belly lay the thick, sweet weight of remembered desire.

She'd spent last night in Chase's arms, and she refused

to regret what she had done. Still, it *had* changed everything.

Most especially it changed her.

Chase had stroked her hair and her face, touched her with praise on his lips and reverence in his hands. He had told her she was beautiful, not just with words, but with the glow in his eyes, and the homage in his kisses. He had taught her how to accept the gift of delight, and how to give it back again. He had let her discover she had nothing to fear from him and held her safe in his arms as she abandoned herself to pleasure.

She blushed now, just remembering.

Chase had made her his wife last night, and Ann had finally allowed Chase to be her husband. No matter what she'd planned before, she could never leave him after this. But there was so much in her past she had to confront in order to stay with him.

Right now, there were more pressing things to see to— namely Christina. Hastily, she wrapped a sheet around herself, and went to look for her daughter. Neither the baby nor her basket were in the usual place. Chase must have taken her with him when he left. But how long ago was that? And where exactly was her daughter now that Chase was undoubtedly busy with his departure duties?

Ann found Christina squalling in Frenchy's arms a few minutes later.

"It is good you came to get this poor girl," he scolded as he handed her the baby. "I rocked her and sang to her—"

"You *sang* to her?"

"Christina likes it when I sing in French," the cook

said with a sniff. "I also gave her a sugar tit. What she wants is her mother."

"I'm sorry you ended up looking after her," Ann apologized and lifted the baby against her shoulder. "I'm afraid I—overslept."

"*Oui.*"

It was a single word, but Ann recognized his inflection. *Frenchy knew.*

A flush blossomed at her sternum and bloomed all the way to the roots of her hair. "What did he say?" she asked furiously.

Frenchy didn't even ask her what she meant.

"Nothing, *chéri*. A gentleman never speaks of his *amours*. But you *did* kiss him right there on deck where anyone could see, and he *didn't* sleep in the officers' quarters."

Which meant every crewman she saw today would have a very good idea how she and Chase had spent last night. Ann buried her face in her daughter's neck. She'd learned months before that there were no secrets aboard the *Andromeda*. Still, she'd hoped to keep what passed between Chase and her private, at least until she'd figured out how she felt about it.

And how Chase felt.

"We are all very happy for you and the captain," Frenchy went on. "He is a good man, *chéri*, the kind of man I would be glad to see my own dear daughters wed when their time comes. And you love him, *non?*"

That was something else Ann wasn't ready to discuss—much less with Frenchy Bertin.

"I'm taking Christina back to the cabin," Ann told him and wheeled toward the door. She nearly collided with Jake Skirlin as she burst outside.

Though the two of them usually stepped around each other like hissing cats, Skirlin hesitated, a sly, knowing quirk pulling at one corner of his mouth. "Mornin', Mrs. Hardesty. You sleep well last night?"

Ann reined in the impulse to turn and run. She made herself face him instead—the first of many confrontations. "How I slept, Mr. Skirlin, is none of your concern. And I'll thank you not to ask such impertinent questions in the future!"

Ann turned with a sniff of dismissal and made her way to the cabin—where she holed up for the rest of the day.

Chase dropped by at mid-afternoon with Christina's basket tucked under his arm. "I thought you might be needing this."

Ann was more conscious of him standing over her than she had ever been of anyone. It was a ripe kind of awareness, heady and filled with possibilities—but new and intense and utterly overwhelming.

She refused to look up from the button she was sewing onto one of his shirts. "Thank you for bringing up the basket."

She couldn't think what else to say to him. She'd exposed parts of herself last night she never let anyone see, lost herself to sensations she hadn't even known existed. How could she carry on a conversation with him when he knew her body so intimately and had shared so much of her pleasure?

Chase seemed unaffected—or undeterred—by this new familiarity. He set the basket on the table. "I missed seeing you at noontime."

"Frenchy sent something up."

He paused, still standing over her. "The weather's particularly fine this afternoon. Will you take a turn around the deck with me?"

She glanced out the door to the cloudless sky and the gold-leafed trees visible at the lip of the horizon. She thought about the serenity of the river, the freshness of the wind in her face. She considered her encounter with Skirlin, and what each crewman would think as she and Chase passed by.

Ann shook her head. "Christina will be waking soon, and I need to be here when she does."

Nodding with what looked like resignation, Chase folded himself into the chair beside her.

That made Ann bend even more intently over her mending.

Finally he reached across and took her hand. "Annie..." he said holding her, thimble, thread, and all. "I know that making love wasn't something you planned to do. Maybe it wasn't something you were even really ready for..."

Ruddy heat washed up her throat.

"...which is why I want to thank you—"

"*Thank me?*" Ann looked up in spite of herself.

"I want to thank you for giving me so much of yourself when I needed you. For giving me so much comfort—and so much joy."

He took a breath before he went on. "Some things that happened yesterday—just didn't turn out the way I hoped. That you believed in me and were willing to stand by me when I needed..." He raised his gaze to hers, and she was caught by the bright blue sincerity of his eyes. "Well, it made a world of difference that you did what you did last night."

Ann clasped her free hand over his. How many times had Chase stood by her when *she* needed *him*? How many times had he fought her battles and lent her his strength? *And how many times had she thought to thank him?*

"Oh, Chase," she murmured, her throat closing around the words. "I wanted to be with you last night. I wanted to help. But it changed—Oh, Chase—it changed so much."

Chase held her hand a little tighter. "It changed things for me, too, Annie. It made me realize I needed to tell you how much I love you. That you ought to know how much you and Christina mean to me."

He looked up at her again. "I'm so proud of you, Annie, so proud you're my wife, so proud you're such a fine mother to our little girl. I'm so proud of the way you've befriended my crew and become such a gracious hostess to our passengers."

Ann hastily lowered her lashes. No one had ever said the things to her that Chase was saying. No one had ever praised her or complimented her. No one but her mother had ever told her that she loved her. Ann wasn't prepared for the power in those words, how they washed over her and left her breathless. She hadn't expected the joy they lit inside or the tears they brought to her eyes.

"I know I haven't done anything to deserve a woman like you, Annie," Chase went on, "but I'm doing the best I can to provide for you—for you and Christina."

Ann stared at him, at this man who said such wondrous things to her, who'd held her with such tenderness and given her such delight. She couldn't tell him that she loved him—at least not yet—but knowing how he felt reinforced her resolve to find a way to be with him.

"Your troubles are my troubles, Chase," she said quietly, aware of the warmth of his flesh between her hands. "Just as you have always made my troubles your own. I know that whatever was bothering you last night can't have gone away. Will you tell me what it is and let me help?"

He looked down at their clasped hands. "You've done so much for me already, Annie. More than I'll ever be able to explain to you. What I need is for you to keep believing in me, keep believing that the choices I've made are for the best, no matter how they turn out."

"I'll never stop believing in you, Chase," she whispered.

"The other thing I need, Annie," he went on, "is for last night to be the true start of our life together."

They were such sweet words, such romantic words, such persuasive words—words that made Ann ache with longing. For a moment she could do no more than stare at him. What Chase wanted was a union between them where they loved each other, trusted each other—*and told the truth.*

But how could she tell Chase the truth?

She knew his family, knew that Chase had been raised to believe that the world was good. How could a man who'd been sheltered from cruelty and deceit all his life understand the kind of betrayals she had suffered? If she told Chase the truth, would he look at her with the same warmth in his eyes? Would he love her when he knew everything? Would he still accept Christina as his daughter?

Chase tightened his grip on her hands, speaking intently. "Hard times come, Annie, and hard times go. Folks get through the worst of things by sticking together. They lie down together every night, wake up in each other's arms every morning, and draw strength from being together. It's what I want for us, Annie."

Ann studied the planes and angles of her husband's earnest face and wished she could open her heart to him. But before she could explain about her past, before she could be the kind of wife he wanted, she needed to face her demons on her own.

"That all sounds wonderful, Chase," Ann said and reluctantly withdrew her hands from his. "But I need time—"

"Time?" The word was tinged with disappointment and, for the first time she could remember, a hint of reproach. "It's been six months since we spoke our vows."

"I know how long it's been." She looked into his eyes,

willing him to trust her. "I'm sorry I've made you wait. I'm sorry I have to ask you to wait a little longer."

He searched her face, the depths of her eyes, and it was as if he were charting every single one of the dark and hollow places inside her.

"All right, Annie," he finally agreed on a sigh. "Take what time you need. I'd just hoped..."

Ann covered his hand with hers again and looked up at him. "Keep hoping, Chase," she whispered. "Please keep hoping just a little while longer."

THE *ANDROMEDA* WAS STILL HALF A DAY SHORT OF KANSAS City on the outbound run, and already Chase could see it was going to be a hell of a trip.

The river was low and, as the dawn light washed pink across the surface of the water, he could pick out the pale fingers of sand inching farther and farther into the channel. The Missouri was a treacherous river to navigate at the best of times, but with the summer's dry spell stretching well into September, even the finest pilots swore they'd resorted to divining rods to find clear passage.

Lucien Boudreau exhibited no talent as a water witch. He'd already run the *Andromeda* aground more times than Chase could count. Sometimes they'd been able to back down and off a reef. More often, they were forced to use the spars—timbers mounted at the bow of the boat—to lever themselves over. Twice they'd had to discharge cargo to lighten the load.

Both times Chase had tried to dump the carbines in the river, but Curry was keeping too close an eye on them.

Those damn rifles.

Chase had been jerked awake almost every night since they'd left St. Louis by dreams of warriors attacking wagon trains, of homesteaders' cabins in flames, of the lives that would be lost if he delivered those Spencers.

Somehow he had to prevent those guns from reaching the Indians. Somehow he had to keep Ann from discovering that the *Andromeda*, that all the Gold Star boats, were running contraband. Somehow he had to put an end to the smuggling without exposing everyone involved—including Ann's father. But if any of that was possible, Chase hadn't figured out how.

Just then the galley door swished open behind him and Chase turned, hoping it was his wife. It was one of the waiters instead, trudging up to the wheelhouse with Lucien Boudreau's breakfast on a tray.

Chase swigged down a swallow of cooling coffee and scowled. He'd been standing right here for the last six mornings, waiting for Annie to come and share the dawn with him. She'd asked for time, and he'd promised her whatever she needed. But he'd have felt so much better able to face his worries about the low water and the smuggling if he had her to talk to.

He scrubbed at his mouth with the back of his hand.

Annie had come to him that night in St. Louis when he hadn't even known how to be with himself. She'd cupped his face between her hands and told him she believed in him. She'd gathered him into her arms, delighted him with the warm, yielding sweetness of her mouth. Then she'd offered him the kind of consolation he'd needed so desperately.

She'd given herself to him.

What incredible courage it must have taken for her to do that. He'd seen by the tremble in her hands and the set of her mouth just how much each new intimacy frightened her. Yet she'd trusted him. She'd responded to him with a shy voluptuousness that made him ache with love and longing even now. She'd abandoned herself and found joy in being one with him.

Annie had given him back himself that night. She'd pleased him and soothed him and renewed him in a way he'd never imagined anyone could. He'd awakened that next morning loving her more than he ever imagined possible.

After that one perfect night, Chase had assumed what they'd shared would grow into a deep and enduring marriage. But Ann had backed away. She'd asked for time, more time. An indefinite period of time while she—

While she what?

He loved Ann, and he believed she loved him, too. They were married, shared a child they both adored, and were standing on the threshold of a wonderful life together. Why couldn't they just go ahead with it?

Chase sighed, downed the last of his coffee, and waited. But Ann didn't come, and what he saw as the *Andromeda* rounded the next bend made him curse under his breath.

In the middle of the stream, a steamer had grounded on a sandbar. Because shipping was a business where time was money, one boat generally ignored the plight of another unless the potential for loss of life was involved. But because this steamer was lodged crosswise to the current, preventing *Andromeda*'s passage, they were going to have to stop and help.

Then Chase noticed the gold star emblazoned on stretchers between the chimneys. He saw the half-moon finial on the pilothouse roof and realized this was the *Cassiopeia*.

It was Boothe Rossiter's steamer that had run aground.

A̲NN KNEW HE'D COME.

She listened all morning to the officers' shouted consultations on how to free the *Cassiopeia* from the sandbar. She watched all afternoon from the safety of the cabin's doorway as the crews off-loaded the smaller steamer's cargo. She felt the *Andromeda*'s floorboards shimmy beneath her shoes as the engines labored to pull the *Cassiopeia* into deeper water. She waited as they reloaded and towed the disabled craft upstream to put in for the night.

Though she knew Chase would have done his best to keep Boothe from bedeviling her, he materialized out of the sunset's sulphurous glow. He loomed up in the cabin doorway, a dark, menacing presence that cast its shadow over Christina and her.

Though Ann had done her best to prepare herself, her stepbrother caught her at a disadvantage anyway. She was trapped in the cabin's single armchair with her daughter asleep in her lap when he arrived.

"I came to see my—*niece*," he greeted her.

"Christina's asleep," Ann told him as coldly as she could. "I won't have you disturbing her."

If she'd expected the admonition to deter him, she should have known better.

"I won't wake her," he promised and sauntered toward them.

As he closed the distance, the smell of the camphor moth-proofing that permeated his clothes became more and more oppressive. So did Ann's memories of that night last fall.

She swallowed the surge of bile at the back of her throat and tried to maintain her composure, but Booth did his best to make that impossible. Each circuit of her chair brought him nearer; each step he took became a further violation. Ann had ample reason to be afraid, but she shored up her courage for her daughter's sake.

As Boothe stopped before her, his menace wrapped around them like a shroud. Ann shivered in spite of herself.

"So our Christina is two months old?" he asked her.

"Nearly three," Ann corrected him. She gathered the baby up in her arms and splayed a protective hand across her back.

Ann knew Boothe liked that she was afraid of him, and though she loathed to give him power over her, she couldn't seem to help herself. He'd bullied her and terrorized her since they were children. Because her mother had never allowed her to retaliate, Ann never thought she had a right to protect herself.

But the regard Ann recognized in other people's eyes when they looked at her, had changed her somehow. Hadn't she won the respect of the men aboard the *Andromeda*? Hadn't the Hardestys claimed her as one of their own? Didn't Chase show in the simple way he draped a shawl around her shoulders what she meant to him?

"Has your husband noticed," Boothe taunted, a narrow smile slithering to the corners of his mouth, "how much Christina is coming to look like me?"

It was an old taunt, one he didn't think she'd answer. It was the opening salvo in a skirmish he thought he'd win.

"Chase hasn't noticed," she answered quietly.

"Surely it's only a matter of time," he purred, "before he sees the resemblance and knows you lay with me."

Ann was beginning to think that though Chase might stroke Christina's night-black hair, remark on her widow's peak or her long-fingered hands, he might never mark the resemblance between Boothe and their little girl. Or even if he did, she wasn't sure he'd fathom what it meant. Chase simply wouldn't expect anyone to have suffered the kind of depravity that made her daughter.

"So what are you going to tell Hardesty," he sneered, "when he asks if I'm Christina's father?"

Ann knew how she must answer him and gathered

Christina closer as if she could draw courage from her daughter's nearness, from the very weight of the child in her arms. Still, her heart fluttered in her throat as she declared herself. "I'm going to tell Chase the truth."

Boothe gave a yip of disbelieving laughter. "You mean to tell your husband you lay with me?"

"I'll tell him you took me against my will."

She knew telling Chase the truth would mark him in a way a man like him ought not to be marked, but it was necessary.

"I'll tell him you forced yourself on me," she said, "to punish me for things that happened when we were children."

Boothe paced away, then turned on her. "Goddamn you, Ann! Why didn't you just stay in Philadelphia?"

"I was wrong to come back," she admitted bitterly. "But I'd missed having a real family, a real home. I thought that if the two of us were grown, the commodore wouldn't have the same power over us he had when we were children."

The commodore always had used what passed as affection to manipulate them. He'd bought Ann's love by cosseting her; he'd wrung obedience from Boothe by withdrawing his favor.

"I remember how you sashayed into the town house that first day," Boothe accused, his voice raw with loathing. "You came all done up in your pretty clothes, with your pretty manners and your pretty ways. With your lovely mama to take my mother's place."

Ann straightened in her chair. "She didn't come to

take your mother's place. All Mama wanted when she married your father was a bit of security."

Boothe went on as if he hadn't heard. "Before you and your mother came, my father took me everywhere. He let me go with him to the warehouses on the levee and onto the boats. When you came, he stopped doing that. You and your mother turned my father against me!"

"We never did anything like that, Boothe. Your father cultivated your jealousy so you'd do what he wanted!"

Boothe shook his head, and Ann knew he'd never recognize the truth.

"Do you know how much I hated you?" he raged, his eyes black with loathing. "How much I wanted you dead!"

"You really did try to kill me, didn't you?" she asked uncertainly.

She'd been out in the stables not long after her mother died. The air had been thick with the tang of fresh-cut hay. Sunlight streamed in the open windows. Boothe's horse had been nuzzling an apple from her hand when he came in and found her.

"Sammy was *my* horse." He blazed at her as if it had happened yesterday. "I hadn't given you permission to touch him."

"You pushed me down and sat on me," she accused, remembering how his knees had crushed her ribs. "You put your hands around my throat."

"I wanted to teach you a lesson."

But it had been more than that. She'd kicked and flailed, but Boothe had been too big and too strong for

393

her to dislodge. Black dots had begun to wink before her eyes when Mary Fairley came into the barn to gather eggs. Boothe had scrambled away, but Mary must have seen what he was doing.

That night James Rossiter had called Ann into his study. He'd examined the bruises on her throat, questioned her about being in the stable, then told her he was sending her away.

He'd punished her as if what Boothe had done had been her fault. But it hadn't been her fault. Boothe's attack last fall hadn't been her fault either.

The rage Ann had held in check for months burst through her, surging through her blood, sizzling along her nerves, clearing her head like a whiff of ammonia. She rose to her feet feeling suddenly vindicated, suddenly purged of all restraints. Suddenly ready to face her stepbrother after all this time.

"You will never threaten me again after today," she said, her voice honed like a blade of steel.

"You will never threaten or harm my daughter." Ann cupped her hand protectively around that small, fuzzy head and stoked her anger with the need to protect all that innocence and vulnerability. "You will never speak a word to anyone about Christina's parentage."

Boothe gave a short, derisive laugh.

"If I hear that you've spread so much as a whisper of scandal about this child"—Ann cut him off—"I'll go to the police and bring charges against you."

"Charges of what?" He sneered at her.

"I'll tell them you raped me, violated your own sister."

Boothe's nostrils flared. "There is no blood be-tween us."

"No," she conceded. "But in the end, that won't matter."

"I could deny that Christina is my daughter."

"Yes, you could," she acknowledged him softly, "but as you say, she looks like you."

"I will say it was you who seduced me."

"And who would believe that a gently reared young woman would know how to seduce anyone?"

Ann waited, knowing she had this one chance to con-vince Boothe how ruthless she could be when it came to protecting her daughter.

"Agree to this, Boothe—" She clasped Christina close, knowing her love for her baby was the source of her strength. "—or I swear, I'll see that no one up or down the river will ever acknowledge or do business with you again."

Rivermen lived by their own code of honor, and Boothe had violated it the night he violated her.

Pinpricks of fear lit in the inky malevolence of his eyes. "Go to hell, Ann," he shouted at her and spun toward the door. "And take your bastard daughter of yours with you!"

Boothe swept off into the thickening twilight.

Ann stood for a moment staring after him, listening to his footsteps *thud* across the deck and clatter down the stairs. Only when they'd faded away did Ann's trembling knees give way. She sank into the chair, lay her daughter against her legs.

Christina was just blinking awake, gurgling and kicking her legs, pulling her tiny, spitty hands out of her mouth and waving them at her mother.

Ann bent above the child and saw for the first time bits of herself looking back. She traced the dimple in Christina's chin and saw that the baby's eyes were shaped like hers. She skimmed her fingertips over the baby's blue-veined brow and her rosebud mouth.

Suddenly breathless, suddenly humming with elation, Ann gathered up her precious girl and laughed as tears streamed down her cheeks.

FOR THE FIRST TIME SINCE THEY'D MADE LOVE, ANN WAS waiting at the railing when Chase stepped out of the galley. She stood silhouetted against the amber brightness of the morning sky, her profile as delicate and perfectly wrought as a cameo.

Chase's heart squeezed inside of him, and he eased the door closed, stealing another moment to drink her in. They'd walked and eaten and spoken together every day this week, yet somehow he'd missed her.

"Morning," he said a little gruffly.

Ann turned from the rail and smiled at him.

It was the kind of smile she should have given him the morning after they'd made love. It rolled over him like a line of breakers, a giddy fizz of exhilaration sweeping through him.

Chase clasped both hands around the mug of coffee to

keep from reaching out to her. He braced his elbows against the rail and tried to convince himself this was just like every other morning.

But it wasn't like every other morning. The sun seemed brighter, the air fresher, the birdsong from the trees along the bank especially sweet. His nerves tingled with awareness—especially of her.

Deliberately he spoke of mundane things. "I didn't see much of you yesterday."

"I was busy looking after Christina."

"I thought maybe you were hiding from Boothe."

She flashed him another quick, dizzying smile, then turned to watch the river.

He sensed an odd agitation in her. Her small, usually quiet hands twirled a button one moment and pushed back a strand of hair the next. She seemed skittish and full of energy.

And somehow more sure of herself.

Before he could ask her why that was, Annie turned to him. "Will they be able to repair the *Cassiopeia*?"

Chase hesitated, wanting to catch her and hold her still long enough for him to fathom the change in her.

"Was the damage to the *Cassiopeia* very serious?"

Chase studied her a moment longer, then allowed himself to be diverted. "It was serious enough. I can't imagine why Boothe tried to run such a treacherous stretch of river in the dark. If the *Cassiopeia* had been going a few miles faster when they rammed that bar, they'd have stove a hole right through the hull."

Boothe had risked the lives of everyone aboard the *Cassiopeia*.

Chase scowled when he realized how much time and hard work it had taken to refloat the steamer. In the course of conferring, towing and sparring, off-loading and reloading, he had made a thorough inventory of Boothe's cargo, looking for contraband. But the *Cassiopeia* was a good long way downstream. If they'd been carrying guns, they'd have made their delivery days ago.

Just thinking about the carbines down in the *Andromeda*'s hold made Chase sweat. He wasn't any closer to knowing what to do about those damn rifles today than he'd been when they left St. Louis. All he knew was that he couldn't live with himself if he sent the guns on their way to the Indians.

"Will the *Cassiopeia* lose much time making the repairs?" Ann persisted.

"A week or two," Chase answered a little peevishly. "Why are you so curious about all this?"

"I suppose I'm not eager to see Boothe again."

Those few words gave Chase the chance to circle back to what he'd meant to ask her earlier. "So Boothe ended up visiting you and Christina, after all."

Ann pushed back from the rail, buoyed up and restless again. "He came right after the boats tied up for the night."

Chase stepped in close, instinctively trying to protect her. "I thought I'd managed to keep him away from you." He shook his head. "If I had any idea he'd come aboard—"

"No." She silenced him with the brush of her hand. "No, it was all right."

"What did Boothe do to bedevil you this time?"

"It doesn't matter what he did." She turned to him, her eyes alight. "What matters is that for the first time in my life I stood up to him! I told him to go to the devil—" She laughed as if she were amazed by her own temerity. "—*and he went!*"

Chase had dealings enough with Boothe Rossiter to know it couldn't have been that simple. "Tell me what happened."

She gave his wrist a squeeze. "I will," she promised. "But not today."

He might have pressed her for more details except that Joel Curry hailed him from the hurricane deck. "Fort Leavenworth to port, sir."

Chase turned his attention to the top of the bluffs where the fort's square, solid buildings perched overlooking the river like a vulture along the lip of a crag. "Order preparations for landing, Mr. Curry."

Begun forty-odd years before, Fort Leavenworth was a citadel worthy of the name, a big sprawling encampment whose primary function was to supply and oversee the string of military outposts that had been built along the river . . . *to control the subjugation of the Indian tribes in the Northwest*.

A gust of realization blew through him; shivers lifted his hair. He'd spent days trying to think of a way to avoid delivering the crates of carbines, and his nights dreaming about the consequences if he failed. Now here was a fort chock full of soldiers who'd be more than willing to come aboard and relieve him of every last one of those guns.

All Chase had to do was explain to Fort Leavenworth's provost marshal that while he was loading cargo he'd spotted some suspicious-looking boxes. The army was bound to investigate, and when they did, they'd find the guns and confiscate them.

Curry and Skirlin would never know Chase was behind the raid, and the army wouldn't learn a thing from the invoices and in the manifests that would involve Ann's father. The *Andromeda* might fall a little behind schedule while the soldiers searched and questioned the crew, but it would be worth the inconvenience to be rid of those goddamn rifles.

Chase squeezed Ann's arm, then pushed away from the railing.

"How big an order do we have to deliver to the fort, Mr. Curry?" he asked as he sauntered toward the hurricane deck.

"Nearly three hundred boxes and barrels, sir. Mr. Skirlin could give you the particulars."

Even from the distance Chase could see how busy Fort Leavenworth dockage was. "How long will it take to off-load that much cargo?"

"A couple of hours, sir," Curry answered.

"Very well, Mr. Curry," he said. "I'll stand the rest of your watch. Go below and prepare to off-load that cargo."

Once they tied up at Fort Leavenworth, Chase was going to go see the provost marshal, tell a few lies, and let the army take those damn carbines off his hands.

THINGS AT FORT LEAVENWORTH DIDN'T GO QUITE THE WAY Chase thought they would. He hadn't gotten rid of the damn guns; he'd acquired a passenger.

The trim little man standing beside him now in a tweed sack coat, corduroy trousers, and high boots might look like a sportsman, but he was really Colonel Richard Follensbee. The colonel had been detailed to accompany the carbines as far as their transfer point. Chase wasn't privy to the colonel's orders beyond that, so what Follensbee meant to do when they got where those guns were going was anyone's guess.

But not knowing was putting Chase on edge.

At the moment, what Follensbee was doing, though, was reeling off a list of things he'd forgotten, things he wanted Chase to get for him while they were wooding up at Hardesty's Landing.

"... shoelaces, and a razor strop," he finished, as they stood together on the *Andromeda*'s hurricane deck. "And maybe a bit of pipe tobacco."

Hardesty's Landing lay half a mile upriver, and as Chase squinted ahead, his mind was not on what Follensbee needed. It was on Rue.

He'd had a note from his mother by way of another of the other Gold Star captains just after they left St. Louis. She had written that his brother was on the mend, but Chase wouldn't be satisfied that it was true until he saw Rue for himself.

"My folks don't stock a proper store, Mr. Follensbee,"

Chase said, addressing the man beside him, "but I'm sure Ma will do the best she can to accommodate you."

He signaled Boudreau to sound the landing whistle, then started shouting orders.

Only after the *Andromeda* was safely berthed was Chase able to turn his thoughts to other matters. When he looked up toward the house, he could hardly believe what he was seeing.

"Rue!" he whooped. "My God! Rue!"

"Managed to finish the run without me, did you?" his brother shouted back.

Rue was balanced on a pair of homemade crutches at the foot of the stone steps. From the way his mother was hovering, Chase guessed Rue might not be as steady on his feet as he looked from here. Still, considering they hadn't been entirely sure Rue would live when they left, Chase was amazed by his recovery.

Lydia waved, too, then something on the lower deck snagged her attention. His family, no doubt.

His family. Chase lit up inside.

For the first time since they'd spoken their vows, he and Annie were coming home to Hardesty's Landing as true man and wife. As people who loved each other and meant to make a life together. He hadn't been sure this day would ever come, but now that it had, he wanted to share his joy with everyone. Especially with his mother.

Ann and Christina were already visiting with Lydia and Rue as he strode toward the four of them a few minutes later.

"I can hardly believe how much you've grown!" he heard Lydia coo as she held her newest grandchild.

"She's three months old," Ann offered, smoothing her daughter's hair. "How is that possible?"

"It seems like only yesterday *this one*"—Lydia gave Chase's arm a welcoming nudge—"was in short pants."

Chase bussed his mother's cheek, then turned to Rue.

"I'm glad to see you're recovering from your dip in the river," he greeted him and slid his arms gingerly around his brother's shoulders. "Ann was worried, but I said you were tough as shoe leather and being batted around by a paddle wheel wouldn't slow you down for long."

"Damn right," Rue agreed and hugged him back.

Still, Chase could feel how bony Rue was beneath his hands, how he wavered on his crutches just standing there.

"I'm going to be all right, Chase," Rue assured him quietly, "so you can stop fretting. But before you leave, we've got some things we need to discuss."

"I figured we might." Chase steered his brother toward the thigh-high ledge that ran across the back of the landing.

Rue sat down gratefully. "So," he said once he caught his breath. "Did you figure it was Curry that pushed me overboard?"

"I was pretty sure what happened wasn't an accident," Chase hedged, glaring across at where the burly mate was supervising the wooding up. Still, he'd hoped there was another explanation. He hated the idea that a man he'd worked with and eaten with for months, a man who slept in a berth barely an arm's length away had tried to kill his brother.

"I've never trusted either Skirlin or Curry," Chase went on. "I should have tossed them off the boat as soon as we began to suspect they were moving contraband."

But Chase hadn't fired Curry and Skirlin. He hadn't wanted to believe that the *Andromeda* was carrying contraband. He hadn't wanted to admit to himself, much less reveal to the commodore, that he hadn't been in complete control of his own boat.

"I'd gone down to settle a bet I'd made with Cal," Rue said, recalling the day more than a month before. "Curry and Skirlin were getting ready to off-load boxes—the kind of crates you and I had been watching for. So I wandered over—and somehow the cover on one of them came lose."

"And there were Spencers inside."

Rue confirmed it with a nod. "Curry was waiting for me when I came out of the engine room a few minutes later."

"And he tried to kill you," Chase offered softly, reaching across to gently clasp his brother's shoulder. He needed that contact, the reassurance that in spite of how fragile Rue seemed, he was going to be all right.

How could he have lived with himself if Rue had died?

"Curry and Skirlin are working for the commodore," Chase went on. "He's the one who devised this scheme, working hand in glove with the president of Overland Freighting. But I swear, Rue," he vowed, "no matter what happens or who else is involved, Curry and Skirlin are going to pay for what they did to you."

"I was counting on you to see to that," Rue acknowledged. "Just the way I used to count on you when we were boys."

"I'm sorry I didn't act fast enough to spare you this," Chase apologized.

Just then, Enoch Hardesty came striding across the landing. "Morning, boy," his father greeted Chase.

"Hello, Pa."

"You have a chance to talk to him about the rifles?" Enoch asked the younger man.

Chase's stomach pitched. But then, Rue would have to have told Enoch about the guns. Knowing there'd been contraband aboard the *Andromeda* would have confirmed every doubt Enoch had ever had about Chase's judgment and his worth.

"Of course I know about the rifles," Chase said, owning up to what he'd done.

"About the carbines in the cave?" Enoch asked him.

Chase's knees wobbled as if he had been sucker punched. "There are guns in one of the caves?"

Enoch's lips quirked with something that might have been satisfaction. "Stuart came across four crates of shiny new Spencer carbines a couple days after you brought Rue home."

"I don't know a thing about those guns," Chase declared.

Or maybe he did.

"When Rue was hurt," Chase began sorting things out

as he went, "I gave orders to head directly for Hardesty's Landing, so we must have steamed right past the transfer point."

"And your smugglers dumped the rifles first chance they got," Enoch finished the thought.

"Which was here at Hardesty's Landing," Rue pointed out.

Chase nodded thoughtfully. That explained why there had been no guns to be found aboard the *Andromeda*.

"James Rossiter is behind the smuggling, isn't he?" Enoch asked quietly.

When Chase inclined his head, Enoch lay one big, rough palm against Chase's shoulder in a gesture of commiseration and council. "What are you going to do about him being part of it?" he wanted to know. "He's Ann's father."

Chase shook his head. "I'm going to do my best to protect her and Christina."

"Chase . . ." There was concern in Enoch's voice. "As much as you need to look after your family, you can't get caught up in running contraband."

"I'm taking care of it, Pa," Chase said, wishing he knew what Follensbee meant to do. "It'll be all right."

Just then, Will came sprinting across the woodlot. "They went to the cave and got the guns, Pa," he told them excitedly, "just like you said! Jake Skirlin and that new mate loaded them right aboard the *Andromeda*."

Chase turned on his father. "You warned me about not dealing in contraband and now you let Curry and Skirlin recover guns you know full well are headed for the Indians?"

"Well you see, Chase, while those guns were here with us we did a bit of gunsmithing."

"What kind of gunsmithing?"

"Will and Silas and me, we filed down the percussion slides." Enoch grinned like the firebrand he must once have been. "Skirlin and Curry may well send those fine rifles to the Indians, but not one of them will ever fire."

chapter sixteen

A DETAIL OF SOLDIERS WAS WAITING ON THE ST. LOUIS levee when the *Andromeda* pulled in. Ann wondered why they were there, then watched with a hitch of apprehension as they quick-stepped up the gangway.

Led by a gangly young lieutenant, they approached the foredeck where she and Chase were bidding good-bye to their cabin passengers. "Captain Hardesty?" the young officer asked.

"I'm Captain Hardesty."

"I'm Lieutenant Ashbrook, sir," the young man introduced himself, "from the provost marshal's office. I'm afraid I have orders to take you into custody and impound your vessel."

Ann clutched her husband's arm.

"On what charge, Lieutenant?" Chase asked.

"Unauthorized distribution of restricted materials to hostiles," Ashbrook answered.

"What?" Ann gasped. "What kind of restricted materials?"

"Guns, ma'am," the lieutenant answered. "Your husband's accused of running guns to the Indians."

"He wouldn't do that!" Ann protested. She turned to Chase, wanting an explanation.

He gave her wrist a gentle squeeze. "There's been some kind of a mistake, Annie," he told her. "I'll just go along with the lieutenant to get it straightened out. It'll be all right."

He sounded so calm, so sure of himself. Ann nodded and did her best to believe his reassurances.

Then one of Ashbrook's men brought out a pair of manacles and clasped the iron bracelets around Chase's wrists. For a moment Ann couldn't tear her gaze away from where Chase—her Chase—was being chained like a common criminal.

"Please, Lieutenant Ashbrook," Ann implored, her voice shaking. "My husband wouldn't run guns to the Indians!"

"I'm sorry, ma'am. I'm just following my orders." He extended the document for her to read.

Ann unfolded the warrant and scanned the jumble of legal phrases. She turned to Chase. "I know you didn't do this!"

He looked at her for one long moment, then averted his eyes. "I'll explain everything when I get back."

Something in that instant of evasion sent a close, panicky heat coursing through her.

Then one of Ashbrook's men grabbed Chase's arm. A second man prodded him toward the landing stage, and the detail moved out, taking Chase with it.

Ann followed them across the deck. "Chase!" she called out. "Chase, I'm going to hire a lawyer."

Chase shook his head as he looked back at her. "Find Richard Follensbee. Tell him what's happened. Tell him to meet us at the provost marshal's office."

"Richard Follensbee?"

"In cabin eight. And, Annie," Chase shouted as the provost's guards loaded him into the back of a high-sided wagon. "This is going to be fine."

It didn't look like it was going to be fine.

As the wagon rumbled across the levee, Ann ran up the stairs, praying this Richard Follensbee hadn't disembarked. Her heels clattered on the wooden floor as she crossed the empty salon, and she pounded impatiently on the door to cabin eight. She waited with her heart in her throat, wondering what she'd do if Follensbee was gone.

As soon as he opened the door, Ann recognized the slim, square-cut man as having come aboard somewhere west of Kansas City on the upstream run, then joined them again for the return to St. Louis.

"Mrs. Hardesty!" he exclaimed, clearly surprised to see her. "Is there something I can do for you?"

"They've taken my husband!" Ann told him in a rush.

Follensbee pulled her into the cabin and closed the door behind them. "Who took Captain Hardesty?"

"Soldiers came and arrested him. They say he's been smuggling guns to the Indians, but I know Chase would never..."

For the first time, Ann realized just how serious the charges were. If Chase were tried and found guilty, he would be sentenced to years in prison. Her knees nearly went out from under her at the thought of losing him.

Follensbee's grip on her arm tightened. "Where, Mrs. Hardesty?" he asked her. "Where did they take him?"

"Chase said to meet them at the provost marshal's office."

Follensbee nodded briskly and grabbed a portfolio from the half-packed valise. "You wait right here, Mrs. Hardesty," he instructed as he turned to go, "until Chase gets back."

Ann watched him go, knowing the very last thing in the world she intended to do was to "wait right here."

Chase hadn't been smuggling contraband, but there was something going on. Something Ann didn't like. She could see that her husband was going to need a lawyer, money for bail, and a place to stay in town until this got settled.

She hated going to her stepfather for help, especially when the *Andromeda* was involved, but the commodore had friends in high places, men who'd be able to advise them.

Ann rushed to gather up her bonnet, reticule, and the things she'd need for the baby, then bustled into the galley. Frenchy had been keeping an eye on Christina, but

Ann knew he had appointments of his own to keep this afternoon.

She'd just bundled her sleeping daughter up in her arms, when she heard footfalls behind her. She turned to thank Frenchy for his help—and stopped dead in her tracks.

Never had she seen Frenchy Bertin wear anything but baggy trousers, a flowing shirt, and a flour-dusted apron. She hadn't once seen him freshly bathed *and* freshly barbered simultaneously.

Ann stared openmouthed.

"Anouk is waiting for me at The Planters House Hotel," he said by way of explanation. "Do I look all right?"

The dark coat and pinstriped trousers hung on his lanky frame like wash on a clothesline. Someone had cut his hair too short, and his ears stuck out. His striped cravat was inexpertly tied and listing to the left.

"I think you look very handsome," Ann lied stoutly. Then, bracing Christina against her shoulder with one hand, she adjusted his tie with the other. "Anouk will be so impressed."

Frenchy blotted the sweat from his upper lip. "I will be glad to see her, too. And, of course, the children."

Ann knew he wasn't entirely resigned to living with Anouk as his only wife, but the priest at the St. Louis Cathedral had been quite insistent. He'd ordered Frenchy to resolve his matrimonial tangles immediately or risk his immortal soul.

Grumbling and reluctant, Frenchy had sent Marie and

Charmaine letters the very next day, offering them annulments and settlements—money Ann was lending him. Both women had agreed, and Charmaine confessed that in his absence, she'd taken up with someone else. Though Frenchy's feelings were bruised, Ann had written bank drafts to both the women and accompanied Frenchy to the post office to be sure he actually put them in the mail.

"So," Frenchy said, shrugging off his own concerns, "are you going to get our captain out of jail?"

"I'm going to see the commodore," Ann answered. "I hope he'll use his influence to get the charges dismissed."

"Smuggling guns to the Indians!" Frenchy said and huffed for emphasis. "Our captain would never do such a thing!"

With a determined nod, Ann headed toward the door. "Good luck explaining everything to Anouk," she called back. "And don't forget to tell her about that business opportunity we talked about."

"*Oui*," he assured her. "That may be the only thing that keeps her from divorcing me outright when she learns the rest!"

Twenty minutes later, Ann rushed up the limestone steps to the wide double doors of her stepfather's town house. Mary Fairley answered her knock, and the moment the older woman saw Ann outside, her round, wrinkled face was wreathed in smiles.

"Oh, Miss Ann, what a dear little thing your Christina's getting to be!" she exclaimed as she ushered Ann into the hall.

The baby stretched and yawned and blinked awake almost as if she'd recognized her name and wanted to be accommodating. Ann nestled Christina against her, traced one soft cheek with her fingertips, drawing calm from the contact.

Mary leaned in close for a better look at the baby. "Oh, what a sweet little thing you are!" she cooed to her. "Wouldn't cook and the girls downstairs just love a peek at you?"

"You may take Christina down and show them, if you like," Ann offered. "I have some business to discuss with the commodore. I'll come and collect her when we're done."

"It'd be grand to keep her for you, Miss Ann!" Mary offered and held out her hands for the baby.

As Ann settled Christina into Mary's arms, the baby gurgled up at her. "Oh, you darlin' girl!" Mary cried and rocked Christina against her. "Don't you worry, Miss Ann, I'll look after her. Take as much time with the commodore as you like."

Ann watched Mary carry Christina down the hall, then burst in to her stepfather's study.

"Ann!" James Rossiter looked up from his paperwork in surprise. "I didn't expect to see you until this afternoon!"

"The provost marshal's men came aboard the *Andromeda* and arrested Chase!" she told him, crossing the room in a bustle of skirts. "They claim he's smuggling arms to the Indians. But you know as well as I do that Chase would never—"

The commodore pushed to his feet and hurried around the corner of the desk. "Sit down, Ann," he offered solicitously. "Tell me what happened."

She perched on the seat of one of the armchairs. "There's not much more to tell! They arrested Chase and took him away in irons!"

The memory of her tall, proud husband shackled like a criminal tore at her. For the first time since the soldiers had come aboard, Ann's eyes filled with tears.

"Please," she whispered imploringly. "Please, can we go hire a lawyer for him? Can we see someone about having the charges dismissed?"

"Of course we'll get him a lawyer."

"Can we do it now?" Ann pressed him. "I don't want Chase spending a single night in jail when I know he's innocent."

"Now, Ann." The commodore settled in the chair beside her and clasped her hand. "As much faith as you have in that husband of yours, you've got to realize federal warrants aren't issued willy-nilly. The provost marshal must have evidence—"

"But how could there be evidence?" Ann's heart squeezed with fear. "Chase wouldn't do this!"

"Are you sure?" he asked her. "Just think about the rough-and-ready life Chase lived before he married you, and the kind of people he comes from. If he had a chance to make enough money to put that life behind him for good—"

"Chase wouldn't do that! He wouldn't smuggle guns to the Indians!"

The commodore's mouth narrowed. "How can you be so sure?"

Because I know Chase! she longed to shout. But she needed to give the commodore reasons, explanations. "Before Enoch and Lydia adopted him, Chase was orphaned in an Indian raid. He would never do anything to put another family in jeopardy."

James Rossiter pushed to his feet and stood over her. Perhaps it was how tall he suddenly seemed, or the cant of his mouth that put Ann in mind of the night years before when he'd summoned her to this very room and told her he was sending her away.

Instinctively Ann braced herself.

"I think you should know," he began, "that there have been rumors circulating for months that someone on the Gold Star boats has been running guns to the Indians. Both the provost and federal marshals have been investigating. They even came here and questioned me."

Fear clawed up Ann's throat. "What did you tell them?"

"I had to tell them the truth, Ann. You understand that, don't you?"

Her heart went still. *"What did you tell them?"*

The commodore shook his head. "After the *Andromeda* made that first packet run of the season, her clerk came to see me."

"Jake Skirlin came here?"

"He said he'd heard rumors about the Gold Star boats running contraband and wanted to report a suspicious landing."

Ann's belly fluttered with apprehension.

"He said that about a day downstream from Sioux City the *Andromeda* made a stop in the middle of nowhere."

Ann remembered that stop and remembered asking Chase where they were. It was barely dawn and the mist was still rising off the river. A man with a wagon had been waiting.

"I was on deck that morning," she said quietly.

"Skirlin said they delivered some big, heavy boxes."

She could see those boxes, even now. How the roustabouts had strained under their weight, how they'd grunted as they heaved them into the wagon.

Had they been boxes of guns for the Indians? The hair stirred along Ann's arms the way the wind stirred the grass on the open prairie.

"Jake Skirlin came here and accused Chase of smuggling rifles?" she asked and rubbed the shivers away.

Her stepfather nodded gravely. "I'm afraid that's what I had to tell the marshals."

Ann stared past him, not able to let the memory go. She'd been standing right beside Chase when the *Andromeda* made the stop, and she'd have sworn he didn't know a thing about the boxes. *Skirlin* was the one who knew about them, and if those were boxes of guns, then he must be the one behind the smuggling.

But that didn't feel right, either. How would Skirlin have been able to secure those rifles on his own? That would have required ready money. He'd have to have connections with the freighters to set up a rendezvous.

Skirlin might be devious, but he wasn't either smart or particularly ingenious.

Ann looked up at her stepfather. "It's you, isn't it?"

She recognized the smug curl of his lips and a chill of certainty swept through her.

"How could it be me, Ann? I haven't left St. Louis. I'm not delivering rifles to the Indians."

"No, but you're behind the men who are. Nothing happens aboard the Gold Star boats without you knowing." That certainty grew in her. "Nothing goes on you don't control."

His black eyes raked over her. "Is that what you think?"

"You and Skirlin fabricated the evidence against Chase, didn't you?"

The commodore gave a low, gruff laugh. "My poor, dear, Ann," he said. "I didn't have to fabricate a single thing. Your husband might not have been with us at the start, but he's as deep in this now as everyone else.

"He knew full well what he was carrying. He took delivery of the guns on this last run himself. I've just received confirmation he delivered them just when and where he was supposed to."

Ann understood now why Chase hadn't been able to look at her this morning. In spite of his assurances, he was guilty.

She sank back into her chair. The commodore had proof against her husband, enough to convict him, to send him to prison for years and years. But why would an honorable man, *why would Chase*, agree to something he didn't believe in?

But then Ann knew: He'd done it to protect her and the baby. He'd done it because the commodore had given him no choice.

"But you—" Ann shook her head, still trying to make some sense of what had happened. "—you arranged for Chase to marry me. You gave your own granddaughter into his care."

"For a time," the commodore conceded.

"You gave Chase the *Andromeda*."

"He never truly owned the *Andromeda*."

Ann's eyes widened. "What do you mean?" she demanded. How else had this man cheated her honorable husband?

"According to the marriage agreement Chase signed, the *Andromeda* doesn't come to him until he's completed the shipping season. He has one more run to make." The commodore leaned toward her as if he were confiding in her. "I don't think he's going to make that final run, do you?"

Rossiter shrugged, clearly pleased with himself. "Besides, I promised the *Andromeda* to Boothe."

Ann shot to her feet. "You're not going to help me get Chase out of jail, are you?"

"No."

"You've arranged for him to be tried and convicted of running contraband while everyone else goes free."

"Exactly."

"But certainly Chase will expose you," Ann cried.

"He'll tell the provost marshal what he knows about the smuggling!"

"Chase won't say a word."

"Why?" That single word seemed to take all of her breath.

"He'll own up to this because your husband is a noble fool. He'll admit his involvement because he believes he deserves to be punished. He'll hold his peace to protect you and Christina."

The certainty in him terrified her. "Protect us?"

"Why, Ann," the commodore said almost kindly, reaching out to clasp her hand. "Chase knows that while he's in prison, I'll be providing for you and Christina. He wants to be certain you're treated—well."

Ann jerked away from him.

"I've already begun making plans for you. Would you like to hear them?"

Ann backed away.

"Once the furor of his trial dies down, you'll divorce Chase Hardesty," he went on anyway. "Then we'll find you a more suitable husband. I have several alliances in mind that might be good for business. . . ."

Ann stared at James Rossiter, repelled by the cold, meticulous workings of his mind. To him, people existed to serve his purpose, each as expendable as a pawn on a chessboard, each a chit he'd used to further his own ends. Odd as it seemed, Ann didn't think it was malice that drove him. It was expedience and the pleasure he took in controlling other people's lives.

Ann shivered in spite of herself.

To accomplish what he'd set out to do, he'd cheated Chase at every turn—in his marriage to her, in claiming Boothe's child, and with the captaincy of the *Andromeda*. Her stepfather had ruthlessly duped and corrupted him, stolen the honor of one of the most honorable men she'd ever met. Now the commodore meant to turn Chase's own guilt against him—*but she wasn't about to let him succeed.*

"I can see," she said, turning on him with icy civility, "I'll have to find another way to prove my husband's innocence."

She sailed across the study toward the half-open door into the hall. The commodore caught her wrist before she reached it.

"Don't be a fool, Ann. Let him go. Let Chase Hardesty make this sacrifice for everyone's sake."

That he thought she'd agree to this, side with him against the man she loved, made her angry. She jerked out of his grasp and stepped back panting. "I'm not going to allow you to betray my husband the way you've betrayed me!"

For an instant he hesitated, seemed genuinely taken aback.

"Betrayed you?" he finally bellowed. "Goddamn ungrateful girl! I *protected* you. I protected you and your bastard!"

"Protected me?" she raged at him. "The way you protected me when Boothe tried to kill me that day in the stable?"

"Of course I protected you! I had plans for you. Even

then it was clear you were going to grow up to be a lovely woman, a woman with connections back East and a flawless pedigree. With those kinds of attributes, there was no limit to the kind of advantageous marriage I could make for you when the time came. So I sent you out of harm's way."

Tears sprang to her eyes. She had been a commodity to him, to the only father she'd ever known. "You made me feel as if what happened was my fault! *As if I deserved the way Boothe treated me!*"

"He was only teaching you a lesson." There wasn't a shred of humanity in those black eyes. "Perhaps you *did* deserve the scare he gave you."

"No," she cried, outrage rippling hot beneath her skin. "I didn't deserve that then, and I most certainly didn't deserve what Boothe did when I came back to this house! You knew very well I was afraid of him, but you did nothing. You never restrained him or tried to prevent him from threatening me. Because you turned a blind eye to what your son was doing—*he raped me!*

"Boothe raped me right here in your house! He got me with child—and the only thing you could think about afterwards was protecting the Rossiter name. You were so desperate to conceal what he had done that you sold me—"

"For not an inconsiderable amount," he reminded her.

Ann punched him. She hit him as hard as she could and felt his nose mash flat beneath her fist. James Rossiter staggered back a step, blood coursing down his chin.

Ann gasped in astonishment. She'd seen the rousters

fight amongst themselves more than once, but she'd never imagined she was capable of hitting anyone. She never thought she'd feel such a rush of satisfaction at doing it. She'd never once imagined how much her hand would hurt afterwards!

"'For not an inconsiderable amount,' you say?" she shouted at him. "You promised Chase Hardesty a steamer you knew he'd never own, a captaincy he couldn't possibly sustain once his boat was gone, and a woman so sullied she might never be able to be a wife to him!

"You didn't offer him one thing of value in exchange for his good name. And now you mean to take his freedom, too. Well, I won't let you do that!" She wheeled like a warrior queen and strode toward the door. "Chase Hardesty might not tell the authorities who's been running guns to the Indians, but I will!"

Ann tore open the door into the hallway and saw her husband standing just outside. From the sick horror in Chase's eyes when he looked at her, she knew he'd heard every word.

Aɴɴ's WORDS PIERCED CHASE LIKE A BLADE OF STEEL.

"Boothe raped me," he heard her shout, "right here in your house! He got me with child—and the only thing you could think about afterwards was protecting the Rossiter name."

Chase stumbled back from the half-open door and braced himself against the wall. A swirl of sickness took him. His ears rang and his mouth went sour. He couldn't move, couldn't breathe. He couldn't think about anything but what Ann had said.

Boothe raped me.

Chase clamped his eyes shut, trying not to see, trying not to imagine, but the visions swirled through his head. Boothe's long-fingered hands tearing at Annie's clothes, bruising her skin as he held her down. Boothe's cruel kisses crushing her mouth, his body...

Chase's throat seared with bile.

He'd seen the shadows in her eyes, recognized the vein of fear in her, and been convinced that someone had taken her against her will. She'd all but confirmed it when they made love. He just hadn't known who it was or understood how terribly she'd been betrayed by her own family.

How had his Annie borne what these men did to her?

"'Chase Hardesty might not be willing to tell the authorities who's running guns to the Indians'"—Ann's voice carried out into the hall—"'but I will!'"

Ann tore open the study door and saw him standing there. She stopped dead in her tracks. Her face paled. Their gazes held for a moment that seemed to verge on forever.

Seeing him standing there seemed to strip the final shreds of Ann's veneer away, her final fragile layer of defense. In that instant he saw all the way to the core of her, her half-healed scars, her tattered faith in a world that had been so cruel to her.

He saw the steel-spined courage it had taken for her to

survive, to become the kind of woman she was, the kind of mother she'd been to Christina. He realized how much she'd overcome to allow herself to care for him, open herself to him.

He could never change the past, change how her stepfather and brother had misused her. Because he hadn't known the truth, he'd been powerless to help her heal what they had done.

Chase was powerless no more. A fervent, fine-grained fury drove through his blood. It prickled along the surface of his skin, collected bitter and hot in the pit of his belly. He saw only one redress for what the men in Annie's own family had done to her. *Had done to his wife*.

The law was going to punish the commodore; he'd seen to that. Now he was going to find Boothe Rossiter and pound him into dust.

"Chase," Ann whispered and reached out to him, as if she knew what he meant to do and was trying to sway him. "Chase."

He refused to give her a chance to change his mind. He turned without a word and strode away from her.

A NN PRAYED HE WAS AN APPARITION.

She prayed Chase wasn't standing just outside the door to her stepfather's study. Prayed he wasn't staring at her as if she was someone he didn't know. She prayed he hadn't overheard what she'd said about Boothe.

But she could tell by his expression he had.

Cold peppered through her. She raised one trembling hand, palm extended in entreaty. "Chase."

His mouth narrowed; his eyes went hard.

"Chase."

He turned from her without a word.

Ann stood frozen, hollow, staring after him as he blazed down the hall and tore open the front door. She clapped her hand over her mouth to hold back the cry that spiraled up her throat.

He was leaving her—doing exactly what she was afraid he'd do when he learned the truth.

After what happened with Boothe, Ann had felt tainted, unworthy of accepting the love of the steady, honorable man Chase Hardesty had proved himself to be. But in these last months aboard the *Andromeda*, Ann had changed. Becoming Christina's mother had changed her. Admitting her love for Chase had changed her. Offering herself to him had changed her.

The woman she'd become had had courage enough to confront Boothe after years of cruelty, to break his hold on her and Christina. The Ann she was now had been powerful enough to stand her ground against the commodore. After she'd fought so hard and accomplished so much, how could she watch Chase walk away?

How could she give up the dreams he had made her believe in?

Ann picked up her skirts and ran down the hall after him. But Chase couldn't seem to get away fast enough.

When she yanked open the door at the front of the

house, he was already down the steps. Though she called to him, Chase banged out the iron gate and stepped onto the street. He strode right past the squad of soldiers clustered around a wagon parked in front of the town house.

Ann would have done that, too, except Richard Follensbee stepped in front of her.

"Mrs. Hardesty," he said.

Ann did her best to get around him. "Please!" she implored, but Follensbee refused to let her pass.

She watched helplessly as Chase stalked off down the street, knowing that he'd heard the truth and he was repelled by it, repelled by her. Wasn't he putting as much distance as he could between them?

"Mrs. Hardesty," Richard Follensbee's voice was insistent. She turned to him, suddenly drained and sagging with resignation.

It was a moment before she noticed the change in him. He stood taller, seemed tougher, more determined and in command.

"Why are you here, Mr. Follensbee?" she wanted to know.

"It's Colonel Follensbee," he corrected her. "I'm afraid I misled you about who I am. I was aboard the *Andromeda* to look into allegations that Gold Star boats were running contraband."

"Chase had nothing at all to do with that!" she declared in a rush, needing to clear her husband's name. "The commodore was the one behind the smuggling."

"We know that, Mrs. Hardesty," Follensbee assured her. "We've come to take your father into custody."

Was that why Chase had come to the town house? Had he meant to warn James Rossiter that the provost marshal was after him?

"What I'd like, Mrs. Hardesty, is for you to let us in voluntarily," Follensbee went on, "and give us permission for a search."

"Is there an alternative?"

"We could break down the door."

Ann let the colonel and his men into the house, but the commodore was gone. A trail of papers strewn down the back stairs seemed to indicate how he had escaped.

Follensbee gestured his men to track him down, then settled Ann in one of the armchairs. Lieutenant Ashbrook returned not three minutes later with James Rossiter in tow.

"He was saddling his horse," Ashbrook reported and handed Follensbee a pair of bulging saddlebags. "Looks like there's some interesting reading here."

The colonel riffled through the bags then handed them back. "Take Mr. Rossiter on out to the wagon. I need a few words with Mrs. Hardesty before we go."

As Ashbrook hustled James Rossiter toward the door, he turned and glared at Ann. "You'll mind your mouth, girl, if you know what's good for you."

"I won't lie to protect you, *Father*," she answered coolly, "when you never once raised a hand to protect me."

Rossiter called curses down on her head as Follensbee's

men led him away. Once they were alone, the colonel turned his attention back to Ann.

"Very well, Mrs. Hardesty," he began. "What do you know about your father's activities?"

"James Rossiter is my stepfather." It seemed a particulary important distinction for Ann to make. "And until this morning, I didn't know a thing about any of this."

"Then why don't you tell me what you've learned?" Follensbee encouraged her.

Because her fate—and Chase and Christina's—had always been in the commodore's hands, Ann had never before spoken about her stepfather. Though she kept her secrets, she told the colonel what she could and did her best to clear her husband's name.

"So you see," she finished, "Chase didn't know about the contraband at the start. He only agreed to carry the rifles on this last trip because the commodore threatened Christina and me.

"Chase is a good man, Colonel Follensbee," she went on. "You've seen what a fine captain he is, and how the men respect him. Please, if you could just see fit to recommend leniency where he is concerned . . ."

"But, Mrs. Hardesty," Follensbee broke in, "didn't Captain Hardesty tell you? He's the one who helped us make our case against the smugglers."

"What?" Ann managed to croak.

"We heard rumors this spring that some of the Missouri River steamers were running guns and started to investigate. But the smugglers were so skillful at passing off the contraband as cargo, that it was nearly impossible to detect. We didn't know exactly how they were doing it until Chase came to see us at Fort Leavenworth three weeks ago."

How difficult, Ann wondered, had it been for Chase to go to the authorities when there was so much at stake? When he must have known he'd be risking his own freedom by telling the truth? Yet he'd done what he thought was right in spite of it, and Ann was proud of him.

Follensbee perched at the edge of the desk and looked down at her. "I boarded the *Andromeda* to see how the smugglers operated, and I stayed aboard so I could deliver my report to Jefferson Barracks. If I hadn't been aboard this morning, Chase would most certainly be cooling his heels in the guardhouse while we got things settled. As it is, we'll round up the other Gold Star officers involved in the smuggling either at the end of their runs or farther upriver."

"Then Chase has cleared his name?" Ann pressed him, needing to be sure. "There won't be any charges—"

"Your husband is completely exonerated."

Ann let out her breath in relief.

Once Follensbee had gone, she climbed to her feet and ambled to the window that overlooked the garden. Though the sun beat bright and warm on the last of the summer roses, Ann felt bleak and gray with exhaustion.

She was drained by her confrontation with the commodore and Follensbee's questioning. The idea of seeing Chase and telling him the truth about Christina and Boothe terrified her beyond all bearing.

She rested her forehead against the glass and blinked back the tears. As long as she lived, she'd never forget how stricken Chase looked standing there in the hall, or how decisively he'd turned from her.

How could she convince him, even after this, that they could pick up where they left off? That they could have a life together?

Ann knew she had to try. If he refused to accept what she had to tell him, then Chase at least deserved to hear how grateful she was for what he'd taught her, how precious her time aboard the *Andromeda* had been to her. Chase needed to understand how proud she'd been to be his wife, and how much she'd cherished being a Hardesty.

He deserved to know just how much she loved him.

She raised her face to the sun, felt the heat of it baking through the glass to warm her, fill her with its strength. Ann basked in the sunshine a moment longer, then turned away.

Chase would show up at the *Andromeda* eventually, and when he did, Ann intended to be waiting. That meant she had to collect her daughter from Mary Fairley and head back to the levee.

When she got down to the kitchen, she gathered Christina in her arms, then took a horsecab back downtown.

She was just paying the driver when she heard the quick triple *thoop* of what she recognized instantly as the *Andromeda*'s whistle. She turned with a jerk and saw that the steamer was backing down. Smoke billowed black from the smokestacks and the stern wheel churned feverishly against the current as the boat hung for a moment in the middle of the river.

Ann's heart fluttered in her throat like a butterfly caught in her two hands. The *Andromeda* wasn't scheduled to leave for Sioux City until noon tomorrow.

Where was Chase going?

She threaded her way through the people gathered on the levee, waving in desperation. She knew how unlikely it was that anyone aboard the riverboat would see her in the crowd, but she ran toward the water anyway.

Then the *Andromeda* blew its whistle one last time and headed north, her wake rolling out behind her like the tea-dyed train of a lady's lacy dancing dress.

Ann was still standing on the cobblestoned slope, trying to decide what she ought to do, when one of the transfer agents came tramping toward her.

"Mrs. Hardesty," he said as he tugged a small square of paper from his waistcoat pocket. "Your husband asked me to give you this."

She nodded her thanks, then shifting Christina on her hip, tore open the folded page. Chase's writing was, as usual, all but illegible, yet somehow she made out the words.

My dearest Ann,

Colonel Follensbee has had word that there is one final shipment of rifles aboard the Cassiopeia. *He has commandeered the* Andromeda *to go after them. There is money in the bank to see you through until I*

*get back. I will ask for word of you at the town house
when we return.*

*Your husband,
Chase*

With her heart in her throat, Ann raised her gaze from the message and watched the *Andromeda* steam out of sight.

chapter seventeen

"IS THAT HER, CAPTAIN HARDESTY?" COLONEL RICHARD Follensbee asked from where he leaned against the breastboard in the *Andromeda*'s pilothouse. "Is that the *Cassiopeia* just beyond the bend?"

Chase squinted into the fierce orange glare of the setting sun, trying to make out the configuration of the steamer half a mile ahead. He raised his hand to shade his eyes.

Was it the *Cassiopeia*? They'd been chasing Boothe Rossiter's boat upstream for six days, ever since Follensbee and his troopers had stormed aboard and commandeered the *Andromeda*.

"The invoices we found in James Rossiter's things," Follensbee had explained to him, "indicate a full dozen cases of carbines are aboard the *Cassiopeia*. If the Cheyenne and Sioux get hold of that many rifles, there'll be a bloodbath from Nebraska to the Rockies come spring. We have to overtake Boothe Rossiter's boat and stop him from delivering those guns."

Chase had scribbled a note to Ann before they left St. Louis and given it to one of the transfer agents. Looking back, he realized he should have apologized to her for the way he'd gone roaring out of the town house. He should have made it clear that his only reason for leaving her behind in St. Louis was because of the urgency of recovering the rifles. But he'd been too riled up when he'd written it and too eager to get out on the river to be thinking clearly.

And in truth, when Follensbee's mission was over, Chase meant to find a way to settle his score with Boothe Rossiter.

"We're catching up!" Follensbee cried, shifting Chase's full attention back to the river. "Can you tell if it's her?"

As they drew nearer, Chase recognized the fancy crescent-moon finial on the roof of the steamer's wheelhouse and her high, rounded stern. "It's the *Cassiopeia*, all right," he confirmed. "If we're lucky, she'll pull into the landing up ahead for the night."

When the smaller steamer slowed and blew its landing whistle, Chase smiled in anticipation. Once the *Cassiopeia* tied up at the cluster of buildings in the crook of the bend, they'd have them.

Then from the *Andromeda*'s own foredeck came a chorus of whoops and a flurry of rifle fire.

"What the hell's going on down there?" Chase demanded.

Follensbee bolted out of the wheelhouse to investigate. When he came storming back a few minutes later, he was sputtering. "That goddamn idiot corporal took odds on when we'd overtake the *Cassiopeia*. The fools who won took it into their heads to celebrate."

"Well, their celebration has cost us our prize." Chase observed, nodding to where the smaller steamer had turned back into the channel. "Rossiter's decided to make a run for it."

Follensbee cursed volubly when he saw the *Cassiopeia*'s tall, black chimneys give a fiery belch of smoke as the steamer picked up speed.

"You want me to go after him?" Chase asked, watching the *Cassiopeia*'s wheel toss up spume.

"What's the river like ahead?" the colonel wanted to know.

Before he answered, Chase put the wheel down to port and glided through the thick blue shade cast by the limestone bluff opposite the town. "Beyond this crossing the bank levels out and the channel widens. We'll need to catch the *Cassiopeia* in that stretch of open water, because just beyond it the banks close in and the channel doglegs."

"If we don't catch that steamer tonight, there won't be a single gun aboard her come morning." Follensbee glanced across at Chase. "Those carbines are why we came."

"You *did* say the government would buy me another boat if we wreck this one, didn't you?"

Follensbee just laughed.

"Well, if we're going to turn this into a race," Chase went on, "you'd better have your men hang tight. Things could get rough before this is over.

"And Colonel Follensbee," Chase added as the colonel turned to go, "would you ask Mr. Boudreau to step on up here? I could use a second pair of eyes for this."

Once Follensbee left the wheelhouse, Chase rang the engineering bells to signal Cal for greater speed. Almost immediately, he felt the steamer surge beneath him.

"I'm coming to get you, you bastard," he vowed under his breath. "And when I catch you, I'm going to make you pay for what you did to Annie."

As the high banks fell away, Chase blew the whistle in a long, loud challenge any riverboat captain would recognize.

The *Cassiopeia* whistled in answer.

The race was on.

As he chased the *Cassiopeia* into the setting sun, Follensbee and Boudreau materialized on either side of where Chase stood. He could hear the *Andromeda*'s boilers roaring two decks below and feel the smooth, muscular stroke of the engines.

Gradually Chase closed the distance between the two boats—from a thousand yards to eight hundred, from eight hundred to five. The tang of anticipation came sharp in his mouth. For as much as this was Follensbee's mission, it was Chase's fight.

The steamers churned into the deepening twilight. Then, just as they came close enough to count the crates of goods piled on the guards, a shower of sparks trailed from the *Cassiopeia*'s chimneys.

"They're pulling away!" Boudreau cried.

"They're burning fatwood," Chase answered and rang the engineering bells, signaling Cal to spike the furnaces.

As he did, Chase could almost hear the engineer's voice ringing in his ears, "Don't you bust up this boat, boy! She's the best ol' gal I ever tended."

The *Andromeda* leaped ahead.

While the river lay straight before them, both steamers ran full out. But when they reached the dogleg half a mile ahead one boat or the other would have to give ground. Whichever boat was in the lead when they made the turn would pull away. The other would fall back or risk running aground in the shallows.

Chase signaled for greater speed. The *Andromeda* strained forward. Her timbers groaned, and her hog chains hummed from stem to stern. She inched up beside the *Cassiopeia*, close enough for Chase to taste her smoke and catch a glimpse of the yelling passengers' faces.

Ahead, the surface of the river shimmered like molten copper, making the channel nearly impossible to read when every glimmer could harbor a threat and every shadow mean disaster. Still, Chase held his course.

As they approached the dogleg, he nosed past the *Cassiopeia*. As he did, he expected Boothe to fall back, to give ground as they roared into the turn, but Rossiter kept coming. Chase steered as close as he dared to the southern bank, but the *Cassiopeia* slid sideways, crowding him.

He gave the other steamer what space he could.

Then, with a groan like lost souls howling on their way to hell, the *Cassiopeia* shuddered and fell back.

"Boudreau!" Chase shouted, not daring to take his eyes off the river. "Tell me what happened!"

The younger pilot dashed to the doorway. "Looks like a sawyer pierced clear through to the Texas," he shouted. "The *Cassiopeia* is sinking fast!"

Chase signaled Cal to bring the *Andromeda* back to maneuvering speed, and they ran half a mile more into the deepening twilight. Then, just as they were making their turn to go back and help, a plume of yellow light shot skyward from the wreck. A thunderous *whuff* of an explosion set the air to shimmying.

"The *Cassiopeia's* burning!" Boudreau cried.

Cursing under his breath, Chase fought the wheel. With a deep-throated complaint, the *Andromeda* came about. As she did, Chase saw a perfect vision of perdition take shape before his eyes.

The *Cassiopeia* had sunk at midstream to the depth of her boiler deck. A bright line of flames licked along the roof of the salon. Half a hundred people were foundering in the water.

Some of them flailed desperately. Others clung to boards and crates and shutters. A few bodies floated motionless.

Chase could see at least a score of passengers still

clinging to the burning boat. Several crewmen were beating at the flames with blankets. A woman and two children waved frantically from the front of the Texas deck. One man had climbed the jackstaff and kept shimmying higher as the *Cassiopeia* settled.

Chase maneuvered the *Andromeda* in as close as he dared, signaled for Cal to hold her against the current, and turned the wheel over to Boudreau.

When he reached the main deck, the hands had already pulled two or three dozen people from the water. They lay shivering in the night air, their stark faces illuminated by the flames from the sinking steamer.

There was the sound of another explosion, the ceaseless braying of a donkey off to their left, and the even more frantic cries of people hoping for rescue. Beck Morgan had launched both the skiffs. He and Colonel Follensbee had taken one. Chase climbed into the second with two of the deckhands.

They maneuvered around the bow to the far side of the *Cassiopeia*. Chase could hear people in the water, but the reflections and the deepening shadows made the passengers almost impossible to see.

"Call out," he shouted. "Help me find you."

"Here!" a woman's hoarse voice answered. "Here."

Chase managed to locate her and her child, clinging to one of the *Cassiopeia*'s bright red shutters. They maneuvered the yawl near enough for Chase to scoop the child into the boat. He hauled the boy's mother over the gunwale after him.

The two deckhands had just put their oars in the water

when something else exploded, blowing the glass out of the cabin windows. Fire licked through the broken panes, illuminating one of the *Cassiopeia's* skiffs bobbing not ten feet away.

At first Chase thought the man aboard it was rescuing people, too. But when a boy about fifteen grabbed the side of the yawl, the man turned and smacked his hands with the flat of an oar.

"What the hell are you doing?" Chase shouted as one of his own crewmen reached out his hands to help.

Abruptly the man in the skiff turned to face him, and Chase's pulse thumped with satisfaction.

It was Boothe Rossiter.

Rossiter recognized Chase, too, and pulled a gun from the waistband of his trousers. He fired at him, the bullet whizzing past Chase's head. As the skiffs bobbed closer, Boothe raised the gun again.

Before he could fire, Chase leaped at him. As he slammed into Rossiter's midsection, his momentum tipped the skiff, dumping both Boothe and him in the river.

Chase grabbed a handful of Rossiter's clothes as they plunged deeper and deeper. Down into the cold, murky darkness. Down where sand swirled and branches ripped at skin and clothes.

Together they slammed into the mucky river bottom. Chase felt the mud suck hard at ankles and shins. They rose toward the yellow, firelit surface of the water.

Chase broke the surface first, sputtering and gasping for breath, his hand still twisted in Rossiter's coat. Boothe bobbed up an instant after, kicking and fighting to jerk away.

Chase held on for Annie's sake. The two of them bashed and flailed at each other. They punched and gouged while the Cassiopeia disintegrated around them.

Then from directly above their heads came the mournful, unearthly wail of failing timbers. Chase looked up to see the entire salon section of the boiler deck tip slowly toward them. It came first in a rain of shimmering orange sparks, then shattered into sheets of flame. Each section pulsed with heat, pulsed with life.

Rossiter screamed in horror.

Chase kicked away and dove deep to avoid the timbers that shot past him, hit bottom, and ricocheted toward him.

One of them slammed into his ribs. Another bashed his knee and agony shot the length of his leg. In the haze of pain the yellow blaze around him dimmed.

Darkness dragged at him, slowly swallowing him down. A vision swirled in his head, of honey hair and gentle hands, of glowing eyes and a soft, plush mouth.

Annie.

The air gushed out of him in a burble of breath.

Annie.

Water rushed into his throat and gurgled in his chest.

Annie.

His ears roared. His thoughts blurred.

Annie.

He reached for her as the vision faded.

Then something—someone—grabbed him by the scruff of the neck and yanked him upward.

Chase's head broke the surface of the water. He felt the air on his face and took a breath.

He puked up water instead. He breathed again and coughed up more. Still, the air tasted good. It might be steamy hot and thick with smoke, but it tasted better than any air he'd ever sucked into his straining lungs.

He hung limp in someone's grasp, breathing, gasping, gagging, hardly believing he hadn't died there in the river. At length Chase came to realize someone was shouting his name.

"Hardesty! Damn you, Hardesty! Are you dead or alive?" Shaking accompanied the shouting. "Hardesty! Damn it, answer me!"

The shaking made Chase realize he hurt all over—his chest and ribs, his legs and back. He moaned and coughed and rolled his head to the left.

Richard Follensbee wavered into his view, leaning over the side of the yawl. Clutching Chase by the collar of his shirt to keep him afloat, shaking him the way a terrier shakes a rat.

"Hardesty!"

Chase moved his arms and legs experimentally. His muscles twitched and knotted, but everything worked.

"You dead or alive, Hardesty?" the colonel bellowed.

Chase blinked Follensbee into focus. " 'live," he managed to croak and set off coughing again.

"Well, you've got no right to be! Half that damn steamer came down on top of you."

"Feels like it," Chase mumbled and closed his eyes. He opened them again a moment later. "Rossiter?"

The colonel tipped his chin in the direction of a steaming pile of rubble. Chase recognized the *Cassiopeia's* superstructure, collapsed and half-submerged in the water. He saw the wheelhouse's crescent moon tilted drunkenly and gleaming in the firelight.

"Rossiter?" he asked again.

"Under there," Follensbee said. "Buried with his goddamned rifles."

chapter eighteen

CHASE RETURNED TO HARDESTY'S LANDING IN defeat.

In spite of receiving a letter of commendation signed by General Sherman himself, which thanked him for his part in stopping the shipments of guns, and in spite of his personal satisfaction in knowing that Boothe Rossiter had paid for his sins, Chase's world had come apart.

Ann was gone when he got back to St. Louis. The town house was shuttered, empty, and had been seized by the bank. She'd left no word for him, no hint of where she'd gone. Chase searched the city from bottom to top. He stopped at every hotel and went from boarding house to boarding house all over town. And found nothing.

The longer he searched the more desperate he became. So many things had lain unresolved between Annie and him the day he left. He regretted storming out of her father's house without a word. He wondered if she was angry with him for going after Boothe Rossiter. He worried that she'd lost faith in him and the life they'd begun to hope for together.

Chase spent another day questioning the ticket agents down at the levee, especially the ones who booked passage on steamers headed East. He crossed the river and inquired at the train depot in Illinois—and found no sign of her.

Ann and Christina had vanished.

He spent the rest of his time trying to verify his ownership of the *Andromeda*. Men from the Mercantile Bank had been waiting on the levee to repossess her when they got back. They'd taken possession of the steamer and evicted Chase from the captain's quarters so fast he barely had time to pack their things.

He'd pressed his claim to the steamer at both the bank and at the courthouse. But no one cared what papers he'd signed, or what James Rossiter had promised him. The bank owned the *Andromeda* now. After two weeks of frustration and disappointment, Chase had begged passage and headed home.

Where else did a man go when he'd lost everything?

He leaned heavily against the railing of Barnaby Greene's sleek little steamer, the *Julie B*, and waited for Hardesty's Landing to come into view. As they rounded the last bend and he saw the house at the top of the bluff, at least some of the weight seemed to lift from his shoulders.

"So you're leaving us, are you?" Captain Greene asked,

ambling toward him across the steamer's closely packed deck. From the quantity of merchandise aboard the *Julie B*, it was clear the stores in towns along the river were stocking up for winter.

Chase gathered up his canvas duffel. "I expect I'll spend the off-season helping my folks."

"It's a shame about the *Andromeda*," Greene offered.

Chase acknowledged the older man's sympathy with a nod.

"If you need work piloting in the spring," the older man continued, "you come see me."

"I'll keep that in mind." It was as close as Chase could come right now to thinking about the future. Then, as the steamer slowed, Chase grabbed up his bag and jumped ashore. "Thanks for the passage, Barnaby."

Captain Greene waved in answer as the steamer eased back into the channel.

Chase slung the bag over his shoulder and started for the house. He'd taken barely a dozen steps when his father emerged from the shed at the edge of the woodlot.

"Chase!" he exclaimed. "You all right, boy? We didn't expect to see you up this way for at least another week."

He watched his father approach. The vigor in his stride made Chase feel old and tired by comparison. "The shipping season ended early this year," he told his father. "At least for me."

"Good God!" Enoch's mouth narrowed with concern. "The *Andromeda* wasn't involved in that big wreck downriver, was she?"

Chase rubbed at the half-healed gash that ran from his eyebrow into his hair. "Not exactly."

"Then what are you doing here?"

Chase hoped he'd have a chance to talk to his mother before he faced anyone else. He needed Lydia to tell him that losing the *Andromeda*—and especially losing Ann—weren't his fault. He needed to be sure that someone still had faith in him.

The last thing in the world he wanted was to confront his father with all of this. But Enoch stood with his hands planted on his hips, as if he were waiting for an explanation.

Chase lifted his chin defensively. "Well, you might as well know," he began. "I lost the *Andromeda*."

His father didn't show so much as a ripple of surprise. "How'd you lose her?"

Chase did his best to swallow the regret wedged in his throat. "The bank took her," he said, then waited for Enoch to say it was because he'd mismanaged his captaincy. "It's what you expected, isn't it?" Chase goaded him, spoiling for a fight. "You never believed I'd prove myself as a captain."

"I might have had my doubts about your business dealings with James Rossiter," his father conceded, not rising to the bait, "but I never once doubted your abilities." He clapped one big hand around Chase's shoulder. "I'm sorry you lost the boat, son. I'm even sorrier you didn't think I believed in you. You make a fine captain, Chase. You'll get a new command."

Chase let his father's words soak in like rain to dry, parched earth.

"I thought the *Andromeda* was where I belonged," he said, his voice rusty with regret. "I thought by captaining my own boat, I could prove myself. I wanted so much for you and Ma to be proud of me."

Enoch scowled and shook his head. "You shouldn't have to prove yourself to anyone, Chase. A man has to have pride in what he does. His opinion of himself is all that matters."

If only it were that simple. Because he'd been the first of the strays the Hardestys had taken in, Chase always thought he had more to prove than anyone else. Pa might not make concessions to any man, but Chase felt obliged to live up to a special set of standards. He'd negotiated the debt himself, built it on gratitude, love, and a load of early responsibilities. Now that he'd failed to meet those expectations, he felt lost.

Chase might have turned away if Enoch hadn't held him still. "I don't want you to mistake what I'm saying, boy. Your ma and me, we've always been proud of you. From the time you were little, you were as fine a son as any man could ask for. You worked hard, played fair, and always looked after the younger children—especially Rue. And we couldn't have asked for anyone to set them a finer example."

Enoch's own voice caught a little as he went on. "If ever there's a man who's proved himself, it's you, Chase. But you ought to know you don't have to be a steamboat captain to make us proud of you."

Chase turned and looked into his father's eyes, seeing not just acceptance but warmth, not just pride but affection—and maybe a glint of tears.

Before Chase could speak, Enoch patted him briskly. "You head on up to the house, now. Your ma will be wanting to know you got home safe."

Chase grabbed up his duffel and headed for the steps.

"And Chase..." Chase hesitated and looked back at his father. "You've had those words coming to you for a good long while. I'm sorry I made you wait so long to hear them."

Chase wasn't sure he could trust his voice, so he nodded in answer and continued on up to the house.

His mother was alone in the kitchen for once, whipping up some concoction that must have taken lots of eggs. There were shells scattered across the tabletop, and she counted her strokes as she stirred. "Seventy-eight, seventy-nine..."

"Afternoon, Ma," he said and closed the back door with a *thump*.

Lydia whirled around, bowl in hand. "Chase!" she cried. "How glad I am that you're all right! We've all been worried!" She tipped her head so he could buss her cheek, then patted him, dabbing his chin with batter. "Ann will be so relieved to see you!"

"Ann!" Chase's knees wobbled, and he had to grab the edge of the table to keep from ending up on the floor. "Is Annie here?"

"Didn't you know?"

"How would I know?" he demanded, furious at being

ambushed. "She didn't leave a single word for me in St. Louis."

Now that he knew Ann was here, he wanted to find her, dress her down for scaring him—then kiss her until neither of them could breathe.

"She's been here nearly a month," his mother said with the reproving lift of her eyebrows. "She came right after you set off after young Rossiter."

"I didn't 'set off after' anyone, damn it! The *Andromeda* was commandeered by the army."

"Well, all I know," Lydia went on, "is that she's been beside herself ever since we heard about the *Cassiopeia*. She was sure you were involved in that terrible wreck."

Chase ducked his head. He wasn't ready to talk about the *Cassiopeia*, either.

"Ann would have had word of me a damn sight sooner if she'd been in St. Louis!"

"She didn't have much choice about staying there, now, did she?" Lydia scolded, banging the spoon against the edge of the bowl for emphasis. "They snatched that house right out from under her. So she came here, *where she belongs*."

That Ann thought she belonged at Hardesty's Landing quieted at least some of Chase's misgivings. "So where would I find Annie now if I wanted to talk to her?"

Lydia whipped the batter a few more strokes before she answered. "She put Christina down for a nap and walked on out toward the point."

The point. With those two words Chase was drowning in memories: of lying with Annie in the grass beneath a black banner of sky, of how beautiful she'd been in the light of the summer moon, of the consolation she'd given him when Rue was hurt.

Somehow that night had been their true beginning.

"Well, then," he said and climbed to his feet. "I think I'll just wander on out to the point and surprise my wife. Since we've got some things we need to discuss, I'd appreciate it if we weren't disturbed."

"Oh, I think I can manage that," Lydia said, then turned and grinned at him. Chase flushed to the tips of his ears and fled from his mother's laughter.

He followed the well-worn path along the top of the bluffs, striding through stands of cedar and pine, through hardwoods rustling in gold and russet splendor. He clambered through the jumble of rocks and found Ann just where he hoped she'd be, settled in the bowl of grass at the edge of the cliff.

He stood one long moment drinking her in: the graceful furl of her skirt and the drape of the sage-green shawl around her shoulders, the dip of her head and the thick, tightly wound knot of hair at the nape of her neck.

"Annie," he called softly.

She swung around and stared at him, then scrambled to her feet. "Chase!" she cried as she ran toward him. "Oh, dear God! Chase, are you all right?"

They came together as if drawn by a force stronger than either of them. Ann threw her arms around his neck. Chase enfolded her in his embrace and lifted her right off her feet.

His mouth closed over hers, and the kiss that swelled

between them was heady and reckless with weeks of sep-
aration and uncertainty. Chase couldn't seem to hold her
close enough, couldn't seem to breathe deeply enough of
her sweetness, or savor enough of her warmth to reassure
himself he'd found her. That she was here in his arms.

"I was so afraid for you when we heard about the
Cassiopeia." Annie clung to him as if she never meant to
let him go. "You were there, weren't you, when Boothe's
steamer ran aground?"

Chase lowered her to her feet, but couldn't seem to relinquish his hold on her. "Colonel Follensbee found invoices in the commodore's papers that indicated the
Cassiopeia was on its way to deliver one last big shipment
of guns before the river closed for the winter. He commandeered the *Andromeda* to go after her. Didn't you get
the note I left you?"

"Couldn't you have refused to go with him?" she
asked, her eyes darkening as she traced the half-healed
gash that ran up into his hair.

"The truth is, Annie, I didn't want to refuse. The truth
is, I wanted to make sure Boothe Rossiter got what he deserved."

"We've heard all sorts of things in these last days," she
offered quietly, taking half a step away. "Will you tell me
what happened?"

Chase looked down at her, trying to interpret the
pucker between her brows and the line of her mouth.

"We chased the *Cassiopeia* upriver for a full six days,"
he told her, "and caught her in the stretch between

Glasgow and Lexington. We could have taken her peaceably enough if Boothe hadn't tried to run."

He could still feel the wind in his face and the hum of exhilaration in his blood as they'd steamed full-out into the setting sun. But the thrill he'd known in the midst of that run didn't come close to making up for the horror and remorse afterwards. Eight people had lost their lives that night, and even if Boothe Rossiter had chosen to flee from the *Andromeda*, Chase had to shoulder his share of the blame for what happened.

"Is Boothe . . ." Ann's words parted the fog of Chase's regrets. "Is Boothe dead?"

Chase smelled the smoke and steam again, saw the orange glow of the burning wreckage reflected in the Missouri's dark surface.

"Yes, he is." He felt a tremor run through her, and he knew what she'd have to ask.

"Did you—" She looked into his eyes. "Did you kill him?"

"No." Chase caught her more closely against him. "I didn't want Boothe's death on my conscience—or on yours. He destroyed himself by running away."

Ann leaned into him. "I shouldn't be glad he's gone," she confessed so softly that he could scarcely hear, "but I'm so relieved."

He looked down at that bent head, at those tightly flexed shoulders and her vulnerable nape. Ann had endured so much cruelty at Boothe Rossiter's hands, yet it had drained away none of her decency, none of her compassion.

"You're only human to feel that way, Annie. Boothe brought what happened on himself. He was part of a conspiracy that dealt in guns. When he knew he was going to be arrested, he risked the lives of every person aboard that steamer to get away. What happened to Boothe had nothing at all to do with you."

She nestled close enough that he could feel the imprint of her forehead and nose and chin against his chest. "Thank you," she whispered, "for saying that."

"It's the truth."

He wrapped her close, contented to have her in his arms, especially when he'd thought she and Christina were gone for good. He could have stood there forever holding her, but he'd been carrying a question around with him for weeks that only Ann could answer.

He turned her back toward that small grassy hollow at the edge of the bluff. "Why, Annie," he finally asked, "why didn't you tell me what Boothe did to you?"

Since that day she'd opened the door to her father's study and seen him standing in the hall, Ann had known this moment was inevitable. She'd known she'd have to tell him everything. But then, hadn't she sworn to do that anyway? Hadn't she vowed to tell Chase the truth the morning she'd decided to stay on the *Andromeda* and make a life with him?

Ann looked up into her husband's face, seeing the concern in his eyes, and a certain disappointment.

She drew in her breath. "I'm sorry. I meant to tell you. I would have told you before, but I was afraid—"

"Of what, Annie?" he asked, cupping her face between

his hands. His palms were rough against her skin, yet warm and infinitely gentle. "Did you think I'd respect you less? Love you less?"

"Yes!" Her voice shredded on that single word. "I thought that everytime you looked at me you'd see not who I was, but how I came to be with you. That when you took Christina in your arms you'd see not her, but who her father was."

He looked into her eyes, and Ann knew her faults and weaknesses lay cast in sharp relief: the shame she'd felt and her terrible fruitless anger, her trepidation about the future and her fears for her daughter.

"Oh, Annie," he murmured, his voice was nearly as ragged as hers had been. "Don't you know that you're the most beautiful, wonderful thing that's ever happened to me? Don't you know how much I love you and Christina? Don't you realize the two of you are more important to me than anything?"

Chase tightened his hold on her. "Oh, Annie," he murmured, "I just wish I'd been there to protect you. That I could make this right for you."

"You are making it right," she insisted softly, "by holding me and accepting me and believing in me. You're making it right by loving me—and by loving Christina."

He wrapped her up safe in his arms.

Ann closed her eyes and abandoned herself to the solace he was offering. A tear breached the rim of her downcast lashes, and she swiped it away. Another scorched down her cheek. She blotted it against his shirtfront. Her tears came harder, faster. A sob pushed up her throat.

Her chest knotted. Shudders took her and her knees gave way.

Chase folded up right there on the grass and gathered her into his lap. For a time, she could do no more than cling to him, weeping shivery and openmouthed, weeping as she had not wept since she was a child.

Chase crushed her closer. "You're all right, love," he whispered. "I won't let anyone hurt you, Annie girl. You're safe with me."

As she burrowed against him, his words became a murmured litany in her ears, a counterpoint to the low, muffled sound of her grief. He held her and rocked her and stroked her. He became her stalwart, her rock to cling to. *He became her husband in a way he'd never been before.*

When the storm finally ebbed, Ann lay spent and sprawled against him. She wasn't sure she could move and was even less sure she wanted to. Still, there were things she had to tell him, truths she needed to speak before she could rest.

"It started," she began in a very small voice, "the very day I came home from Philadelphia."

Though Chase didn't move, she could feel his muscles tighten, turn to granite beneath her. "How? How did it start?"

"He touched his tongue to my cheek when he kissed me hello," she said with a shiver. "He watched every move I made through dinner. When we passed on the stairs, he brushed against me."

Chase bowed his shoulders and raised his knees around her like a barricade.

"From that day on, when I looked up from my sewing or reading or correspondence, I found him watching me. I discovered things in my bedroom had been moved. He started leaving gifts: a dead rose, a butterfly pinned to my pillow, a nightdress he'd ripped to pieces."

"Did you tell the commodore what he was doing?" She could hear the anger in his voice.

"Of course I did."

"What did he do to stop it?"

Ann shook her head.

"Boothe opened the door to my bedroom one night while I was undressing, so I stole the housekeeper's key and kept my bedroom locked. Still, I'd hear him try the latch at night. He'd rattle it just enough to wake me, just enough to let me know he was there."

Chase swore under his breath.

"The commodore was away the night he kicked in the door."

"Oh, Annie."

She began to cry softly. "I tried to push him away. I fought so hard." She raised her gaze to his. "I hit him, and I kicked him. I scratched him so deeply he must have scars. But no matter what I did he ..."

The tears came in a flood, but Ann was angry now. She wept rigid and cursing, shivering with rage and revulsion.

"I'm sorry, Annie," Chase whispered, rocking her. "I'm so goddamn sorry he hurt you."

She ground her face into the soft, well-washed fabric of his shirt, breathed the smoky masculine scent she'd come to associate with safety. There wasn't much more to tell, and she wanted to get it over with.

"When he was gone," she whispered. "I burned what was left of my nightclothes and all the bedding. I scrubbed myself until I bled, but I could smell him on me for days after.

"I had bruises everywhere he touched me. Those bruises had hardly begun to fade when I realized he'd left something a good deal more permanent to remember him by."

"Christina."

"Oh, Chase," she went on. "I look at her now and can hardly believe I didn't want her, but I pretended she didn't exist for as long as I could. I couldn't stand the idea of Boothe's seed growing inside me. I couldn't bear that I was carrying his child.

"Then when she was born she looked like him, and I was sure everyone would see him in her and realize—"

"All I ever see when I look at her," he told her softly, "is our Christina."

Ann smiled at the tenderness in his voice, the stroke of his hand against her hair. Chase loved the baby every bit as much as she did.

"How is it that something as wonderful as Christina can come from what Boothe did to me?" she asked in wonder.

Chase shook his head as if he were as much at a loss to explain it as she was. "You've been such a fine mother to her, Annie. You could so easily have turned away, but you've embraced her, taken such good care of her."

"It's you who taught me."

"To be a mother?"

"To love Christina for herself."

"I did that?"

Ann warmed at the memory and smiled up at him. "The morning after Christina was born, I found you sitting out on deck. You were holding this tiny dab of a baby in your two hands and whispering how wonderful the world was going to be for her. I'd never seen anyone touch a child the way you touched her, with such assurance and such tenderness. I'd never seen such love in any man's face, especially for a child that wasn't his."

"Christina's mine in every way that matters, Annie," Chase insisted, his voice resonating with conviction. "And so are you."

She looked up at him, up into those fierce blue eyes. "I want so much to be a good wife to you."

"You get better at that with every day that passes," he said, teasing her gently. He bent his head and kissed her with vast and transcendent tenderness. "I love you, Annie," he murmured. His words were a caress, his acceptance the wondrous gift he'd given her. "I'll always love you."

"I love you, too."

He closed his eyes as if he needed to savor her words, to take them deep into himself. She'd waited too long to tell him how she felt, to tell him how deeply she cared for him.

"I love you," she whispered again, then stretched up to kiss him back. As she did, she sought deeper access to his mouth, took pleasure in the way their lips lingered and clung, in the faintly nubbled texture of his tongue brushing hers.

She ran her hands over him, delighting in the sinuous flow of his shoulders beneath her palms; the broad, graceful slope of his back; the solidity of him against her. That night aboard the *Andromeda*, Ann had discovered the wondrous rightness in the way their bodies wove together. She needed to feel that rightness again, to seal and celebrate this deepening bond between them.

At the thought of lying with him here in the grass, a deep and provocative yearning rose up in her. Something sultry and viscous, demanding yet almost unbearably sweet.

Chase seemed to sense what she was feeling, because as his mouth lingered over hers, he trailed his fingers down her cheek and throat. He gathered her breast in the palm of his hand and caressed her gently.

Ann moaned into his mouth as he sought the bud of her nipple through the folds of her clothes. He circled that tightening nub and Ann felt as if she were circling, too. Her head went light and desire unfurled in lush, slow curls at the base of her belly.

She wanted him.

Chase seemed to want her, too, because he sprawled back in the cool rustling grass and pulled her over him.

Ann followed, instinctively fitting her body to his, feeling the urgency of his need stir against her. Once she'd been afraid of his desire, but now she relished his heat and hardness, the proof of how much he wanted her.

The knowledge that he longed for her turned her soft inside. It made her melt; it made her ache with a need she knew she could trust Chase to meet and satisfy. She pressed her hips to him, inviting him to come to her, inviting him to be with her in a whole new way.

"Oh, Annie, love." Chase's eyes darkened. "Do you know how much I want to make love to you?"

"Do you know—" Ann felt the heat scorch her cheeks, but continued anyway, "—how much I want you to?"

Basking in the sultry warmth of that Indian summer afternoon, they slowly removed each other's clothes. Here at what seemed like the top the world, they bared themselves and came together.

Once he was fully joined with her, Chase caressed her with trembling hands. He cupped the swell of her breasts, traced the curve of her back, clasped the flare of her hips and drew her more tightly down on him. He stroked the thick, downy hair at the apex of her legs, opened the bud of her femininity with the stroke of his thumbs, sought the very heart of her feminine pleasure.

As he did, Ann seemed to rise in a wondrous swirl of sensation. She threw back her head in delight, caught up in wanting him. She lifted her hips and took him even more deeply into herself. She spilled forward and over him, bracing herself on her arms.

They surged together, kissing with new and ravenous intensity, stoking each other's needs and inciting new sensations.

Chase moaned, caught up in their mutual pleasure. Ann drew that vibration into her mouth, letting it resonate through her body. She was one with him, wholly and completely joined with him. Wholly and completely in love with him.

She looked down into his eyes as they began to move together. "Oh, Chase!" she whispered. "You're the one who took my fear away; you showed me all the wonders a woman could feel."

"I love you, Annie girl," he whispered. His face was flushed. His mouth was bowed with anticipation. His blue eyes were aglow with his need for her.

"I love you, Chase. I'll always love you."

They moved in a slow, sinuous dance, took up the age-old rhythm of life, of creation, of people who loved each other and belonged together. And in that union they found glory and wonder and surcease, found joy and communion and resounding satisfaction. They found that no matter why they'd come together, the love they shared transcended everything. It united them as man and wife forever.

They lay curled together in the aftermath, languorous and replete, with only the warmth of the sun as their coverlet.

Ann sprawled against him, muzzy and sated, nuzzling the whiskery hollow at the turning of his jaw. "I love you," she murmured lazily. "Now that I've discovered what a fine, virile husband you are, I'd marry you all over again."

Chase shifted sideways and traced his thumb along the corner of her mouth. "*Will* you marry me all over again, Annie?"

With a laugh, Ann raised her head and looked at him. "Do you mean it?"

"So much has happened since we spoke our vows," he said and she could hear his growing conviction, "it seems right to make new promises. We could do that, Annie. We could speak our vows, just the two of us, here, together."

What he wanted seemed suddenly right to her. She was wholly a woman now, sound and complete in a way she hadn't ever dreamed she'd be the day they'd stood up together in the town house parlor. The months aboard the *Andromeda* had changed both their lives, united them in a way she might never have believed was possible.

"It would be like starting again," she whispered, her eyes misting with tears. "Only starting it right, this time."

"Yes."

"I—I think marrying you again would be wonderful," she whispered.

They helped each other clothe themselves. Ann turned Chase's trousers right side out. Chase guided Ann's chemise down over the curve of her hips. She buttoned up the shirt she'd all but torn off him earlier. Chase knelt and laced her boots.

They stood hand in hand in the very center of that grassy bowl at the edge of the bluff. There in the golden glow of afternoon sunshine, beneath a perfect dome of cerulean sky, they said the words that would bind them forever.

"I, Chase," he said looking down with love bright in

his eyes, "take thee, Annie, to be my lawful wedded wife..."

Ann felt the happiness well up inside her. "I, Annie, take thee, Chase, to be my lawful wedded husband..."

They made their pledges, one to the other. Each vow they spoke took on a truer meaning, each word seemed imbued with purer love and deeper devotion.

When they were done, Chase bent his head and kissed his wife. They settled back down in the grass again, holding each other, whispering, dreaming. Beginning to plan.

"I thought we'd stay on for a spell at Hardesty's Landing," Chase murmured after a time. "I'll help Pa with the winter work, and in the spring—"

"In the spring we'll go back to St. Louis and board the *Andromeda*...." Ann finished for him. She was already imagining what their next season on the river would be like, all that beautiful country rolling out before them, all those people to meet, places to see, and towns to visit.

Chase sat up and squeezed her hand. Ann could see how grave his face had suddenly become.

"I'm not sure how to tell you this, Annie," he began, "but the *Andromeda* is gone. The bank took her away from me, right along with the town house and everything else the commodore owned."

"Oh, Chase, no! I know what the *Andromeda* means to you." She reached to cup his cheek and tried to smooth away the creases of resignation around his mouth.

"I know what she means to you, too, Annie, and I'm sorry we lost her. But we'll be all right." He turned his head and pressed a kiss into her palm. "I'll get a berth piloting some other boat."

"I know you will."

"We won't be together much during the shipping season—" He took her hand in his and clasped it to his heart. "—but we'll make do. You can stay on here at Hardesty's Landing, or we'll find you a flat in St. Louis. We'll save our money and in time we'll buy another steamer."

Ann tightened her grip on his hand. "Or," she said, sliding him a sideways smile. "I could buy you the *Andromeda* as a wedding gift."

"Oh, Annie!" Chase laughed and brought her knuckles to his lips. "As generous as that offer is, I know you haven't a penny to bless you any more than I do."

Ann shifted a little uncomfortably, wishing now she'd been more forthcoming about the news Mr. Throckmorton had brought her.

"Well, actually," she said and swallowed hard, "I *do* have a penny to bless me. Quite a few pennies, as a matter of fact."

"What?"

Ann dipped her head. "I—I guess I should have mentioned my inheritance."

"Your inheritance? I guess you should have!"

Ann couldn't tell by the tone of his voice if Chase was shocked or angry.

"Just how many pennies are there in this inheritance?"

After all they'd been through, he wouldn't be upset to

find that she had thousands and thousands of dollars at her disposal, would he?

"Annie, *how many pennies?*"

She glanced up and could tell by the trim of his jaw he wanted an answer.

"Enough—" She moistened her lips with the tip of her tongue. "Enough to buy back the *Andromeda.* Enough to pay off Frenchy's other wives and invest in his bakery."

"You mean Frenchy really does have more than one wife, and he's opening a bakery?"

Ann nodded. "And I'd have money left over after I paid for all of that."

Chase stared at her. "As many pennies as that? And how exactly did you come into this inheritance?"

"Do you remember when that lawyer came to see me when we returned from Fort Benton?" When Chase nodded, Ann went on. "Well, he was executing my mother's will. It seems she stipulated that the money was to come to me only after I was wed."

He pursed his lips and took a moment to think that over. "And you want to use that money to buy me the *Andromeda?*"

"Yes."

"Well, I'm not sure I can let you do that, Annie."

"Why?"

"A man earns his own keep," he insisted stubbornly. "A man takes care of his own family. A man doesn't ask his wife to finance—"

Ann broke in before he could talk himself out of

something she knew he wanted. "I'd be buying the *Andromeda* for both of us."

"Both of us?"

"You said before you knew how much that steamer means to me. It's what brought the two of us together. It's where Christina was born. It's where we fell in love. I wouldn't be here with you today if it weren't for the *Andromeda*."

How could a man nod and still seem patently unconvinced?

"Buying the *Andromeda*," she persisted, "is a promise we'd be making to the future. To our livelihood as well as to Christina and our other children."

His eyebrows rose and his voice softened. "Our other children, Annie?" he asked. "Are we going to have 'other children?'"

"Don't you think that after doing what we just did, having other children is a distinct possibility?"

He lowered his gaze and she could see the ruddy color come up in his face. "I suppose it is."

"So can we make this promise to the future, Chase?" she asked hopefully. "Can we reclaim the *Andromeda* for all of us?"

His deep blue gaze rose and locked with hers. "Oh, Annie, if you're sure..."

"I'm sure, Chase." Annie leaned across and kissed him. "I've never been surer of anything in my whole life."

About the Author

ELIZABETH GRAYSON was published for the first time in the fourth grade and hasn't stopped writing since. She wrote while she earned both a BS and MS in Education, while she taught art in elementary schools and children's classes at the St. Louis Art Museum. Elizabeth delights in telling rich, romantic stories set on the frontier and received the Romantic Times Career Achievement Award for Historical Romances set in America. *Painted by the Sun* was also a finalist for the prestigious Willa Cather Literary Award.

Elizabeth lives in Missouri with her devoted husband, Tom, and indolent cat, Simba. Readers may contact her through her website elizabethgrayson.com or at P.O. Box 260052, St. Louis, Missouri 63126.